MW01154922

About the Author

S. R. Sway is an avid reader and lover of all stories. When she is not reading or writing, she can be found camping with her family and dog, Beau.

Theft in the Blood

S. R. Sway

Theft in the Blood

Olympia Publishers
London

www.olympiapublishers.com
OLYMPIA PAPERBACK EDITION

Copyright © S. R. Sway 2025

The right of S. R. Sway to be identified as author of
this work has been asserted in accordance with sections 77 and 78 of the
Copyright, Designs and Patents Act 1988.

All Rights Reserved

No reproduction, copy or transmission of this publication
may be made without written permission.
No paragraph of this publication may be reproduced,
copied or transmitted save with the written permission of the publisher, or in
accordance with the provisions
of the Copyright Act 1956 (as amended).

Any person who commits any unauthorized act in relation to
this publication may be liable to criminal
prosecution and civil claims for damage.

A CIP catalogue record for this title is
available from the British Library.

ISBN: 978-1-83543-170-2

This is a work of fiction.
Names, characters, places and incidents originate from the writer's imagination.
Any resemblance to actual persons, living or dead, is purely coincidental.

First Published in 2025

Olympia Publishers
Tallis House
2 Tallis Street
London
EC4Y 0AB

Printed in Great Britain

Dedication

To my husband: I couldn't have done this without your encouragement and support.

Sydney

It was dark. All she could hear was the soft snore of the man in the bed. The room smelled like stale beer and sour whiskey. He was the son of a rich politician. Daddy, in her opinion, was a crook who was making money the easy way, taking advantage of hard-working people. She had studied him like she did all her prey. He was a drug user and a womanizer. He often got in trouble and Daddy usually bailed him out. She felt no guilt for what she was doing.

It was four in the morning and she knew by his party habits that he would be passed out from drugs and alcohol. She had watched him earlier in the night and she wasn't too worried about him waking up.

She let the door softly click shut behind her. She waited a minute, making sure all was as it should be. With her running shoes not making a sound, she crossed the hotel room, the penthouse to be exact—another benefit of being the politician's son. She had followed him to Manhattan for a fundraiser and he'd gone out after to party.

Sydney Wright went through the living area and over to the open bedroom door. She could hear him sleeping.

Through the window, the dim streetlights showed another figure in the bed passed out, most likely the woman she had seen him with earlier. He must have snuck her in the back. Wouldn't want to ruin his reputation. She rolled her eyes in the dark.

Through her research, she knew that this guy always carried large quantities of cash on hand. For many bad dealings and to get himself out of trouble, she was sure.

Silently and slowly, she made her way over to the dresser and started to search the top. There was nothing but a comb and some change.

Sydney looked up and caught her reflection in the vanity mirror. Her long black hair was pulled into a bun on top of her head. She was dressed in black jogging leggings and a black, tight, zip-up hoodie. No loose clothes on a job, and that's exactly what this was.

Her fanny pack, which was a must, hung tightly to her hips. In it, she kept a small flashlight, a lock picking tool, and a few other essentials.

She slowly pulled open the top drawer and it was completely empty. She did the same to the next; again, nothing. *He officially hadn't unpacked,* she thought, and turned to scan the room.

She saw the woman's pink, high-heeled stilettos thrown in the corner along with her dress. The stilettos were designer and the latest fashion. She wondered what size they were? *Stay focused,* she told herself.

Forgetting the pretty shoes, she continued to scan the room. She saw the open lid of a suitcase between the bed and the window. She started over, and when she got to the corner of the bed, she heard the rustling of the sheets. She dropped down to a squat, hopefully out of sight.

"Move over." She heard the politician's son groan.

The woman said something inaudible. There was some more rustling of blankets, and then a thud.

"What the…" the woman began, then a slap.

Sydney's adrenaline spiked. *Shit*, she thought. *They better not start fighting.*

There was some more mumbling, and then it was quiet. Sydney waited. She wasn't going to risk it and waited to hear snoring again. A few minutes later, she heard it—the soft rumble. She slowly rose from her squatted position and walked over to the suitcase in front of the window. She took one more look at the couple in the bed and then silently glanced down at the designer suitcase. She was impressed by the quality and made a mental note to look into buying one of her own.

She unzipped the large compartments on the lid of the suitcase and shuffled through the expensive clothes, but there was nothing. She searched the whole thing and still nothing but clothes and shoes. Getting frustrated, she took another look around. Surely, there was a safe somewhere. Getting up, she crept back out of the room and into the living area.

Most hotels were the same, usually a safe in the closet or behind a picture in the fancier hotels. She took her pen light out and ran it across the walls. She noticed a large landscape painting on the far side of the room with green rolling hills, something you never saw in Manhattan. She quickly walked over and pulled up on the corner of the frame. It lifted easily, but there was no safe. She was getting increasingly frustrated. This was taking too much time, and she needed to hurry it along. She did a quick sweep of the room. Then she noticed the coffee table in the living area.

There was a small travel bag on a shelf underneath. She walked over and grabbed it. She opened it, and there it was: stacks of money.

"Bingo," she whispered.

There were three stacks, all labeled $10,000. She made the decision to just take the whole travel case instead of trying to shove it all into her small fanny pack. She noticed a Rolex watch that was thrown on the side table, and that went in the bag also. She opened the drawer on the table and, shifting through some papers, she saw a gun; she wasn't sure what kind. Her first thought was that she should take it and throw it in the dumpster out back of the hotel. After a short debate in her head, she thought better of it and left it there. She closed the drawer and decided she'd been there long enough. She tiptoed back to the front door and let it close softly behind her.

Back in the hallway, Sydney made for the back staircase. At this hour, she knew that no one would be there, and if she passed anyone, she would pretend she was doing a stair workout. As she quickly moved toward the stairs, she removed her gloves and put them in her fanny pack. She unzipped her black hoodie, revealing a bright pink tank top. She put the travel bag with her take between her legs and quickly tied the hoodie around her waist. She then hit the stairs at a jog. It actually felt good to jog down the stairs, her adrenaline still pumping like it did on all jobs; it helped to keep moving. She turned down one flight and, on the landing, there was an older man in a robe carrying an ice bucket. He jumped out of her way, and she gave him a small smile.

She heard him say something about crazy health nuts and it being too damn early. *Perfect*, she thought.

At the bottom of the staircase, she took the back exit leading to the parking lot.

Once outside, she slowed down and started to walk and catch her breath. The cool spring air hit her face, and she took in a deep breath of the sweet air. It calmed her nerves and refreshed her body. The streets were quiet; not many people were out yet. She put her hoodie back on but didn't zip it. She hailed a cab and headed out of town.

She gave the cab driver an address to a small motel on the edge of the city.

She stayed in different motels and always used fake names. As she watched the city whirl past the passenger window, she was impressed. She loved the city, with its big buildings and thousands of people. She thought that it was always easy to disappear in a place like that. Unlike the small town where she lived as a child, where everyone knew everyone and their family history.

The cab soon pulled up to the small motel. She paid with cash from her wallet, grabbed the travel bag she'd taken and went inside.

Once in her small, cheap room, she stripped down and hit the shower. As she rinsed the long night away, she thought about the job. It was a simple one, easy in and out. She didn't need the money, thanks to her sister's useful computer skills, so she would give an anonymous donation to a charity. She decided to donate it to a woman's abuse shelter; she was pretty sure that woman in the bed at the hotel was on the receiving end of the slap that she heard.

She got out of the shower and dried off. She dressed quickly and decided it was time to get out of the city. She had spent the last month there, and even though she loved it, she'd done four jobs, and she didn't want to overstay her welcome. She had left New York almost a year earlier, but being back was nice. It was time.

She only hit the rich. Most either don't know that they were robbed or were too embarrassed to call it in. *It would be front-page news*, she thought. *The Senator's Son's Drug Money Stolen*. She laughed at her own joke.

Maybe a trip to Miami, she thought. She'd never been there before, and the beach sounded wonderful. She'd get a nice hotel this time and take a little vacation.

With the thought of a warm, sandy beach, she packed her clothes. She used her phone to make plane reservations and find the nearest woman's shelter. She placed the money she stole in a large brown envelope and wrote the address down, planning to mail it on her way to the airport.

As she was grabbing her things, her phone rang. Seeing the contact on the screen, she debated whether to even answer it. It had been a while since she'd talked to her twin sister. Her stomach pitched, but she answered it anyway.

"Hello?"

"Hey, Syd, it's me. I've got some bad news."

*

"Syd, wake up." Sydney rolled over to see her twin sister's familiar face an inch from her own.

"What, Roxy?" Half-awake and annoyed, she pushed her away.

"Can you hear that?" Roxy was in her nightgown. She sat back on her knees and smiled.

She could hear Guns N' Roses, her dad's favorite band. He always played it when he was in a good mood.

"Do you smell that too?" Roxy asked, jumping off her bed.

She sniffed the air. The warm, sweet smell hit her nose. Chocolate chip pancakes! Their favorite.

She threw the covers off, and together, they ran down the stairs. They headed down the hall of their old house, bumping and pushing each other as they passed the little living room and headed straight into the small kitchen.

There, standing with his back to them, was Gabe Wright. He was bouncing to the music and in the middle of flipping a pancake. He was wearing his standard white, dirty T-shirt and blue jeans, and he was barefoot. His black hair was a mess, like he, too, had just gotten out of bed. He spun around and faced the girls. With the spatula as a microphone, he sang, "Knock knocking on heaven's door!"

Both girls laughed.

"Dang!" He put the spatula down. "Thought you girls were going to sleep through your whole birthday." He threw up his arms for a hug. Sydney couldn't help but smile. Her dad was her hero and the most handsome man she knew. Both girls giggled again in happiness and ran to his open arms. He picked them both up at the same time like he always did and swung them from side-to-side, whispering to both, "Happy twelfth birthday."

Her heart swelled with love for this man, her father. She breathed in his old spice smell mixed with pancake batter.

He put them down. "All right, I got chocolate chip pancakes for the birthday girls!"

They ran to the table. It was old and wobbly; it had dents and scratches from years of use. But she didn't care. Right now, it was set for both girls. There were plates, forks, and napkins laid out, and a big stack of pancakes in the middle with all their favorite toppings, including maple syrup, peanut butter, and raspberry jelly. It was perfect.

They sat and started filling their plates with the sweet breakfast.

Dad had turned the music down, making Sydney think he had done that just to wake them up. He flipped the last pancake on the stack and sat to join them.

"Margie is coming over today." He piled his plate high. "She baked you girls a big birthday cake.

"Yay!" Both girls cheered.

"I hope it has white frosting," Roxy said, her mouth full of pancakes. "I asked for it."

After they had their fill of pancakes. They started to put their dishes in the sink. Sydney turned from the sink and realized her dad had left the kitchen.

"Where did Dad go?" she asked Roxy. The two girls weren't identical twins, but they looked quite alike. Roxy always kept her hair short while Sydney kept it long. But they had the same blue eyes and black hair that matched their father's. They had very different personalities, too. Roxy didn't care about dressing nice or looking pretty like she did. Instead, the only thing Roxy cared about was the stupid computer.

"I don't know," Roxy said, putting the peanut butter back in the pantry.

"Girls, I have a surprise for you!" came a loud, deep voice.

They looked at each other wide-eyed. Dad had always tried to make their birthday special, but sometimes there just wasn't enough money.

They ran from the kitchen and followed his voice to the living room. He was standing by a small table in the corner and on it was a brand-new computer.

"Holy cow!" Roxy all but screamed as she ran to the table. Examining the flat screen computer, she said, "It's the newest addition! It even has Wi-Fi!"

Sydney watched Roxy.

What a nerd, she thought. She didn't really care about a stupid computer and was always confused with Roxy's fascination with them.

"Now, no taking this one apart, you hear?" Dad said with a smile. "I know how you like to do that." He chuckled.

Margie, their beloved babysitter, had given Roxy her old computer and Roxy had taken the whole thing apart, and tried to put it back together. She was still working on it.

"I won't, Dad." She hadn't taken her eyes off the thing. She started booting it up then looked up, realizing that he was still standing there watching her, a smile on his face. She stepped over and gave her dad a big hug. "Thank you, Dad, I love it."

"You're such a nerd," Sydney said from across the room.

She couldn't help but feel a little bit of jealousy creeping in. The computer was a great gift, but she wondered how her father had afforded it. Roxy looked up at her and stuck her tongue out.

Dad laughed. "I got something for you too, kiddo." He picked up a small package off the table. Sydney walked over, admiring the small gift. It was wrapped in pink paper and had a huge gold bow. Dad handed it to her.

"Margie helped me wrap it," he said, beaming.

Sydney couldn't speak. It was the prettiest thing she had ever seen.

"Well, open it. The gift is inside, silly," Dad said.

Sydney gently undid the bow and slowly unwrapped the paper. Inside was a small white box. Sydney opened the lid. Inside on black velvet was a gold locket on a gold chain. It had a red ruby in the middle shaped like a heart. Sydney looked up in admiration at her father.

"Do you like it?" he asked, smiling.

"I love it, Dad." She ran and gave him a big hug. But doubt crept in.

"Dad, you didn't, you know, pick it?" She used the slang word that the three of them used to describe their hobbies. It was no secret to them; hell he had just showed her how to pick a lock the day before. He had been proud at how well she had done. He wasn't just a car mechanic.

He bit his lip briefly, then smiled.

"Heck no! Paid cash money for these presents. You wear that necklace with pride, my girl. I got myself a good gig coming up. Enough to pay the bills and, who knows, maybe get us out of this old town. Here, let me help you put it on."

Sydney gently took it out of the box and handed to her dad. He placed it over her head and did the clasp in the back. Sydney looked down at the locket and smiled.

"You mean it?" she asked; hope filling her voice.

Even Roxy looked up from her computer. "We can move out of Fuller?"

Her dad gave a small smile that didn't reach his eyes. He looked to Roxy and then back at Sydney. "Of course. We can't live in this small, nowhere town forever. I have great things planned, just you wait and see." He smiled big this time and put his arm around her shoulders, giving her a light squeeze.

This was the best birthday ever.

*

"Excuse me. Miss?"

Sydney startled. "What? Where?" She looked around, trying to orient herself to her surroundings.

She was on a plane.

"Sorry, I didn't mean to startle you." The flight attendant was leaning over the seat. "But we have landed and you need to exit the plane."

"Right, sorry," she said. The flight from New York to Seattle was long and because of her early morning, she was tired.

The call from Roxy had her on the next flight to Seattle. But not without much hesitation.

Roxy had told her that their neighbor and grandmother figure from their childhood had passed away.

Margie had lived in the house across their field. She was a widower. She helped her father take care of her and her sister when he had to work. She was a kind lady; she worked in her garden and had always grown lots of vegetables. She also always had cookies for them and taught them how to play poker in the evening when their dad had to work late.

Sydney and Roxy's mom had passed away in childbirth, leaving her father to take care of them by himself. Margie had been in her life as long as she could remember. She had been with them through their whole ordeal with their father's death as well.

The news of her passing had been a blow to her heart.

Sydney walked through the terminal and headed for the car rentals. She rented a red convertible Mercedes and started the long drive to the small town of Fuller in eastern Washington. She stopped at the first Starbucks she saw, which didn't take long in Washington State. She was going to need the pick-me-up.

She was meeting Roxy at the only motel in the small town. When she finally hit the freeway, her mind went straight to her memories of her father and the tragedy that had hit her family.

She did not want to go back.

After her dad died when she was twelve, she and her sister had been sent to a girl's home in eastern Oregon. Margie had tried to foster them, but the state had declared that she was too old and not financially able to take

16

them. Margie had visited them as much as she could and often wrote them and sent packages of her homemade cookies. The only good thing about the girls' home was no one knew who she and her sister were or the story of what had happened. All the girls there had stories of their own.

The dream she had on the flight was a reminder of the beginning of the end of her childhood.

Her twelfth birthday was one of her best memories. But a few weeks later, her dad had been murdered in their home. The police had suspected criminal activity, but she and Roxy had been there, and they knew he was murdered, but no one would listen.

The sheriff in town, Sheriff Stone, had his suspicions about her father being a thief, but he had no proof. Dad was very good at what he did. When their mom died, she had left big hospital bills. Her dad's job at the auto body shop hadn't paid well, not to mention her dad had two babies to take care of. He would take side jobs as a thief. She never thought twice about what he did. He was good at it. He had taught her and Roxy everything he knew. How to pick wallets and jewelry, how to open locks and to play the mark. He had said, "You have to do what you have to do for your family."

She held herself to the same standards. She did it to help others. Lately, she had been liking the thrill and the challenge. She hadn't stolen for herself in years, not since she first left the girls' home and eventually the state. She was accepted at a design school in New York. Her first year was paid with the jewelry she lifted from Upper Manhattan. It wasn't more than a year later that Roxy's hacking skills ensured her a constantly full bank account. With banking all online, it was easy for Roxy to create accounts for them that never ran out. When she asked her about the taxes and the IRS, Roxy said not to worry, so she didn't. She just wished that Roxy had those same hacking skills when her father had been around.

On her twelfth birthday, when she had asked her dad about their gifts, he had said that he had a big job and she believed that was what got him killed. The sheriff's department had investigated, but had come up with nothing. They had found that her father had been killed with a single gunshot wound to the head and the house had been set on fire, possibly to cover the murder. Sydney and Roxy were the only witnesses to anything. Sheriff Stone had told the newspapers that there might have been criminal involvement. That was when the rumors started.

People said that her father was a criminal and a thief. That he was dealing with drug dealers and she even heard a rumor about a cartel.

The sheriff had let them stay at Margie's as the investigation continued and tried to have the social workers get them placed. Those two weeks had been the worst. The first week, they stayed at Margie's and cried. People had come to give their condolences, and she often heard what they were saying about her father. The next week, they went to school. The sheriff's daughter, Marcy Stone, had been in her class and knew about the murder through her father. She called Roxy and Sydney the daughters of a criminal. She had said that her dad told her that their father was nothing but a drain on society.

She had punched Marcy right in the nose, and she had felt satisfaction when she saw the blood drip down her chin.

The school had suspended her. Margie had picked her up, and as they left, Marcy and her friend were standing outside the door to the office.

"Just like her father," Marcy had said with a tissue covering her bloody nose.

Tears had stung her eyes. "You know nothing of my father!" she had yelled back.

Margie hadn't made them go back to school after that. She was sure Margie knew they wouldn't be there much longer.

*

She was so lost in her thoughts about the past that she almost missed the "Welcome to Fuller" sign. She immediately felt her back tighten up and her chin go up in defiance. She could do this. She owed Margie.

The motel was close to the freeway so she thankfully didn't have to drive through town. She pulled into the small parking lot that was all but empty. She wondered if Roxy was even there yet.

Roxy had been living in Seattle, working freelance computer stuff. Sydney wasn't sure exactly what that meant.

The motel was a dump even in the bright, late afternoon sun, and the place looked depressing. The one-story building stretched around the parking lot in a U-shape. The building was painted an off-white color with brown trim. There were flower boxes under the windows with small, colorful flowers planted in them, surely to try to brighten up the sad-looking place. The building only added to her already negative attitude.

She took the first parking spot she saw and pushed the button to put the top back on the car. She grabbed her bags from the back seat. She didn't have much.

She never kept clothes for long; this kept her traveling light and kept her wardrobe up-to-date. She had expensive taste. She liked her designer clothes; she knew it stemmed from being poor when she was a kid. Even though no one knew she had dropped out of school her last year, she spent the last year traveling the east coast and sharpening her skills as a thief. It was a lifestyle that kept her entertained. Keeping her luggage small only made it easier. Today she had on her yoga pants and Ralph Lauren sweatshirt, and her Nikes were the newest style. These kinds of clothes she usually considered essentials. She had one black dress that she always kept; a girl always needed one black dress. Her heart fell when she realized she was going to have to use it in a couple of days.

She carried her bags to the front door of the building labeled office and opened the door; the door gave a loud squeak.

The office was a small room with only a few chairs in the front and a long desk that had a small TV behind it. The Mariners game was on at a low volume. The desk clerk turned from the game when he heard the door. He was a tall, skinny man with white hair that was thinning on top.

"I need a room." She pulled her wallet out of her large purse.

"Okay. How long of a stay?

"Um, I don't know." Her shoulders dropped. She wasn't sure what she needed to do in town. Roxy had said that they had to plan the funeral and sign some legal paperwork. She was hoping that her stay wouldn't be long.

The clerk looked at her with annoyance. She started to pull her phone from her purse to call Roxy when the squeak of the door announced another guest. She turned to see her twin sister standing in the doorway. Her black hair was cut short and pulled into a stubby ponytail. She had on a pale blue T-shirt that brightened her blue eyes and old, faded jeans. She wore black Converse shoes which were her go-to for as long as Sydney could remember. Unlike Sydney, Roxy didn't care about fashion. She and her sister were the same height, but where she considered herself curvy, her sister had more sharp edges to her small, skinny frame.

"Hey," Roxy said, giving a shy smile. She tried to close the door quietly behind her.

Sydney hadn't seen her sister in years. The two had been close when they were younger, and they always had each other's backs, especially at the girls' home. But when she left for New York, besides some short phone calls, they hadn't really kept in contact. She surprised herself and felt uncomfortable.

"Hey," she said. *Though it sounded fake*, she thought. "How long are we going to be here?"

"I'm not quite sure yet. A couple of days is what I paid for."

"Two days." She turned to the man behind the counter, handing her card over.

He leaned his head slightly to the left and gave her a stare, then looked at Roxy.

"You're the Wright Sisters," he said, pointing at them with her credit card.

"Thought maybe you girls would be showing up with Margie's heart attack and all." He swiped her card fast.

They both smiled, but neither of them offered any more information, and he didn't ask.

She felt a little relief. Just a couple days and then she would be out of town and hopefully on her way back east.

The clerk handed her a room key and her card with a smirk and raised eyebrows. She snatched them from his hand and turned with her head held high as she pushed past Roxy.

"What room are you in?" Roxy let her pass and they entered the parking lot.

"Room 5."

"Good, I'm in 6. We'll be right next to each other." Roxy smiled nervously.

Roxy looked just as uncomfortable as Sydney felt.

They walked the short walk to the rooms in silence.

She stopped in front of her room, then looked at the key.

"Can you believe it's an actual key and not a key card?" she said.

Roxy chuckled. "This town doesn't change much."

The room smelled musty. Sydney dropped her bags on the bed and went to the one and only window and slid it open. She walked over to the small fridge and opened it too, finding it was empty and that it smelled even mustier than the room. She scrunched up her nose.

"Damn. That stinks."

"Forget this isn't a fancy five-star hotel." Roxy sat on the end of the bed.

Sydney sat down at the table under the window thinking how she could use a drink.

"Ugh, this town." She looked up. Roxy just nodded, knowing full well what she meant.

"So, tell me what happened." She leaned against the table. It was sticky and she pulled her arm away in disgust.

"The mailman, Mr. Jenks, found her." Roxy leaned back on her hands.

"I guess she had a heart attack in the front garden. She was there for about an hour. Mr. Jenks spotted her when he brought her mail."

Sydney covered her face with her hands and rubbed.

"I should have called more."

Roxy just looked down. "I called her once a week she never said she was feeling ill or anything. I was contacted by her lawyer late last night. He said that she finished her will just two weeks ago."

She snapped her head up. "Do you think she knew?"

Roxy just shrugged and stood up.

"We have a meeting with her lawyer tomorrow at nine o'clock, then the funeral home later at noon. You're probably pretty jet-lagged." Roxy got up and walked to the door.

"I'll let you rest. See you at eight-thirty. You'll have to drive." And just like that, Roxy was gone.

Roxy

The next morning, Roxy slowly opened her eyes and looked at the digital clock on the table. It was already eight in the morning. She had stayed up too late working on her computer.

She had signed on to a private contract for a large firm in Seattle and was doing a sweep of a computer for a high-profile case in Chicago. It was easy stuff for her, but it kept her busy, plus what she found on his hard drive was going to put this perv in jail for life. What a scumbag.

She pulled the covers off and jumped in the shower. She was going to have to hurry to make it to the lawyer on time.

She'd been nervous to see Sydney. She had been looking out her motel window yesterday, waiting for her to arrive, and in typical Sydney fashion, she had pulled up in a car that screamed attention. She would never rent a car like that; drawing attention wasn't what she liked. Staying under the radar was more her way. It was why she enjoyed computers so much. No one really knew you.

She and Sydney called each other about once a year around their birthday. Sydney would talk about school, even though last year, she got more and more vague about it. She would talk about work and what she was working on.

She had gotten a surprise call a couple of months ago from Sydney asking if she could hack into a camera and erase a security video of her leaving a hotel in New Jersey. Roxy figured Sydney was bored and had started picking again. She had hoped her bottomless bank account would have stopped these activities.

But she didn't ask why and just did it. She didn't want her sister getting into any trouble. She was hoping that it was a one-time only thing.

Besides the account she set up for Sydney, she was staying away from that lifestyle. She didn't have the stomach for it like Sydney had. Her dad and Sydney had both told her that she was good and had a knack for it. But in reality, she hated it.

After she finished with her shower, she threw on the first sweatshirt she found and the jeans she had on the day before. She found her Converse shoes by the door and she slipped them on. She looked at the clock and noticed she was five minutes late.

The sun was out and it was warmer than she thought. It always impressed her how different the climate was in this state by just going over the mountains.

As she walked up to Sydney's car, she saw her standing there drinking coffee and holding a brown paper sack.

"I was up early," Sydney said. "Thought you might like some breakfast."

She handed her a cup. "Black coffee, just cream, if I remember, right?" Sydney said with a smile.

She was wearing a very expensive-looking red sweater and skinny jeans with ankle boots. Sydney always looked like she had just stepped out of a fashion magazine.

"Thanks." Roxy took the cup and sipped. "What's in the bag?"

"Muffins." Sydney handed her the bag.

"I braved it and drove toward town, got lucky though and found a coffee shop just a mile up the road. The lady running it was a friend of Margie's. Her name was Bev. Do you know her?"

Roxy searched her brain, but the name was unfamiliar.

"No, I don't think so."

"Well, she was surprisingly nice." Sydney opened the door to the car. "She recognized me and said the whole town has a bet on whether we show up or not. I guess we've been the talk of the town lately."

Roxy's stomach tightened. "Seriously?" She blew out a breath. She was not looking forward to this week.

*

They drove slowly down the main street; Roxy had been to visit Margie many times over the years, but she tried to just stay at Margie's house which was on the outskirts of town. It had actually been a couple years since she had been downtown. She looked to Sydney who hadn't been back since the day they came home from the girls' home. Even then, she left for New York the next day.

Sydney's jaw was clenched and her knuckles on the steering wheel were white.

"Hey, relax," she suggested.

"I can't." Sydney flexed her fingers. "I hate it here."

"I know. Me too. But that was a long time ago."

Roxy looked out the window. They were on Main Street at eight-thirty in the morning and there weren't many people out. The town looked almost the same as she remembered. There were all of the same buildings, but the store names where different.

They passed the storefront where the old ice cream parlor was and it made her think back to her father. The three of them would walk to the ice cream shop; it was on the corner, down the way from the auto body shop where her dad had worked. They had gone over there after school a couple times when Margie wasn't able to watch them, and it was the few times they got to hang out with their dad at the shop. She loved watching him as he worked on cars. She would hand him tools , and his boss, Tim, was always real nice to them, and most times let them sit in the office and play on his computer.

One day, he had let Dad take a long break and they went to get ice cream. She remembered holding her dad's hand and Sydney holding the other. He would swing them high, making them both laugh as they walked.

On their way back, she had stumbled on the curb and had dropped her cone. She remembered tears welling up in her eyes as she looked at her Rocky Road ice cream smeared all over the street.

"Here, have mine," he had said, handing her his mint chocolate chip cone.

She remembered looking up into his smiling face. She still remembered his kind, blue eyes and shaggy black hair that often fell across his forehead and into his eyes. How her heart had sung with love for the man.

"I think this is it." Sydney pulled her from her memory.

*

Inside the lawyer's office, they were escorted into a small room in the back. When Brad McKnight, Attorney at Law, stepped in, Roxy remembered him from her childhood. He was the lawyer Margie had hired to try to get custody of her and Sydney. His hair was laced with white now, but he was clean-cut and looked ever the lawyer. He wasn't much help and in her opinion wasn't very good considering how it ended up.

"Good morning, ladies." He sat behind his very organized desk. He placed a thick file down on it and looked up at them.

They both forced a smile.

She rubbed her sweaty palms down the thighs of her jeans. She didn't want to be in his office. She didn't know Margie had a will, and Brad McKnight was very short on the phone. She didn't know what to expect.

"I'm sorry for your loss," he began. "It's great to see you girls again. It looks like you both are doing well. How is school going, Sydney?" he asked, opening the file.

"Fine," Sydney replied sharply as she adjusted her sweater, pretending to pick off lint.

"Good," Brad said. He was quickly realizing this was going to be strictly business.

"I just want to start by saying that when Margie came in to start her will, I wasn't surprised to hear that she wanted to include you ladies in it."

He folded his hands on top of the thick folder making him look friendly and professional, she wondered if that was something, they taught in law school.

"She loved you guys very much. The whole town is feeling her loss as well."

Sydney's crossed leg started to nervously swing.

"Thank you," Roxy said softly.

"It's good to see you guys back." He smiled.

"I'm sure." Sydney snorted and rolled her eyes. "Did you win the bet?"

Mr. McKnight looked a little taken aback. "I mean, I know things were rough around here with your father's death and all."

"You mean our father's murder," Sydney said, sitting up and unfolding her legs. "So, how much did you win?"

Mr. McKnight started unfolding his hands on his desk and shuffling papers again.

"I assure you I have no idea what you're talking about. Plus, the Sheriff exhausted all his resources to find out what happened to your father."

"My father was murdered and this whole community spread rumors and lies about him. I'm glad we got shipped out of here. No, thanks to you." Sydney looked like she was about to get up. Then she thought better of it and she fell back in the chair, folding her arms and shaking her leg.

Roxy's mouth dropped. She hated confrontation. She felt sick. She quickly turned to Mr. McKnight who was sitting there calm and collected like a lawyer in court.

"I'm sorry that you feel that way," he answered in a cold, calm voice.

There was an awkward silence. Not knowing what to do, Roxy filled it. She tried to keep her voice from shaking.

"So, the will, Mr. McKnight?"

"Yes." He looked relieved to be moving on.

"She left you guys everything. The house, the car, and all her assets. She left instructions that whatever you didn't want would go to the local thrift shop in town. The house is paid for and she stated that if you guys don't want it, sell it."

Roxy was surprised. Margie had left everything to them? She had no other family and no kids. She took a second to bring it all in.

She guessed their stay in Fuller was going to be a little longer than what they both hoped for.

Two very long hours later, Roxy and Sydney left Brad McKnight's office. It was official. They were the legal owners of a house and everything in it. They even had the keys to the house. Mr. McKnight, if nothing else, was efficient, and Margie had dotted all of her I's and crossed all of her T's. He stated that they had full access to the house and he would email the rest of the information to them.

"Geez." Roxy buckled her seat belt. "Did you really have to be like that? I mean, he's probably on the phone right now, telling the whole town how the Wright sisters came in and were starting trouble again. We haven't even been in town for twenty-four hours."

Sydney huffed. "I don't care, Roxy. I'm here for the funeral and will help you sell the house, then I'm out. No later than the end of the week."

"It's going to take longer than a couple of days, you know that, right? I mean, we have a ton of paperwork alone, not to mention packing up over thirty years of stuff in Margie's house."

Sydney looked toward her. "I can't make any promises."

Sydney

They decided that they would stay at Margie's house that night so between the lawyer's appointment and the funeral director, they would pack their belongings and check out of the motel. She was glad. The motel had to have bed bugs.

Even though going to Margie's was going to be tough, it was going to be one step closer to leaving town.

They piled their bags in the trunk of the car, checked out of the dumpy motel, and made their way to the funeral home.

The funeral director meeting went smoother than the one with the lawyer. She had kept calm.

Margie had stated that she wanted to be buried next to her husband and she had already paid and picked out the headstone. There wasn't much for the girls to do but pick the date. They decided to have the funeral in two days, which was a relief to Sydney.

The short, bald funeral director reminded them that the townspeople were going to want to pay their respects and not to be surprised that people were going to show up at Margie's house after the funeral.

She saw Roxy rub her forehead.

"So, are you okay with people showing up at the house after the funeral?" she asked Roxy as they walked to the car. It was late afternoon and the town seemed to be in full swing.

She couldn't help but notice a couple walking across the street who pointed over at them. She ignored them.

"I guess that's normally what people do. She did have lots of friends." Roxy stopped on the passenger side of the car.

"I mean, after we left Margie, she still went to town and church. She stayed involved."

She just nodded and looked around.

"The town looks the same. But different too, you know?" she said.

"Yeah." Roxy studied the town too.

She watched a woman and man walk together and go into a restaurant.

He held the door for her. She saw a lady trying to round up two young kids who were not happy about leaving the park. People were everywhere. She wondered how these people got to where they were? Why her life had been so different and not normal like these people's seemed to be.

They both got in the car. She reached to start it but soon stopped. Was she ready to go to Margie's house? She hadn't been there since she was eighteen, four years ago, and that was when she had just gotten out of the girls' home. The next day she left to go the other side of the country. Roxy looked over at her.

She could feel the tears welling up in her eyes. One fell and she realized that was the first since she heard the news. She was so concerned with coming back to town that she hadn't let herself feel the loss of her beloved family member, because that's what Margie was. She looked to Roxy.

"I don't know if I can go back to her house."

"I know." Roxy looked down at her hands. "You want me to drive?" Roxy asked.

"No, I'll be fine. It's just been a long time. I thought I would never come back here. Never thought Margie would pass away. Pretty stupid, huh?"

"No," was Roxy's short answer. Then Roxy placed her hand on Sydney's shoulder. She had the need to shake it off but stopped herself. She looked at her sister. Her blue eyes were sad and she had a small smile. She had forgotten how her sister's eyes were always soft and caring looking, unlike hers.

She gave a weak smile back. She turned the key and put the car in gear. "So, where is the nearest liquor store?"

"That is the best idea of the day." Roxy sat back in the seat.

*

It turned out the town of Fuller didn't have a liquor store. After Roxy's search on her GPS, they ended up at the grocery store, which Roxy pointed out was probably a good idea to get food as well. Neither one of them had eaten anything but coffee and a muffin all day.

When they arrived at the store, she headed straight for the wine and beer aisle. Roxy followed with the cart.

She placed a bottle of gin for herself and she grabbed three bottles of wine for Roxy.

"I don't need three bottles," Roxy pointed out.

"Don't worry. You can share with me." She smiled and they went to find food.

They filled the cart with various food items, considering they didn't know what Margie had and if it had gone bad. They rounded the corner, looking for the coffee creamer, when she heard her name.

"Oh my god! Sydney and Roxy Wright!"

She froze, even after ten years. That voice made her blood boil.

"Marcy Stone." She spun around with a fake smile across her face.

"Oh, well, it's Harris now." She brought her hand up and wiggled her fingers, showing off a large diamond ring.

"Well, look at that rock, Roxy." She smiled quietly, calculating how much she could get for it. Roxy gave her a warning look.

"Hello, Marcy." Roxy's knuckles turned white on the cart handle.

Marcy was pushing a stroller that had a small baby swinging around a slimy stuffed dog.

"Well, you sure have your hands full."

"I know." Marcy stepped out from behind the stroller. "And another on the way." She was rubbing her hand down her beach ball of a belly.

Roxy wrinkled her nose.

A small arm shot out of the stroller and threw the stuffed dog on the ground. Neither of them went to pick up the wet stuffed animal.

Marcy bent to pick it up. It was the most uncomfortable deep squat she had ever seen. It almost made Sydney feel bad for her. Almost. She put the stuffed dog in the pocket of the stroller and looked up.

"So, I heard you two were back in town. So sorry for your loss." Marcy's face fell into a sympathetic pout. "Margie was a great woman. It was sad to hear how she was found by Mr. Jenks. He said that she was all alone."

Guilt rose in her throat. Sydney almost choked on it.

"Thank you," Roxy said quietly.

"I will definitely be at the funeral. I heard that it was two days from now at noon."

Her mind went blank.

"How did you know that? We just finished the meeting with the funeral director."

Marcy laughed. "I'm friends with the funeral director's daughter. Our kids go to daycare together. But it's on the funeral home's website too. It's under the schedule section."

Marcy tapped on her phone and showed them the screen. Right at the top. *"Margie Simms' Service,"* it read.

"What?" They both stepped closer and stared at the screen. It had the date and plot number as well.

Roxy stepped back and pulled her phone out, then started to flip through it.

Marcy pulled her phone back and placed it on the stroller.

"I know that most of the town will be there, and many plan to pay their respects later at the house." Marcy ran her hand over her stomach again and Sydney noticed a diamond tennis bracelet. She wondered if her guy in Seattle was still there.

"We should go," Roxy said as she started to push the cart toward the next aisle.

"I heard you were doing well over in New York, Sydney." Marcy continued ignoring Roxy's attempt to escape.

Marcy glanced at Roxy. Sydney swore she saw something predatory in her eyes.

"Yep, New York is great." Marcy waited for further information and when Sydney didn't comply, she turned to Roxy. Sydney's back straightened.

"So, Roxy? Margie said that you were doing computer stuff in Seattle. How is that going? Working for Microsoft or something?"

"Nope, mainly private contractor work."

Marcy looked her up and down quickly.

"I take it there isn't much money in that kind of work." The evil smile that she remembered from her childhood formed on Marcy's face.

She could feel the anger bubbling up and she shuffled her feet.

"Well, actually…" She was ready to tell Marcy how successful Roxy was or maybe she was going to punch her. Either way, she stepped forward, but Roxy grabbed her by the arm and pulled her back.

"We need to go. Lots of stuff to do." Roxy yanked her arm again.

"Of course." Marcy grabbed the stroller and turned to leave.

"I'll talk to my designer friends in New York and have them send you some new maternity clothes." Sydney couldn't help herself.

Marcy looked a little taken back.

"My husband special ordered these for me from Seattle. You remember my husband, Mark Harris. He was the quarterback for the Fuller High School Hornets. She gave a little cheerleader fist pump. "Oh, wait, you didn't go to Fuller High. That's right. You two were sent off to a girls' home or orphanage or something like that." She chuckled.

Sydney saw red and she took a step forward again. But Roxy tightened her grip on her arm.

Marcy laughed again. "It's been a treat to see you girls." She looked down at her phone. "But I have to go. Running late. I'll see you two at the funeral." She tilted the stroller and left.

"I'm going to kill her." Sydney spun on her heels and started down the aisle. She wanted out of there—out of this store, out of this town.

"Wait." Roxy started to run after her with the cart. "Sydney, just wait!" It was the loudest she had heard Roxy talk all day.

She turned, unshed tears in her eyes.

"Marcy's not worth it," Roxy said.

Sydney looked back behind her, trying to shoot darts at Marcy's back.

"Who does she think she is?" She wiped the tears from her eyes. "She hasn't changed. She gave us so much crap in school."

Roxy took a deep breath. "I know, but if it makes you feel better, just look at her."

Sydney looked over at Roxy in confusion.

"She's married to a guy she went to high school with. She lives in a small town that she's never left and is popping out kids in what seems to be in a very unhealthy amount of time."

Sydney's laugh was soft. "I guess you're right. Can't beat up a pregnant lady."

Roxy chuckled. "That won't help our reputation. Come on, let's get creamer and get out of here."

Together, they headed for the front of the store.

"Did you see her ring?" She looked to Roxy who was placing the flavored creamer into the cart. Roxy just nodded.

"I bet I could get at least two grand for it." She smiled. "Plus, that bracelet too. I bet Yuri in Seattle will give me more. If he's still there."

"He is." Roxy pulled the cart into the closest checkout line. Roxy remembered Yuri from the one time she had gone to his shop with Sydney.

"But I have a better idea. Let's not get caught stealing in this town."
Roxy leaned in close to Sydney. "I brought my computer."

She looked over at Roxy slowly.

"Roxy, you genius. Let's mess up her credit score."

Roxy wiggled her eyebrows.

They left the store and as they headed to the car, an older woman approached them.

"Sydney Wright!" They heard the woman yelling. Then the woman started to wave her hands over her head.

Sydney waved back. "That's Bev, from the coffee shop," she told Roxy, trying to erase the annoyance from her face.

Bev made her way over. She was a short, round woman with a blonde cap of hair. She was smiling and it was almost comical how she was waving her arms.

"Hello, this must be Roxy." Bev stopped right in front of them and held her hand out.

"I've heard so much about you girls. Margie was so proud of you."

She let go of Roxy's hand.

"I heard the funeral is in two days. Are you guys ready for people to stop by afterward?"

"We really don't even know what to do." Roxy was wringing her hands.

"Well, you girls, don't worry, I'll take care of it. I promised Margie I would help you guys out as much as possible. Most people bring food, so don't worry about that. No decorations. It's not a party."

She couldn't tell if Bev was even talking to them or reading off a list in her head.

"I'll bring some wine and drinks. Just make sure you guys have ice. Easy enough, right?" Bev gave a big smile.

"I think we can handle that," Sydney said and smiled. "Thank you."

Bev waved her thanks away. "I'll see you girls later."

Then Bev turned and threw her arms up again. "Trudy! Hey, Trudy!" she yelled and darted off after someone else. Roxy looked over at her. Sydney smiled and said, "I kind of like her."

*

They rode to Margie's house in silence. When they pulled into the driveway,

32

her heart quickened. *It looked the same*, she thought. The one-story rambler house was still white with blue trim. The paint was chipping in a few spots and the grass was overgrown. The trees cast shade over the side yard where Margie had set up a small table with two chairs, but the late afternoon sun shone on the front yard.

Margie always said that she was grateful for that. It meant she could grow beautiful flowers. Except there were no flowers blooming. She never had time to plant her spring bulbs.

Sydney felt her eyes water up but forced it down. She didn't want to cry in front of Roxy again. She took a deep breath.

"When was the last time you were here?" she asked, not taking her eyes off the front of the house. She squeezed the steering wheel.

"Two months ago. She seemed fine. She was happy and full of energy. I wish I had known, maybe I could have helped her. I skipped the last couple of times I was supposed to visit; got caught up in work. Told her I had a deadline to make." Roxy's eyes filled up with tears this time, but she blinked them away. She grabbed the door handle. "Let's get this over with."

She got out of the car and together they walked around to the trunk. They each grabbed their luggage and the grocery bags. They walked to the front door.

Roxy shuffled her bags and took the key from her pocket.

Sydney turned to the front of the yard, facing the two-lane road. There was a field of yellowing grass, and out from that, you could just barely see the main road that led out of town. She turned left and looked at what was a large field full of acres of the same bright yellow grass, but there was a bare spot, a spot where the grass didn't grow. It was the space where their small, barely two-story house used to sit. She didn't know who owned it now and didn't care. She didn't wonder why no one had built on it either. The thought of the night her dad died slammed her in the chest, making her take a big breath of the evening's air.

Turning away from the memories of the worst night of her life, she walked into the house.

Roxy

The house was dark. She flipped on the foyer light. She didn't know what she was expecting—maybe death. But it looked the same as it did the last time she was here. She blew out the large breath she was holding. She swore she heard Sydney do the same.

The living room was in front of the house. It had just a plain tan couch against the wall and an old TV in the corner. She remembered sitting on that couch watching movies with Sydney.

Margie had some pictures on the wall of her and her husband on vacation or their wedding day. There was also a picture of her and Sydney from their twelfth birthday. They had on paper hats, and their big, white, frosted cake sat on the table in front of them. They were both smiling and wide-eyed. That had been a good day.

They walked into the kitchen to find it looked the same as it always had. A small dining table was off to the left and all the simple appliances made it look like any other kitchen.

She put the grocery bags down on the counter and saw Sydney's face looked pale, and her eyes were dark and sad. "You all right?" she asked her sister.

"Yeah." Sydney looked up, a little dazed. "Yeah, fine."

Sydney's face was pale and Roxy was worried for her sister.

"Are you sure? You don't look very good."

"I'm fine." She grabbed the wine bottle from the bag. She marched to the cupboard and started looking for wine glasses. Then she stopped. Sydney looked at her. She took a deep breath. *Lots of memories.*

They were both silent. She wanted to hug her sister, but thought she shouldn't. Sydney always stiffened when she touched her.

"Why doesn't Margie have wine glasses?" Sydney forced a laugh.

"The other cupboard." She pointed.

Sydney found them in the back, poured two large glasses, and brought one to Roxy. She put the wine bottle on the table between them. She flopped down on the chair next to her at the table.

"What a day." Sydney took a big, long drink from her glass.

Roxy followed her lead. To her surprise, the wine was good and she took another sip.

She watched Sydney. She was looking around a lot, being fidgety. She hadn't seen her like this since they had been in the girls' home.

Roxy thought back to Sydney sitting on the end of her bed in their room on the first night. She was twelve, her hair pulled back in a ponytail, wide-eyed and staring at everything like she was looking for an escape.

She shook the memory; it was a time in her life she tried not to think about too often.

"It's like the whole town just came down on us all at once."

"It did, didn't it?" Sydney agreed. "Can you believe Marcy Stone? I mean Harris." She said the last part with her nose in the air.

She remembered what Marcy had said about her clothes. It had made her feel self-conscious and caused her to wonder if something was wrong with her, because she had never really cared before.

"Do I really dress that bad?" she asked Sydney, pulling her shirt down and trying to look a little nicer in her black sweatshirt. She couldn't help it.

"Hell no! You're fine. Don't let her get to you. You know, I read an article one time that said smart people often don't care about what they wear. Their brains don't care about insufficient stuff like that. You have better things to think about."

She smiled and looked down at her glass. "Thanks, Syd." She looked back up. "I think that's one of the nicest things you have ever said to me."

"Yeah, well, whatever." Sydney's face flushed; she refilled her glass then topped off her own.

"So, what are we going to do about this house?" Roxy looked around. "I guess we get rid of everything and sell it? Or do you want to keep it?"

"Nope. I don't want any more ties to this town. Sell it online. Then we can take a vacation to the Caribbean. And donate the rest to a charity that Margie would have liked."

Roxy started to think of what channels she could take to sell the house online. It would be easy. She wanted to go get her computer.

"I guess we have the funeral, then clean the house out, and we'll be done with this town for good."

She got up to get her computer from her bag that she had dumped in the foyer.

"In the meantime, let's check what kind of credit cards Marcy uses. Let's show her what a girl that dresses poorly can do."

Sydney laughed wickedly. "Yes!"

*

It had been a week since their dad's funeral. It was small and quick. Not many people had attended. Tim, Dad's boss, was there. A few other people from town and the auto body shop attended. Sydney and Roxy arrived, holding Margie's hand.

Tim had told the girls that he had loved their father and that if they ever needed anything, all they had to do was call. He had asked Margie where he should send Gabe's tools. Margie had looked at the girls and when they gave no response, she told him just to keep them.

The girls hadn't spoken to anyone. The next few days after the funeral, they had stayed inside Margie's house all week and watched movies and cried.

But Roxy was getting antsy and could see Sydney was too. They had asked Margie if they could walk down to the playground that was two blocks away. Margie was hesitant, but the girls pleaded that they needed to get out, so Margie had given in.

"The sun feels good." Sydney turned her face up. They had only walked a block so far, but it felt good to be out.

"Yeah," Roxy replied absentmindedly. She had been thinking about the phone calls she had been eavesdropping on between Margie and someone else. It sounded like they weren't going to be staying at Margie's much longer.

"You think we will have to go to the girls' home?" she asked.

"I hope not. I don't think Margie will let that happen. She loves us and told me she wants us to stay."

She shook her head in agreement, but little flares of panic still clutched her chest.

They walked another block in silence. They entered through a small gate to get to the playground and headed for the swings.

"Shoot!" Sydney hissed.

She looked up and sure enough, Marcy and her little gang of girls were already by the swings.

"Let's just go." She grabbed Sydney's arm and tried to pull her back.

"Why? They don't own the park."

Marcy was always making fun of their hand-me-down clothes and bargain brand shoes. Roxy didn't want to deal with them right now. But Sydney didn't stop. She walked right over to the swings and sat down. Roxy had no choice and followed.

Roxy started to swing. She was too nervous to talk. She was trying not to bring attention to them and was hoping the other girls would just leave.

She heard giggling from them. Roxy looked over and found that they were all staring at her and Sydney. Marcy had actually pointed. Roxy slowed down her swing.

Marcy and her friends walked over.

She stood up like she was ready to run. But Sydney stayed in her swing.

"Hey girls," Marcy said, her voice sounding high-pitched.

"I heard about your dad. Tough break, huh?" She had a fake frown on her face.

"Heard your dad was shot in the head," a girl named Brandy laughed.

"Yeah, by a drug dealer," another girl said. Roxy didn't know who she was.

Sydney stood up. "You shouldn't talk about things you know nothing about."

The girls all started to laugh.

"My dad's the sheriff. I heard that you guys have to go to an orphanage, because you're homeless and have no parents." They all laughed again.

Sydney jumped forward and grabbed Brandy by the hair. She pulled her head down, throwing her to the ground. Marcy came back in full attack mode and grabbed Sydney by the ponytail.

Roxy jumped in and started to hit Marcy on the back with her fists. The next thing she knew, they were all on the ground, rolling in the dirt. Roxy was just throwing punches at any and everyone.

She felt herself being pulled up by big, strong hands and she started to kick wildly.

"Whoa girl, calm down."

She looked up and saw Sheriff Stone. He and another deputy were breaking up the fight. She looked around frantically for Sydney. She saw her sitting back on her hands. Her hair was hanging loose from her ponytail and her eyes were wild.

The sheriff put her down. "What's going on here?"

"Daddy, they attacked us," Marcy pouted.

Roxy wanted to spit at her. She turned to Sydney to see if she was all right.

"Now, you stay here, girl," the sheriff said as he grabbed her by the arm and held her back.

"They were saying mean things to us." Sydney stood. "They were talking about our dad."

The sheriff looked over at his daughter and her friends. He was a large man with a big stomach. His uniform was always wrinkled and that day he had some kind of stain on the front of it.

"Were you guys being mean?"

"No, Daddy. They just attacked us."

The sheriff nodded his head. "Deputy Grosser, why don't you take my girl and her friends back to my house and I'll take care of the Wright sisters."

Roxy's stomach tightened. She didn't want to be left with the sheriff. He always gave her a bad feeling.

The deputy gathered up the other girls and herded them toward his patrol car.

Sydney walked over to Roxy and stood next to her.

"Now, girls, I know that you have been having a hard time lately. But that doesn't mean you guys can go around picking fights."

"Your daughter is mean," Sydney said. She stood up taller. Roxy stepped in closer, letting them be a united front.

The sheriff laughed. "You girls got guts, just like your old man." His face went serious. "Let me give you girls some advice. Your daddy was a crook, and when you live like he did, you end up like he did."

She started to shake and tears of anger welled in her eyes. She felt Sydney stiffen up next to her too.

"Don't follow in your father's footsteps. You hear?"

*

Roxy woke with a start; the room she was in was all wrong, different. It took a second but it all came back. She was at Margie's house in one of the spare bedrooms. She sat up. Her head spun and she remembered that she had a lot of wine last night. She fell back in bed, thinking maybe she should sleep more. But her dream came back, filling her mind. Her eyes filled up with tears. She hated the sheriff from that day forward. It wasn't that much longer after that fight on the playground that Sydney had punched Marcy in the nose and they stopped going to school. She had pushed that memory away for a long time.

Seeing Marcy must have brought it back and she wished that she could forget it again.

She laid in bed waiting for the dizziness to pass. She had to admit she had fun last night with Sydney; they had canceled Marcy's American Express and then even dropped her husband Mark Harris' credit score a few points. She felt a little guilty, but not enough. She'd change it back in a couple days.

She got up and shuffled down the hall to the kitchen to make coffee. She needed it. She was used to late nights but not wine. She wasn't a heavy drinker, but it felt good to be with her sister. The two of them had been inseparable when they were younger, and when Sydney left to go to school, it had hurt Roxy more than she cared to admit. But they were together now and she was going to make the best of it.

She started the coffee pot and then turned her computer on. She caught up on her emails and told her boss that she was taking a few days off because of a death in the family. She got up to pour coffee when she turned and saw that Sydney was standing at the end of the hall.

"Good morning," Roxy said, trying to hide her smile behind her mug. Sydney looked like she had a rough night. Her hair was in a big, tangled mess and her eyes were puffy.

"It looks like you could use some coffee," she said.

But Sydney kept staring into the living room.

"What are you looking at?" Roxy asked, craning her neck around the corner.

"Nothing," Sydney said, still staring. "Just forgot about the ducks."

When Roxy didn't say anything, she continued.

"Those porcelain ducks," Sydney said, pointing.

Margie had two life-size white ducks that sat in the living room. One was bent over like it was eating and the other stood tall, his head up. She never knew why, but Sydney would always turn them to face the wall.

Sydney shook her head and finally walked over to the coffee pot.

"They're still facing the wall," Sydney said, pouring a large cup.

"Margie would always ask, 'What have they done now?'"

Sydney smiled. "I would make up some story about how they did something bad, and Margie would laugh and say it serves them right then."

"I turned them the night before I left for New York." Sydney looked into her coffee mug.

"I should have visited. Not one time did I visit after that. I'm horrible," she said, looking up, tears filling her eyes.

"Margie understood." Roxy closed her laptop. "She knew what Dad's death did to us and what people were saying. I think she felt guilty for not protecting us from it. She felt she failed us too."

"That doesn't make me feel better." Sydney reached over and grabbed a bagel from the bag that was sitting on the counter. They sat in silence.

"So, what do we do today?" Roxy tried to change the subject and gain some type of purpose.

"We start boxing stuff up, I guess."

"Let's start in her room. People are coming over tomorrow for the wake and we will need the main house to be suitable."

Sydney looked over to her. "Look at you. I thought you didn't socialize, and here you are planning."

Roxy felt a blush. "Whatever. I'm just ready for this to be over."

*

They spent the morning going through Margie's bedroom.

After an hour of going through the closet, Sydney got bored of her small-town wardrobe and started going through the jewelry box. Roxy kept at the closet.

"I take it you don't want any of these clothes?" she asked Sydney.

"Nope." Sydney pulled a shelled necklace out with a frown. Roxy couldn't help smiling. Sydney threw it in the box marked "Donate."

Her plan was to keep some clothes, but every time she pulled something out, she couldn't stand to think that Margie once wore it, and she found herself throwing it in the donate box.

Sydney threw a couple cheaper bracelets into a box, then got up. "I'm getting us a drink."

She usually didn't drink this much and didn't think Sydney did either, but it sounded good.

Memories of Margie were all around and she was having a hard time believing Margie was really gone. She pulled out an old, faded flannel that Margie wore all the time in the garden. She couldn't help the tears that came. She envisioned Margie in the garden on her hands and knees, scraping the dirt with a small shovel. A box of flowers next to her waiting to be planted. The sun shining, she remembered the way Margie taught her to tickle the roots of the flowers before planting and how she had laughed at the thought of the flowers being tickled.

Sydney walked in and handed her a glass half full of gin.

"Here," she said and went back to the bed. Sydney didn't say anything about her tears and she was grateful.

Sydney gulped her whole glass without even a flinch and with the bottle she hadn't seen her bring in with her, filled her glass.

Roxy hated gin. She thought it tasted like pine needles. She followed Sydney's example and threw it back fast.

Her throat burned. "Gross." She gasped for air. "How do you drink this all the time?"

"Low carb," Sydney said. She had the jewelry box again and pulled out a small ring.

Roxy studied it from the floor. "Do you think that is her wedding ring?"

"I think so," Sydney replied, turning the ring in her fingers.

"What do you think her husband was like?" Sydney squinted her eyes to get a better look at the small diamond.

"I don't know." She tried to picture them together. The pictures around the house were few, but they showed a happy couple, both young, the man in military dress and the woman in a simple white gown. Both were smiling. "They looked happy."

Sydney sighed. "He died young, right out of the Gulf War. They didn't have much time together. Margie must have really loved him considering she never remarried." She paused. "You think Margie ever dated?"

Roxy just shrugged.

"How about you?" Sydney asked, taking a sip of her drink. "Any dating?"

"Nope," Roxy said quickly. "You?"

"No, no time."

Sydney stared at her with a smile. "Are you still a virgin?" she asked with a hint of a devilish gleam.

She could feel her cheeks redden. They used to share everything.

Sydney had lost her virginity and had told her that night in their junior year of high school.

"No. I'm not." She was folding a T-shirt.

Sydney sat up on the bed.

"When, who, where?" Sydney was literally leaning forward, ready for answers.

"Wait, why didn't you tell me?" She noticed the quick look of hurt pass over Sydney's face.

Roxy put the shirt in the donation box.

"His name was David and we worked together on a project a couple years ago."

"Well?" Sydney made a "keep going" motion with her hand. "How did it happen?"

"I'm sure you're familiar with how sex works."

Sydney rolled her eyes. "Yes, but I mean, how did it happen? Were you working late together or maybe you caught eyes over your monitors and it was true love?" Sydney fluttered her eyelashes and then laughed.

"We had just finished the project and everyone went out for drinks to celebrate. I wasn't going to go, but somehow he talked me into it. He was very good looking. We started talking and we went back to his place." She shrugged and threw another T-shirt into the donation box.

"You dirty computer nerds." Sydney laughed. "Did you ever see him again?" Sydney refilled her drink again.

"We keep in touch. We had dinner once. It was okay, but that was it. No love between us, but we're still friends."

"That's it, huh? Did you do it after dinner?"

"Yeah!" Roxy laughed.

"How about you?" she said, handing her glass back to Sydney for a refill, Margie's closet forgotten for the moment. "How are the guys in New York?"

"I don't know, been pretty busy with classes." Sydney looked away. There was a guy freshman year, but that fizzled out fast. Sydney shrugged.

Odd, Roxy thought.

"And I've kind of been picking a little bit. Plus, guys ask a lot of questions when you leave in the middle of the night and come home with big diamonds and large amounts of money."

"I thought you might be doing that again." She frowned. She wanted to ask how long when Sydney cut her off. "So, tell me, was David good?"

Sydney

She woke up in the small guest room. She groaned, thinking how it was the day of the funeral. How was she going to get through this? She rolled over to face the window. It was cracked open a bit, but the curtains were still. She could see that it was going to be a nice day.

Sydney and Roxy had pretty much gone through all of Margie's bedroom. They had several donation boxes already and planned on selling her bed and dresser.

That was only one room and it had taken forever. They had talked and it felt good to laugh with her sister. It had been too long. But they had to speed up if she ever was going to get out of Margie's house and the town.

Maybe, we should just burn it down? she contemplated, then moaned.

She rolled herself out of bed and put on a robe that she had found in Margie's closet over her large T-shirt she had worn to bed. When she opened the door, she smelled the glorious aroma of coffee. "Thank God." she cried.

Roxy was in the kitchen, typing away on her laptop.

"I made a large pot this morning. I think we are going to need it today."

Sydney noticed the bags under Roxy's eyes and wondered if hers looked as bad. Sydney showered first; she tried to keep it short. Margie's house didn't have a very big hot water tank, something she had complained to Margie about when she was younger.

Margie would respond, "It's only me. I don't need to save water for anyone." She always said it with a smile, but that smile had never really reached her eyes.

She slipped on her black dress and, since the weather was nice, decided to go with her black wedges that wouldn't sink in the grass. She also decided to wear her long black hair down and put on some makeup. She went to the kitchen to grab another cup of coffee.

Roxy walked into the kitchen. She was wearing a pair of black slacks and black button-up blouse. She had on her black Converse.

"Do you even own another pair of shoes?"

Roxy looked down. "Yeah. I have red ones too. I left them in Seattle, though."

Sydney couldn't help rolling her eyes. She went to her room and came back holding a sweater in black and her spiked black heels.

"Here, put these on. At least you'll look a little more put together."

Roxy slipped the sweater on. It did help, a little.

"I can't walk in these." Roxy held up the heels. "I'll break my ankle."

She took a sip of her coffee. "Very true. Here, wear these wedges. They will be easier to walk in." She slipped her feet out and kicked them over to her.

Roxy took her shoes and socks off. She shoved her feet in the wedges.

"Christ, Roxy! Look at your toes."

"What." Roxy looked down at her unpainted toes poking out of the wedges.

Roxy looked over at her pink toenails. "I don't ever get a pedicure. I don't like my feet touched."

Sydney sighed. "I don't have any closed-toed shoes besides my Nikes with me." She wasn't going to tell Roxy that she had sold them when she had dropped out of school.

"I think Margie had some flats in the donation box. Go get those."

She noticed Roxy was getting irritated.

Roxy turned to go to Margie's room and rolled her ankle in the wedges and almost fell. Sydney held her laugh in till Roxy was out of earshot.

*

The funeral was at the Fuller Town Cemetery. When they pulled in, the place was packed.

"Wow! You think all these people are really here for Margie?" Roxy looked at her from the passenger seat, her face white.

"Relax, it's going to be fine, don't get all anxious on me." She leaned over the steering wheel and looked out the front windshield. There had to be a hundred people there.

They looked at each other and sighed. "For Margie," Roxy said and pushed open her door.

The town must have been slow on the drama lately," she whispered to Roxy as they walked to the plot.

They were just getting to the crowd when Bev pushed her short, round body through. "Girls!" She was waving her arms and jumping up and down.

"Oh my god," Roxy looked down, avoiding eye contact with everyone.

Sydney gave a little wave back, so that at least Bev would stop screaming their names.

"I got spots for you girls right up front." She grabbed both girls by the arms and started to push them through the crowd.

"Move, Freddy." Bev elbowed a man in dirty jeans and a black T-shirt. "Margie's girls are here."

She scanned the crowd as she was being pulled and saw no familiar faces, which wasn't a surprise.

She heard Roxy next to her whispering, "Excuse me" and "Sorry" as she bounced through the mob.

She caught a glimpse of Marcy and a couple other women standing on the other side of the crowd. They made eye contact. Marcy made a sly little half smile. Sydney wanted to flip her off, but before she had a chance, Bev pulled her and Roxy down into some folding chairs, right in front of the coffin.

"Here, sit, I got these chairs just for you guys."

"Thank you." She'd much rather have been in the back of the mass, watching from afar. She assumed Roxy felt the same.

But it was thoughtful, and Bev had gone out of her way for them.

The smell of dirt and freshly mowed grass filled her nose. She looked over at Roxy.

Roxy was wringing her hands in her lap. She reached over and grabbed her sister's hand. Roxy looked up and smiled. Together, they listened to the pastor as he gave his short speech.

When it was time to lower the casket into the ground, they both stood, still holding hands. They watched Margie's casket being lowered. She felt hot tears in her eyes. Roxy wiped one off her cheek with her free hand.

Both she and Roxy dropped a rose into the hole and together they silently turned and headed for the car. No one tried to stop them or try to talk to them. The crowd all but parted for them as they went.

When they reached the parking lot, Bev trotted up to the car.

"That was a beautiful service." Bev gave a sad smile.

"It was," Roxy said, giving her a soft smile back.

"Everyone is going to start making their way to Margie's. But it will take some time in the traffic mess this will be. I'll meet you guys there as soon as I can. Did you get ice yet?"

"Of course." They didn't want to say that they had forgotten the ice.

"Well, get going unless you want to be stuck." She made a shooing gesture with her hands, and they jumped into the car. She pulled out in a large swerve and gunned it to the exit.

"Man, we forgot the ice." She shook her head.

"We had one job." Roxy held up her finger and chuckled.

They did a quick stop at the gas station and bought eight bags of ice.

"I hope this is enough," Roxy said through gritted teeth. They were struggling carrying four bags each.

"Me too. I don't want to run out," she said as they threw them into the truck.

They were halfway to Margie's when she noticed the long line of cars start to form behind them.

"You don't think they are all coming to our house, do you?" Roxy's eyes darted from the road to the side mirror.

"Bev better be right about them all bringing food." Roxy still had her eyes glued to the mirror.

Sydney turned in to Margie's drive.

They were barely out of the car when cars started to pull in behind them. Some people were parking on the street also.

They both got out and headed for the trunk for the ice. When she slammed the door of the trunk, Bev was standing right next to her and Sydney jumped.

"Geez, Bev, you scared me."

"Sorry, I'm just surprised I made it here so fast." She was carrying two large bags full of what sounded like wine bottles. Every time she shuffled her feet, they clinked together.

Roxy ran over and took one and they headed for the door.

After two trips, Sydney had carried all eight bags of ice in and found Bev and Roxy in the kitchen.

Bev was fully in host mode and Roxy was doing whatever she was told.

"Looks like you ladies are going to have a full house." Bev was pulling paper cups from one of the bags.

People were already streaming in without even knocking.

Bev noticed too. "Hey Mindy! Glad you're here. Place your salad on the table and have your Aaron set up the coolers in the back yard."

"On it, Bev," the woman named Mindy yelled back.

"Thanks, Bev," Roxy said, looking relieved.

Sydney realized that neither of them were ready or had the know how to do this.

"You're welcome, dear." Bev patted Roxy on the shoulder. She then pulled a small bottle of whiskey from another bag.

"I figured the three of us could share this. We'll hide it from the guests."

Sydney smiled. She loved Bev even more.

*

It felt like for the last two hours she was opening the front door to townspeople, receiving condolences and casseroles. She said her thanks and placed them on the table or counter as she went. She checked on Bev several times, but she was busy socializing and running their wake. She seemed to be in her element.

"Thank you" seemed to be the phrase of the night, and Sydney continued to do her part. Most people were polite, and they only caught people staring or whispering to each other a couple of times.

She walked by the kitchen and caught Roxy, her head in the freezer.

She grabbed a cup from the table and made her way over.

"Please," she whined, handing Roxy her glass.

"It has to end sometime," Roxy said as she poured.

"Well, there you guys are." Both Roxy's and Sydney's shoulders tightened. They turned together.

"Hello, Marcy," Roxy said with a little bit of bite.

"What a nice service. I was all teared up." Marcy placed her hand on her chest.

They both smiled at her.

Marcy took a look around the house. "You girls sure have your hands full with this old house. What do you plan on doing with it?" Marcy took a drink from the paper cup she held.

Sydney noticed that she was wearing the same tennis bracelet as the other day. The diamonds sparkled in the kitchen light.

"Not quite sure yet. Probably sell the house. Why, you interested?"

"Oh, heavens no." Marcy laughed. "Mark and I already own our house, and looking for a vacation place, we wouldn't have the time to restore this old place."

She thought of the credit check she and Roxy had done the other night and knew they had bought a house but it hadn't been paid off yet.

Sydney smiled. "Here. Let me freshen your drink." Sydney grabbed one of the bottles of Diet Coke off the counter.

"Sure, thanks." Marcy held out her cup with one and rubbed her large belly with the other.

Sydney went to pour but she stumbled a little and the soda missed the cup and splashed on Marcy's wrist.

"What the hell!" Marcy stepped back, trying not to get any soda on her shoes.

"Damn! I'm so clumsy." She grabbed the towel that was on the counter and started to wipe Marcy's arm.

Marcy wrenched back. "I got it. You haven't changed much, have you?" Marcy turned and grabbed a roll of paper towels and started to wipe her dress.

"So sorry," Sydney said again and turned toward Roxy.

Roxy hadn't missed it. It was one of the first moves their father had taught them.

Sydney smiled.

Roxy looked to Marcy and saw that she was at the sink, using water to wash out the stain. Roxy leaned in to Sydney and whispered, "She wears that all the time. She's going to notice it's gone."

"I'm not going to keep it," Sydney said blandly.

Dad had always taught them not to steal from people they knew.

She looked over to the foyer and saw coats hung on the rack. She noticed a pale pink petticoat worn by Marcy's blonde friend. She always giggling when she and Roxy walked by. She walked over to the coat rack and dropped the bracelet into the pocket. She walked back to Roxy.

"Let's see how strong their friendship really is."

*

An hour later, people were finally slowly leaving. Marcy had left shortly after the accident and that helped her relax a little.

Bev was in the kitchen tidying up and she spotted Roxy through the backslider door awkwardly talking to an older man who was smoking a cigar. Sydney had no idea who he was.

She went to the living room; it was empty. The sun had set and the room was dark. She walked over to the lamp on the side table and flipped it on. She slipped her shoes off. The feeling of setting her toes free from her tight wedges had her letting out a sigh of relief.

"Wow! Your feet must have been hurting to get a moan like that," a deep male voice said.

She spun and there was a man walking into the living room.

She plastered her fake smile on her face but it slowly turned to genuine.

He was handsome. Tall, well over six feet, with wide shoulders. He had dark brown hair and a strong jawline under a trimmed beard. His smile was slow and mischievous. His gray eyes were hidden by thick lashes.

"Yeah, I guess it's been a long day." She felt a little unsettled by his smile.

He looked her up and down quickly and held out his hand. "I'm Asa Hallows."

"I'm Sydney Wright." She took his hand and gave it a small shake. She couldn't help notice how large his hand was.

"I'm sorry for your loss." He let her hand go.

"Thank you." She gave a small smile. "So how did you know Margie?"

"She did some business with my family a little while ago. When I heard of her passing, I wanted to give my condolences to her family. Sorry I'm late, but work keeps me busy."

"Would you like something to drink?" she asked politely.

She noticed that his dark suit was designer, looked Italian, and so did his shoes. She wondered what kind of business Margie would have with a man in Fuller looking like that.

"I already did. Thank you. I met your sister when I first got here and I left some flowers on the table." He pointed to some pink roses on the kitchen table. "But I wanted to meet you before I left. Margie talked about her girls all the time."

He looked at her and his gray eyes looked mindful and a little too knowing. Like he already knew all her secrets. She crossed her arms over her chest.

Her dad had taught her to read people and the room. But Asa Hallows wasn't that easy. He looked like a man who couldn't be fooled.

"You know, when I got here, there were two women out front, yelling at each other, something about a bracelet and how the blonde was always jealous of her. Pretty weird thing at a wake." He shot her a huge smile. She only smiled back.

"Well, I better get going. It was nice to meet you." He turned to the door, but not before he gave her a wink; then he left.

She flinched at the sound of the door closing and just stared.

Soon the house was empty except for Bev who was at the sink washing up the last of the dishes. Both Roxy and Sydney cleared the table of the paper plates and cups that were left scattered.

"Thanks, Bev," she said it for the millionth time as she sat the last of the clean paper plates back in the cupboard.

"You don't have to do that. We can take it from here." Roxy took the washcloth from Bev's hands. Bev looked over at the clock on the microwave.

"Yeah, I guess we are pretty much done here. My favorite show is on soon and I would like to kick my feet up and watch it."

Bev went to gather her stuff. They both followed her to the living room.

"We owe you big time." Sydney handed Bev her purse. "We couldn't have done this without you."

Bev waved them off. "It was my pleasure. Margie was my friend." Bev looked away and sniffed. "It's hard to think that she's really gone."

Sydney went in and gave Bev a hug.

"If you ever need anything, you just call," Roxy said and wrote her number down on a Post-it note from the counter and gave it to Bev.

She took it with a smile. "I'm glad I got to meet you girls. I can see why Margie loved you so much." She opened the door and turned to the sisters. "She was proud of you both. I'm sure I'll see you both again." Bev turned and started down the walk to her car.

They watched her go, making sure that she made it to her car all right. When Bev pulled out, they shut and locked the door.

Roxy

"Well, at least we know one nice person in this town." Sydney sat at the table and kicked her legs over to the other chair across from her. She looked exhausted.

Roxy walked to the fridge and pulled out a dish with leftover mac and cheese. She grabbed two spoons. She placed it on the table, sat on the other side, and slid a spoon to Sydney.

"This should be good cold." She took a bite. "I heard Marcy yelling at her blonde friend in the front yard earlier." She took another bite.

Sydney smiled; her cheeks full of mac and cheese. She swallowed.

"I heard." Sydney scooped up more noodles. "By the way, I heard about that from a man named Asa Hallows. Did you meet him?"

Roxy thought for a second. She had met a lot of people throughout the day. His face jumped into her mind. "He was a tall, handsome man. Business partner or something, right?"

"Yeah, he said he was a friend of Margie's. He left these flowers." Sydney pointed to the roses on the table.

Roxy thought the pink roses were really pretty and stood out among the rest of the flowers scattered throughout the house.

"But you don't know him? You've never seen him with Margie or heard Margie talk about him?" Sydney asked.

Roxy shook her head no.

"Why?" She studied her sister.

"I don't know? He seemed…" Sydney paused. "I'm not sure. He kind of snuck up on me. Gave me a weird vibe."

"You think he was looking around?" Roxy spooned up another bite. She was a lot hungrier than she thought.

Sydney just shrugged. "I don't know. He just made me nervous, I guess."

"He did have a nice smile." Roxy looked at her sister. "Maybe it's been too long since you got laid."

Sydney looked shocked, then gave her a death stare. It made her burst out laughing, and she accidentally spit out a noodle.

"Gross." Sydney threw a napkin at her, smiling.

*

The next day, they decided to tackle the attic. She pulled the string on the hatch for the stairs. Musty, dusty air came down, and she sneezed.

"I don't think anyone has been up here in a while." She started to climb the rickety ladder at a slow pace. Sydney followed. The attic was dark. A little light came from a vent on the far side. She pulled the cord on the bare bulb hanging from the ceiling.

"Yuck!" Sydney said, waving the dust from her face.

The attic was full. It was packed to the ceiling with boxes and old furniture. There wasn't anywhere to even walk. This was going to take a while.

Three hours later, they had made a small dent in the boxes. They found boxes containing Margie's husband's clothes, old vinyl records, and dishes. They would donate most of what they had found so far. They pulled out old chairs and side tables that were also going to the local thrift store. When they finally cleared a small walkway through the clutter, she sat down on an old, wooden stool. She was tired and didn't even care that it was covered in years of dust. She was pretty much already covered in it, anyway.

"So how is school going?" she asked Sydney as she pulled a box over to her and opened the lid.

"Fine." Sydney didn't look up and continued to go through her box.

"Grades good?" She smiled over at her sister. Sydney still didn't look up.

"Need me to hack your records and change any of them for you?" She paused. Sydney didn't say anything. "I can give you straight A's."

"No, they're fine," Sydney said flatly.

Sydney pulled a framed picture out of the box.

"Look, it's Margie, and that's not her husband." Sydney laughed. "Go, Margie."

She looked over to study it. It looked like an old prom picture. Margie and a young man were standing close, and Margie had a huge smile on her face.

Sydney studied the picture with a sad smile. "I'm going to miss her."

Roxy looked over to Sydney. "Why are you changing the subject?" she asked. They had seen a million photos already.

"I'm not." Sydney went into defensive mode. It was something Roxy had seen her do many times.

"Yeah, you are. What's up with school?" She wasn't going to let it go.

"Nothing." Sydney tossed the picture into the box.

"Now that I think about it, you've hardly mentioned anything about it."

Sydney looked away.

"So?" she asked again.

Sydney's shoulders sagged and she turned to her. "I dropped out."

She was taken by surprise and couldn't help but feel a little disappointed. She had never been to college but was proud of her sister for going.

Sydney blew a long breath out of her nose.

"How long ago?" She felt worry spread through her stomach.

"About a year," Sydney said quietly.

She didn't say anything.

"I was bored." Sydney looked a little deflated. "I swear if I had to study the different patterns of fabric one more time, I was going to scream."

"You've been picking in New York for a whole year?" It wasn't really a question, but more of an astonishment.

"Not just New York. I have been traveling around the east coast."

She knew Sydney was picking; she had told her as much. But she thought it was fewer and farther between. She didn't know she was doing it full-time.

"Sydney, that's dangerous. Even Dad didn't do it all the time."

"Maybe I'm better than he was. I do my homework. It's exciting and I'm donating it all to charities." Sydney sat up straighter, defensively.

"Hey, I get it." She held up her hands. "But you can't do that forever. I thought you were going to be some great designer?"

"Well, it turns out I'm not very good, and it's boring. Sydney's face turned red in anger. She grabbed the lid to the box and slammed it shut, then pushed the box away with her bare foot.

"Every day, the same thing. Get up; go to class. Learn about colors and patterns. With the same people who then go to the coffee shop across the way to do homework. It was just so…" She paused, then continued, "Blah. When I'm picking, that's when I feel good."

"So, what do you plan on doing? You can't do it forever."

"I don't know. I'll figure it out."

"So what? You're just going to go around stealing until you get caught. We all know how that ends." It was her fear talking now.

"This isn't what Dad would want you doing with your life." She regretted it the minute it came out.

Sydney stood up from the floor. "Who do you think taught us this life? I'm good just like him—better even. I think he would be proud of me; I only steal from the people who can afford it, and I donate it to the people who need it. He would have liked that."

"But you forget that he wasn't proud of his lifestyle. It was just a means to survive."

"Roxy, don't act like you're better just because you hide behind your computer and steal instead of going into the trenches. It doesn't make you any less of a thief." Sydney crossed her arms over her chest.

It always stung when Sydney said that she hid behind her computer. She jumped to her feet.

"This computer, that I so call hide behind, saves your butt more times than you can count. You would be in jail if I couldn't do what I do. Plus, you wouldn't be able to donate that righteous money you steal if it wasn't for my banking program keeping you in your fancy designer clothes."

Sydney looked away, her arms still crossed.

Roxy turned her back to Sydney and walked to the other side of the attic. "I don't steal anymore." She paused, and when she turned back around, Sydney looked shocked.

"Do you use the fake bank accounts?" Sydney asked.

She shook her head no. Sydney looked down.

"I don't need to. I have a job." Roxy's voice was low.

Sydney looked up. "Well, I guess you're better than me. Just like everyone else in this town. I guess I'm just a criminal like Dad was."

It hurt. "That's not fair," Roxy said. She felt the anger build up. Don't act like I didn't grow up here, or spend my teenage years in a girls' home too. I don't pretend like I didn't hear the things people said about our family. I don't think Dad was a criminal. He did it to put food on the table; you're doing it for entertainment. That's dangerous."

"I won't get caught." Sydney's voice rose.

"You could end up dead!" she yelled this time.

Sydney froze.

"I don't want to lose you too." Her voice hitched.

Sydney looked down, then turned toward the ladder and went down, not saying anything.

She let her go. She rubbed her hands down her face. She replayed what she said over in her head. Had she been too mean? It was true she had bailed Sydney out of trouble a hundred times. She still felt horrible. Sydney was her sister, and all they had was each other. She would always bail her out.

She turned toward the pile of boxes, and something caught her eye—something she hadn't seen in years.

"No freaking way!" Excitement pumped her up, her thoughts of their fight forgotten for the moment. She stepped over boxes and pushed others out of the way. She all but tripped over another that was further into the darkness.

"Oh my god! I knew it," she said it out loud to no one. It was her old computer. She grabbed the old, flat screen.

She pulled the monitor out and placed it in the small circle that they had cleared.

She turned back around and dug in the box again. There were all the wires and a couple other smaller boxes.

She slid the big box out, and written on the side was "girls' stuff."

"What is all that?" Sydney was climbing up the ladder, a bottle of wine and two coffee mugs in her hand.

She looked up at her sister, wondering if they were still fighting.

Sydney set the wine down on the floor.

"I don't want to fight. I'm sorry, Roxy." She looked down.

"I'm sorry, too. I didn't mean…"

Sydney cut her off, saying, "It's fine."

She shook her head in agreement, knowing they were fine for the moment. She wasn't done with the subject yet, but now wasn't the time. Emotions were too high.

"What is that?" Sydney pointed with her hand that held the wine.

"It's my old computer, the one Dad gave me for our birthday."

"I thought that thing went up in the fire." Sydney pulled the corner and looked in.

Roxy started pulling the wires out when one of the small boxes fell out. It was pink and had a big gold bow.

Sydney gasped.

She grabbed the box and pulled the lid off. Sydney's face lit up with surprise.

"My locket." She touched the ruby heart in the middle, then looked up at Roxy.

"I thought this was lost in the fire too." Sydney had tears in her eyes. She took it out of the box and went to put it on, but it didn't fit over her head anymore. She laughed. "I guess it's not as big as I remember. She stared down at it. She popped the locket and opened it. It was empty. Sydney never had the time to put pictures in it.

Sorrow swept in for her sister.

"Here, help me," Sydney said, holding the ends of the chain out.

She helped her clasp it and smiled. She knew how much Sydney had loved that thing. Sydney brushed her fingers over the locket. She then grabbed the coffee mugs and poured them a glass of wine.

"What's with the coffee mugs with wine?" She picked hers up and took a sip. She let the sweet wine rinse the dust from her mouth.

"They have handles," Sydney said simply. "Easier to carry up the ladder."

She took another sip, agreeing with Sydney's logic.

She brought her attention back to the box. She couldn't believe it—her old computer. She wondered what she had on it. It still had the apple sticker she had slapped on the back, along with the Vans skateboard sticker. She had stolen that sticker from the shoe store at the mall. She tilted the monitor to the side to admire the sticker when she saw that it was missing two screws that held the back of the monitor.

That's weird, she thought. Dad had told her not to take the computer apart, and she had kept her promise. She gently pushed the plastic backing to put it back in place, but she heard a strange click, like something had fallen inside. Maybe the things broke. That was going to be disappointing. She thought about getting it up and running again and seeing what she could do with the dinosaur of a machine that held happy memories for her, even if it had only been for a few months. It was the best birthday present anyone had ever given her. It also had come with a promise from her dad for better times. Not that it had mattered. Which made her wonder how this had gotten into Margie's attic. Had her dad brought it over?

She walked over to a box that she had gone through earlier and had seen some basic tools. She grabbed the small screwdriver and went to open up the monitor. She wanted to see what the issue was and if it was even worth it.

"Why are you taking it apart?" Sydney was still holding the locket, sliding it across the chain.

"I think this thing might be broken. Something is clinking around inside."

Sydney took a seat on the dusty chair, holding her mug of wine in one hand and her locket in the other, content on just watching her sister work on the machine. She figured Sydney was done packing for the day.

When she finally got the last screw out, she gently removed the back cover and she placed it to the side, and looked in. It looked normal to her. She pulled out her phone from her back pocket and turned the flashlight on, and shined it in. Resting on the bottom behind some wires was a small purple velvet pull-string bag and a folded-up piece of paper.

"What the hell?" She reached in and pulled them out.

Sydney bent forward on the chair. She placed her mug on the floor, clearly interested in the find.

She looked to Sydney. "What is this doing in the monitor of my old computer?"

"Open it." Sydney jumped up on the seat.

She pulled the strings loose and dumped the contents out in her open hand.

It was a ring. She turned it in her hand. It had a large, smoky white, oval stone in the center, and the sides had diamond-shaped white gold pieces on the sides of the stone.

Sydney was leaning on her shoulder to get a better view.

"It's beautiful." Sydney reached out to grab it. She let Sydney take it from her hand.

"Where did this come from and whose is it? Why was it in the computer? How come Margie never told us our stuff was here?"

There were a million questions running through her head.

"I wonder how much we can get for it?" Sydney was holding it up to the bare lightbulb.

She picked up the paper and unfolded it. It was a confirmation for American Airlines for three boarding passes.

"What is this about?" she asked more to herself than Sydney.

Sydney looked over. "What does it say?"

"It's a confirmation for plane tickets. For us and Dad." She paused, then added, "To Portland, Maine."

"Seriously?" Sydney put the ring down on the chair and went to look over her shoulder.

"Look at the date." Sydney pointed. "March 5. That was two days after Dad died."

"Do you remember Dad ever talking about Maine? Did we have family over there that we didn't know about?"

"Slow down." She stood up and started to pace. "We need to find out what this is and where the ring came from, how it got here? Let me do some research before you go and try to sell it. It might be important. There has to be a reason it was hidden in my computer." She went for the stairs, all thoughts of clearing out the attic forgotten. Sydney jumped up from her chair, clearly excited.

When they got downstairs, she immediately went for her computer.

"Remember how Dad would sometimes hide stolen objects?" She paused, remembering. "The tickets were set for two days after his death. This isn't a coincidence."

She already had her laptop set up on the dining room table and started to boot it up. Sydney refilled her mug with more wine and, considering she had left her glass up in the attic, Sydney poured her another in a real wine glass this time before placing it on the table. She didn't touch the glass, but instead dove right into the computer; she was going to start with a simple Google search.

Sydney sat the ring on the table so she could get a good look at it. She grabbed her phone and took a several pictures of it from different angles, and sent those to the computer as well to help her search.

Google brought up no exact images of the ring but lots of images of similar items.

"I'm going to have to do a deeper search. This might take some time. I want to search this flight too."

Sydney sat back in her chair and took another sip of her wine.

Roxy started to think out loud. "Let's see, it was in the computer monitor which means he was hiding it or maybe thinking of a way to transport it undetected. Plus, he put the ticket confirmation in there too. Dad was keeping it a secret."

Sydney looked at her wide-eyed. "You really think this was Dad's?"

She sat back in the chair. "It makes sense; it was in my computer which was at our house. You think before the night, you know, when Dad died, he brought the computer over here for safekeeping? Putting the ring and the ticket confirmation in the computer so no one would know it was in there? How come Margie never told us it was here? You'd think she would have mentioned something."

Sydney looked up and started at the light fixture hanging over the table.

"The day of the fire, Margie babysat us. Remember, Dad said that he had been called into work, so Margie took us to the movies in the next town over. Dad even gave her money, telling us to have fun. It was the only time she had ever taken us; I remember because we had large sodas and I almost peed myself on the way home." Sydney paused.

"You think Dad didn't have to work but was bringing our stuff over here and buying plane tickets?" She picked up her wine and took a large sip.

"He said he had some big plans, and we were finally going to get out of this town." She ran her finger down the side of her glass. "You think this ring was a job?"

"If it was, then this ring is worth big bucks," Sydney said. "Maybe he got some heat from it, and that's why we were going to the other side of the country."

She looked up to her sister. "That means this ring could be the reason why Dad is dead."

*

There was a pounding on the door; it was loud and aggressive, and it woke her. She looked around, wondering what was going on. Her childhood bedroom was dark. Was it the middle of the night? She saw Sydney sitting straight up in her bed. She, too, had heard the pounding.

"Hey Gabe!" It was a man yelling from somewhere outside. "Get your ass out here!"

She ran to the window. The streetlight in front of their house was lighting up the driveway, which really just was the side yard, graveled, and she could see four or five black cars filling it up. There were men she had never seen before getting out. There were a couple of them walking to the

60

house, while others were just hanging around the front. *They were all wearing dark suits, like businessmen*, she thought. She noticed one had a baseball bat he was smacking into the palm of his hand.

Fear seized her. Why were these men screaming for her dad?

Sydney joined her at the window.

"What's going on? Roxy, look, that guy has a gun." Sydney pointed to the man in front. He was standing forward, his hands crossed in front of him, the gun pointing downward.

She heard fear gripping Sydney's voice like it was gripping hers.

"We need to find Dad!" Sydney turned to the door.

"I don't know. Maybe we should just hide?"

Then they heard pounding feet come up the stairs, and their door flung open.

Dad stood in the doorway; his face shadowed by the hall light, his hair pointing every which way, his stance rigid.

"Girls!" was all he said.

Relief filled her. It was Dad. He would know what to do.

"Dad, what's going on? Why are there people at our house?" He walked over. He slowly peeked through the curtains and looked out the window.

"Girls, come here." He stepped away from the window and came down on one knee. He gathered them close. He wrapped his arms around them, hugging them tightly to his sides.

Just then a window crashed downstairs and a man yelled, "We got a lot to talk about, Wright. You think you can steal from us and get away with it?"

Dad broke his hug; he placed his large, calloused hand on her face and the other on Sydney's.

"I need you to go to Margie's." He started to talk fast. "But you need to go through the window in my room and walk the roof to the lean-to where we keep the firewood." Another window crashed. He spoke faster.

"Jump down and run to the back of the field. When you get to the very back, you run as fast as you can to Margie's. Don't stop. You hear me?" He looked her in the eyes, then he looked into Sydney's. His face was lined with worry, and there was fear in his big blue eyes. They both shook their heads in agreement.

"Good, now let's go."

There was another crash, but not a window this time. It sounded like the front door falling in.

Dad gave them both a short hug, then pushed them to his room, across the hall. His room was dark. She could see from the light from the already open window. His bed was a mess like he had just jumped out of it. He had clothes scattered all around, and it smelled just like him, grease and old spice. "Girls, I need you to be brave now. Don't let anyone see or hear you, and no matter what you hear or see, you keep going. Don't stop till you get to Margie's." She could feel the tears running down her cheeks.

"Dad, come with us, please." Sydney was pulling on his white shirt, begging him.

"I can't, Syd; I need you guys to go." He paused. "I'll meet you there."

She knew her father, and that was the face he made when he was lying. His normally happy, relaxed face was betraying him now, the fear washing it out. She only cried harder.

There were footsteps running up the stairs. Dad picked them up and dropped them outside the window and onto the roof. He slammed the window shut. She flinched from the loud thud, sounding like their final goodbye.

Sydney grabbed her hand, and they made their way over to the edge where the firewood lean-to was. There was shouting behind the closed window. Her dad's voice came through, too. "Hey guys, come on now, we can talk this out."

She heard shuffling and her dad's grunts. She looked back as Sydney dragged her to the edge of the roof. The drop to the lean-to was maybe two feet. But she hesitated.

"We should go back and help Dad." She looked to Sydney. They heard more crashes coming from inside.

Sydney paused, looking back over her shoulder. Roxy thought she was going to agree for a second. "No. We do what Dad says. He said he would meet us there."

Her heart was beating so hard it felt it was going to burst out of her chest.

She wanted to believe it. Sydney did. But she had seen his face. Sydney was only fooling herself.

Sydney took her hand. "Let's go."

They jumped onto the lean-to. The plywood that was the roof was soft, and she thought she might fall through. Taking it slow, she walked to the edge and jumped down to the ground, mud squashing between her toes.

They went straight to the side yard that led to the back of the property. They ran.

The grass was wet, and her bare feet were cold, almost numb. Her favorite red nightgown with all the stars was sticking to her legs as she ran. When they got to the back of the field to the tree line that separated their property from the neighbors in the back, they cut across. The grass was tall and they ran hunched over. It was dark back there and she hoped the scary men couldn't see them.

They made it about halfway when they heard it—a single gunshot. She almost yelped out loud but fear kept her quiet. Sydney pulled her to the ground, where they laid on their bellies, soaking the front of their nightgowns.

"Was that a gunshot?" Sydney's breath was coming fast.

"I don't know. Where is Dad?" she stammered; her voice riddled with fear.

"He's fine," Sydney said with a shake of her head. "Dad is always fine. He's got this. Come on, let's go."

Roxy paused, fear paralyzing her. What if the men came after them? What if they had Dad, and now they wanted them? What if they killed him? She looked over to her sister, the face that was so similar to hers. She had fear all over it, but determination too. Sydney wasn't crying like she was. She believed Dad would come get them. It was then when Sydney looked her sister straight in the eyes.

"Dad wants us to go to Margie's; that's what we are going to do. Now let's go." Sydney tugged her hand painfully hard. It was enough to pull her out of her fear and back onto her feet. They ran.

It felt like it was taking way too long to get to Margie's. Her lungs hurt, and her legs felt like rubber. When they finally got there, they cut through the row of trees that separated the two properties and stopped on Margie's manicured lawn. They looked back at their house, and that's when they both saw the glow of flames. Their house was on fire. The amber flames were shooting up into the dark night sky.

"No! Dad!" she screamed and fell to her knees. Sydney dropped to her knees too and wrapped her arms around her sister.

She heard Margie's front door open and heard Margie screaming both their names. But neither girl cared. They both just clung to each other, softly crying. They knew in that moment that their dad was dead.

Roxy awoke and shot straight up in bed, tears streaming down her face.

63

Sydney

Sydney awoke to the smell of coffee. She rolled over and looked at the small clock that was a hundred years old. It said six a.m. *What the hell*, she thought. Roxy never gets up this early. She debated whether to go back to bed or not, but the smell of the coffee was divine, and she was wondering if Roxy even went to bed last night or was up all night researching.

She made her way to the kitchen, where she saw Roxy already dressed and on her computer.

She wasn't wearing the same clothes as yesterday, which meant she had gone to bed.

"What are you doing up?"

Roxy looked up from her computer. The dark circles under her eyes were vivid.

"I had another dream," Roxy said simply.

"What was it about?" She poured coffee into a mug.

"The night Dad died."

She sat down at the table.

"I'm sorry." She understood. She'd had the same dream many times. "You want to talk about it?"

Roxy shrugged. "Why? We were both there. You know what happened." She looked back down at her computer.

"What's more frustrating," Roxy kept typing, "is that I can't find anything about this damn ring we found. No one has filed it missing or stolen. There isn't any record of it in any jewelry inventory or museums. No royalty, no nothing. Expect I did find a short folklore tale about a man who brings a stone to his true love. The stone is described as similar to the stone in the ring, but it's a super old tale, and the description could be any stone that is white with smoking gray in it. I mean, we could probably go outside and find the same description of a rock in the backyard." Roxy blew out a breath and continued, "There was nothing special about the tickets to Maine either. It was a normal plane. Dad paid with a credit card. The only thing I know is that it was out of his price range. He didn't have online banking back then, so I have no way of seeing how he got the money." Roxy turned to face her.

Sydney picked up the ring that was sitting on the table and slid it on her finger. It felt cold. She took it off and placed it back on the table.

"I'm pretty sure this is white gold." She continued to stare at the ring.

"This stone could be nothing, but why would Dad hide it and why would it be put into a white gold setting?"

She took a drink of her coffee. "I say we take it to Seattle. I'll call my guy down there and have him look at it. He could even ask around see if anyone knows anything. If not, we might get a little money from the setting and we can go to dinner and maybe hit up the club, find a couple of marks." The thought of stealing with Roxy made her think of the old days. Roxy was great at lifting jewelry and wallets. Her theory was that no one suspected the shy one. She smiled excitedly at Roxy. It was exciting to think of watching Roxy lift.

But Roxy just sat back in her chair and looked at her sister then back at her computer. I told you; I don't do that anymore." She sighed. "Syd, I think we should hold off on taking the ring anywhere. It was Dad's and he hid it for a reason."

"We don't know if Dad put it there." She was feeling a little embarrassed about Roxy's disregard at the idea of hanging out together. "I mean, Margie could have put it there too. Hell, it could have been in there when Dad bought the computer."

"Then why were there plane tickets in there? Let's just hold off for a little bit." Roxy rolled her shoulders. "Plus, I have to finish filling out some of this paperwork for Margie's estate. While I do that, you can finish the attic." Roxy gave her a big smile.

*

It was early afternoon, and she had been in the attic all day. She thought she was going to die. She had gone through tons of old junk by herself, while Roxy had been doing work on her computer.

She was bored and restless. She ran her finger through the chain of her newly found necklace. She was so glad that they had found it since she had thought it was gone forever. It brought back old feelings of her father—the good ones—and it was nice to have something to hold and remind her of him. She stood. She needed to move. She needed fresh air.

That's it, she was going for a drive or maybe stop at the mall a few towns over and buy something new. She needed to rotate her clothes anyway. She had been in Margie's house for way too long.

She headed downstairs and found Roxy still glued to her computer.

"I want to go shopping," she said out loud to Roxy. "I'm bored and we both need fresh air."

Roxy waved her hand at her, not looking up. "Go. I don't want to, plus I'm busy."

She sat down at the table. "Please, I'm begging."

Roxy finally peeled her eyes from the laptop.

"No, I'm looking for realtors to sell this house for us, not to mention places that will come and pick up the furniture, and the lawyer, McKnight, still has paperwork for us fill out, so unless you want to handle this, I suggest you go back up to the attic or go shopping by yourself. Plus, I still want to research that ring some more. Something about it isn't sitting right with me."

"Fine." She was upset that Roxy wouldn't hang out with her. It was an old feeling that she hadn't had in a while. But she needed out. She looked over and saw the ring still sitting on the table where she had left it that morning. She grabbed it and put it on her finger. She ignored the icy feeling. The idea popped into her head that she would call her contact, Yuri, in Seattle. She could get some information about it, and then maybe Roxy would stop worrying about it.

She stood up with the ring still on her finger. "I'll go shopping by myself." She turned. "I'm going to buy you some new shoes and some nail polish. You're getting a pedicure tonight." She smiled over her shoulder, but Roxy was already back to staring at the screen.

*

Sydney jumped into her Mercedes, and even though the weather was nice, she left the top up. *Maybe*, she thought as she pulled out of the drive, *when I'm in Seattle, I'll trade this rental in for an SUV or truck—something that can move boxes and small furniture*. That will help out. She smiled to herself again, thinking that Roxy would be happy.

The drive through town was uneventful. When she hit the freeway, she rolled the windows down, turned the music up, and was ready for the almost two-hour drive to Seattle.

When she pulled into the parking lot in downtown Seattle, she parked close to her favorite place—the first Starbucks. She walked in excited for her sugar-free vanilla latte. She was tired of just drinking drip coffee.

She went in, ordered her latte, and sat at a table in the corner. She scrolled through her contacts; Yuri was at the bottom. She hadn't seen him since right before going to New York for school. She had pawned a few pieces so that she would have cash on her in the city. She remembered how Yuri was a no-nonsense guy, then made the call.

"Hello," said the grumpy, heavily Russian-accented voice on the other end of the line.

"Hello, Yuri?" she said.

"Who is this?" Yuri now sounded annoyed, making her smile.

"Now you're hurting my feelings," she said jokingly.

"I have no time for games."

"It's me, Sydney." It annoyed her that Yuri knew her real name. She never gave it to pawnshops and other people who bought stolen goods, but she had met Yuri when she was young, and it had been a beginner's mistake.

"Oh," he sounded a little taken back. "I wonder where you been. Why you call?" He got right to the point. "You have hot piece?"

"No, actually, this is a family heirloom, I inherited it. You in the shop?"

"I be there in an hour. You meet me there." He hung up.

"Nice talking to you, too," she said to the silent phone.

She placed the phone in her purse along with the ring. She sat back. Well, she had an hour to burn. *Looks like I'm going shopping*, she thought to herself. She grabbed her purse, slung it over her shoulder, and decided to go to the nearest department store.

She walked the couple of blocks, enjoying being back in the city. She loved the loud traffic and the busy streets. There were thousands of people in the city. It almost felt like New York, but not quite. A little more relaxed. She figured that's why Roxy had moved here.

When she entered the store, she felt a little normal again and lost herself in the process of shopping, looking for the latest fashions. She picked the colors and styles she liked and what looked good on her. It brought some normalcy that she hadn't had in a while.

She ended up with three new tops, a pair of designer jeans, and a new skirt. She passed the shoe department and found a pair of pink Converse shoes. She almost bought them for Roxy, but knew that she would never wear them. Next, she hit up the makeup counter and bought three of the latest colors of nail polish. She was going to paint Roxy's toes, even if she had to tie her down. She bought a new shade of lipstick and some more of her favorite foundation.

When she grabbed the bags from the cashier, the conversation she had with Roxy flashed in her mind. Roxy didn't use the fake accounts anymore. Guilt stung her. She sighed deeply. Pushing the feeling away for the moment, she thought how she had needed this trip; she needed this small amount of time to just be and clear her mind. She checked her phone for the time.

"Perfect," she said out loud. She would get her car and make it to Yuri's right on time.

When she arrived at Yuri's pawnshop, he was already there, sitting behind the glass counter. He was an older, tall, and skinny man with thinning hair.

When she came up, he smiled and leaned over the display case, taking her hand. The warm welcome was a surprise.

"So good to see you," he said.

"Likewise." She hadn't realized how much she had missed him. She gave him a bashful smile, and started to rummage through her bag.

"I inherited this from a family member. I don't think it's worth much," she said as she pulled it out and placed it on the counter.

Yuri stiffened.

"I know it's kind of lame but was wondering if it looked familiar to you? Maybe some kind of rare stone?" He only stared. She was a little embarrassed. "I guess it could just be some rock? That's white gold; I do believe it's set in; it could be melted down."

Yuri didn't say anything. He picked up the ring and was turning it in his fingers. He looked up at her, his face still.

"Right," he finally said.

She was feeling foolish. "It is real? White gold, right? I'm not mistaken, am I?"

"Yes. Yes. I take in back and weigh it, I give you fair price for gold. I think rock worth nothing." He turned and went into the back room, shutting the door.

He was acting weird. His warm welcome was nice but he turned cold fast.

She would just see how much she could get. She most likely wouldn't sell it.

She looked through the glass case and was admiring some of the nice pieces he had in there.

After about ten minutes, she had looked at everything, and there was still no sign of Yuri. She was starting to get irritated. How long did it take to weigh the thing?

She was starting to wonder if he was okay when he finally came out. He had placed the ring on his finger. It didn't fit and was sitting above his hairy knuckle. The creamy stone hung off the tip of his finger. "This ring a good find," he said.

"You had me nervous there for a minute." She felt a little relieved, "So, any idea?"

"That I can't say. Scale in back not work. How about I hold ring here and you come back tomorrow and I give you money."

"I don't know; I'm not staying in the city; maybe I should…"

The door to the shop swung open, and two men walked in, the bell over the door jiggling loudly. They were both wearing navy-blue slacks and white button-up shirts. The man in front had a navy-blue blazer unbuttoned.

"Ah, Yuri!" the man in the blazer said, throwing his arms up in celebration.

She looked to Yuri. His back was rod straight, and he took a step back, fear clearly in his eyes.

"You, my friend, have brought me good news. Let me see the ring." The man in the blazer walked up and leaned against the counter right next to her, the other hanging back.

She watched as Yuri handed him her ring.

"What's going on? Is he some kind of specialist or a buyer?" She was confused.

The man ignored her and took the ring. He studied it. He turned to his partner, who was just behind him and smiled. His partner smiled in return, showing a gold incisor.

The man in the blazer turned to her.

"Nope. I'm not a buyer. A specialist on this ring, yes. You have found something that I have been looking for a very long time."

69

The man with the gold tooth stepped forward and grabbed her arm roughly. She stumbled back and she gave a little squeak of pain. She looked to Yuri; he had retreated to the far corner behind the counter. He immediately turned his head and looked away, avoiding eye contact.

She looked down at the man's hand holding her arm with confusion and saw a scar on his wrist; it was V-shaped with slashes, and it looked dark.

He leaned in, rubbing his nose in her hair. He took a deep breath.

"Ummm," he hummed. "She smells nice."

She jerked her head away and stared at the man in disgust, but he just stared back, a dark look in his eyes. Strangely, she couldn't help but notice that he smelled like mint.

"Play nice, Cal," the man in the blazer said, smiling. She looked over at the man, and she couldn't tell if he was giving a warning or was joking around. It seemed like he was in a really good mood. He looked her right in the eyes. They were burning with intensity.

"I have been looking for this ring for a very long time, and you, girl, just walk right into a pawnshop with it." He paused and looked down at the ring in his hand. He looked back up at her. "Which I bet means you are one of Gabe Wright's daughters?"

She tried to take a step back, fear seizing her. The man called Cal held tight to her arm.

"I take it from the look on your face, I'm right. Which one are you? Sydney or Roxy?" His face was growing serious.

When she didn't answer, fear paralyzing her, he stepped forward, eyes full of anger, "Do you know how long I have been looking for this? How many lives of my brothers have been lost because of this ring?" He shook the fist holding it. He, too, had the same scar on his wrist.

"The night your father stole this from us, five of my friends lost their lives. My boss was so angry." He drew back with a jerk. He started to pace around the small shop.

"He made us look day and night, told some of us not to come back without it or we would die."

He looked back at her. "Lucky for some of us, after a while he calmed himself and let us return, but we still have been looking for it." He grew still and silent. His stance loosened, and he leaned on the counter. His mood shifted again.

"Who would have thought that a stupid girl and a Russian pawnbroker would make this day finally come? This all ends today." His head snapped up. "Ten years." He tossed the ring up, then caught it.

"Thank you, Yuri, for making the call." The man in the blazer reached into his inside blazer pocket and took out two stacks of wrapped money.

"Here you go." He tossed it on the counter. Yuri took a step forward and swiped the money from the counter before retreating to his corner.

He then looked to her. "We already killed Gabe for his theft. Should the daughter pay for the sins of the father? For the lost lives of my brothers, for the anguish her father has bestowed on the Brotherhood?"

Her chest tightened in fear; her head felt fuzzy.

What was she going to do? No one knew where she was, Roxy thought she was shopping at the mall. Then she heard Cal speak, his head close to her ear again.

"I think you should let me have some fun first. She is very pretty."

Cal looked over at the other man and all but sang, "I could teach Gabe's daughter a lesson."

Fear had her turning. She looked over at Cal, his gold tooth gleaming from his smile. Fear ripped through her body. His face was sinister, his eyes like the devil himself lived in there. If she survived this, she would see them in her nightmares.

She started to panic. She frantically tried to pull her arm away, but he held tight. She looked to Yuri. He looked up from the money in his hands, his eyes full of shame. His mouth moved and he whispered, "Sorry."

No, she thought as she tried to yank her arm away from Cal's grip again. This time, he tightened it and reached for her other arm. She started to kick and pull, trying to free herself from his strong grip, but he didn't let go, and a smile grew on his face the more she struggled.

"I like it when they fight back." Cal smiled.

The man in the blazer reached into his coat and pulled out a silver pistol. Her heart sank and she started to feel tears run down her cheeks.

"No, please. You don't have to do this. You can have the ring. I'll leave and I won't tell anyone. I'll disappear."

She was sobbing, meaning every word that came out of her mouth. They both just laughed.

Cal pulled her in close so that her back was against his chest and her arms were pinned to her sides. The smell of mint filled her nostrils.

She tried dropping to her knees, using her weight to bring him down,

71

but he was stronger than he looked and lifted her and held her up.

The man in the blazer walked up, holding the gun to her face. "There has to be justice for the Brotherhood and my friends." Cal whipped her to the side, taking her from the barrel of the gun.

"Come on, man, let me take her to the back; it won't take long. Besides, the boss wants her alive, remember?"

The man in the blazer paused.

"It wasn't the boss' friends that died for this ring, and I'm sure he would be okay if we only brought the ring back. We'll say her death was an accident. There's still one more daughter out there."

What the hell? she thought. *Are they going to go after Roxy too?*

All of a sudden, a stack of wrapped money flew, hitting the man's hand, knocking the gun, and making him swing to the side. Unfortunately, he didn't drop it.

Yuri yelled, "Run, girl, now!"

But before she could do anything, she heard the deafening sound of gunfire. She screamed, and her ears rang. She saw Yuri's chest bloom red. He stared at her for a moment, his eyes sad, then he slowly slid to the ground.

"No, no, no!" she kept screaming over and over, thrashing her legs and her body, her eyes filling with tears. Yuri was dead, and she was most likely going to be raped and killed. She didn't let up, just kept moving, hoping that Cal's arms would loosen just enough to slide out.

"Get a hold of her now!" the man with the gun yelled. "Take her to the back before we draw attention to ourselves."

Cal shook her and tightened his grip. The other man lifted the counter door with one hand and let her and Cal pass. She kicked her leg up again.

"No, please, no!" she kept yelling as she twisted and pushed, trying to get free. As she passed, she looked over and saw Yuri slumped against the wall, blood pooling around his legs.

Then the bell on the door jiggled, and the door was thrown open so hard that it slammed the glass behind it, making a creaking noise. All three of them looked over to see a man in a light gray jacket running at full speed toward them. He hit the man in the blazer like a defensive lineman, taking him down hard, the gun flying out of his hands. The stranger punched him in the face over and over, blood spraying the floor.

Cal, seeing his friend in trouble, slammed Sydney down on the ground behind the counter and went to his aid.

Her knees hit first, skidding across the dirty, rough carpet. She stayed still on the floor, ignoring the sting and listening to the sound of fist hitting flesh and deep grunts.

This is my chance, she thought, getting up and peeking over the counter. The man in the navy blazer was out cold, blood running from his nose and a gash on the side of his head. Cal and the stranger were wrestling. The stranger had him in a headlock, and Cal was throwing punches like a rabid animal. The stranger looked up at her. She realized that she recognized his face. Stunned, her plan to run was forgotten.

"Asa Hallows? What the hell?"

"Run, now!" he said, his voice strained.

She just stared.

"Go now!" his deep voice screamed. It startled her, and she made her way from behind the counter to the front of the store, but Asa and Cal were blocking the front door. Panicked, she jumped over the counter and went for the back door. She pushed the door open when she heard a crash. She looked over to see Asa and Cal rolling on the floor on top of a display of DVDs that had been knocked over. She whipped her head around, panic driving her into confusion. She had to help him. She couldn't just leave him there; he was a friend of Margie's.

She looked around. The silver pistol was on the floor; she ran around the counter again and grabbed it. But the man in the blazer on the floor came to and grabbed her leg, tripping her, and she fell to the floor, her knees screaming again, the gun still out of her reach. She rolled over and started kicking, but he blocked her foot. He was able to grab her other leg. He started to pull her down to his side. She clawed the rough, dirty carpet, trying to get a hold of something, the dirt sticking to the underside of her fingernails.

He wrapped his arm around her waist, and in a blind panic, she threw her elbow out and made contact with the top of his head, causing him to howl in pain. She scrambled to get up, but she stumbled over and felt his hands grabbing at her clothes. She turned and bent to throw a punch, but he grabbed a hold of her locket and he yanked her down. The chain broke with a snap, but she was free from his grasp and stood up. *The bastard*, she thought. He broke her necklace, and she had only just gotten it back. Her dad gave her that. She went to reach down and grab it. The man shoved it in his coat pocket and grabbed her hair. Blood was running from his nose, and his eyes were glossed over. Asa had really worked him over. He pulled her head down, and her scalp burned with pain. Her ear was inches from his mouth when he said, "I watched as they killed your father. We made him fall to his knees. Made him beg for his life as we held a gun to his head."

Her eyes filled with tears, and anger raced through her body. She saw red. She wanted to make him bleed and wished Asa had hurt him more. Instead, with the very skill her father taught her, she reached into his pocket and grabbed her locket and the ring that was resting next to it. Without breaking eye contact, and with the skill of her trade that her father had practiced with her daily, she slipped it into her own pocket.

Fueled with anger and ignoring the pain radiating from her scalp, the necklace and ring safe, she lashed out, hitting him in the chest and stomach as hard as she could. He got a hold of her arm and yanked her until she fell over unbalanced. She fell to the side and looked up just in time to see Asa pistol whip Cal and watched him fall to the floor. Asa ran over and pointed his gun at the man on the floor.

"Let her go." When the man only laughed, Asa brought the gun down to his forehead. "Now." His voice was low and stern, full of authority.

The man let her go, and she stumbled back, falling on her bottom. She watched as Asa got down on one knee and, in a low voice, asked, "Where is the ring?" His eyes were intense, not leaving the man's face.

She stumbled back in shock. "What the hell?" she whispered. He wanted the ring, too? She shook her head, trying to grasp the situation.

The man laughed and held his hands up in surrender.

Asa bent over and started to search the man's pockets. When he came up with nothing, he looked over to Cal, still lying unconscious on the floor.

"Don't move," Asa commanded.

He turned and started toward Cal.

But then a phone rang. She startled and turned, and the man on the floor started to laugh. It was coming from his jacket.

He was still on his back, his face a bloody mess. He looked up at her.

"That's my friends calling." The man coughed, spitting blood onto the floor.

"If we don't answer, they will come to our aid, then you both will be dead. I promise, honey." He looked her right in the eyes. "You'll wish that my friend Cal had taken you instead."

She stood up, fear making her body vibrate. She wanted to run. She felt light-headed.

Asa stepped toward her. "Don't run. I'm here to help you. Trust me." He looked right into her eyes, his gray eyes changing to soft and pleading.

He had saved her from Cal, but he wanted the ring, just like these men did.

The man on the floor started to laugh.

Asa stepped to the side, still holding the gun on him.

The sound of screeching tires filled the small store. All three of them looked up to see a black SUV with tinted windows pull in to the front and come to a sudden stop.

The man started to laugh harder, making himself cough again.

"You're in trouble now, my friends. They will cut you down, man, and then we will all take turns with the girl." He spit blood on the floor again.

The loud bang had her jerk in surprise.

Asa shot the man in the head. The laughter stopped as his head fell back.

She gave a small scream and started to back up. Bile and the coffee she had earlier began to rise in her throat.

Asa turned to her. "I'm sorry." He held his hand out. "But we need to go, now!"

She only shook her head, trying to erase the image burned into her eyes.

Asa grabbed her hand and headed for the back room. She turned one last time as she was being pulled. She saw that Cal was rolling over from his back, and she watched as he looked at his dead friend. With bloodstained teeth, he smiled over at her and then winked. "We will find you, Gabe Wright's daughter! You will pay!"

She followed Asa through the back door.

"Move faster." He was pulling her past boxes and shelves and ignoring Cal's laughter from the front of the store.

They made it to the back of the storage room and to the exit door. Asa stepped back and kicked the door hard; it flew open with a loud bang. He stopped at the opening and looked down the alley both ways; he then pulled her through and she followed. The sun was setting, and the alley was full of shadows. She couldn't help herself and kept looking back down the alley, expecting someone to shoot her in the back. But Asa kept a firm hold on her hand and she kept moving.

"My truck is parked at the corner of the block."

They were keeping close to the wall of the building. When they reached the corner, he stopped. Asa swung his arm out, holding her against the wall as he looked down the street. She was ready to make a break for it, still not sure if she could trust this guy. She heard the loud bang, and then a chuck of the brick wall came raining down on her head. Dust and pebbles littered her hair.

She ducked, placing her hands over her head to protect it from the debris.

But Asa didn't hesitate; he grabbed her hand and swung her around the corner, then turned back and fired two shots down the alley. He pushed her to a blue truck parked about ten feet away. She heard the beep of the lock and saw the lights flash.

She swung the door open and jumped in. Asa ran around the backside. She heard two more gunshots, and she quickly ducked her head down below the dashboard. The truck door swung open and Asa jumped in. He hit the ignition button, threw it in gear, and swung the truck into oncoming traffic.

There was a car coming, and she placed her hands on the dash to brace herself for the crash. But Asa took a left and went down another alley, just in time.

When they came to the end of the alley, he took a left going the right way, and then entered the freeway heading east toward Fuller.

"What the hell just happened?" She was looking down at her hands. They were dirty and had blood on them. She didn't know if it was hers.

"Oh my God! Yuri is dead." She whipped her head and looked at Asa. "I watched them shoot him, and you shot that other guy. What's going on?" Her voice trembled and tears welled in her eyes. "Who are you? How did you know I was at the pawnshop?"

He looked over at her. He studied her face.

"I'm not a friend of Margie's." He looked back to the road.

"Obviously." She wiped her eyes.

"I was following you. Tracing the Lojack I put on your car the day of the funeral." He said it bluntly, and he reached for his phone.

"What? You were following me? With a Lojack?" She was secretly relieved that she knew what that was.

"Who are you?"

"I'm an independent investigator."

"What?"

He pushed some buttons, then the truck filled with the sound of a ringing phone.

She noticed that his knuckles were bleeding and swollen. He flexed them once on the steering wheel. He had gotten those beating the life out of those two men. The ones who wanted to take her and worse. She felt sick.

The realization that she could have been raped and killed hit her hard. If he hadn't shown up, she was sure she would be dead. She looked up at his face. It was serious but not hard. The thought had her relaxing a little.

"Hey, did you get it?" A man's voice came over the speakers, filling the cab.

"No, but I ran into some trouble. I'm pretty sure it's the Brotherhood."

"Damn, are you okay? What about the girl?"

"I got her, and we're fine. But brother, they knew her." Asa paused. "They want the girls, too."

She turned in the leather seat to face him.

Roxy.

She thought of her alone at Margie's house.

"Do they know where we live?" she asked. "They knew our names and my father's name."

"Most likely," said the man on the other line. She flinched, forgetting that he was there.

"How far are you out?"

"Still an hour plus." He paused. "Brady, you need to go get her."

"On it." The man named Brady didn't even hesitate.

"But wait," she said. "Roxy isn't just going to go with some stranger that shows up at the house with some crazy story. She'll call the cops."

Both men were silent.

"Just go; we don't have time," Asa replied. "I'll have Sydney call Roxy now."

He looked to her. "You'll have to convince her. We don't have time." He must have seen the look of unease on her face. "Look how fast they showed up at the pawnshop." When she didn't say anything, he continued, "I do want the ring. I have my reasons which I will explain when we have more time. But if I wasn't here to help you, I would have searched for the ring longer and left you with them."

He was right. He could have just left her. She only nodded, deciding to trust them for now. She started to think of what she was going to say to her sister. Hell, she didn't really know what to think of it all yet.

"Call me when you got her," Asa said into the phone and hung up.

He handed the phone to her, and she started to dial Roxy's number with shaky fingers. As the phone rang, she looked to Asa. He was staring straight ahead. He was running his hand down his beard like he was straightening it out. Is he thinking? she wondered, observing his movements.

"Who is Brady?" she asked. The phone started to ring.

"He's my cousin, you can trust him."

"Can he protect my sister?" she asked.

"Yes," he said it with confidence. He stopped tugging on his beard.

"Hello?" Roxy said, her voice not as loud on the speakers as Brady's had been.

"It's me, Sydney. I need you to listen. Roxy, this is very important. I was just attacked trying to pawn that ring."

"Seriously." Roxy cut her off. "I said to wait on the ring."

"No, listen," she cut her off. "There are some bad people that are pissed at us. I need you to go pack our bags and wait. There is a man named Brady. He is coming to pick you up, and we will meet you…" She stopped and looked over at Asa.

"He'll take you to our hotel in the valley. It'll be safe there."

"Who is that?" Roxy immediately asked.

"That's Asa Hallows. The man from Margie's wake."

Roxy was quiet for a few seconds. "The one that gave you weird vibes?"

She could feel the blush run up her cheek.

She side-glanced Asa. He flashed a grin at her, then looked back at the road.

"Yes, I need you to trust me; this is no joke."

"I'm confused," Roxy said, unsure.

"These men knew we're Gabe Wright's daughters, and they want revenge, I guess Dad stole that ring from them, and they're the ones that killed him. Now they want to kill us too." Her breath hitched on the last part.

Roxy huffed out a breath. "Are you sure? If this is a joke, Syd, it's not funny." She didn't sound like she was taking it seriously, and it was making her frightened.

"Please!" she said, noting how she could hear the desperation in her own voice.

"Fine. I'll leave with a total stranger because someone wants to kill us. Sydney, you better not be pulling a con on me."

"I have never been more serious in my life. They wanted to rape me; I wouldn't joke about that. Now go pack and hurry. He'll be there soon."

"I think he's already here," Roxy said, sounding confused.

"Wait!" There was panic in Asa's voice. He looked at the clock on the dash.

"Look out the window, Roxy." His voice was softening, calm. "But don't let them see you. What kind of car is it?"

There was some shuffling on the other end.

"It's some kind of black SUV," Roxy said.

"Listen carefully," Asa said; his voice firm and filled with authority now instead of calm.

"That is not Brady. You need to go out the back quietly and head out into the field behind the house."

"What, are you crazy?" Roxy asked.

"Just listen to him," she yelled. "Roxy, just get out of there!" Panic had her sitting up in the seat and her eyes filling with tears.

"All right," Roxy said quietly. The panic in her voice was finally making Roxy take it all seriously.

Asa broke in. "Don't hang up. Don't have us on speaker. You need to be quiet." He was being patient and was staying calm. Unlike her, she felt like she was going to explode.

"I need to text Brady. Let him know to pick you up in the backfield. So, once you get there, stay. Let him find you." Asa held out his hand and she put the phone in it.

"Are you outside yet?" Asa started to text one-handed with his thumb.

"Yes," Roxy whispered. "I'm heading to the back field."

The sound of branches and dried grass cracking filled the truck.

He continued to type while looking between the phone and the road.

"What way are you headed?" he asked.

Roxy sounded like she was running when she answered, "West."

"Are you in the back field yet?"

"Yes, shit, they have flashlights and they're scanning the field."

"Get down!" Sydney yelled.

The truck filled with the sound of crunching grass.

Asa dropped his phone down in his lap and looked over at her.

"Brady is ten minutes out."

"You hear that, Roxy?" she asked her sister.

"Yeah," she whispered. "I think they're…"

The phone went silent.

"Roxy? Roxy?" There was no answer. Her mind went fuzzy with fear, panic filling her blood.

"Roxy, are you there?"

Still no answer.

Tears filled her eyes and she met Asa's. He dialed her number again; it went straight to voicemail.

He punched the gas.

Roxy

"Hello? Hello?" She looked at her phone, but the screen was dark. Damn, she forgot to charge it again.

She was laying in the field, covered in grass and mud. She just had this dream the night before too, so it was only adding to her fear. If Sydney was right, she was running from the same thugs as last time.

Fear gripped her. She was alone, waiting for a stranger to come get her, and her father's murderers were searching the field for her.

Lucky for her, the field was overgrown and the grass was thigh high. It was almost dark, and she was having a hard time seeing. She needed to get up and start to make her way back to the tree line. It felt like the flashlight beams were getting closer.

She got on her hands and knees and started to crawl. She knew there was an access road a little further back. Instinct had her reaching for her phone to GPS it. But she stopped, remembering it was dead. She would be too if she didn't get moving. Her stomach tightened.

She crawled about five yards on her hands and knees. Mud soaked through her jeans, and the smell of dirt and grass filled her nose. She then heard voices.

"Go to the back. She has to be here somewhere. She left the back door open. Remember, the boss said, alive."

"Alive?" she whispered. Fear had her picking up her pace.

A beam of light went over her head, and she froze. She slowly lowered herself all the way to the ground, trying not to move the grass.

She waited. The light kept moving, and she listened. She could still hear crunching grass, but faintly. She wanted to peek her head up and see where they were, but fear had her staying down.

After a minute, she started to crawl again. She stopped when there was the sound of heavy breathing, not more than a couple yards away. She froze, and it seemed like everything else did too. Then a twig snapped. Closer. Fear paralyzed her, and she flattened herself to the ground.

Had they found her? Adrenaline fueled, she started to get up and make a break for it when the sound of thunder boomed over her head. She fell to the ground. It was a gunshot. She heard a thud a few feet to her right. She laid there, fear gripping her chest. *Were they shooting at her?* She lifted her head slightly above the grass and found there was no one there. She went to stand and turn for the tree line, when a hand clamped down on her mouth and her body was thrown to the ground. She was pinned down.

She tried to scream but nothing except a muddled noise came out. She started to kick her legs, but to no avail. The man on top of her had her pinned down. Her clothes were heavy with mud, but she didn't quit.

"Shhhh!" the male voice said. "It's okay, I'm Brady."

Still frightened, she didn't stop kicking.

"Please," he said. "Sydney is your sister, and she and Asa, my cousin, sent me to pick you up."

The information had her legs growing still.

"I'm going to remove my hand. Do you promise not to scream?"

She nodded her head, feeling the mud drip from her cheek.

He slowly removed his hand.

She looked up but couldn't make out his face in the dark.

"We need to get out of here. Are you okay? Can you run?"

She just nodded.

"Follow me."

Instead of crawling, he stood hunched over. When he reached down with his hand, the far off light from the house's back patio reflected off his glasses, and she reached up and took it.

"Let's go. Before they find out about the access road. That's where the car is."

They started to run; he hadn't let go of her hand. She was feeling exposed with her back to the house, and she had fear gripping her chest. She started to slow her pace. Brady looked back. "We're almost to the tree line."

He tightened his grip on her hand, and she pushed herself forward.

When they finally hit the tree line, he pulled her behind a large maple tree. She rested her back against it and tried to catch her breath. Brady kept close to her, and the closeness made it hard for her to breathe easily. He smelled like cloves and mud. He peeked his head around the tree, and sounding only slightly winded, he whispered, "I don't think they saw us." He turned from the field and looked at her. "You good?"

She nodded. By the little she could see, his hair was disheveled, and he had black-framed glasses. He was tall and slim.

Without another word, he grabbed her hand again, and they weaved their way through trees and bushes. When she stumbled over a root, he swiftly pulled her back up, his eyes scanning the tree line behind her. "You still with me?" he whispered.

"Yes." She was irritated. The fact that he kept asking her that and she was stumbling around in the dark made her feel helpless. Especially considering he was having no problems.

They hit the access road, which was really just a gravel road overgrown with grass. There was a small, black, two-door hatchback car. He let go of her hand and picked up his pace, running toward the car while pulling the keys from his pocket. She had no choice but to run after him.

When she reached the car, he was already sliding into the driver's side, and she swung the passenger door open and slid in. He turned the key and hit the gas. He swung the car in a tight, small U-turn to face the entrance and then gunned the small car down the road.

When they got to the intersection, he took a right, and they hit the main road.

They were about two blocks from the house when he finally turned the headlights on, and they began to head toward the edge of town.

She finally took a large breath. She noticed that she was covered in mud, and when she touched her face, she could feel it all over. She wiped it, but it only flaked off.

She looked over to the stranger named Brady. He had black-framed glasses and light hair. It was sticking up all different ways. His jaw was prominent like Asa's, and she believed his comment that they were related. He was lanky but muscular, and she thought he was quite handsome like his cousin.

"Thanks," she said.

"You're welcome." He gave her a huge grin. "Nice to meet you. Sorry, it couldn't be under better circumstances."

She just smiled, feeling confused.

He checked the rear-view mirror.

"You think they'll follow us?" she asked.

"I hope not." He stopped at a red light and checked the mirrors again.

She noticed that a black SUV pulled up to the red light on the other side of the intersection. She froze.

Brady noticed her intake of breath and looked forward.

"Shit."

Just then, the light turned green, and they both took off. She stared at the SUV when it drove past, but the windows were tinted and she couldn't see in.

"Do you think that was them?" She gripped the door. "A black SUV, just like that one, pulled into my driveway."

"Keeping going," he whispered, dragging out the last word. He was looking back and forth between the road and the mirror.

His whispers had her checking her mirror too.

She watched as the SUV taillights glowed red and it stopped. It did an illegal U-turn and headed their way.

She let out a little squeak.

"Dammit." Brady reached behind him and pulled out a gun from the back of his jeans.

"What the hell are you going to do with that?" She stared at the black pistol.

"You ever used a gun before?" He placed it in his lap.

"No." She had never held a gun before and didn't know the first thing about them.

"Well, hopefully I won't have to use it again." He placed both hands on the steering wheel.

"Again?" she asked, confused. He looked at her with a grievous smile.

It dawned on her then that the shot she heard in the field was him.

"You shot one of them?" she asked.

"They were going to catch you," was all he said, taking the corner, a little too fast.

They drove down the main street, forced to do the speed limit. People were still walking around the streets when the SUV caught up.

"We should go to the police," she said, the headlights shining into the car and lighting everything up.

"We think that the Brotherhood has ties with the local police here. Your father's murder, for example." He looked over at her.

"How do you know about my father?" She was taken aback.

Brady looked over at her and grimaced like he had just been caught.

"My grandmother was the one who hired your father to steal that ring."

"What does the ring have to do with all this?"

Before Brady could answer, he took a sharp turn onto another street leading to the other side of town. She quickly looked to the side mirror and, sure enough, the SUV turned too.

"What if they run your plates?" she asked. "They'll know where you live and just go there."

"No worries," he said. "They'll find that the car is registered to an elderly man that passed away two years ago."

"Is this car stolen?" She side-eyed him.

"No." He looked at her with a toothy grin. "Let's just say we have something in common."

She was confused. She didn't ask further questions because they hit another street, taking them further out of town.

"What are we going to do?" she asked again. The SUV was staying on their tail, but not making any moves.

"We are going to have to try to lose them." As he said that, the light at the intersection turned yellow, and he stepped on the gas, but to their dismay, the SUV ran the red light. This time, Brady took the first right and sped down another residential road, going way too fast to be safe. She grabbed the handle above her door.

The SUV stayed right behind them. It hit her then, seeing the SUV relentlessly following them, their headlights blinding her through the mirror, that this was real and these guys were after them. That Brady, this guy she didn't even know, might have to use the gun that was sitting in his lap. Her eyes wanted to fill with tears. No wonder Sydney sounded so frantic on the phone. These guys meant business and they were way over their heads.

Brady kept taking random turns, not slowing down, and she was being thrown about in the car. But the SUV stayed right on their bumper.

After being whipped to the right, she saw the mud from her hands flake off and fall to her dirty knee. She looked to Brady. His eyes were in serious concentration, and if he was scared, he didn't show it.

She hoped he had a plan. She kept quiet and let him drive.

There was a four-way stop coming up. It was a busy one, because it led back into town on the other end.

"Hold on," Brady said in a stern voice. He hit the gas and he didn't hesitate and went for it. She braced herself. There was a big white truck that was about to take off, but he saw them and slammed his brakes. It let out a whale of a blast from his horn. Their little car swerved just a little bit, jerking her to the side, and the headlights of the big truck temporarily blinded her. She trapped her scream in her mouth as they went by. When they made it to the other side, she checked the side mirror and, to her relief, the SUV was trapped by the truck, and more horns were singing. Brady took another turn, speeding even faster, trying to get as far as possible. He turned onto Main Street and then backed into a dark alley halfway before cutting the headlights,

He sat there, staring straight ahead.

She was breathing heavily. "Do you think we lost them?"

He picked up the gun, but kept it below the steering wheel.

"Are you going to shoot them?" she whispered as if they might hear, feeling a little stupid.

"Only if I have to."

Just then, a black SUV with tinted windows drove by slowly. She ducked down. They were in the shadows of the alley, and the streetlights didn't reach their spot. Brady shifted in his seat; his gun held a little higher.

Her stomach tightened. "Please don't see us," she whispered over and over, almost like a prayer.

The SUV stopped. Its white backup lights flipped on and the SUV went in reverse. It turned down the alley.

She pushed back in her seat and reached for the door handle, ready to run.

Brady turned to her. "Stay here." He exited quickly and slammed the door, leaving her ears ringing in the now-silent car.

She watched as he held the gun up with both hands, walking toward the SUV. But the black truck didn't hesitate. She heard its engine rev loudly, and the tires screeched as it jerked forward.

Brady stopped, stood tall and confident, and took aim, firing three fast shots. She saw the glass crack. The engine growled. The SUV hit the side of the alley and bounced off. It hit the opposite side and struck a dumpster, where it finally stopped. Brady stayed where he was for a second. When nothing happened, he quickly turned and came back to her. He jumped in, dropped the gun in his lap, and threw the car into reverse. He backed all the way to the end of the alley and whipped the car around to face the direction to get out of town. Then he gunned it. He took the turn and drove straight for the freeway. He took the ramp and they were out of town.

Once they hit the freeway, both of them kept checking the mirrors, constantly. After about ten minutes, she broke the silence and said, "You killed those guys in the SUV?" She didn't know if she was asking or stating a fact.

He looked over at her and frowned. "I'm sorry you saw that. I had to. Please don't be scared."

She just turned and faced forward in her seat. She didn't know what to think just then. Even though she knew what he said was true, she couldn't process what was happening.

"We need to call Asa and your sister. When I hit the access road, I got a text from him that they lost contact with you. Your sister is worried."

She nodded and went to pull her phone out of her pocket, but it wasn't there. "Damn, I think I lost my phone in the field." Then she remembered that it was dead.

Brady hit the small screen on the dashboard and placed the call to Asa's phone.

It barely rang once.

"Brady, tell me good news, brother?" His voice was tense with fear.

"Yep, I have Roxy and we are both okay."

"Thank God." She heard her sister in the background sigh with relief.

"Any trouble?" Asa asked.

"Nothing I couldn't handle. But they know my car; I need to ditch it."

"Where you at?" Asa sounded serious.

"Headed the opposite direction of home on I-90." He started pushing buttons on the small screen, pulling up the GPS.

"There is a small gas station about ten miles from here." He paused as he moved the screen with his finger. "There's some woods behind it." He pinched the screen and widened his search. "We'll park behind the dumpster. Come pick us up back there. I'll drop you a pin."

"Got it. We will be there in..." The other line beeped, indicating that Asa got Brady's pin drop. "Be there in thirty." The line went dead.

"He's not much for goodbye, is he?"

"Not when he's stressed, and this just got a lot messier than we originally thought."

"What did?" She looked over at him.

"Getting the ring for our grandmother."

"Your grandmother wants the ring?"

"It's a family thing and a long story."

She didn't ask and they rode in silence.

Brady took the exit, and they found the gas station. It was on the main road, but not much else was around it. It was a rundown station and meant for the last ditch effort to get gas before going over the pass.

He pulled around to the back and parked next to an old dumpster. The one streetlight out front didn't reach back there, and he cut the engine.

He looked around and then sat back in the seat, and looked over at her.

"Good thing we're ditching the car. You got mud all over the place." He gave her a silly grin.

She looked down and noticed that the floor had dirty footprints and grass everywhere. The handle above her head was covered in mud also.

She dusted her pant leg off. "You did tackle me."

"Sorry about that, but I didn't want you to scream and give our position away. They were close." He frowned.

"You couldn't just try to get my attention somehow?"

"Like what? Yell, 'Hey, Roxy, its Brady, a stranger. Come with me if you want to live.'" He made his voice sound like the Terminator at the end and laughed.

She couldn't help it; she laughed too. "It would've been less frightening."

He smiled again. He reached onto the seat behind him and pulled out a computer bag and placed it in his lap.

"You brought a computer?" she asked.

"Never leave home without one." He opened the glove box, pulled some paperwork out, and slid it into the side pocket. Then he took a couple more items out of the center console. He then placed it on his lap and the gun on top of that.

She realized she had left hers at the house. "I don't think I shut mine down," she said out loud.

"It's okay," Brady said. "When Asa gets here, I'll access it and move your information to a cloud and erase what I can."

She huffed. "Yeah, right, you're going to access my computer? Good luck."

Brady just turned and gave her a smile.

"How did you learn to drive like that?"

"I was in the army after MIT. Was there mainly to do tech. They still make you go through boot camp; they don't teach defensive driving, but they do teach you how to stay calm in stressful situations. I even did a tour in Iraq."

She was surprised, as he didn't really look like a soldier to her.

They sat there for a couple of minutes in silence. She was anxious to see Sydney and try to understand what was going on. To fill the silence, she asked, "You were in Iraq?"

He kept his eyes forward, scanning the parking lot. "I don't talk about Iraq."

"Oh." She looked away, feeling embarrassed for asking.

They both tensed when a pair of headlights shone into the car. They watched with relief when they saw a small white sedan pull into one of the pumps.

"You want something? I can go into the station. Maybe some water?"

The thought brought a sharp ping of panic to her chest and she immediately answered no. The thought of being left alone right then petrified her.

He just nodded and went back to watching the gas station.

She looked down at her dirty hands. She would much rather be in this car with a stranger, who she watched kill at least the driver of that SUV, then be left alone right now, and that was a new thing for her. She usually preferred to be alone, and normally she would have said yes just to have a second to herself in the car. All of a sudden, her hands were too dirty, and she tried to wipe them clean on her pants, but her pants were just as dirty, and it wasn't helping. Memories of what had just happened came flooding back. They had come to her house, and she ran through the field again, hiding from men who wanted to hurt her. She had to trust a stranger. She was chased through town. Her eyes filled with tears, and she kept scrubbing her hands. She started to use the seat to do so, not caring that it wasn't her car.

She looked over at Brady. He was a stranger, and she was waiting with him at a nowhere gas station. She wondered how this had happened.

He looked over at her. "Hey, it's okay." He took his hand off the gun and placed it on hers. He picked it up, trying to get her to stop scrubbing.

"It's going to be fine. Your sister will be here any minute. You're safe."

She looked up, tears falling, she couldn't see what color his eyes were

89

in the dark, but she could see the softness in his expression.

It was a look she hadn't seen in a long time. Her heart slowed.

"I must look crazy right now." She let out a little laugh.

He gave her a warm smile. "I don't think you look crazy at all. Quite the opposite, actually." He winked, and she felt a blush climb her cheeks. She was glad for the dark and the mud.

Another pair of headlights flashed into the car, but this time they blinked three times.

"There's Asa. Stay here." He grabbed the gun and opened the door before turning to her. "Everything is going to be okay." Then he turned and exited the car.

She turned in the seat and watched as he slung the computer bag over his head and tucked the gun into his belt at the small of his back. Asa got out and gave his cousin a one-armed hug. Just then, the passenger door of the truck flung open, and Sydney jumped out. Asa threw his arms up in defeat and she heard him give a muffled, "I told you to stay in the car."

But if Sydney wasn't listening, neither was she. She too flung the door open and ran to her sister.

Sydney's jeans were ripped, her eyes were red-rimmed like she had been crying, and her cheeks were flushed.

Sydney grabbed her in a huge hug, and she hugged her back. This wasn't normal for them to show such affection to each other, but she was so relieved to be there with her sister.

"Roxy, I have never been so scared. What happened? Your phone just cut out. I thought they had you."

"I forgot to charge it again." She pulled back from her sister. "The battery died."

"Jesus, I've been out of my mind. You're covered in mud." Sydney straightened her arms and pushed her back to examine her clothes.

"Girls!" Asa all but boomed, "We need to go."

She looked over and Brady was loading his computer into the front seat, and Asa was at the driver's door.

They broke apart, but to her surprise, Sydney didn't let go of her hand, and they walked together to the truck.

Sydney

She was so relieved to have Roxy next to her in the truck. She thought she had lost her sister, and the thought had sent her in a spiral of fear.

From the back seat, she could see Brady's side profile. His hair was light and messy. His face was clean-shaven and angular, but where Asa looked tough and serious, Brady had a boyish charm. She owed this man for bringing her sister back to her safe.

As they drove, Brady told their story of what happened in Fuller.

When he talked about shooting one of the men in the field, she glanced over at Roxy who looked frightened. It twisted her gut, making her want to reach over and grab her sister tight. Then Asa told their story, and Sydney filled in the parts that Asa wasn't there for.

Brady pulled his computer out in the front seat. He pushed some buttons on the screen in the dash and turned the hotspot on. He then started typing.

"They haven't accessed your computer yet. Hopefully it went into energy save mode before they could get in."

"Wait what?" Roxy grabbed the back of Brady's headrest, pulling herself forward and looking over his shoulder. Mud fell from her arms onto the floor of the truck.

"How do you know that? No one can access my computer. I know this because I designed the firewall myself."

Brady looked over his shoulder, sporting a boyish smile.

"Are you serious?" Roxy leaned further over Brady's shoulder.

She couldn't help but laugh. Roxy was pissed.

"Well, it wasn't easy," Brady said reassuringly. "It took me a couple days, actually."

This time, Asa chuckled. It surprised her to hear him laugh. He had been serious the whole way to the gas station. He had relaxed a little since Brady had gotten into the truck. He seemed more like the man she'd met at Margie's house.

Asa leaned over. "Most programs don't challenge Brady; he was pretty frustrated. I think he stayed up for like three days trying. The cuss words coming out of this guy would make a felon cry."

"I would hope so," Roxy chuffed. "How did you do it?"

She didn't know if Roxy was still mad, but she looked like she was pouting.

Brady started to talk computer while Roxy listened intently over his shoulder.

She tuned it out and stared out the window. The day had been long, and she had a feeling it wasn't quite over yet; there were lots of questions still to be answered. She felt the weight of the ring in her pocket. She looked up and caught Asa looking at her in the rearview mirror. She held his stare for a second before he looked back to the road.

*

The Valley was a slightly larger town than Fuller and twenty minutes away. It was still small but had large chain retailers and restaurants. There were only a few hotels in the town, and they pulled up to the Calli, which was the more expensive and upscale hotel compared to others in the area. This made her think that Asa and Brady liked and could afford comfort. She looked at the two of them sitting in the front of the truck. Brady had put his computer away, and they both were scanning the parking lot as they pulled in.

She wondered if she could trust them. They both did help her and Roxy. She didn't think they wanted to hurt her and her sister. But they did want the ring, just like these people that they kept calling the Brotherhood.

She looked to Roxy who was sitting back in the seat, arms crossed, lips pouty, looking irritated. She was still fuming over the fact that Brady had hacked into her computer. The more she thought about it, that too made her nervous. Roxy was good; she was a genius when it came to computers, yet Brady had gotten in. She wondered if going to their hotel room was the right decision. They could easily hurt them; they did have guns. Maybe they should run? When they parked, she would grab Roxy's hand and make a break for it. They could get a cab, maybe head to... she paused. Head where? Feeling the heavy weight hit her shoulders made her sink back into her seat. They had no one.

Margie was gone, and they couldn't head back to her house. The

92

Brotherhood was there now, doing God knows what. They couldn't head back to New York; she had nothing there either. She didn't even have her dorm room. They surely knew where Roxy lived in Seattle. They would have to hop from one hotel to the next. She had been doing it for a year now. It hit her hard and sadness filled her chest, making it tight and heavy. She did it knowing that some day, when she was done, she could always go to Margie's. But not anymore. Tears welled up in her eyes. But before one could fall, Brady spoke.

"There's a black SUV out front."

"Yeah, I saw that, but people drive black vehicles all the time." Asa was staring at the vehicle. He stopped the truck in the corner of the parking lot and backed into an empty spot.

"I'll go check it out," Asa said. "I'll text you." He opened the door and stepped out.

She studied him as he headed for the entrance to the hotel. She hadn't noticed before, but he was wearing a light gray suit jacket that fit comfortably over his wide shoulders and jeans that looked tailored to his legs. She couldn't help but look.

His walk was of a man comfortable in his own skin, and she watched until he disappeared behind the door.

They all sat there quietly. Brady had his phone in his hands. She noticed that Brady kept scanning the parking lot but was mainly keeping his attention on the black SUV.

When Brady's phone buzzed, she immediately looked up. The phone lit up his face, and she watched as it turned up in surprise.

"Go time." Brady swung up the center console and slid into the passenger seat. He started the truck. Before she could ask, he was gunning the engine and whipping out of the parking spot. He headed right for the entrance.

"Hold on," he said as he slammed on the brakes.

The truck door swung open, and Asa jumped in.

"What's going on?" She grabbed the door handle as Brady gunned it again and made for the exit.

Asa turned to Brady. "They're here. About ten of them."

She and Roxy sat forward. "What? How?"

"I don't think they noticed me. It looked like they were waiting for us.

"Did they have security at the pawnshop?"

"I don't know. I didn't really have time to study the store," Asa retorted, frustration in his voice. He looked over his shoulder.

"They did," she said from the back. "Yuri was paranoid. He didn't trust anyone."

"Then they have your face." Brady turned to Asa.

"It's not hard to do face identification. They know who you are, and that means, I'm sure they know who I am too. They traced us here."

"Then they know this truck through the rental company," Asa said.

"They probably know everything." Brady got on the freeway. He checked the rear-view mirror every couple of seconds. Asa did too. "I don't think they're following us."

"Where are we going to go?" she asked. She was at a complete loss. Her mind felt blank and black with no solutions, and it made her hands shake with fear. She felt like a skittish animal running from one side of the road to the other.

"Bev," Roxy said, leaning back.

The truck was silent.

"I don't want to bring her into this. She was a nice lady, but we will end up scaring her and bringing all this crazy to her doorstep."

"She was a friend of Margie's," Roxy said. "She has no connection to us until the last few days."

"It's too dangerous," she said again.

"I don't know," Asa said, looking toward Brady.

Brady looked back from the side mirror and out to the road. "If the Brotherhood can't connect the girls to her, it might be our best shot."

Asa ran his hand down his beard. "We need to regroup and talk about our options."

Brady looked up in the mirror. "If they know who we are, they will be watching our bank accounts, credit cards, and phones." Brady paused. A frown crossed his face. "We need to get rid of all our tech."

They all looked to him.

She looked over to Roxy, and she was nodding in agreement. "If they have the technology to do face recognition, then they can trace cell phones."

She sighed. "I don't have my phone. It was left back at the pawnshop."

Asa reached over and grabbed Brady's phone from the center console. With his phone in his hand, he threw them both out the window.

She watched as they hit the ditch on the side of the road.

Asa looked over to Brady. Brady was looking over at his computer bag. "That thing is going to have to go too."

Brady sighed long and hard. Asa grabbed it from the computer bag, and she watched as he tossed it out the window.

Roxy

They decided to park the truck at a nearby fast-food restaurant about twenty miles in the opposite direction of Fuller and take random buses back. They agreed that Bev was their only solution. They needed a plan and Bev's was the safest. They had no credit cards and no IDs.

She all but rolled out of the high truck. She was wet, muddy, and cold. Her shirt was sticking to her back with mud, and it was becoming hard and flaky.

She looked over at Sydney. When she jumped out of the truck, she winced. She noticed that Sydney was favoring her knees, and by the look of the holes in her skinny jeans, it looked like she was hurting.

She watched as Asa grabbed personal belongings out of the truck and noticed he placed a gun in the small of his back. Asa saved Sydney's life, she told herself, trying not to be nervous at the sight of the gun. She had seen more guns in the last few hours than in her whole life.

Brady placed the now lighter computer bag over his shoulder and made his way to her. The restaurant's neon sign lit the whole parking lot. His black-framed glasses were designer and gave him a smart, sexy look. He was tall and thin but had muscle. She could tell by the tightness of the sleeves of his white T-shirt; it, too, was stained with mud and grass. His jeans were worn over black high-topped Converse and, for some irrational reason, she liked that they wore the same kind of shoes.

He saw her staring and he smiled. "Ready? The bus stop is just at the end of the street."

She quickly looked away. "Yep."

The four of them walked in silence. They reached the bus stop, and she took a seat next to Sydney on the bench.

"You okay?" she asked. "Your knees look pretty bad." Up close, she could see blood soaking through.

"Yeah, just skinned knees. The guy threw me down pretty hard."

"I'm just glad you're okay," she said, surprising even herself. "That sounded intense."

Sydney looked over at her. "Yours sounded scary too. You, okay? You're covered in mud and you're wet." Sydney slid over on the bench and sat closer, leaning shoulder to shoulder. That, too, was surprising. "Are you cold?"

Trying to keep the shock off her face, she just smiled. It felt good to be close to her. She didn't realize how much she needed the comfort.

Sydney leaned in and whispered in her ear, "Do you think we can trust these guys? I mean, they want the ring too. We can't take them to Bev's and put her in danger."

She looked over at them. They were talking softly to each other, but they weren't looking at each other, and she couldn't make out what they were saying. Both were standing straight with their shoulders back, like they were just waiting for a fight. Neither one was relaxed and their eyes were hard.

She thought about the last couple hours. They knew nothing of these strangers. They wanted the ring. It had something to do with their family and her dad. If it was true, then she wanted answers. But Bev was a single older lady and a new friend.

She looked to Sydney. "I want answers and I don't think we have any other option. Brady and Asa saved our lives. They could just ditch us and find the ring. They don't need us. We're just extra baggage. I think we will be okay."

Sydney broke their eye contact and looked down at her bloody knees. "We don't really have a choice, do we?"

They both sat in silence for a minute, pondering their situation.

"If we take this to Bev's doorstep, then we need to be prepared to protect her," Sydney said.

"Agreed," she said.

Sydney looked up. "We call the police if these guys seem like trouble."

"Brady said that the Brotherhood has contacts in the Fuller Police Department." She felt nauseous. This was sounding unbelievable. If she wasn't living it, she would think it was a huge joke.

"If they are conning us, then we know that's a lie."

They both looked up as a bus pulled in to the stop with a loud hiss. She looked to Sydney. She saw uncertainty on her face, just like she was sure it was written on hers. Then they stood, and just like their father had taught them in any con, they moved like they knew what they were doing.

The bus ride was long and uneventful. They took two random buses in opposite directions of Fuller. Then started to circle their way back.

By the time the last bus dropped them off in Fuller, she was tired, cold, and hungry. She wanted nothing more than a shower and a hot meal. She could tell by the way Sydney kept running her hand across her face that she, too, was ready to be off the bus.

They were in the heart of town, and Asa and Brady were on high alert. The sudden realization that a few hours ago she and Brady had been chased through the town by the Brotherhood had her forgetting her grumbling belly.

They took an alley that ran parallel to the backside of Main Street. They were all silent as they made their way. She watched as Asa pulled his gun from his back and kept it at his side. She also noticed Brady stayed behind them, his gun also resting at his side.

Fortunately, Bev lived just a couple blocks away, and they found her house quickly.

They stood out front and stared up at the small rambler. It was just like she thought it would be.

The house was painted bright yellow with white trim. Even with the dim streetlight overhead, the house glowed. She had large rosebushes in the front, under all the windows. She had small garden gnomes spread out all over the lawn, looking like a small army protecting the house. The porch light was on, but all the windows were dark except one. It had the flicker of what looked like a TV still on.

"Let's see if she is even awake," Sydney said as she walked up to the heavy white wooden front door.

She stayed close behind her, and Asa and Brady followed.

Sydney rang the doorbell, and she could hear them tinkle softly.

After a minute, they all looked to each other.

"Do we knock?" she asked.

Sydney just shrugged.

Brady looked back over his shoulder, surveying the yard.

"I think we might need another plan." Asa took a step back.

She didn't know what else they could do.

She was just about to say that much when a light in the window flipped on and the front door swung open with a quick jerk.

Bev stared out. She was dressed in sweatpants and a bright pink T-shirt.

Her hair was disheveled but her eyes were bright.

She was just about to apologize for the late hour when Bev looked her square in the eye.

"I guess you guys found the ring."

Sydney

Shock filtered through her body. *What the hell?* she thought. She looked to Roxy, whose face was just as surprised.

"Are we the only ones that didn't know about this damn ring?"

Bev smiled and eyed the two strangers behind them. She pointed at Asa.

"I had a feeling about you when I saw you at Margie's funeral. I said to myself that's a Sinclair man if I ever saw one." She smiled.

Asa took a step forward. "I don't mean to be rude, but we need to get out of the open."

Bev smiled and took a step back. "Of course." She gestured them in.

The house had an open floor plan, with the kitchen in the back, the dining room to one side, and the living room in front. It was full of colorful knickknacks, covering every open space. The furniture was old and mismatched but gave the room a homey feel. She liked it. It was so Bev.

Bev walked in behind them and drew the large blue curtains closed. She then turned on the lamp and looked at the four of them.

"So, you kids want coffee?" She smiled and then took in their appearance. "Maybe something a little stronger. Come on, I'll put the coffee on. You guys sit and take a breath. There's fear in your eyes."

They followed her to the dining area and sat at the table. It was old and scuffed from many family gatherings. She had a moment of envy at the thought of sitting here with Bev, laughing over a family holiday.

Bev came back with a bottle of Bourbon and glasses. She sat at the head of the rectangular table.

She poured them each a shot and slid them over. Asa grabbed his and studied it. She was accepting him to shoot it, but instead he took a small sip then smiled. "You've got good taste, Bev." He then took another small sip, savoring the flavor.

She smelled it and took a small sip. It went down like liquid fire and burned her throat. She couldn't help it and blew out her breath. Asa and Bev laughed. She decided not to take another sip but instead held it to steady her hands.

"So rough night?" Bev asked with a smile over the rim of her glass.

Asa leaned forward. "You could say that. I'm Asa Hallows," he said and stuck his large hand out to Bev, who was sitting right next to him. Bev took it with a large grin. "Beverly Thompson, but everyone calls me Bev." Bev looked over and winked at her.

"Brady Sinclair." Brady stood and leaned over the tabletop to shake Bev's hand. "Me and Asa are cousins." When he sat back down, she noticed Brady hadn't touched his Bourbon.

"So, tell me everything," Bev shuffled in her seat, getting comfortable, "starting off with where you found the ring."

The story took almost an hour. Bev had lots of questions; some they couldn't answer. When it was all said and done, Bev stood and got the coffee.

"I think it's time to switch to this instead." She handed everyone a mug.

Sydney had questions swirling in her head. Then it hit her.

She turned to Asa and Brady. "Sinclair?" They both looked at her.

"As in the Maine Sinclairs? As in the 1800s steel, Sinclair family?"

Brady gave a small flinch. "Yes," he said quietly.

"I don't get it. Why do you keep saying their name like that?" Roxy was looking around the table at everyone. Soon, her gaze landed on her sister.

"The Sinclair family is one of the richest and oldest families on the east coast. They had a hand in the steel industry back in the 1800s. Among other things." She looked over at them. "They are a pretty quiet family now. Rumor has it they have an in with the Rothschild family."

Asa smiled over his coffee mug.

Brady huffed out his breath, his face a little red. "That's just a rumor. How do you know so much about my family?"

Sydney shrugged. "I like to read the gossip magazines." She didn't want to mention that she made it her business to know about the rich circles. She and the Sinclairs had never crossed paths. As far as she could tell, they were honest in their dealings.

Asa looked at her with those all-knowing eyes again, the ones from the night of the funeral. She shifted in her seat.

"So," Asa quickly tore his eyes off her and looked over at Bev, "what do you know? You seem to know about us and the ring?"

Bev took note of the change of subject and started in. "Well, I remember when your father died." She looked at the girls with sympathy. "Margie was so worried about you girls, and she came to me. She was full of fear and uncertainty. She told me everything. Mary Sinclair contacted her about the job that your father did and that she was pretty sure it was the Brotherhood that killed him. Mary worried that the Brotherhood would come after you girls. Margie had no idea where Gabe had hidden the ring, and it seemed you girls had no idea that it even existed. She wanted to keep it that way. With no help from Sheriff Stone, Margie took Mary's offer to send you girls to the girls' home in Oregon and seal your records." She looked over at them.

"It was a decision that she didn't take lightly. She really wanted you guys to stay with her, but she felt she couldn't protect you like Mary and her money could. It broke her heart. She loved you girls like her own." Bev stopped and looked into her mug of coffee, then took a sip. "She told me all this because she was scared that if the Brotherhood came after her, she wanted to make sure someone knew and took care of you girls. She gave me Mary's number." Bev put her coffee down.

"After a while of nothing and you girls were off doing your own thing, Margie told me that she thought it might be over. That the Brotherhood realized that you girls knew nothing. Margie told me that she prayed that the Brotherhood found the ring on their own and that the whole thing was over." Bev ran her hands through her hair. "But I guess not."

She continued, "When Margie passed away, I thought of contacting Mary Sinclair just to let her know. But Margie had believed it was over, and I was hoping it was too. I mean, what was I to say? 'Hey Mary, you don't know me, but I know your secret.'"

"I helped with the wake to watch over you. That's when I saw you, Asa." She looked over at him. He was sitting back in his chair, listening. He had one arm resting on his chest and the other hand stroking his beard in a thoughtful way.

"I was hoping that Mary sent you to check up on the girls. I figured that Mary, being who she was, would send someone. It actually made me feel better knowing Mary was keeping her promise to watch over the girls." Bev looked at the whole table. "I guess it's not over."

The room was silent. Sydney broke it. "I can't believe that Margie knew this the whole time and didn't let us know. I mean, we are involved.

This lady, Mary, who I had no idea about, was paying for our schooling? She was watching over us?" She paused, letting it sink in. She had hidden them away, and Margie let her? She looked back up at the people sitting around the table.

"Our father died because of this. And what's worse," she said, throwing her hands up, "is that the ring was in her house the whole time. She was in more danger than anyone else."

No one said anything.

Roxy spoke up. She looked to Asa and Brady. "Why do you guys want the ring?"

They looked at each other. Brady gestured to Asa.

"Our family has ties to this ring, or really the stone, that date back hundreds of years. To an ancestor named Henry Slate. From the 1600s." Asa ran his hand down his beard, then leaned forward in his chair. "Our grandmother asked me to find the ring. As an independent investigator, she knew I had the resources, and I brought Brady in because of his MIT background.

"What's an independent investigator?" she asked.

Brady turned and smiled. "He's a private detective."

Asa rolled his eyes. "It's not 1950." He looked over at the table. "I used to be a cop, but I retired early and started my own business. It doesn't really matter. The Brotherhood has the ring now. We'll most likely never get it back." His face was stressed.

When he looked over at her, she nervously squirmed in her chair, something she realized was completely out of her control, and she berated herself for letting this stranger make her break confidence.

"We'll get it back; this isn't over yet." Brady shuffled in his chair, looking antsy. "It wasn't going to be this easy, and we knew that going in." He looked to Asa.

Asa nodded.

"Tell them the story. I'm going to watch the front." Brady got up and walked over to the front window. He pulled the curtain aside. When nothing caught his attention, he stayed and waited.

"Our family is cursed."

The room was quiet. Everyone was staring at Asa.

"So, tell us about this curse." Bev said, leaning forward, excited for a good story. "Why does your family need this stone?"

"It's really just an old tale passed down through the generations."

They all looked at him, waiting. "We want to hear it," Bev said.

Asa took a sip of his Bourbon.

"Back in seventeenth-century England," Asa began, "Brady and I had an ancestor named Henry Slate, and one day while he was in the market, he ran into a woman named Abby. The story goes, it was love at first sight. They spent all their free time together. When Henry went to ask for Abby's hand in marriage, her father declined and said that Henry was too poor and had nothing to offer. Abby's family were farmers, and even though they weren't rich, her father had plans to marry her up.

"Later that night, against her father's wishes, Abby snuck out and met Henry in the barn. He promised her that he had a plan to convince her father to let him marry her. His plan was to find the stone of prosperity.

"The tale was old, but it had intrigued Henry for years. His father would tell him the story before bed when he was a boy.

"There was a stone said to have magical powers to give the possessor whatever they wanted. But it was hidden on the side of a cliff near a small fishing village in Ireland. The cliffs of Ireland supposedly had magic, and the stone would only show itself to someone who was pure of heart. He told Abby that his love for her was pure and that the stone would surely show itself to him. He was going to Ireland to get the stone and exchange it for her hand in marriage. For surely, her father wanted it. Abby excitedly agreed and promised to wait for his return. They spent the night together in the barn, making plans for their future.

"The next morning, Henry walked Abby home. He gave her promises of winning her father over, saying that he would only be a couple months. He went to his house and convinced his younger brother Edward to go with him. Their parents had both passed away years before, and only having each other, Henry was worried for his brother's safety and well-being. Henry had told him that it would be a great adventure, and Edward agreed. They packed as many provisions as necessary and started out that day.

"They walked and caught rides with wagon caravans. The trip was slow and took longer than Henry thought it would. When they finally made it to the sea, they were both half-starved and out of money. They took jobs fishing the water and, after another month passed, they were able to pay their way to Ireland. But on their trip, the boat was caught in a storm and thrown off course. Instead of landing in Northern Ireland, they were in the south.

"They had just added weeks to their trip. But Henry was determined. He couldn't let Abby down. He would think of her at home waiting for him to return, and he would carry on.

"But as they made their way through Ireland, it seemed like bad luck was all around them. The first week into their journey, both were laid up with sickness. They had barely made it to a village, where a family nursed them back to health. The family ended up robbing them, taking what little money they had and all their supplies.

"When he confronted the family, they were run off by the father with an ax and received several wounds. They took small jobs and even stole food and clothes to get by. One night, while trying to steal horses, Edward was kicked in the leg. It shattered his bone. Henry carried Edward for miles—his mission and the thought of Abby gave him strength. After weeks of pain and hunger, they finally arrived at the small village on the northern shore of Ireland. They were tired, broken, and feeling defeated. They went to the nearest pub and asked around about the stone. They quickly discovered that the Irish loved to tell stories, and soon he had heard all the theories of where it might be. Henry got a job as a fisherman. He soon was able to get Edward to a doctor, and he paid for a room in the nearby inn and began his hunt."

Asa paused to take another sip of his drink. He looked around the table and noticed everyone was waiting to hear the rest. He took a breath.

"No one really knows what happened to Henry on his search. Edward was riddled with an infection and was laid up in an inn for weeks. Edward was delirious and never knew how long Henry was gone. When he returned, Henry was thin and pale. His was missing patches of his hair and he was missing a thumb. But he had brought the stone back with him. He slept for three days straight. As Edward healed, he stated that Henry didn't say much other than mumbles. He would stare out the window at night, humming a soft tune. One night, Edward woke to his brother's screams. Henry was at the window again, and when he turned to Edward, his face was possessed, his jaw open in a silent scream, his eyes black and hollow. Edward was so scared; he left the inn and slept in the barn. When Edward returned the next morning, Henry was sleeping peacefully in his bed. Edward was worried and wanting to get his brother away from the town, thinking if he could just get Henry to Abby, everything would be okay."

"It took them twice as long to get back home. Edward said that the way back was the worst months of his life. The weather was bitter cold. Henry was tired all the time, and he couldn't put weight back on. But he started to sleep again, and the screaming had stopped. It was a slow walk home. They again had to work to pay for passage back to England."

"When they finally made it home, over a year had passed. Henry's first stop was to Abby's house. When he showed up, Abby was sitting in the yard. When Henry approached, he saw a small baby in her arms. Abby turned and saw him. She was taken aback he looked so sick and beaten."

"Henry just stared, confused. She had a baby in her arms. 'What's going on?' he asked."

"Then a man stepped out of the front door. He was dressed in fine clothes. He asked if everything was all right."

"Henry looked to Abby, and he whispered, 'You promised to wait for me.' He backed up slowly, pain stretched across his face. 'I was gone a little over a year," he said."

"'No, wait,' she had replied. 'It's not what it looks like.'"

"But Henry took off. Some say that he wasn't thinking clearly, that the pain and trauma he had experienced from his travels rotted his mind. Others said that he was being toyed with by the demons that guarded the stone."

"He ran straight from Abby's house and up into the hills. One witness said that he had the stone in his hand and his eyes were dark. That he was mumbling. Another witness said he was talking to someone, shaking his head, and speaking in tongues."

"No one ever knew what he really said, but they did know that it was a curse on Abby and her child."

"Three weeks later, a pair of hunters found his body at the bottom of a ravine deep in the hills. No stone in his hand or around his body. He was naked and half-eaten by animals. Tales from Edward had many men searching the mountains for the stone of prosperity."

Asa looked at his now-empty glass and pushed it away.

"The thing was, the baby Abby held in her arms was Henry's. They conceived that night in the barn, right before he left. Abby's father, seeing his daughter in an unholy way, forced her to marry another man. Abby refused at first. She really tried to keep her promise to Henry, but the longer he was gone, the more she worried he was dead. With the baby on the way, she feared she would be shunned from her home and town. She finally gave in to her father and married a nice man who owned the general store in town; his name was William. The man accepted the child and considered it his own."

"Abby and William ended up having another child. William unexpectedly died in a hunting accident right after birth.

Abby told her mother that she had nightmares after William's death. She would see Henry muttering words as he walked deep into the hills. Other dreams had her in a boat, and she would look to the bottom of the lake, and Henry would be under the water, chanting that his blood was cursed and all she needed was the stone. Then the stone would magically float to the surface, and when Abby reached for it, Henry would reach up and pull her under."

"The family lore is that Henry cursed his bloodline, the stone of prosperity, giving him his dying wish. Every child born through his lineage that has fallen in love and married has had their spouse die in a strange way."

Asa stopped and looked at everyone. "Brady's bloodline is a direct line from Henry. My bloodline comes from William's side." The room was quiet.

"So, what does that mean for you?" She looked to Asa.

"Both my parents are alive. It's only through Henry's direct bloodline. Brady and his sister, Haley are my cousins, and we were all raised together after Brady's mother passed away, Brady's dad had Haley and him move in with me and my family. We're all very close."

"Your whole family believes this curse?" Roxy was trying hard to understand.

"No," Brady said, walking back to the table. "Half our family believes, and the other half does not. But our family history shows it. Everyone with a direct blood tie to Henry has lost a spouse." Brady reached for his coffee. "My mother passed away when I was young. Our grandfather also passed away before I was born. It's all there; I can show you the family tree."

"Were you going to steal the ring from us?" she asked.

"We are willing to offer you money for the ring," Asa said, looking at both girls.

She sat up. "Really? Why?"

"Our family was going to pay your father; it only seems like the right thing to do."

"No. You guys take the ring. I don't want it," Roxy said, panic in her eyes.

"Well, it doesn't matter. We don't have the ring." Asa looked to Brady. "The Brotherhood has it, which means it's gone. Who knows where it could be?" He ran his hands through his hair. Stress was written all across his face. He stood up quickly, the chair almost falling over. "I failed," he said. He started to pace the room.

Brady stood. "A, relax." He placed his hand on Asa's shoulder. "We'll find it. We just need to find out more about the Brotherhood." Brady paused. "There has to be a way we haven't tried yet."

Asa spun and faced his cousin. "Granny has been trying for years to find them, and she can't touch the damn Brotherhood."

"We'll figure it out," was all Brady said. "It's not over yet. We need to get the girls to Maine. If the Brotherhood has the ring, then the next thing, if you're right, will be them. Then we hammer down. We try. I won't let you give up yet."

Asa closed his eyes and ran his hand down his beard. When he opened his eyes, he said, "You're right. First thing is to get the girls to Maine. Make sure everyone is safe."

She watched Asa. She could see he felt failure. It had guilt welling in her chest. Their next plan was to get them to safety, and they were serious about it. She knew now she had to give them the ring.

She stood up in her chair, and she felt everyone's eyes on her. "I have something." She reached into her pocket and pulled out her take. She placed the ring and her locket on the table.

Everyone was quiet. All eyes left her and turned to the table.

She looked down at her locket. The chain was broken. She tried to hide her despair.

Brady was the first to break the silence. "Is that it?"

"You had it the whole time?" Asa looked shocked.

"He told me how he watched my father die, and I was so mad." The anger rose again. She pushed it down. "Plus, I wanted my locket."

Asa stepped over and picked up the ring with his bruised hand. He studied it for a good thirty seconds. "This is it." He gave a little smile to her and then looked at Brady. "We have it."

"Let me see that." Brady stepped over, and Asa handed him the ring. He gave a quick look, then handed it back. "I thought it would be…" He

paused. "I don't know; I thought it would glow or something. After all the damn stories I heard."

"How did you get this?" Asa looked at her suspiciously. "I checked his pockets."

"I took it." When he only stared, she shrugged.

"Why didn't you tell us?"

"I don't really know you. I still don't know if I can fully trust you guys yet." She saw a look that briefly crossed his face. She couldn't tell if it was hurt or annoyance.

"But you guys say you'll take us to safety, and I guess I believe you. So…" She trailed off.

"We take the ring to Maine and give it to our grandmother, and she'll take it to England," Asa said matter-of-factly. He looked relieved.

"To do what with it?" Roxy asked.

"To break the curse," Brady said.

Roxy leaned over toward her. "I need to talk to you in private."

Those words had drawn Brady's attention, and Asa sat back down in his chair. He looked lighter and in a better mood.

Roxy stood, taking Sydney's arm. They made their way over to the kitchen area.

"Roxy, calm down." She knew her logical sister was freaking out and panicking.

"We made a deal," Roxy whispered. "Remember? If it gets dangerous, we get Bev, and we go. They are talking about glowing rings and curses. We fell into a crazy town." Roxy's whisper was getting louder. "We need to go to the police."

She leaned in and took Roxy by the arms. "Just take a deep breath." Roxy's fear was feeding her own. She looked over at the table.

Asa made eye contact with her. "Before you try to run, you should know your dad believed in the curse. That's why he stole it."

She paused. He was right. Dad had started this. She wanted to know why. She looked to Roxy. Her brain was going; she could see it. She pushed her own fear down.

"Let's just hear it out. This is the reason Dad died. We make the Brotherhood pay for what they did to him." Her sister's eyes were filled with fear. But the comment about their dad had soothed her rigid body.

She looked over at the table again. Asa was looking at her still with a spark in his intense gray eyes. That made her nervous. Brady was wiping his glasses on his dirty T-shirt, surely eavesdropping. Bev just stared over at them, mug in hand and a large smile on her face.

She looked away. "Come on, Roxy." She took her arm this time. She leaned in. "This is the only option we have right now."

Roxy took a deep breath. "I just can't believe this is happening. You lifted the ring from the Brotherhood guy?"

She smiled. "It was easy; Asa had already messed him up. Come on."

They sat back down. "Go ahead," she said nervously and took a sip of her now cold coffee. "Tell us the rest."

Asa continued, "Our grandmother, Mary, asked me to find the ring. I brought Brady in to help with the research." Asa sat back in his chair; his feet crossed at the ankles, looking like a man comfortable in his own domain.

"Brady saw Roxy's searches on her computer, and we knew that meant you guys had found it. But apparently you guys couldn't wait."

She felt the blush spread up her cheeks.

"I was actually on my way to come give you guys an offer when Brady caught movement on the Lojack that you were headed to Seattle. I couldn't take the chance of you selling it." He paused and took a deep breath.

"The trip to the pawnshop has put you guys back on the Brotherhood's radar, and they now know that you have it and will do anything to get it back." He sat forward and folded his hands together.

"That's why you need to come with us to Maine. Granny has the best security money can buy. Brady designed it himself. You'll be safe there. Then we take care of the Brotherhood."

"So, we just put our lives on hold," she said.

"I'm sorry," Brady said, sliding his glasses back on. "But like Asa said, they are looking for you."

She thought of her life. Really, she had nothing going on. No school and no Margie. Roxy was here with her. She thought about her father.

The Brotherhood had murdered him.

"I'll go if I can help take the Brotherhood down too," she said.

They both nodded.

Roxy didn't look surprised, but deep in thought. "I already told work I was taking some personal leave. I'll go if I can help too."

Asa nodded, as he already knew that they would go, and Brady smiled.

Bev smiled, looking around her table. She knew what she saw and was happy, not to mention grateful that Mary had sent these two to take care of Margie's girls.

"So, how did Gabe get involved with this?" Bev asked Brady, leaning in. She was enjoying this too much.

"Yeah, how was my father involved?" Roxy asked.

"Well, actually, it started years before. Granny started the search after our grandfather passed, which wasn't long after my father was born," Brady said. "He was coming home from a business meeting overseas. The weather was clear, and the pilot was a seasoned veteran. It crashed over the Atlantic Ocean. The official report was engine failure, but my grandmother believed it was the curse. She believes she can break the curse with this ring. She has been searching for it for years. She spent all her free time researching folklore and our family history. She hired private investigators, detectives, and antique dealers to find it. A little over ten years ago, one of them came to her and said they think they found it in a private estate in Japan and that it was going up for auction. She was outbid by a private trust. That's when she hired your father. She found the cargo ship that was carrying it and learned that it was docking in Seattle. One of her contacts recommended your father for the job. He was considered an honest thief."

She smiled.

"Mary told him the whole story and offered him a new life for you girls in Maine. He took it. She figured the bidder wanted the expensive art and antiques, not the ring. It has no money value. But she was wrong. Still, to this day, we can't figure out why the Brotherhood wants this ring so bad they would kill for it.

"After your father's death, she stopped looking, riddled with guilt, till Haley's engagement announcement last winter. Now she wants it more than ever. She wants to find it quietly. Under the Brotherhood's radar."

"She is not getting that anymore," Asa said with a frown.

No one said anything.

Bev broke the silence. "Roxy and Brady, you guys look like you need a warm shower." Bev stood. "Brady, you take the bathroom at the end of the hall. Towels are in the closet. You can drop your dirty clothes outside the door. I'll wash them. You can wear my late husband's clothes till then. Roxy, you take the bathroom in my room. I'll wash your clothes, too." She looked to Sydney. "Get some ice for Asa's hand out of the freezer, and I'll grab the first aid kit and will clean those knees of yours."

Everybody did what they were told. Their brains were heavy with folklore, curses, and revenge.

Roxy

She followed Bev into her bedroom. The large bed was covered in throw pillows of all possible colors. She had pictures of her family all over the walls, along with old concert posters that looked like they were from Woodstock.

"Here is a towel and some clothes of mine to wear till yours are clean." Bev handed her the pile, and Roxy looked up to her.

"I'm sorry we came here and got you involved."

Bev just smiled. "Margie involved me a long time ago. I'm just glad I can help."

"Thanks." It was all she could say. She turned to the bathroom.

"Roxy?"

She turned to the short woman who was being so kind.

"I think you can trust these two. Margie trusted Mary. I think their intentions are noble." She nodded her head and closed the bathroom door.

The shower had been just what she needed. She not only felt cleaner and warmer, but she processed Bev's words, and they had made her feel better, as though maybe she could trust Brady and Asa. She wiped the mirror of the condensation and realized that the shower had made her feel better, but not look better. Her eyes had dark circles and she looked tired. There were a couple small scratches on her face, most likely from crawling around in the field.

She huffed out a breath and put on the clothes Bev had left her. The pajama pants were too wide, but she pulled the drawstring tight and tied them in to a knot. The sweatshirt was too big also, but it was cozy and soft.

She went to the bedroom door and opened it to find Brady right on the other side. She startled, not expecting anyone to be there.

"Oh, hey," he said, looking nervous. "Bev told me to throw my towel in the hamper."

She stepped back. The smell of his warm, clean skin assaulted her nose and made her stomach twist.

She nodded and threw her towel in too.

She looked at Bev's late husband's clothes. He must have been a short man, because the sweatpants rode high above Brady's ankles and the T-shirt of a mystic wolf howling at the moon was barely covering his flat stomach. She laughed while looking him up and down. "Nice."

He looked down at his clothes. "You like?" He wiggled his eyebrows at her. "You know, I think I had a shirt like this in first grade. Matter of fact, I think it was the same size too." He tried tugging it down to cover his belly button.

She laughed. When she looked back up at him, he was smiling down at her. She noticed he had straight teeth, and his bottom lip was fuller than his top.

Not breaking eye contact, he gestured toward the hall. "Come on, let's see if anyone has a plan yet."

She turned and realized that she actually felt at ease.

When they came back into the dining room. Asa had a bag of frozen corn on his hand and another glass of Bourbon. He looked deep in thought.

Bev was sitting in a chair across from Sydney, cleaning up her knee. It looked like Bev had lent Sydney a pair of shorts, and Bev was just putting the last bandage on.

"All patched up," Bev said, standing up.

Brady walked over to the front window and scanned the yard.

She took a seat next to Sydney at the table and, not caring whose Bourbon was in the glass in front of her, she threw it back. It burned, but she let it.

She shook her head and slid the glass across the table.

"We'll have to drive to Maine," Asa said, giving a light laugh.

Brady, being satisfied with the outside, walked over to the table.

She looked up at him. He gave her a reassuring smile.

"We'll get you guys there; you'll be safe. Then we take the Brotherhood down."

Sydney looked up. "You can do that?" She paused. "Can we prove my father was murdered? Bring them to justice?"

"We can and we will."

Asa stood. He started to pace. "We can't fly without IDs and credit cards. I have cash."

He looked over to the girls. "It was the money I was going to buy the ring with."

She watched Sydney eye Asa. "How much?"

Asa only smiled. "Enough to get us to Maine."

"I have Bill's old Suburban. You guys can take that." Bev stepped forward. "It's old and a gas guzzler. But it's registered in his name. So, if the plates are run, they won't know it's you."

Asa nodded. "Thanks, Bev."

"I have camping gear too. Like sleeping bags and a cooler, in case you need to pull over and sleep. I'll load the cooler with food and water."

Brady stood too. "We'll have to navigate the old way with maps. But we can take back roads and head south, then back up north." He looked to Asa. "What do you think, brother?"

"I think it's the best we've got for now."

He looked around the room. "We'll leave early tomorrow morning."

Sydney and Roxy helped Bev pull the camping gear from the shed and filled the cooler. Brady and Asa were in the garage, making sure the Suburban was ready for the trip. Other than being a quart of oil low, they announced that it was ready. Bev's generosity wasn't going unnoticed, and the four of them thanked her nonstop.

At two in the morning, they were all exhausted and decided that they were as ready as they were going to be.

Bev gave her and Sydney the spare room, and the guys could sleep in the hobby room. They had found the air mattresses in the camping gear, and she went to set it up for them.

The hobby room was packed. Half the room was a table filled with a sewing machine, yards of fabric, ribbon, and other sewing necessities. The other half was filled with fly-tying material. Feathers, hooks, and magnifying glasses were all spread across the table. It was set up for them to work together back-to-back. It had made Roxy smile to think of Bev and her husband being together, doing their hobbies.

She placed the last of the blankets down on the air mattress and was leaving the room when Brady came in.

"Whoa," he said, looking around the room.

She followed his eyes. "I think it's nice. They had different hobbies but still spent time together."

Brady stepped over the air mattress and studied the fly-tying stand. He brushed the dust of the table. "You know, I have never been fishing."

"Really? Isn't that a common hobby for young boys?"

Brady smiled. "My father was off at work all the time and Asa's father was more into sports like football and basketball. So that's what we did."

"I did once," she said. "Fished."

Brady turned and looked at her. "Really? You don't seem like the fishing type." He gave her a lifted eyebrow and a knowing smile.

"Once. My dad took me and Sydney on one of his rare days off. Sydney and I were so excited. Mainly because we were going to spend the day with Dad."

She walked over to the fly-tying table and picked up a hook as she thought of that day. "I remember going to the river. It was a warm day and we had two fishing poles. We stopped at the corner store to get bait. Dad didn't tell us what the bait was, until we got to the river and all set up. He pulled the Styrofoam container out and showed us the worms. Sydney started freaking out and refused to touch them. But Dad only laughed. He baited her hook all day."

Roxy paused. That had been fun and she hadn't thought of that day in a long time.

"How about you?" Brady asked quietly. "Did you bait your own hook?"

"I tried. I wasn't scared to touch the worms, but I didn't have the heart to push the hook through them. The first one I just placed on the hook, but it fell off after the cast. Dad just laughed. He tried to bait it for me and I just kept saying, 'No, don't hurt them.' We had sandwiches, and Dad used the crust of his sandwich instead." She smiled.

"Did you catch anything with bread crust?" Brady was now sitting on the edge of the table. He was watching her and listening. Her nerves kicked in when she noticed the attention. She was so lost in the memory; she had forgotten that she had an audience. She placed the hook down.

"No. It was probably for the best." She smiled at him, then straightened up. "I'll let you get to sleep." She headed for the door.

"Hey Roxy?" Brady said, still sitting on the edge of the table. "Your father seems like a good guy."

"For the most part, he was," she said and slipped out the door.

Sydney

She tossed and turned. Roxy was next to her in the bed and she was trying to be still. But she would close her eyes and see Yuri, his chest red with blood, laying on the floor.

She'd roll over and try again, only to see the man with the gold tooth smiling like the devil himself. She'd hear the other man call him Cal, and his gold tooth would sparkle. She could smell the mint. Her eyes flew open. Sleeping was out of the picture. She slowly rolled out of bed, trying not to wake her sister.

She padded barefoot down the hall to the kitchen.

It was dark and she decided to turn the small oven light on. She turned to the cupboard, looking for the coffee. It was then when the deep male voice made her jump.

"I think the coffee is in the cupboard over the sink."

She whipped around to see Asa sitting on the small, old couch. He was fully dressed, even with shoes, and he had a book in his hands.

"You startled me," she said, turning for the other cupboard, but not before she noticed the way he looked at her bare legs in Bev's shorts.

She wasn't a stranger to men checking her out, but Asa's stare was different. It made her feel uneasy, like a man not scared to be caught looking. It made her skin heat up.

"Why aren't you sleeping?" She reached for the coffee bag on the shelf.

"I'm keeping watch."

She looked at the book in his hands.

"Just passing time," he said casually.

She filled the coffee pot with water.

"Why aren't you sleeping?" he asked, placing the book upside down, saving his place.

"Couldn't," was all she said. Then, she changed the subject. "What are you reading?"

"A book I found on the shelf," he answered, looking down at it. "It's a detective mystery novel."

"So right up your alley, huh?" She dumped the grounds in and started the pot.

He smiled in the dim light. "Haven't solved it yet. Have my suspicions, though."

"Only halfway done, and you think you can solve the mystery?"

When he didn't answer and only smiled, she looked at him, curiosity getting the better of her. She leaned on the counter that separated the kitchen and the living room. "So why did you quit being a cop?"

He leaned back on the couch. "Lots of reasons."

While she waited for a real reason, he leaned forward again and placed his elbows on his knees.

"I was tired of the system, really. I wanted to help people make the world a better place, you know. But it wasn't what I thought it was at all. It was paperwork and technicality. I watched the guilty set free and the innocent suffer." He shrugged. "Now I help on my own terms."

"Being a private detective has less rules?"

"Independent investigator." He pointed out with a laugh. "I'm not Dick Tracy."

She laughed.

"You know Dick Tracy?" He looked surprised.

"Yeah, it was one of Margie's favorite movies. The one with Madonna." She laughed. "Not the comic book."

"Of course," he said with a smile. "And yes, less rules."

The coffee pot clicked. She went over and poured two mugs and looked over at him. He was sitting back, his arm draped over the back of the couch, the other lightly tugging his beard.

"Creamer?" she asked.

He looked up at her and his hand dropped from his beard. "Just black, thanks."

She poured a healthy amount of creamer in hers and wondered if all cops drank their coffee black for a reason. She brought both cups to the living room. He gave her a soft smile when he took his. Her stomach tightened, making her frown.

"I could get used to this," he said and took a sip.

The couch looked small with him on it and the reaction she had at his smile had her taking a seat in the recliner on the other side of the room.

"What's that?" she asked. She pulled the shorts down her leg.

"It's been a while since a woman served me coffee in the morning."

"What, being an independent investigator leaves you no time for the ladies?"

"Basically. Ever since Haley announced her engagement, Brady and I have been researching this damn ring. It's been all-consuming."

She only nodded and took another sip. They sat in silence for a moment.

"Do you want to talk about it?" Asa said, getting her attention again.

She looked over at him, confused for a second. "What?"

He placed his mug on the table. "You know what all happened today. Or I guess yesterday. That was a heavy situation. I figured that's why you're not sleeping."

"I'm fine," she lied. She looked at him and remembered how he had shot that man. It dawned on her that watching him shoot someone wasn't what made her scared, but what brought her comfort. She tightened her grip on her warm mug to fight the chill it gave her.

He leaned back. "I'm here when you're ready to talk. I'm a good listener." She didn't reply. He looked down at his watch. "We better wake the others; we should hit the road soon."

She went and woke Roxy and changed back into her torn jeans. She was glad that holes in jeans never really went out of style. She looked around the room, her intentions to get ready to leave on a long road trip. But she quickly realized she had nothing. No clothes, no purse, not even a toothbrush.

She made her way out to the living room. Bev was making breakfast sandwiches. She said they would be a good on-the-road breakfast. The news was on the TV. Asa and Brady came in from the garage.

"Cooler is packed," Asa said. "I guess it's time to go."

Bev came over with the sandwiches wrapped in paper napkins.

Just then, a special bulletin on the TV caught everyone's attention.

"This just in." It was a good-looking reporter behind the news desk. His blazer had pin stripes, and his hair was neatly combed back.

"A shooting in Seattle yesterday has police looking for answers," he started. "The pawnshop on 38th was robbed and the owner was shot. Brian has more on the story." The report switched to Yuri's pawnshop. It had yellow tape and a couple of police cars surrounding the front.

"Oh my god." She took two steps closer to the television. She watched as a picture of Yuri appeared on the screen. Asa came up next to her and watched the broadcast.

"There are two people wanted for questioning as of right now. They were seen entering the pawnshop right before the security cameras cut off. The man and woman are unknown at this time."

A blurry close-up of her face appeared on screen. Next to it was a side profile of Asa. It was even harder to see.

"If anyone has seen or knows who these people are, please call Seattle police."

The reporter came back on screen, and they moved to the weather.

"What the hell, they have footage of us but not the other two?" Asa said, surprised.

"People in town will know that's me," she said, turning to face the others. "Fuller will have no problem turning me in."

"We need to go now," Brady said. "Before they start looking for you guys."

She turned to Bev.

"Don't worry, I won't say anything, though I'm sure I'll hear all about it." Bev rolled her eyes.

"Will they connect you to us?" Roxy asked.

Bev handed Roxy a sandwich. "You mean Margie's girls? I just met them yesterday at Margie's wake. They seem like nice girls. But no, I don't know them personally."

"I guess that's all you can do, huh?" Brady said as he took his sandwich.

"You don't worry about me. Even though we just met, I've been living here my whole life."

"Thanks, Bev," Asa said. He handed her a piece of paper. "This is the phone number for Max, our head of security. If you have any problems or suspect the Brotherhood knows you helped us—and I mean any worries—you call. Tell them I sent you and say the password I wrote down. It's the word we use when we need help. No questions asked."

"I'll be fine. They want nothing to do with this old woman," Bev said and patted Asa on his wide chest. "What I need is to know you will take care of the girls and get them to safety."

Asa's eyes narrowed. "We will."

She watched as Bev's shoulders relaxed.

119

Asa turned and went for the garage.

She turned to Bev and gave her a big, grateful hug. "Thanks, Bev, you're the best." She didn't pull away and neither did Bev.

"Trust them," Bev whispered in her ear.

For some reason, she could feel her shoulders relax in the same way Bev's did.

"Okay, Bev." She patted her back then pulled away. "We'll call you when we get there." She turned to leave, but stopped short.

"Bev?" she asked and pulled her locket from her pocket. "Could you hold onto this for me, please? I can't wear it and I don't want to lose it."

Bev smiled. "Of course." She took it in her hand. "It will give you a reason to come back."

"Thanks." She turned and went to the garage to let the others say their goodbyes.

The sun hadn't come up yet, but the night was starting to fade. The air was cool, and it felt good. She took a deep breath, letting it fill her lungs, then turned to the red Suburban. It was old; it had to have been made in the mid-nineties. It was nothing like the new ones—no tinted windows, no automatic anything, and everything was very square.

But beggars couldn't be choosers. She kept her face down as she hurried to the backseat of the truck, hoping no one saw her. She and Asa were wanted by the police now.

She looked over at Asa. He was keeping his head down also has he got into the driver's seat. When he sat down, he turned to face her. "Things just keep getting more complicated." The passenger door swung open and Brady jumped in. "Damn it." He pulled his seat belt on. "They only mentioned Yuri, not the Brotherhood guy you shot."

"Maybe they pulled their guys out," Asa said.

"Makes sense," Brady said. "They probably messed with the security footage also."

Roxy got in next to her. She leaned closer to her, and they stayed that way all through town. They were off to Maine, like her father had planned for them years earlier.

Roxy

The first few hours were quiet. They spoke little, and everyone but Asa, as the driver, was in and out of sleep.

They needed to stop for gas, and when Asa announced it to everyone, Brady mentioned a map and Sydney mentioned toothbrushes, so she seconded the motion. They decided to stop in a small town along the freeway. Once they had a map, they were going to stay off the main highway and stick to back roads.

They pulled off right after the Oregon/California border and found a small town; it was a pass-through town, and they felt it was safe.

The gas station was small, with only two pumps and no bathroom. They all got out wanting to stretch. The air was warm and she couldn't help but raise her face to the sky to feel the sun on her skin. She was tired and stressed. She was worried for Bev. If the Brotherhood found out that she helped them or knew where they were going, she could be in danger. She didn't like bringing Bev into this and the guilt was eating away at her. But how could they know or connect Bev to the ring? At least that was what she kept telling herself. The long, quiet ride didn't help her mind from spinning.

Across the narrow two-lane road was a pharmacy and a few other small businesses squeezed between two small parking lots.

After the tank was full, they piled back into the truck to make the small ride across the street to the pharmacy.

When they entered, she wasn't surprised that the store smelled of dust and water damage. She was surprised that it was still in business. The old woman with big glasses behind the counter looked up when they entered and gave them a slight nod. She then went back to flipping through her magazine.

Brady grabbed a basket, and together, they headed to find their supplies.

They found the hygiene aisle quick enough, and they each grabbed a toothbrush and toothpaste. Sydney threw in a hairbrush and hair ties.

As they made their way down each aisle, grabbing just the basics, she grabbed Sydney's arm.

"We can't let them pay for us," she said.

Sydney's face twisted in confusion. "You're right. What are we going to do?"

Brady came up behind them.

"Don't worry. We got this."

"We can't ask you guys to do this," she said.

Brady just shrugged. "Asa has the cash he was going to give you guys for the ring."

They both looked at him, surprised. "Well, not all of it," he said, hurriedly noticing the girls' faces.

"Just how much were you guys going to give us for it?" Sydney asked quizzically.

"A hundred thousand," Brady said simply and picked up some baby wipes from the shelf and tossed them in the basket.

When they both just started at him, he shifted uncomfortably. "So, we can wash our hands and faces." He looked down at the basket.

"Asa's carrying around a hundred thousand dollars in cash?" She was astonished. "How rich are you guys?"

"No." Brady shook his head. "Only ten."

When neither of them spoke, he turned his attention on them. "We were going to give you ten thousand in cash and when we had the ring, we were going to give you the rest. The rest is sitting in a suitcase back at the hotel. Some maid's going to be happy." He looked off.

"Why so much?" she asked Brady.

"That's how much Granny was going to give your father. Thought it was only fair."

Asa stepped up behind them and dumped four black, plain baseball hats into the basket.

"It's actually only eight now. I gave Bev two for the Suburban. We need to wear these hats in public," he added as he pointed to the security camera in the back.

Brady looked up. "I bet it's not live," he said, looking away quickly. "Come on, we need to hurry."

He looked down into the basket. "Asa, you and Sydney find some kind of change of clothes, and Roxy and I will look for maps and prepaid phones." They all agreed and they split up.

She and Brady made their way through the aisles. They found some maps in the back. They found one of California and one for Nevada.

"Man, I wish I had my computer," Brady said. "This old school GPS sucks."

She smiled. "I can help you read it."

Brady rolled his eyes. "Please, I know how to read a map."

"That's right. You know everything, like how to hack my computer."

He looked over with worry written all over his face. "I didn't do it to be nefarious. I simply needed to see if you knew anything about the ring. It wasn't easy, if that makes you feel better. It took me days, and for a while, I really didn't think I could. It's a great system. I just happened to find a little chink in its armor."

She took the map of California off the rack. "I know; it's just that I worked really hard on that system. Years even."

"When we get to Maine, I'll show you that chink, and we can work on it together." He looked over at her. "You're a smart woman. I admire your computer skills."

He winked. Thoughts of her computer forgotten, she felt a blush run up her cheeks. *He was cute and smart*, she thought, with his glasses, muscles, and kind words. She turned back to the rack of maps, trying to hide her red face and thoughts.

"Come on, let's see if this place has phones and meet up with the others." He reached down and took her hand. When she stiffened, he let go. He didn't say anything, and they made their way to the next aisle.

As luck would have it, the small store had prepaid phones, and when they met up with Asa and Sydney, Brady threw four in to the basket. "I want to try and call Max and let him know what's going on," Brady said. They headed for the front.

Asa and Sydney had found cheesy tourist shirts for everyone and a package of leggings for each of the girls. Sydney couldn't help but comment on how anyone would buy a package of leggings. But they also found socks with colorful pictures and patterns. They had added two backpacks from the school supplies section to carry their stuff.

They made their way to the front, and Asa paid the old woman, who said nothing. Then, they made their way out.

They each took a bottle of water and brushed their teeth. The simple act had her feeling better and ready for the next stretch of the ride.

After they loaded all the gear, they made their way further south.

Brady opened up one of the phones. It was an older model of a flip phone, with only a small display and basic functions, and no Internet connection.

"Who is Max again?" she asked while she watched Brady set up the phone.

"He's head of Granny's security and one of my close friends. We were in Iraq together." He plugged the charger into the cigarette lighter. "He had a hard time when he returned. But with Granny's help and the job, he's doing better." Brady paused. "Max saved my life over there; I owe him." Brady dialed a number and put it on speaker.

"Yep," came a deep voice over the line.

"Hey man, it's me," was all Brady said.

"What the hell, man? We were getting worried. Your granny was about to send the whole goddamn U.S. Army out to find you guys. What the hell is going on?"

"Brotherhood," was all Brady said.

"Shit. Where you at?" Max asked.

"Can't talk about it over the phone. They know who we are, and they're tracking us. We're coming to home base and will be there in a couple days."

There was some shuffling in the background, and Max started talking to someone.

Brady looked down at the phone. He frowned. "What's going on?"

"Clint's here. Says your system's lighting up like a goddamn Christmas tree."

Brady looked over at Asa, the frown still on his face.

"Let me talk to Clint," Brady said into the phone.

There was shuffling and then another male voice came on. It wasn't as deep and had a slight Midwest accent. "Brady, man, I think someone's trying to hack the system right now."

Brady pushed his glasses higher on his nose. "Is the system holding?"

"Yeah, for now. But I don't know how much longer."

"It's got to be the Brotherhood," Asa said.

Brady nodded in agreement.

"Okay, man, keep the system going. Tell Granny we'll be there in a couple days. I'm losing this phone. So don't try to contact us."

Brady hung up, then pulled the battery out of the phone. He rolled the window down and threw both out the window. She watched as the phone shattered on the road behind them.

"You think your security program will hold?" Asa asked.

"The warnings should only be going off if whoever is hacking in is getting close to breaking in." He paused, then continued, "The Brotherhood has some high-tech equipment and some good hackers." Brady leaned back in the seat. "I wish I had my computer." He slapped the door panel. "I bet they are watching Max's phone looking for odd numbers." He stopped, then turned to the window. "They shouldn't be able to track that phone. They were probably just trying to eavesdrop." He ran his hands through his hair.

"Don't worry, brother. We will be home in a couple more days," Asa said.

Brady just continued to face the window. "Unless they find us first."

*

Both she and Sydney fell asleep, and when she woke, the sun was starting to set.

She sat up. "Where are we?" Her voice was low and raspy.

"Somewhere in California," Asa whispered. She looked over and Brady was asleep too.

"You must be tired?" she asked him.

"I'm fine." He adjusted in his seat. He was wearing the black baseball hat backward, and she could see the bags under his eyes.

She looked out the window and watched the sky with its orange and pink hues. The sun had just passed the horizon. They were driving through a heavily wooded area. The trees were big and green, the air cool.

"It's beautiful," she said.

"This is my favorite part of the day." Asa took his eyes off the road and looked out the side window. "It's like the day is settling down." He looked back at the road.

She had to ask the next question. It had been on her mind all day.
"Asa?"

He looked in the rearview mirror at her.

"Why are you guys helping us? I mean, you have the ring now."

She watched his eyes squint in confusion at her questions. "Why would you ask that?"

"Well, we're causing a lot of problems for you guys. You could just walk away, take the ring."

"What kind of people do you think me and Brady are?" he asked.

She shrugged. "It just seems like we're getting you into a lot of trouble, is all."

"You think we would just leave you guys to the Brotherhood? Let them rape and kill you? What kind of people do you think we are?" he asked again, then paused before continuing. "Plus, you girls are growing on us." This time, he turned in the seat and smiled.

She smiled back. "Me and Syd, we wouldn't be alive right now if it wasn't for you guys." She hesitated for a moment, then said, "I want to thank you."

Asa just smiled.

"Thanks for being there for Sydney at the pawnshop, too."

"You're welcome. I'm just glad I made it in time."

She watched his mouth turn down.

"Would they have raped her?" she asked.

"Yes."

Roxy sat back and turned to the window. She tried to not imagine her sister being beaten and raped.

"My grandmother," Asa started, "was very upset about what happened to your father. She blames herself every day, thinking she was the reason you and your sister were orphaned. She is very ashamed of herself."

She looked up in surprise. It was hard picturing their grandmother. The more she learned about her, the more she learned about the influence she had in her life. She had never even met her.

"My father made his own decisions." She thought of her dad, his blue eyes smiling. "He always did."

"My grandmother would disown me and Brady if we came back without you girls, knowing what kind of danger you two were in."

She didn't know what to say to that.

"You want me to drive for a little bit?" She watched his puffy eyes in the mirror.

"There's a rest stop up here about an hour away. We'll stay there for the night."

*

When they pulled in to the rest stop, she couldn't have been more relieved.

"Syd, wake up." She gently nudged Sydney.

Sydney jumped forward, smacking her head against the window.

Sydney was wide-eyed, looking around. "Where are we?"

"It's okay. We're stopping for the night."

Brady and Asa were already out of the car, stretching.

"You want to go use the bathroom?"

Sydney nodded and rubbed her forehead.

Brady shot his head into the window. "You girls getting out or what?"

They both got out and stretched. The night air had a slight chill, and it felt good on her skin.

"We're going to use the bathroom," Sydney said.

"We'll all go." Asa and Brady turned toward the restrooms.

"They're never going to let us out of their sight, are they?" Sydney whispered, leaning in to her. She figured that for a while, she and her sister were going to have shadows.

After they used the restrooms, they had a small snack of granola bars and water. They pulled the back seat down, and she and Sydney laid their sleeping bags in the back. The guys reclined in the front seats and laid their sleeping bags over them.

Roxy listened to the traffic on the freeway behind the rest stop, wondering if she was ever going to fall asleep.

"Did you guys think, when you started looking for the ring, that this was what was going to happen?" Sydney asked.

"No," Asa answered. "When we found out you had the ring, I really thought that we would just buy it and bring it home, and the Brotherhood would never know any different."

"We actually thought," Brady shuffled under his sleeping bag, "we were going to talk to Margie. We hoped that she would lead us to where we needed to go. If she couldn't, we were then going to track you girls down." He grew silent. "But she passed away before we could talk to her."

"This is all my fault. I should have never tried to pawn that damn thing." Sydney's voice cracked at the memory.

"You didn't know," Brady said. "We should have come to you guys sooner. Told you what was going on."

Sydney sniffed and said, "When we get to Maine, we'll find the Brotherhood, and we will bring them down. Make them pay."

She found Sydney's hand in the dark and whispered, "We'll put Dad's murderer away."

Sydney

The next day, they drove for hours, cutting over from California to Nevada.

But, to her surprise, the conversation flowed. Asa joked about Brady only wearing white T-shirts. Roxy came back with the remark about how geniuses don't worry about their clothes. She gave Roxy a smile.

Then Roxy and Brady ganged up on Asa and her about always caring about what they wore. Joking about how much time and energy they wasted at the mall.

She enjoyed forming a team with Asa, and she found herself relaxing. The stress of the last couple days began to fade away.

Roxy had asked more about their family. They were told that even though their family had money, they were expected to find jobs of their own and earn their keep before they got their trust. It's why Asa had gone into the police force and Brady went to MIT. Brady also talked about how his dad was a military man and he felt that he had to follow in his footsteps.

They talked about Haley, Brady's younger sister, and how her wedding planning was crazy. Marcus, her fiancé, was a good man, and even though he let Haley run the show, he still knew when to reel her back in. It seems both of them approved of him and were happy for their sister/cousin.

She found out Asa was a big sports star in high school, football being his main sport. He was a quarterback. He also played basketball and baseball. He convinced Brady to play basketball together and got Brady to work out. Brady had put muscle on finally, and Asa said that the kids stopped calling him a nerd. He had graduated early and headed for MIT, leaving Asa to all the sports glory.

*

That afternoon, they needed to stop for gas again. She was ready for a break and needed to stretch. The Suburban was getting cramped. They found a small gas station in a small town, somewhere near the New Mexico border. They all headed into the station; Asa to pay for gas, the girls to use the restroom, and Brady was going to grab them all drinks.

She used the restroom first and studied her face in the mirror. She had bags under eyes from the restless sleep in the back of the Suburban. *Her skin was going to hell*, she thought, the baby wipes were drying out her skin. She washed her hands and dreamed of a hot shower.

When she exited, Asa was still in line to pay for gas, and she decided to join Brady as he picked out snacks and drinks. She went and stood next to Brady and studied the fridge.

"Hey!" she heard Roxy yell. She turned and let the door to the fridge slam shut. The clerk and one other customer in the store turned their heads toward the window.

Two men, both wearing white hats, baggy T-shirts, and jeans, jumped into the Suburban. They hit the gas and took off, fishtailing out of the gas station.

"They're stealing the truck."

Both Asa and Brady dropped what they were doing and ran for the door, she and Roxy right on their tails.

They were greeted with a cloud of exhaust and dust.

"Dammit!" Asa yelled, throwing his arms up and placing them on the top of his head.

Brady had started to run after the truck but, realizing it was fruitless, he stopped and turned to them.

His face looked seriously stressed, and his voice was low. "The ring is in the glove box."

Her stomach dropped. She tugged on the annoying baseball hat and watched as Roxy rubbed her forehead.

"What do we do? Go after them?" She looked around, her first instinct to steal a car.

But the clerk and the one other customer had come out of the store to see what was going on. She feared that they might call the police.

"Yeah," Asa said and looked to Brady. "The gas tank was on E. They won't get far. Let's just hope they don't find the ring."

"Or our guns," Brady added.

She looked over. "Someone's going to call the police. We need to get out of here."

They turned and saw the clerk pull his phone out.

"It's all right." Asa turned to the two people. "I'm a police officer, and there is no need to call the police. Me and my partner," he gestured to Brady, "will take care of this." Brady pulled out one of the prepaid phones and pretended to call for backup.

The clerk went back in and the customer milled around.

Asa turned and said they should get going. He looked out to the road. "I guess we're walking."

The road was surrounded by desert and random houses or shops scattered along the road. The sun was warm and was starting to heat up.

They had been walking for almost an hour when Brady said, "Well, we keep the ring on us at all times from here on out."

"If we get it back," she said. She was starting to think they were going to be out on the road forever.

She wiped sweat from her forehead. She and Roxy had taken the baseball hats off, and she had begun to fan herself with it.

Roxy had been quiet most of the walk. "I think this ring is bad luck. I wish that I had never found it."

Brady looked over, "Really? I'm glad you found it. Granny will be happy; she'll finally relax about Haley."

"I agree with you, Roxy," she said. "Nothing has gone our way since we found it."

"Just think," Brady started. "If you hadn't found it, you guys would never have met us." He smiled his large, goofy grin.

"Yeah." Asa shifted his hat. Sweat had started to run down his face. "And we wouldn't be surrounded by all this positive attitude."

She gave him her best snotty look, but all he did was laugh at her.

"Look," Roxy said, pointing ahead. They were coming up on a building with several vehicles parked out front.

There happened to be a large red vehicle parked on the side.

"That has to be it," Asa said, and both him, and Brady started to jog.

She looked down at her heeled ankle boots and sighed. She and Roxy started to jog too.

As they got closer, Brady grabbed Asa's arm, and they slowed down.

"I don't think they're with the Brotherhood."

"I don't think so either. They just look like punks."

Asa scanned their surroundings. There was really nothing but open desert scattered with shrubs.

When they got closer, they could see that the building was an old, rundown bar. It was falling apart and in need of paint. It had an old porch out front, and it looked like it should be shut down. There were a couple cars out front and on the side was a red Suburban.

They made their way over, and she looked into the back seat. Their sleeping bags were still in the back; they were open and sprawled all over. Bev's cooler was open and dumped on its side; water had spilled out, and it looked like everything was wet. It was their truck.

Asa and Brady made their way to the front and opened the doors. Brady made his way to the glove box. "The ring's gone."

Asa looked under the seat. "So is my gun."

"My computer bag is too," Brady sighed with frustration.

"Good news is they left the keys in the ignition," Asa said, pulling them from the slot.

"You think they're in the bar?" she asked. "Maybe we can get our stuff back."

Asa looked over at the run-down dump. "We don't know what we're up against."

"We have to at least try," Roxy said. When everyone looked at her, she flushed. "We didn't come this far just to let some jerks steal our stuff."

Brady smiled. "I guess we better check it out."

Asa's back straightened up. "Okay, everyone, stay close. If anything seems dangerous, we're out. Keep your eyes out for the ring. Roxy, you saw the guys that jumped into the rig, so let us know if you see them."

They made their way inside.

Roxy

The inside of the bar was dark and smoky. Little light was coming through the dusty windows. There was low country music playing on the jukebox.

They headed for the bar. Brady and Asa immediately started to scan the room. She leaned back on her stool, and she, too, looked for anyone who looked like the guys who had jumped in their truck.

The bartender came up behind them.

"Want anything?" he said roughly. She turned to see a man a lot younger looking than he sounded. He was thin, and his blue shirt was grease-stained and had wet spots on the front.

"Four beers," Sydney answered quickly. Sydney eyed him. "In bottles, please." Sydney looked over at her and gave a quick lip curl of disgust.

The bartender dropped the four bottles on the bar. He took the twenty that Asa held out. He then turned and went through the swinging door that led to the back.

She turned to her group. Brady was sitting and studying the scene, his leg bouncing up and down. Asa had his back to the room and was whispering questions to Brady, who would answer with short, quiet, one-word answers. Sydney took a drink of her beer and disgust crossed her face. She looked down at the bottle, then slid it away from her. Sydney turned to her.

"There aren't many people here," Sydney said. "You see the guys that stole our truck?"

"Nope." She scanned the room again. There was an old man at a table by himself eating a sandwich, watching whatever baseball game was on the TV up in the corner of the room; there were also two middle-aged men quietly playing pool at one of the pool tables, and a woman sitting in the corner smoking a cigarette while looking at her phone, her head down. Her hair was bleached, and her roots were showing.

She leaned over so the guys could hear her too. "Maybe the ring and the men that stole our truck are gone. Are we just wasting time?"

Just then, the door from the back kitchen swung open. It startled her, and she looked over, just as two young men came out. They were loud and laughing about something.

"Man, it's a good day," one said while looking over at the other. They walked from behind the bar and into the room. They headed for the empty pool table.

She recognized the one in the hat. It was the same white hat and shirt that one of the punks who stole their truck was wearing.

She turned and whispered, "I think that's them."

The three of them swung over and looked where she motioned.

She watched as the one in the hat grabbed a pool stick and a small blue cube of chalk. He started to twist the cube on the end of the pool stick when she saw it. Right on the man's pinky finger sat the ring. The white stone shone against the man's tan skin.

She grabbed Sydney's arm. "I see it, too," Sydney said, and they both looked over at Brady and Asa.

She watched as realization crossed Brady's face. Then, just as quickly, his face grew hard.

The four of them slowly turned and faced the bar. They all put their heads down.

"How are we going to get the ring from him?" she asked.

"What if we offered money for it?" Asa said.

"Isn't that weird?" Sydney asked. "Besides, what if he says no?"

"We could take it," Roxy said.

Everyone looked at her in surprise.

"No, not like beat him up. But we pick it."

Sydney looked up, thinking. "We would have to get close to them. They're young, maybe flirt with them a little. It would take some time, but Roxy and I could pull it off."

"No, I don't think that's a good idea," Brady said, frowning.

Asa didn't say anything. Instead, he turned to the pool tables. She turned, too. She wasn't excited to have to run a con, flirt with them. She watched as they were chugging beer and slapping each other on the backs, and making jokes. She watched as the kid adjusted the ring on his finger. He looked up and caught her staring. He winked. She turned on her stool, dread filling her.

"Yeah, that's dangerous," was all Asa said. Brady looked relieved and even gave a little smile.

It made her wonder, *Who was the one in danger?*

Asa leaned forward. "I'm pretty sure our guns are gone. They most likely sold them in the back there, and that's why these guys are so happy. They made some money. But the ring is worthless to any buyer. That's why they still have it. I still think we can buy it from him."

She heard some laughter, and she looked over.

The kid wearing the ring yelled, "Hey, Donna!"

The woman with the bleached hair looked up from her phone. The man grabbed himself and stuck out his tongue.

Donna just rolled her eyes and looked down again, content to remain in the corner.

"I think we just take them out back and beat the hell out of them and take the ring." Brady sighed and took a drink of his beer, frowning.

She reached for her beer. She remembered a con she and Sydney practiced in high school. It was simple. She was pretty good at it, and it had worked the one and only time she had run it on a mark. But she was rusty and hadn't picked in a long time. She wondered if she could pull it off. Sydney had never mastered it, though she had.

She looked over at her group. Asa's forehead was lined with stress, and his fists were balled on the counter. She couldn't tell if he was trying to think of how much he should offer or start a fight. Brady's leg was bouncing; he looked pissed. She wondered if he would really drag those punks to the back and beat them. Sydney's brain was going too. Roxy didn't want her to try anything stupid and get herself hurt. They needed that ring back and with little to no attention. She needed to do this. She took a deep breath. "Asa, can I borrow some money?"

Sydney

She looked up at Roxy. Her mouth turned down in a frown, but she could tell her sister had a plan. It was written all over her stressed face.

"What are you thinking?" she asked.

"I know how to get the ring," Roxy said, frustrated.

"I'll go with you." Brady leaned forward, looking worried.

"No, you better stay here." Roxy looked over at the pool tables.

"Well, tell us," she said. She was excited. Roxy was going to pick it somehow, she just knew it, and she wanted to know what kind of con she was going to pull.

"Just trust me. I'll get the ring. Just be ready to leave."

She put her hand out to Asa. He hesitated and eyed Brady. Brady just sat back in his stool.

Asa pulled out his wallet. "How much?"

"A twenty is fine."

She stirred in her seat with excitement. It had been a long time since she'd seen Roxy in action and not just behind her computer.

Roxy took the twenty from Asa and walked over to the pool table.

She watched carefully to see if she could catch what Roxy was going to do. She felt Asa watch her. She looked over at him.

He smiled. "Wow, this is quite the event for you."

"Roxy is amazing at picking, but she never does it. Just watch."

Roxy walked up and dropped the money on the ground as she walked past the men at the pool tables. She took two steps forward, then stopped suddenly, turned, and picked it up.

"Is this yours?" she asked sweetly.

The kid turned and looked her up and down and smiled.

"Hi there," he said and took a step closer.

Sydney didn't like the look he gave her sister. She saw from the corner of her eye that Asa placed his hand on Brady's shoulder, pulling him back down in his seat. Apparently, Brady didn't like it either.

Roxy blushed and held up the twenty. "It was on the ground. Thought maybe you dropped it."

"Yep, it's mine. Got paid today." He took another step forward, and she could tell Roxy wanted to take a step back, but she held her ground.

"Well here, don't want to lose any of it." Roxy held the bill out to him.

She sat forward in her seat. She remembered this con. They had practiced it together many times at the girls' home. She could never get it, but Roxy had, and it had frustrated her to no end. She wanted to see it in action.

The kid reached for the twenty and she watched Roxy's hand.

He took the bill, and with speed and true talent, Roxy slid the ring from his finger as he drew the bill from her hand. It was tricky, but part of the con was to make it look like a flirty move.

Roxy looked up at his face and smiled her innocent smile. The kind that made you think maybe she was testing him to see if he liked her. There was a slight blush on her cheeks. Sydney watched as Roxy palmed the ring and looked bashfully away.

"What's your name?" the kid asked, pocketing the cash, completely oblivious of what had just happened.

"Sara."

Sydney smiled. That was the name Roxy always used when they were kids.

"Okay, Sara, can I buy you a drink?"

"I would like that," Roxy said excitedly.

He looked over at his friend and jerked his head. Apparently, it was the "get lost" look because the man frowned and threw his pool stick on the table. The friend looked at Roxy. "Gotta take a piss," he said and walked away.

"Beer?" he asked Roxy.

"That sounds good," she said with a slight smile and a tilt of her head. *Damn*, she thought, *my sister is good.*

He walked up to the bar, right next to Sydney. She slowly turned her body toward Asa and Brady. She didn't want him to notice that she and Roxy looked alike. It had complicated lots of cons in the past.

"Jack!" the kid yelled and pounded the bar. "Get your ass out here. I need two beers."

Sydney looked over and watched as Roxy walked right out the door.

She looked up at the rest of her group and nodded. Asa threw down a ten on the bar, and together, they followed Roxy out the door.

When she stepped outside, the light from the sun blinded her. She placed her hand on her forehead and searched for Roxy. She found her headed straight for the Suburban.

"Let's get out of here," she said and started to jog toward the truck.

They all jumped in, and Asa backed the truck up. When he pulled toward the front of the bar, the kid was standing out front.

Roxy slid down in her seat.

"Hey!" he yelled. "That bitch and her friends are stealing my truck!"

Asa hit the gas and sprayed gravel; the guy stumbled back.

Brady stuck his hand out the window and flipped him off as they left. They were back on the road.

She turned to her sister. "Roxy!" she all but screamed. "That was amazing." She reached in and gave her a hug. "You still have it. You did it so effortlessly. I'm a little jealous," she admitted. "But also, very proud of you, you have true talent."

"Yeah, I feel dirty. That guy was gross, and I think he was on drugs; his eyes were all dilated."

She reached up and held the ring out. "Here, I don't want this."

Brady took the ring and put it in his pocket. "This stays on someone at all times."

They all agreed. They hit the next gas station to fill up, and this time they all stayed with the truck.

*

They drove for another couple hours. Maybe it was the action and stress from the bar, but they all started to get restless. She had to pee along with Asa, and they took a side road and pulled over in a vacant lot, looking out to the desert.

She made her way out to the one and only bush and did her business. She stood and looked out. The sun was getting ready to set, and she felt a little peace take over. She thought about Roxy perfectly executing one of the harder cons they knew and saw how much her sister had hated it. She blew out a breath. It stirred up feelings of guilt and judgment and even a little bit of jealousy.

She turned to make her way back when she caught Asa making his way over to her. Brady and Roxy were sitting on the back of the truck, eating a snack and drinking water.

No privacy, she thought, pulling her thoughts from Roxy. She found a rather large rock and decided to sit. She was sure he would come join her.

He did.

She looked up at him. "Coming to check on me?"

"You took a while. Just wanted to make sure you didn't get eaten by a coyote."

She looked at him in surprise. "You think there's coyotes out here?"

He laughed. "Probably." He sat down next to her and looked out to the horizon. "Don't worry; they're more afraid of you than you are of them." He bumped her shoulder with his.

They sat in comfortable peace for a while. She didn't feel awkward or have the need to fill the silence. She looked over at Asa, and even though he was still watching the horizon, he held a peacefulness as well. She felt contentment.

The desert was beautiful. The sky was blue, and the sun was close to the horizon. Pink and orange were on their way. It was strange due to their circumstances, but there was a moment of serenity.

Then Asa pulled the ring out of his pocket and started to roll it through his fingers.

"It's amazing how something so small can be such a problem. I wonder what the Brotherhood wants with it." He slipped it over his finger, but it barely made it to his knuckle.

"I have been thinking the same thing," she said. "Wondering what the leader of the Brotherhood is thinking. Why is he willing to kill for a cheap ring? What does he say that convinces people to follow him and kill for him?" She paused. "Do you think we will ever find him?"

Asa looked up from the ring and out at the desert. "I hope so." He closed the ring in his palm.

She laughed. "I picture the leader of the Brotherhood like Gollum. Hairless, bent over, looking for his precious."

Asa smiled. "You read *Lord of the Rings?*"

"Saw the movies."

"The books are better," he said. He turned to her.

"Not to change the subject," he said as he put the ring back in his pocket, "but how come you dropped out of school last year?"

She was taken aback. "How do you know that?"

"Through our research. I told you that me and Brady have been doing background checks on you girls. You stopped going to school and emptied your dorm."

"Honestly, designer school is boring," she said flatly.

"So, what have you been doing?" He looked interested.

"You know, just traveling around the east coast."

"You were stealing, weren't you?" he said it bluntly. He didn't take his eyes off her. When she didn't answer, he continued.

"Pretty sure your dad taught you how. You both have a couple minor shoplifting charges when you were younger. Obviously, Roxy knows how to." He shrugged. "I think it's in your blood."

She felt uncomfortable. He was an ex-cop, after all.

For the first time, she felt almost ashamed. She never felt that way, not even with Roxy. She didn't like it.

"I donate the money," she said quickly. "I help people with my picks. I don't keep any of the money." Her words were coming out fast.

"Hey, it's all right." He put his hands up. "I'm not judging you. We all live our own life." He looked at her, and his head tilted to the side. "You seem a little defensive about it?"

"I'm not being defensive." She crossed her arms over her chest.

They were silent for a moment. They both looked out at the sunset. The sky was pink and orange now, the sun almost gone.

"So, you're like Robin Hood?" Asa chuckled. "Which is another good book, by the way."

"I saw the movie." She uncrossed her arms. "You like a book nerd or something?'

"I like to think I'm well read." He stared at her.

"Which one? Kevin Costner or Disney?"

"What?" she asked confused.

"Which movie? The Kevin Costner version or the Disney one?"

"Disney," she said and turned slightly away from him on the rock. She didn't like the emotions swirling in her. He was making her feel ashamed about her life choices, and the worst was that she was realizing that she cared what he thought, and she didn't know why.

"You know what you're doing isn't safe?" he said, this time looking out into the desert.

She'd heard it before, and just like before, she didn't reply.

Asa stood. "Your father was considered an honest thief, and I assume you feel the same way."

She opened her mouth but no words came out; he put his hand out to help her up.

"You can live your life however you want. Being lost is part of it. But you can't run forever. Sooner or later, life will catch you. You have to figure out what you want." She just stared up at him.

The sky was pink behind him, his face serious. She took his outstretched hand and stood. His hand was rough and big. He didn't let go, but instead continued to stare down at her. When she let go, he looked away quickly. They walked back to the truck, quietly.

*

"You okay?" Roxy asked, sitting next to her in the truck. "You're being quiet."

She just smiled. "I'm fine, Rox. Just tired." But Asa's words ran through her head. Was she lost? Was she just living life on the run? What did she want?

A few hours later, they found a rest stop and spent the night.

*

The next day, they drove all day. Everyone seemed to be distracted by their own thoughts. There were conversations here and there, but that would end, and they were back to their own thoughts again.

They made it halfway through Texas by the early evening, and they were talking about another rest stop.

"Let's get a hotel." She sat forward in the seat, looking between the two in the front.

Brady and Asa looked to each other.

"We all need showers and beds. I don't even care if's a motel where you pay by the hour."

"Great, she's whining," Roxy said. "That means she wants her way, and she isn't going to let up."

"You think we should?" Brady asked Asa.

"We've made good time today. I could use a shower," Asa said.

"It does sound good," Brady agreed.

"Yes!" She sat back in the seat, a smug smile on her face.

They pulled into a motel off the side of the freeway; it was an absolute dump. The dark green paint was fading. There was an empty pool, unless you counted the large number of leaves laying at the bottom and the fact that it looked like it was starting to grow grass. Asa had gone inside to pay, and they waited in the truck.

"I bet there are roaches as big as my fist in there." Roxy was staring at the old motel.

"I don't care," she said. "As long as I have a shower and a bed."

Asa came jogging out and jumped in. "We're on the back side."

It was dark on the other side; there were no streetlights, and the sun had set. Their rooms were next to the dumpster. It was overflowing with garbage, filling the air with a terrible smell.

They pulled into a spot, and Asa threw a key card that landed in her lap.

"We get our own room?" she said with excitement. This meant she didn't have to share a bed with Roxy.

"Damn, are we really that bad?" Brady laughed, opening the truck door.

"No! No!" she quickly replied. She didn't want them to think she was ungrateful.

But Brady just laughed again and got out of the truck.

"It's just that you guys won't leave our sides," Roxy said, coming to her sister's aid.

Asa started pulling the two backpacks out of the back. He handed theirs to Roxy. He then handed each their black hat. She placed hers slightly on her head and rolled her eyes. Asa smiled at her. "We can't get lazy." She pulled it down further; she didn't want to admit it, but he was right.

"We're in the room right next door," Asa said. "If there are any problems, bang on the wall or call us. Brady handed her one of the phones.

Brady had set up the remaining phones so they could at least keep contact with each other if they were separated. He said that it would be safe to only call each other.

"Don't answer the door for anyone. We'll knock three times, so you'll know it's us."

"Got it, boss." She gave him a smartass smile this time, and she and

Roxy walked to their door.

"Gross," she said as she stood in the doorway of their room, looking in. There was brown shag carpeting, and the bedspreads were grass green.

"I wonder how many prostitutes made money in this room?" Roxy stepped in.

They had two queen beds and she threw herself down on one. "I don't even care how many Johns got VD in this bed. I'll sleep forever."

Roxy laughed.

"I get first shower." She jumped up and ran to the bathroom. She heard Roxy's sigh.

The lime green bathtub didn't hinder her long, cool shower. She let the water rinse the Suburban smell right off of her. She washed her hair twice with the motel shampoo.

After a while, Roxy was pounding on the door. "Hurry up! You're going to use up all the hot water. I'm going to have to take a freezing shower now." She turned the water off and got out. A towel wrapped around her, she opened the door, and Roxy pushed past her with a frown.

She got dressed in a clean pair of leggings and a loose black T-shirt that had an embroidered image of California on the pocket. She brushed her hair and started to feel human again. *I guess I didn't use all the hot water*, she thought, because Roxy seemed to be taking an even longer shower than her.

There were three knocks on the door, and she smiled to herself. They were already checking up.

She opened the door and there was Asa. He had taken the hat off and his hair was wet from his shower, and he had slicked it back. His beard was thicker, making him look even more rugged. He had on a T-shirt that had the word "California" pulled tight across his wide chest. She tried to ignore the butterflies in her stomach.

When she realized she was staring, she looked up. He smiled. "You look clean and refreshed."

"You too. Where's your hat? I thought we can't be lazy," she replied. He only grinned.

"We ordered Chinese takeout, and got a couple of bottles of wine from the store across the street. You girls want to come over and have dinner with us?" He shuffled his feet after he said the last part.

"Sure. As soon as Roxy gets out of the shower."

He did a quick nod and turned to leave, but not before scanning the parking lot.

She shut the door and went to the bathroom. The water had stopped running, and she yelled through the door. "The guys got Chinese food. Let's go. I'm starved."

The door whipped open, and Roxy stepped out. She was also wearing a pair of leggings and a red T-shirt; her short black hair was wet, and she pushed it behind her ears.

"Chinese food sounds amazing."

Roxy found her Converse while Sydney slid her feet into her only shoes—her ankle boots—and, for the first time, envied Roxy's choice of shoes. Her feet hurt from the long walk they'd taken the day before.

They went to the next room and knocked on the door three times.

"I felt stupid doing that," she said to Roxy.

"I like it. It means they're being safe." Roxy turned and scanned the parking lot.

The door swung open and they entered.

There were Chinese food containers stacked on the cheap brown table and two bottles of wine.

She could have wept. Brady had let them in, and Asa was looking through the backpack.

She could smell shower and men's deodorant filling the air, and it smelled completely male in the room.

They spent the next couple hours talking and laughing. It was clear that the showers and thought of sleeping in a bed had lifted their spirits.

Asa told a funny story about Brady taking apart his mother's computers, and she told the same story about Roxy. Roxy was quick to tell a story about her and her narrow escape from the candy shop, where she had picked three candy bars when she was ten. Their father ended up paying for them. Roxy left out the part where Dad had ended up teaching them a better sleight of hand grab.

They ended up drinking both bottles of wine. Then, after a while, the conversation died down.

"I want to learn some defense moves," she said, standing up. She swayed a little, and Roxy laughed at her. Apparently, her sister was feeling the wine too.

"I'm serious. I don't want to be manhandled by some jerks in a blue suit again."

"I think that's a good idea," Asa agreed. He put his glass down and stood in front of her. He jumped right into it.

"There are pressure points on the human body that are extremely painful when hit." He pointed to his nose. "Here, the throat, the groin, the knees, and the tops of the foot."

She looked at him. "Okay. Show me what to do."

He lightly placed his hands on her shoulders and spun her around. He stepped up behind her.

"If they have you from behind, stomp their foot." Asa wrapped his hands around her chest, pinning her arms to her side. She froze; the last man who did that threatened to rape her and she started to panic. Asa must have felt her freeze up because he bent down and whispered into her ear. "It's okay, it's just me." His breath was warm on the shell of her ear, and his words didn't relax her but set butterflies in her stomach.

She lightly stepped on his foot, and together they practiced more moves. He was teaching her to do a strike to the throat when she heard laughter from Roxy. She looked over, and Brady was trying to teach her how to knee him in the groin. She couldn't get it right and he kept dodging her knee.

Brady looked over at them with a smile. "Maybe we shouldn't show them that move anyway."

Asa laughed.

Feeling the fun atmosphere, she joined in.

"What if he comes at me like this?" She couldn't hide her grin, and she ran at him. He simply shifted his stance and picked her up over his shoulder.

"Whoa there, girl," he said, laughing and spinning her around. "So rough."

She started to laugh.

"Hey!" Roxy said, laughing. "Put my sister down!" Roxy stepped forward to help but Brady grabbed her by the waist and threw her up on his shoulder too.

"Don't be going after my cousin," he said.

Both girls were laughing and screaming as they were being spun around.

Asa finally went to drop her on the bed, but she grabbed his shirt and took him with her. He landed half on her and half on the bed, laughing. She looked down at him. His chin was resting on her stomach and he had a grin on his face.

"Can't win a fight with me," he said.

"Someday, I will," she said.

He looked up at her and they locked eyes. All of a sudden, she became very aware of his weight on her and her stomach tightened. He broke the stare first and got up.

He held a hand out and helped her up. She straightened her shirt.

Roxy was lying on the bed laughing; Brady was on his knees on the floor beside the bed. He, too, was laughing.

She looked around, trying not to be awkward. She felt something had passed between her and Asa.

"I guess we should clean up this mess. It's starting to get late." She started to pick up paper plates and napkins.

Brady and Roxy stopped laughing, noticing the shift in the room.

"Here, I'll take the garbage out," Roxy said, pulling the overstuffed bag out of the small trash can.

"I'll go with you," Brady said, standing and taking the bag from Roxy's hand. She grabbed the empty wine bottles and the empty containers that hadn't fit in the can. The two of them left the room to take it to the dumpster.

She sat on one of the chairs from the table and she leaned back, taking a deep breath.

She took a sip of someone's wine that was sitting on the table.

"I overheard your conversation with Roxy the other day, and I want to thank you for your help, too," she said. She looked to his knuckles; they were scabs now.

He was sitting on the bed closest to her and he leaned over and placed his hands on top of hers.

"Like I told your sister. It's no problem. I was a cop once and took an oath to protect and serve, and even though I don't work for them anymore, I still take it seriously."

His hands squeezed her lightly, and she looked down again at his scabbed knuckles; she took one of her hands from under his and placed it over his knuckles and smiled. "I owe you my life. No one has ever done the things you and Brady are doing for us. We are thankful."

Asa looked over at her and then stood. He pulled her up slowly and into a hug. His big arms wrapped her in tight to his chest, where she rested her head.

She softened and let herself be held. She wrapped her arms around his mid-section and hugged him back. She melted into him; she couldn't remember the last time anyone had hugged her—at least not like this. She felt tears swell in her eyes. She realized she had no one left to care about her and her sister anymore. She shut her eyes tight to keep the tears back. She turned her face into his shoulder and breathed in his smell. Soap and trees.

He pulled back, keeping his hands on her shoulders, and looked down at her. He saw her wet eyes and placed his hand on the side of her face. She felt a tear slip from her eye and roll down her cheek. His thumb rubbed her one tear away. He looked down at her lips and then bent forward, and she went to meet him.

Then the knock on the door sounded, and it was only one. Asa pulled back waiting to see if another was going to sound. She felt his body go rigid. Then two more fast knocks and laughing on the other side.

"Dammit," he said under his breath and let her go. He opened the door. Roxy and Brady all but fell into the room.

They were laughing. When they realized she and Asa weren't, they straightened up.

"Sorry, we forgot. We didn't mean to scare you guys," Brady said.

He shut the door. Both Roxy and Brady sat next to each other on one of the beds, smiling.

She studied her sister who looked relaxed and happy. She figured it must be too much wine, as she was feeling fuzzy too. The hug and playing defense on the bed with Asa had left her stirred, and she needed space.

"It's getting late. Roxy, let's go to bed."

Roxy hesitated. She side-eyed Brady, but then agreed.

She stood up. Brady was right behind her.

"Thanks for dinner." She looked at Asa.

"You're welcome," he said, holding the door. She gave him a soft smile which he returned, and they left. When she used the key to open her door, she turned and saw Asa watching from his door.

*

They left early the next morning. She and Roxy had both taken another shower before they left for fear that they didn't know when the next one

146

would be.

The morning was quiet, and no one really spoke. Asa drove, and Brady studied the maps. Roxy was staring out through her window, a slight smile on her face.

She felt rested. Spending the night in a bed and taking two showers made her feel more awake and less on edge. She thought of Asa, too. She thought of last night, and it made her wonder. *Was she really that lonely? Did he like her? Or was it just the wine?* It had felt good to be in someone's arms to feel safe and cared for. Asa's big, strong arms had held her tight. He had almost kissed her until the knock on the door. She could still see his eyes looking soft, staring into hers. His face slowly moving toward hers.

Damn, she thought, shaking her head. Maybe she had been alone for too long? She sighed out loud. She saw Asa's eyes move to the rearview mirror and look at her. She locked eyes with his gray ones, feeling a pull in her chest, he broke the stare and looked away.

She stared back out her side window. Maybe she was lonely. She barely stayed in contact with Margie and Roxy. A few phone calls and no visits. She had kept herself busy with research. She had studied the news and social media for signs of people getting away with terrible things. It had kept her mind occupied, and the picking kept her hands busy. She had told herself that she was doing good, bringing justice to the ones who had been wronged.

In an attempt to make her feel good about herself, she thought of the drug dealer who had the cherry-red Mustang. He liked to sell his drugs to kids on the playground. She had stolen that car and took it to a chop shop; they had given her ten grand for it and she had anonymously donated it to the YMCA in his town. She smiled to herself, wishing she had seen the man's face when he opened his garage door.

Her daydream made her think of the conversation on the rock with Asa. He had known what she did. Doubt crept in. Why did she feel so insecure about her lifestyle? He hadn't even said anything remotely judgmental.

It was the look in his eyes, she thought. She saw it, just like the others. The disappointment and the disapproval. She had never cared before. But for some reason she cared with him. She looked away from her window and glanced at him from the backseat. His black hat was on backward. His window was down and he was resting his huge elbow on it. She looked at his side profile in the side mirror. His jawline was slowly disappearing under the thickness of his beard, and it was shining in the sun. His gray eyes

147

were always scanning, and he would randomly tap his thumb on the steering wheel. He was good looking. She had this urge to make him proud of her. It was weird. She hadn't felt like that since she was a kid. Where had that come from?

Her thoughts were interrupted.

"We need to stop and get gas." Asa was looking down at the dash.

Brady shuffled the maps around and studied them. "There's a small town up ahead, about five miles."

They took the exit and pulled in to the first gas station.

"I need to use the restroom." Roxy opened her door and stretched.

She did the same and waited to see which one was going to escort them there.

"Don't forget your hats," Asa said, looking up at the surveillance camera in the corner of the store.

She shoved the hat on her head. She didn't know how people could wear these all the time. It made her forehead itch, and it felt like her peripheral vision was blocked.

"I'll pump," Brady said and walked over to the pump.

The three of them made their way inside. Asa paid the cashier for the gas first and they headed toward the bathrooms.

When she was done, she looked around. Something cold to drink sounded good. The ice in the small cooler was melted and the waters were lukewarm.

When Asa came out, they waited for Roxy.

"I need something cold to drink," she said, looking up at Asa. It kind of annoyed her that she had no money and had to rely on him. *He was always generous and had no problems handing it over.* The thought gave her another pull in her chest.

"Iced tea does sound good, and we should get more ice for the cooler too," he said, looking over at the fridge.

She decided to make her way to the fountain drinks. She wanted lots of ice.

Asa came up next to her and started to put ice in his cup. She playfully bumped him with her hip, trying to get to the Diet Coke. He didn't look at her but gave a half-smile. She felt a little disappointed. Guess he wasn't in a playful mood. Maybe last night was just the result of the wine. Disappointed, she filled her cup.

As they walked out of the store, Asa threw a bottle of tropical juice to

Brady who was leaning up against the truck waiting for them. He caught it one-handed.

"My favorite." He popped the top and chugged at least half.

They got back in and drove off.

Roxy

The sun was getting low in the sky when they hit Tennessee. Her thoughts all day were of last night. Brady had kissed her. Right in front of the smelly dumpster. It wasn't the best spot, but the kiss had been great. It was a slow, soft kiss and had made her ears hum.

Brady had only given her a small smile when they had loaded up in the morning to leave. She was starting to wonder if it had been just a drunken mistake. But they hadn't had any time alone either. When he offered to pump the gas instead of walk into the gas station, it made her wonder if she was making a big deal of nothing.

But it was amazing, she thought. David, the guy she had dated a little from work, hadn't made her feel that way. She was confused.

She wanted to talk to Sydney about it. Sydney would know and give her advice. She had more experience with men. Even just to talk about it would be nice; she was driving herself crazy.

She paused her thoughts. This was stupid, she sounded like a schoolgirl with a crush. They had bigger problems.

She looked out the window. Evening was moving in fast, and she was ready to stop for the day. There were trees again instead of desert, and it was a nice change. The air was cooler also. Brady had his window down, and she let the air brush her face.

"I think we should stop for the night soon," Asa finally said.

"We're going to need a map of Tennessee next time we stop." Brady was looking at the map on his lap. "There's a rest stop about ten miles up here." He folded it up and put it back.

When they made it to the rest stop, Asa pulled in to the far corner. It had trees on two of the sides and a picnic table a few yards away.

They did their normal rest stop procedure—stretch, rest room, and then food.

They sat at the picnic table and ate trail mix and Cliff bars, which she actually didn't mind.

"I want to learn some more defense moves," Sydney said, getting up from the table. "I need to move also."

Asa nodded. He stood and dusted the crumbs from his hands. They moved a few feet away and started to show her how to throw a punch.

"You should probably learn this too," Brady said. "Come on."

She stood nervously, wiping her hands on her leggings.

He showed her how to make a fist so she wouldn't break her thumb. He wrapped his hands around her fist and was giving advice. She wasn't really listening. All she noticed was how his hands were rough, considering he was a tech. Asa had made a comment about them working out together, and she wondered if he lifted weights.

"Are you even listening?" he asked, looking down at her.

"Yes, hold my hand like this." She was flustered and feeling ridiculous.

"Okay, here, punch my hand." He held out his hand, palm out. She stepped back and threw her fist out as hard as she could. Maybe she needed to burn off this frustration.

When her fist hit his palm, hot pain shot through her arm.

"Ouch!" she yelled and grabbed her wrist.

Sydney and Asa looked over.

"I'm fine." She waved them off.

Brady stepped closer. "Are you okay? I told you not to hold your hand that way."

She was embarrassed by her weakness. Sydney was throwing punches left and right into Asa's palm, and she wasn't in pain.

"I need some water," she said, turning to go to the truck.

Brady followed her.

She reached the back and swung the doors open. She reached into the cooler and pulled out a cold water. She rolled it on her wrist.

"Are you okay? Let me see. I hope you didn't sprain it." He reached out, but she pulled her hand back.

"I'm fine." She jumped up and sat on the back end of the truck. The pain was already fading.

Brady sat next to her. He reached over and pulled the side hair that never reached her ponytail back and put it behind her ear.

She was surprised that she didn't awkwardly shy away from his touch. But instead, she wanted to lean into it.

He took a deep breath and got her attention. "I have been wanting to talk to you alone all day." This time, he looked down.

Her heart jumped; she had wanted the same thing.

"I wanted to make sure that you were okay with what happened last night. You know, between you and me."

She just kept looking at him. Was he going to tell her he was sorry, that he had just been drunk? She didn't say anything.

"I know we had a little too much to drink. But I don't go around kissing pretty girls when I'm drunk." He blushed and stumbled over his words. "I mean, it wasn't a mistake. I really wanted to kiss you."

Her stomach unclenched, and she smiled.

When he saw her face, he relaxed. "Me too." She fumbled. "I mean, go around kissing guys drunk."

"Good." He nodded and smiled. "I have been wanting to kiss you ever since I saw your pouty face after you found out I hacked your computer."

"Seriously?"

He chuckled. "You were so pissed." He laughed harder.

She lightly pushed him. He grabbed her hand and stroked his thumb over hers.

She instinctively looked over to Sydney and Asa.

Brady noticed and let her hand go.

"You didn't tell your sister? I thought sisters told each other everything?"

"I haven't had time, plus me and Sydney's relationship isn't like other sisters." She paused. "I didn't know what was going on. I mean, you could go around just kissing girls when you drink; how was I supposed to know?"

He laughed. "I told Asa last night, right after you girls left."

"Oh yeah, and what did he have to say?" She actually was a little nervous. She respected Asa.

Brady frowned, and he pushed his glasses up on his face.

She felt her nerves tingle.

"Honestly, he said that I needed to be careful. That the stuff going on between us could affect my thinking and jeopardize our job to get us home safely. He also said that we were in a stressful situation, and it could be making my feelings stronger."

"Making your feeling stronger? How?"

Brady shrugged. "Being in an intense situation causes emotions to heighten or something, I don't know." Brady shook his head.

She took a drink of water and wondered if that could really happen.

"I don't think that's true." He looked at her. "I started liking you the first hour I tried to hack your system. I thought you were a genius. If I couldn't hack your computer, I was going to show up at your doorstep and throw myself at the mercy of the Queen of Tech."

She laughed. "Well, you did hack it. So, I guess that makes you the king."

He smiled. "The King and Queen of Tech right here. I like it." He looked over at Asa and Sydney, then back at her.

"Do you feel stressed right now?" he asked.

"Not really stressed, no." She placed her empty water bottle in the bag they used for garbage.

"Good." He grabbed her hand and pulled her to the other side of the truck, opposite of the others.

He pushed her up against the truck gently and placed his hands on either side of her head, pinning her to the dusty Suburban.

"I don't feel stressed right now either. Let's test Asa's theory." He leaned in and touched his lips softly to hers.

It was slow, like the one the night before. He broke away. He looked down at her. His voice low, he said, "I don't think my mind is muddled. If anything, I know exactly what I want."

He bent down again, and this time the kiss was a little harder. His hand came off the truck, and he placed it behind her head. When she felt his tongue, she grabbed his waist, balling his T-shirt in her hands and pulling him closer. He brought his other hand to her face and had his body pinned hers to the truck. Her legs went weak. A need she never felt took over her and she pulled him in closer.

When he finally pulled away slowly, her heart was pounding. He placed his forehead against hers. "We need to stop." His voice was husky.

"No," she whispered and brought her lips back to his. He did a low hum deep in his throat and kissed her back. She let out a soft sigh, and he pulled her in tighter. Her head spun, and her body warmed. This time, she pushed him away. Her eyes were still closed, and her knees about ready to collapse. "You're right."

She smiled with regret. "We need to stop."

She felt him lean in, and he whispered against her mouth, "I still know what I want."

She opened her eyes and stared into his. They were intense. He stepped back. He ran his hand through his hair.

"Let's go practice with A and Sydney. I need to work off some of this frustration."

They again had gotten an early start to their day, leaving before the sun had even come up. They had practiced defense moves till it was too dark to see and then crawled into their sleeping bags. She had a restless night. Her stressed mind was jumping through her emotions, between fear and lust.

*

They had been on the road for more than a couple hours. Brady was telling them about his childhood.

"My father was in the army, and we moved around a lot," he said. "After my mother passed away, he was a mess. Haley was complaining about moving so much, and Dad had no one to take care of us anymore. He took us to his cousin's house. That's Aunt Jenny, Asa's mom. She took us in without a second question." Brady's face filled with love for his aunt. "So, Dad would travel around, and me and Haley stayed with Asa."

"We grew up together. Brady and Haley are more like siblings to me," Asa added.

"So, are you guys like blood cousins?" Sydney asked.

"Technically, we're like tenth cousins or something," Brady said. "Something removed, not quite sure. But all our family is close and stays together." He turned to Asa. "Isn't Granny really like your great-aunt or something?"

"I think so," he said and took his hands off the steering wheel and made finger quotes. "Because of the curse, our family is small, but we stay close."

"What about your parents? Any siblings?" Sydney asked Asa.

"I'm an only child. Parents are retired and traveling. They are currently in Europe. They should be home for the holidays, though."

She was wondering where in Europe, but before she could ask, she heard a quick chirp of a siren.

She saw Asa and Brady both look in their side mirrors, and she whipped her head around to look out the back. There was a cop behind them, his lights flashing red and blue.

"Were you speeding?" Brady asked, turning to look at the dash.

Asa rolled his hand on the steering wheel and peered down. "I don't think so."

"We're about to hit state lines. Can they pull us over on the other side?" Brady was opening the glove box and pulling out the map.

"They can and then hold us till the locals get there," Asa said.

"He started to slow and pull over to the shoulder.

"What are you doing?" Sydney moved to the edge of her seat. "Don't pull over. What if they recognize us?"

"It's going to be okay. We're far from Fuller," Asa said. He spun his hat forward and pulled it low.

When they came to a stop, she turned and watched as an overweight cop walked up to the truck. She leaned back in her seat.

"Good morning." Asa leaned on the open window.

"Do you know why I pulled you over?" His accent was thick like his waistband, and he had a clean-shaven face.

It made her want to roll her eyes. Why do they always have to ask that?

"I'm sorry. I don't, Officer," Asa said.

"You were speeding back there, got you at seventy in a sixty."

"My apologies." He looked down at the dashboard. "This truck is old. and the speedometer could be off. I'll have my mechanic look at it when we get home."

The cop looked in the back window at Sydney. He squinted to look further back, and it made her lean back in her seat.

"License and registration, please."

Her chest tightened with panic. They were going to jail. The Brotherhood would find them.

"Sorry, Officer." He put his hands out, palms up. "I lost my wallet."

The officer stared. She was about to lose her cool. She could feel the pressure. But the officer nodded and brought out a small notebook. "I need your name and birthday."

"It's Marcus Whitney, and my birthday is March 26, 1996."

Brady shifted in his seat.

Wasn't that Haley's fiancé's name? Maybe it would work, she thought.

The officer nodded again and left to walk back to his car.

"What the hell!" Brady said. "They better not pull up a picture. You look nothing like Marcus."

"I know, I know!" Asa was panicked. It did nothing to alleviate her fear. He was always the calm one. He kept his eyes on the side mirror, watching the cop.

"I hope they don't have our faces from the pawnshop," Sydney said, her leg bouncing.

She was too scared to move.

"Shit!" Asa threw the Suburban into drive and floored the gas pedal. The tires began to squeal, and gravel went flying. He was chanting "shit" under his breath.

She saw Sydney grab the handle above the door.

The cop's siren went full volume. She turned to see the cop hot on their tail.

I can't believe we're running from the cops," Sydney said.

Brady pulled the map up and started to scan it, looking for the best exit. They were almost out of Tennessee and about to enter the western tip of Virginia. "I don't have a map of Virginia yet." Brady started to pull the big map of the U.S. out.

He was mumbling under his breath about technology and missing his computer.

"Come on, baby girl!" Asa was whispering to the truck. She could hear the engine revving up. She scooted forward, looking over at the speedometer. It was pushing ninety and the whole truck started shaking.

"We're not going to outrun him in this thing," he said.

She saw Sydney reach for her hat. Her hair was blowing all over her face from Asa's open window.

She tried to think, *What should they do?*

The truck was shaking and the engine was winding up. It sounded like it was going to explode.

She looked again behind them when she noticed that the cop was slowing down.

"I think he is backing off," she said, a little hope spreading through her body. "Maybe he can't pull us over across state lines?"

Asa looked at the rear mirror. "Or he has cops waiting for us up here."

Then, like a nightmare, she saw it.

A black SUV with tinted windows pulled out in front of the cruiser. The cruiser backed off, letting the SUV take the lead.

It looked just like the one that had followed her and Brady through Fuller.

"Shit!" Asa hit the steering wheel with his hand.

He pressed the gas, and the truck wound up again. They passed over the state border and into Virginia.

The SUV pulled right up to their back bumper.

"That's them, isn't it?" Sydney sounded defeated.

"Well, we know they have more than just Fuller cops on their payroll," Asa said.

All of a sudden, Brady yelled, "Take this exit here!" Asa swung the truck and took the exit; it led to a small town, and the area was open with little buildings.

"There is a bus station just north of this town. They know the truck now. We'll have to ditch it and take the bus."

They were going down a long, two-lane road. It was heavily wooded on one side with a few buildings on the other side. Asa pushed the truck and ramped up its speed, swerving around cars as he went.

She was thankful it was late morning and there was little traffic. The road seemed to go on forever.

She heard the crash of breaking glass when the truck jerked, and they were sent into a fishtail, ending up in the other lane. Asa quickly corrected the Suburban. She whipped her head back and saw the SUV's headlight was broken. The black SUV quickly ramped up its speed, and they hit the back end again. They jerked forward, but this time Asa was ready, and the truck barely swerved.

Up ahead was a streetlight and what looked like a small part of a town. Asa ran the light. She heard horns blaring and cars skidding to a stop around them. She watched as the driver of a small red car jerked his wheel, causing his car to spin out, just barely missing their Suburban. The black SUV slammed on their brakes and had to come to a stop among the pile of cars.

Asa took a hard right and whipped the Suburban into a parking lot. She looked around to see they were at a small grocery store. He found a parking space in the middle and threw the car into park.

"We're going to have to run for it." Asa swung his door open.

She grabbed her hat off the floor of the truck and jumped out. Asa and Sydney were already at the back. Asa swung one backpack on his back and gave the other to Brady.

"Into the front of the store and then out the back," Asa said, tugging the straps of the pack.

Brady grabbed her hand, and the four of them ran for the sliding doors. Inside, they ran with their hats down. They bumped and jumped between people, ignoring their shouts and complaints. Her adrenaline was pumping, and she was scared that she would hear gunshots. They made their way to the back. She didn't even care that people were staring. They saw a door for employees only and Asa hit it with his shoulder at a full run. The door swung open and hit the wall on the other side with a bang.

"Hey! You guys can't be back here." He was a small, pimply teenager holding a box of apples.

"We're leaving," Brady said as they ran by.

They found the back door and ran past the loading area of the store. There were semi-trucks parked up and down the side of the building, and they used them for cover.

"The bus station is north." Brady pointed toward the right.

She scanned the area. Nobody was around.

"Let's stay behind the buildings and make our way. Everyone stay close together." Asa grabbed Sydney's hand.

They ran along the backsides of buildings, and when they got to cross streets, they paused and waited till it was clear. They came across an alley, and they decided to go down it.

They were at a full run, and halfway down the alley, when she watched in horror as a black SUV with a broken headlight pulled into the alleyway headed right for them, cutting off their exit. She saw two men in the front. They were wearing dark suits; the driver had a goatee, and she watched as a smile crossed his face. The one on the passenger side was a large man; he looked like a WWE wrestler. His nose was flat and wide.

She froze and gripped Brady's hand tighter.

The four of them took a step back. She saw Sydney poised to run. "No." Asa pulled Sydney back, still holding her hand. "Don't run. They have guns."

She watched as the two men in the front opened their doors and got out. The door behind the driver swung open and a third man stepped out. He was tall and slim in his navy-blue suit; his face was scrunched in tight, and his eyes were beady.

All three had guns. The driver was the only one not pointing at them. Instead, he took a step forward and crossed his hand in front of him, pistol pointing down. He looked comfortable. She noticed a V-shaped scar on the hand facing them.

"We were wondering if you guys were going to come through our neck of the woods." The driver's voice had a slow, heavy southern drawl. "Gave us quite the ride, didn't they, boys?"

The large WWE man grunted, his face hard. The slim man bounced from one foot to the other. "They did, boss, they did." His smile scrunched his face more.

"Now, calm down, Travis," the driver said with a smile.

But the man named Travis was noticeably excited. "We found them, the black-haired witches. The boss is going to be so happy." He continued to bounce on his feet. "I knew it was true."

The driver straightened his navy-blue jacket, looking annoyed.

Brady let go of her hand, and he and Asa slung their backpacks off before they both stepped forward.

"Well, well," said the driver, "looks like we got some alley cats ready to defend their kittens." He laughed. "I do like a good fight, boys, but I'm afraid that we are…" he paused and waved his scarred hand. "Short on time. I want the ring and both girls. Then you two tomcats can walk away."

Travis looked over at the driver. "But boss? He said to kill them. These guys are bewitched."

The driver's face filled with annoyance and he closed his eyes. "I know what he said, Travis. Now shut your mouth!"

He looked back to them. "Please excuse my associate. He has a tendency to get excited. I will let you boys walk away. As long as you cause me no problems."

She froze. She didn't understand why they wanted her and her sister. Sydney side-stepped and ran her arm through hers, holding her close.

Asa put his hands up. "You guys can have the ring." He gestured to his pocket and pulled out the ring. All three men stared. Travis' mouth even dropped open.

"But the girls stay with us."

Looking away from the ring, the man with the goatee focused his gaze back on Asa. "You're quite the gentleman; I can see that, but I must insist that I have all three."

When they didn't move, the driver's face filled with impatience. "Or we can kill you guys and take them. This is your choice."

Sydney pulled her closer and whispered in her ear. "We have to go with them. They'll kill Asa and Brady. I don't think they can kill us, at least not yet; it sounds like their boss wants us alive."

She started to shake. "I know." Was she really going to do this? She'd never been so scared in her life. But she couldn't live with Brady and Asa dying because she was a coward. She owed them.

"We can try to escape at the first opportunity," Sydney said, her voice cracking.

All she could do was shake her head in agreement. Fear rippled through her.

She looked to her sister. Sydney was scared, just like her. "Ready?" Sydney said.

Together, arms still entwined, they stepped through Brady and Asa.

"We'll go; we don't want anyone hurt," Sydney said, her voice shaky.

Brady grabbed the arm of her shirt. "No!" he hissed.

She looked him in the face. "I don't want you to die." She pulled her arm free.

Asa had a tighter hold on Sydney's arm and he anchored them back.

"That's right, girls," the driver spoke up. Then, pointing at Asa with the gun, he said, "You, big guy. Let the lady go and hand her the ring."

"Please," she heard Sydney plead.

Asa looked to the driver, his stare hard. It didn't leave the driver's face even when he dropped the ring into Sydney's hand.

They stepped forward. The next thing she knew, the big WWE guy ran forward and grabbed her arm. She and Sydney were ripped from each other, and he yanked her toward the SUV.

As she was pulled, she watched Travis grab Sydney and pull her toward the goatee man who grabbed her wrist and pulled the ring from her hand. Then Travis yanked her hard toward the SUV.

The driver stared down at the ring in amazement. He was mumbling, "I can't believe it," over and over again as he turned it in his hand.

The big WWE fighter yanked open the back door. He pulled her in front of him to shove her in the seat. That's when she saw the opportunity, and she seized it. She picked her Converse-covered foot and brought it down as hard as she could on his black shiny dress shoe. He howled in pain. When he stepped back, she turned and, pulling her fingers in, she heel-palmed him right in his big, flat nose. She heard a crunch that almost made her gag. He bent forward and covered his face with his hand. She tried to push him back

160

and make her escape, but he was big and heavy and he stood his ground. She looked up at him, the blood from his nose seeping between his fingers, and he stared down at her. He looked to his hand that was full of his own blood. He raised his big, beefy fist up and she turned her face, ready to take the blow that would no doubt knock her out. Before she knew it, though, some shuffling noise had her looking back up.

Then there was Brady. He came at the big guy, shoulder down, and knocked him to the ground. They fell in a large heap, arms and fists flying. She looked over at Sydney. She was bringing her arm back; it looked like she had elbowed the beady-eyed Travis in the gut. Asa had seized the moment too, and he had brought a hard upper cut to Travis' face, knocking him down.

She turned back to Brady, just as he scrambled up off the big guy. He picked up the dropped gun and stood. He pointed down and fired.

The shot made her flinch. The noise was deafening in the small alley. It echoed off the brick walls. She watched as the big man went limp, and the blacktop behind his head turned red. She put her hands to her mouth; he was dead, and Brady had been the one to shoot him. But Brady ran to her and yanked on her arm, pulling her hands away from her face.

"We need to move," was all he said. She agreed, and on shaky legs followed him back to the front of the SUV. When she looked up, her blood turned ice cold.

The driver had Sydney. His fist was balled in her hair, her hat having been knocked off and laying at her feet. He was pulling her head back, exposing her neck, where the barrel of his gun was resting right under her chin.

Travis was lying on the ground either knocked out or dead—she didn't really know.

Asa was standing about ten feet away, pinning them to the wall of the alley. Travis' gun was in his hand, poised to shoot. Brady pulled her behind him and let go of her hand. He stepped up next to Asa, his gun directed at the driver. She took a step to the side; she wanted to see her sister. Wanted to make eye contact. Let her know that she was going to be okay. She was going to make sure she was, that she wasn't leaving without her. She watched as tears fell from her sister's wide, fearful eyes.

The driver looked over to the SUV. "Well, that sure is unfortunate. I liked Bruce. He was dumb, but a loyal man."

He rubbed his chin on the side of Sydney's head, his goatee catching her hair. Asa jerked forward, lifting the gun higher. She thought he was going to take a shot for a second, but he hesitated.

"Yeah, you don't want to do that. Might hit this pretty girl." The driver pushed his gun harder into Sydney's neck, making her groan in pain.

He was holding the gun with the same hand that had the large V-shaped scar; it was surprisingly bright in the dim alley light.

"I have the ring and one girl. I just need the other, and I won't kill any of you."

She looked to the driver's face. He looked right at her, his stare cold and demented. The hair on the back of her neck rose. This time Brady raised his gun and took a step closer.

Still looking at her, the man leaned into Sydney's ear. "He warned me. Said you black-haired witches would be beautiful. He said that you bewitched these men to protect you. They are, aren't they?"

He brought his tongue out, slowly licking the entire side of Sydney's face, his stare still on her. She felt the bile rise in her throat. Sydney tried to pull her face away, her eyes tightly shut, while she groaned in disgust.

Asa tensed and took two steps forward, gun held high. "Let her go or I will kill you," he said, his voice rough.

"No, you won't." The driver took the gun from under her chin and pushed it on her temple, twisting her head back more.

She couldn't help but let out a gasp. "Please stop." She stepped out from behind Brady.

"So, the other sister finally wants to play," he laughed.

He whispered something close to Sydney's ear. His eyes rested on the three of them standing in front of him.

Sydney's eyes widened and her face went deathly white.

But as the driver continued to whisper in her ear, something snapped in Sydney's pale face; it went hard, and her eyes focused.

Sydney's hand shot up grabbed the wrist holding the gun, and she pushed up with all her strength. The gun fired into the air over her head. She rolled out from under his arm; it opened up the front of his body and Asa took a shot. It hit the driver right in the shoulder, spinning him back and dropping the gun. He fell back on the wall, taking Sydney down with him, his hand still clutching her hair.

She fell to her side, the gun landing at her feet. She stretched out, grabbed the gun pointed up at the driver, and fired.

The black hole appeared right above his left eye. Blood and brain matter sprayed the concrete wall behind him.

The three of them ran to Sydney.

Asa made it first. He shoved his pistol into the small of his back, and he dropped to his knees next to her. Sydney's arm was still stretched out, the gun shaking in her hand. Asa slowly placed his hand on her trembling arm and gently brought it down. "It's okay. You're all right. I've got you," he whispered. He placed his arm around her shoulders, pulling her in close. The other hand slowly took the gun from hers. Still facing her, he swung his arm out. Holding the barrel of the gun out, Brady took it, and Asa wrapped his other arm around Sydney to pull her close. She buried her face in his chest and sobbed.

She didn't know what to do. She wanted to comfort Sydney, but Asa seemed to have it covered. He was softly talking to her, and she was nodding to him, obviously finding comfort in his words. She turned to Brady. He was putting one of the pistols in the small of his back. The other was still in his hand. He walked over to the beady-eyed Travis and took his pulse. He stood back up and pointed the gun down at his head. She looked at him; he wasn't the goofy-grinned tech genius she knew. He was the soldier. The man he kept hidden from everyone. The one he didn't talk about. His face was hard, his mouth drawn into a tight frown, his body rigid.

"Wait." She stepped up next to him. "Please don't. I don't think I can see another person die today." Brady turned his head over to her. His face was tight and his eyes were dark. He just stared at her, not really seeing her. She wanted to take a step back in fear, but she knew that the Brady, who had called her a tech queen and had kissed her on the backside of the truck, was in there. She wanted to tell him how, when he kissed her, she felt every muscle in her body both relax and tighten, how her need was overwhelming, and how, for the first time in her life, she felt real. But instead, she took a step forward and placed her hand on his arm. She slowly pulled it down.

"Please?" she whispered.

Brady blinked and let her guide his arm down. He turned and grabbed her in a fierce hug. "Are you okay, are you hurt?" He pulled her away, his eyes softening, and he started to examine her. He ran his hands down her arms and then turned her face, looking for injury.

"I'm fine."

He placed his hands on either side of her face. He kissed her hard and unforgiving. "Don't ever do that again. I have never felt that kind of fear before. I saw you walk toward that SUV. I thought I was going to lose you. All I could think about was how I was going to kill them and get you back."

She was speechless. He kissed her forehead roughly and then her cheek, then her mouth.

He pulled her in and held her close. "Don't ever do that again," he reiterated simply and just held her.

She let him and she felt safe again.

"Hey A!" Brady softly yelled over her head. "We have to go now. Someone would have called the cops by now."

She turned and saw Asa helping Sydney to her feet. He gently placed her hat back on her head. He then bent down and pulled the ring from the dead man's pocket.

Brady let her go and started to go through the pockets of the man on the ground, and she ran to grab their packs.

Brady pulled out an extra clip and shoved it in his pocket. She put one pack on her back and handed the other to Brady. Asa held Sydney close, and they made their way to the end of the alley.

"The bus station is about five more blocks north. You guys ready?" Brady looked around the corner of the building and took her hand.

Sydney

They made it to the bus station. Besides the sounds of sirens in the distance, they had no run-ins.

They went into the bus station with their heads down.

She and Roxy went to the restroom, claiming they needed to use it. But really, she needed a moment to rinse the blood from her hands and wash her face.

The guys were waiting by the door. The restroom was quiet. Only one of the stalls was occupied.

She went to the sink, and Roxy went into a stall. She splashed cold water on her face. She looked at her reflection. The low lighting and teal tiles of the bathroom gave her face a greenish look. Her eyes were wide and dark. She spotted blood splatter on her face; she grabbed a paper towel and scrubbed it. Had she really just killed a man? She scrubbed harder. She needed to get him off her. She scrubbed till her cheeks were red. She felt his tongue on her face, and she scrubbed some more. He had smelled like oregano, and it permeated her nose. She felt her stomach heave. She blew her nose into the paper towel. She threw it in the trash and splashed more water on her face. She tried to think of the way Asa had smelled when he was holding her. He smelled fresh, like a forest, and a hint of metal. It had cleansed her nose, and now she wished she could breathe him in again. She looked in the mirror.

What had her life come to?

The man had whispered how, in vile and torturous detail, he was going to rape Roxy and that he was going to make her watch. Her blood had run cold. Then, all of a sudden, it was like her fear disappeared, and she only saw red. Fueled by anger, she decided that wasn't going to happen. She just moved. She didn't think.

The memory of his words sent a shiver down her body. She looked at her tired face. She was just going to push them away, lock them in her mind, and never think of them again. She had to.

Roxy came out of the stall and walked to the other sink, watching her through the mirror.

"I'm okay. Stop looking at me that way." She felt foolish.

"I'm just worried." Roxy grabbed a paper towel and dried her hands.

She looked at her sister. She was glad it was her who had been grabbed and had pulled the trigger. She thought Roxy could probably handle it, but she didn't want her to have to live with the pain she now felt. She didn't want Roxy to have blood on her hands. She was too kind and gentle, and she wanted it to stay that way.

Roxy pulled her pack off her shoulder and pulled out a hairbrush. "Here, let me brush out your hair. It's a mess."

She turned and let Roxy do it. She was gentle, and the smooth strokes helped to calm her body.

The other stall opened, and a woman in a red suit came out to the sink. "Long trip?" she asked.

Both girls smiled and nodded. "Yeah, me too. You guys are lucky to have each other." The woman gave them a sad smile and left.

The slow strokes of the brush calmed her mind.

"I wouldn't want you walking around in public with your hair looking like this," Roxy said.

She looked at her sister in the mirror. Roxy was trying to cheer her up and make a joke.

"I love you, Rox," she said before she even realized it, and for a second, Roxy froze. She loosened just as quickly. "I love you too." She smiled.

"All right, I think you're acceptable for public display." Roxy zipped the brush back into her bag. "I'm glad you're okay." Roxy looked up from the pack. "I was so scared for you."

Sydney looked over at her brave sister. "You saved me. I saw you stomp that big guy's foot, and it motivated me to fight back." She had seen her gentle nerd sister take on a guy three times her size and was amazed.

She motioned for the pack, and Roxy turned. She pulled out a sweatshirt. She needed to hide the blood that had sprayed all over her T-shirt. She pulled it over her head. "Let's go before they storm in here looking for us."

The guys were standing outside the doors, and even though they were facing and staring at the bathroom, they were deep in conversation. They both stopped when the girls started to walk toward them.

"You guys look like creepers, staring at the women's bathroom," she said when they reached them.

Asa looked around. "Really?" She chuckled at his discomfort.

"We need ID to buy tickets." Brady readjusted his hat. She knew he disliked wearing it just as much as she did.

"We need to be careful." Asa scanned the area. "The Brotherhood will look here, knowing that this could be our only other option of leaving. We need to figure it out and get out of here."

The thought of the Brotherhood finding them again set her nerves on edge. She wanted to get back on the road fast.

She started to scan the bus station, ignoring what her group was discussing. People were either standing in line or gathered in small groups, waiting for their buses. She noticed a group of older women sitting on a bench. She could tell they were on vacation just by the way they were dressed. They had bright clothes in pink and purple along with big droopy hats and rhinestone visors. They were laughing and joking. One lady was sitting on the bench, her purse resting next to her. She saw several bus tickets hanging out of the side pocket.

"I have an idea," she said. Brady stopped talking, and they all looked at her.

"Well?" Brady said.

"I need some money."

"You have a way to buy tickets?" Asa shifted his stance.

"Kind of." She rolled her head back and forth. "In a so-so way."

"You're going to steal them?" Roxy said, looking around for the mark.

"Yeah, but I'll leave them with more than enough money to buy new ones."

No one said anything.

Frustrated by their uncertainty, she turned to Asa. "Can I please have some money?" She hated asking him that.

With a frown, he pulled out his wallet.

Roxy studied her. "If you want, I'll do it."

She looked at Roxy, who was studying her. Did she really look that bad? Maybe she hadn't gotten all of the blood off her face.

"I'm fine," she said, ignoring her thoughts.

"Where are you going to be?" Asa had concern on his face.

"I'll be right over there." She pointed to the group of women.

"I'll go with you. Brady, you and Roxy stay here. Keep a lookout."

Brady nodded. He placed his hand on Roxy's lower back and guided her over to the window.

Asa handed her several hundred-dollar bills. "Is that enough?" He looked in his wallet.

"I think so. You don't have to do this. I work better alone anyway."

He started down at her. She thought maybe she saw pity in his eyes. "Follow my lead," was all she said and she turned to walk to the ladies on the bench. Asa followed close behind.

She sat down next to the woman, and Asa sat down next to her and leaned back on the bench before placing his arm behind her along the backrest. He looked relaxed, but she knew he was nervous and didn't like her idea.

She scooted to the edge of the bench and pretended to adjust the leg of her pants; with sleight of hand, she picked the tickets and, in one swift move, turned to Asa and laughed at an unspoken joke. He looked at her in confusion. She gently slid the tickets out and placed them behind her back. She went to slip the money in and the woman moved.

"Excuse me?" Sydney said as she stuffed the bills into the purse. "Do you know what time it is?"

The lady looked over and smiled. She looked at her cheap gold watch. "Why, yes, dear. It's twelve-thirty."

"Thank you," she replied, a large smile on her face. She turned to Asa as she did and slid the tickets around to the front of her. She slipped them into the front pocket of her sweatshirt. She placed her hand on Asa's large thigh, and she felt his muscle give a slight jump. "You hear that, dear? It's twelve-thirty. We better go before we miss our bus. Asa stood quickly.

She stood and turned back to the lady. "I like your visor," she said. It was bright purple, with rhinestones all over the top.

"Thank you; I made it myself." The lady touched the top, feeling the small stones.

"It really sparkles in the fluorescent lights," she added. The woman smiled.

Asa held out his hand, still standing next to her. "Come on, dear." He emphasized the last word. "We don't want to miss our bus."

"Such a handsome couple you two make." The old lady was staring up at them. "You guys remind me of me and my Sherman fifty years ago." She had a reminiscent look on her face. "He passed away three months ago."

168

Her smile faded.

"I'm sorry to hear that." Asa softened his face. "Sorry for your loss."

The little old lady inhaled.

"That's why we're going on this trip. My friends say I need to get out of the house and have some fun. So, Atlantic City, here we come." The lady gave a half-excited wave of her hand.

Sydney's heart squeezed. Asa pulled her hand.

"Have fun and good luck," she shouted as Asa pulled her along.

"Thank you." The woman waved goodbye.

Heaviness settled over her. Guilt sank in.

Asa looked down at her. "You all right?"

"I feel bad," she stated. "That woman was nice and a widow. She was just trying to have fun with her friends."

He gave her hand a soft squeeze. "We'll have Brady find her address, and we will write her, explain our actions, and apologize. We'll make sure she is doing okay."

She was confused. She hadn't ever apologized for being a thief. But she had never felt this way about stealing either.

"I guess," she said, feeling unsettled and looking up at him. He gave her a smile. It was warm and just like when he held her after she shot that man. She started to feel at ease. He was still holding her hand, and she wanted to lean into his arm and just be.

"So, Atlantic City it is. What time do we leave?" he asked.

She took the tickets out of her pocket. There were five, and it made her feel worse knowing that they didn't need all of them.

"In twenty minutes." She handed them over to him.

Together, they went to find Brady and Roxy.

*

The bus was crowded. Apparently, Atlantic City was the place for Virginians to go. She and Roxy took their seats, and Asa and Brady sat behind them.

She made herself comfortable and watched out the window. She was looking for the Brotherhood's signature navy suits and evil smiles.

She hoped they hadn't even discovered their friends in the alley yet, and it would buy them some time.

169

Roxy shifted in her seat. "This is going to be a long ten hours."

Sydney sat back in her seat.

"There is only one break." When Sydney only stared, Roxy continued, "I'm tired of being on the road. I'm ready to be somewhere, you know?"

Sydney nodded in agreement and rested her head back. But in reality, she had been living like this for the past year. Not in fear, exactly, but on the road. She hadn't realized how tired she was of it. She was glad she wasn't alone. She patted Roxy's hand and gave her a smile. "Soon," was all she said.

The bus hissed and the doors closed. Sydney was tired; the adrenaline was wearing off, and she rolled her head back to the window. She sat straight up when she saw the woman whom they had stolen from. She and her four friends were surrounding what she assumed was an employee as he had a red-collared shirt and Bus Line embroider on the shoulder. The woman was holding her purse up and pointing to the bus. Sydney slid down in her seat, shame washing over her. She just ruined those women's vacation. She peeked over the window seal and saw the bus employee shrug his shoulders. The five women's body language all fell in disappointment. Their floppy hats literally drooped. She wanted to turn to Roxy for comfort but realized she had to take the blame for this one. She had never seen the aftermath of her theft, at least not from the people who didn't deserve it.

The bus jolted forward and her eyes teared up as she watched the women watch their bus pull away, her in their seats.

*

She was in a dark room, except for a single light hanging from the ceiling. In the middle was a body. She tried to walk to it but instead bumped into some kind of window or barrier that wouldn't let her get close. The person on the floor swung their head around and she saw Roxy's face. Her eyes went wide with fear, and she tried to get up. But Roxy's hands and feet were tied.

"Help me!" Roxy screamed. Then her head jerked the other way, like she heard something.

"Roxy!" she screamed, but Roxy didn't turn her head. She pounded on the invisible wall separating her from her sister. "Roxy!" she yelled again.

She still couldn't get through. Just then, a man walked in. His stride was slow and relaxed. When he looked up, she could see that it was the driver of the black SUV. His goatee was shiny in the light from the bare bulb above. He had a black hole going through his forehead and blood dripped from it. He knelt down over Roxy and ran his hand over her head. Roxy jerked but he only laughed.

"No, get away from her!" she yelled, pounding harder on the clear wall.

He slowly looked up, blood running down his neck. "I told you I would make you watch."

He lifted a long knife up over Roxy.

"Please don't," she pleaded. She dropped to her knees. "Please," she said again, begging, tears falling down her face.

He smiled, his mouth full of blood-soaked teeth. "We need both the black-haired witch's blood. Don't worry, you're next."

He brought the knife down fast and hard.

"No!" she jerked forward. Her hands came up. Instead of a clear barricade, it was a rough bus seat.

"Hey. Hey. You're okay." It was Asa. He was in the seat next to her and she remembered she was on a bus headed to Atlantic City.

Asa reached over and placed his hand on hers. "Hey, it was just a dream. You were sleeping."

She swung her head around, surveying her surroundings. When she was sure she was still on the bus, she looked up at him. "It was a nightmare." Panic filled her. "Where's Roxy?" She quickly scanned the bus again.

"She's sitting behind us with Brady. They wanted to talk about computers or something. You were sleeping."

She rubbed her hand over her face. She leaned back in her seat.

"You want to talk about it?" Asa asked.

She turned her head; he had turned his hat backward again which she took as a sign they were safe for the moment. His eyes showed genuine concern, and for a second, she did want to tell him. Tell him everything. Everything that she was feeling—everything that these last few days were making her feel. Making her question her life, making her scared for her sister's life, and those feelings that stirred within her when he looked at her like that.

"No," she said, defeated. She looked forward. She could handle it on her own.

"Does your dream have to do with today?" he asked.

She rolled her head and looked at him. "Yes, but I don't really want to talk about it yet."

Asa just nodded. "I get it."

"I was plagued with nightmares after my first time killing a man too. When Brady came back from Iraq, he had night terrors for months."

She looked at him, stunned. She forgot that Brady was in the war, with his fun, happy-go-lucky self. He made you think he didn't have a care in the world.

Then she remembered, both Brady and Asa had guns trained on the man holding her hostage. Brady had looked all the soldier then.

"Brady had therapy. My mother made him at least try it out. He did it for a while. Don't let his boyish good looks fool you. He has been through some scary stuff."

"Has he told you about it?"

"Not really; I got a few beers in him a while ago, and he started to tell a story. He clammed up halfway through." Asa frowned. "His therapist said he was progressing fine, and that some people just don't talk about stuff, and there is nothing wrong with it."

Asa copied her, and he rested his head back on the seat. "I find talking about it helps, gets if off your chest and out into the open. Sometimes I forget, though, and bottle it up."

"Will you tell me about your first time killing someone?" She found herself really interested and wanting to know more.

A sad smile crossed his face, and he looked at the back of the seat in front of him.

"I was a rookie in New York. It was early morning, and I only had an hour left on my shift; it had been a long, boring night and all I wanted to do was go home, drink a beer, and sleep. Then a call came to me and my partner—a domestic depute. I figured we'd go take care of it and then head home. We pulled up to this small house; it was in shambles, paint peeling, the roof sinking in on itself. My partner knocked on the door, and this small, five-year-old boy answered. He had blood all over the front of his blue footie pajamas. He looked me straight in the eye and said, "Help my mommy."

We drew our guns and entered the residence. The boy led us into the living room, where a woman was lying on the floor; both her eyes were swollen shut and she was covered in blood; my partner turned to call for an ambulance, but before he could get to his radio, a crazy-looking man rushed him from the hallway, taking him down. His shirt was covered in blood, his hair standing up, eyes wide; he raised a knife and went to bring it down on my partner's back. That's when I fired two shots, both right in the chest. The man fell back but didn't go down." Asa turned and looked at her. "I had to fire three more times before he stayed down. The ambulance came, and the woman and boy ended up okay, same with my partner. It turns out the man was a junkie high on crack cocaine and PCP. He had come to beg his ex-wife for money, and when she said no, he beat her.

Asa took a breath and looked at his hands.

"I was claimed a hero. I stopped the bad guy, saved the boy, his mother, and my partner." He paused again. "I didn't feel like a hero. For months, I had dreams of him coming back for me. Sometimes he killed me; sometimes he begged me to not to shoot. I told myself it was him or me. Him or the young boy. I don't think you ever really come to peace with it. But it gets easier."

She reached for his hand, needing comfort for herself and for him.

"I'm sorry that happened to you," she whispered.

"I'm sorry." Asa looked her in the eyes. "I'm sorry you had to shoot that man in the alley. I tried to get a shot on him. But I was so damn scared I was going to hit you. I should have gone for the head instead of his chest. Then you would never have had to pull that trigger."

She shrugged. "It happened, and we can't take it back. If it wasn't for your shoulder shot, he would never have let go of the gun, and I would never would have had the chance. It all worked out."

Asa frowned. "I really should have knocked the driver down first. Not that other guy. But I was panicking; the driver was so mesmerized by the ring I didn't even think he knew what was going on. I went after Travis because I didn't want you to get in that car."

She watched his face. He was frowning deeper than normal, and she was concerned that there was more to his thoughts than he was letting on. She was going to ask when she heard Roxy giggle and Brady laugh.

That's weird, she thought. She hadn't ever heard Roxy giggle like that. She had the urge to turn around and look.

"Are computers that funny?" she asked Asa.

"Yeah, I don't think they're talking about computers." Asa rolled his eyes.

She wanted to ask him what he meant when the bus driver announced a short, twenty-minute break and pulled over to let them out.

Roxy

When they finally arrived in Atlantic City, she was glad to be getting off the bus. When her feet hit solid ground, she stretched her whole body. She felt tight and stiff. Brady had entertained her through most of the ride and she was thankful for that. She had fun talking tech with him, and he promised he would show her a program he had designed that sounded very promising to the security of personal information on the web.

When they exited the bus, he had grabbed her hand. It wasn't the urgent have to escape handhold that she was used to, but the normal one, or so she thought; she had no real experience. Was she falling for him, or was she just nervous and scared? All she knew was that she wasn't feeling shy around him, and she was happy when he was near.

They made their way down to the main strip. They kept their hats and faces down. There was a ton of surveillance in this city, and they had to be careful.

She wasn't sure what time it was, but it was late, and they all decided to find a hotel for the night and make plans the next day. They found a pay-by-the hour motel that didn't ask for ID only a little way down the main strip. They were only able to get one room. They didn't care; they were all tired and just wanted to crash for the night. They even ignored the wink the desk clerk gave Brady and Asa when they were paying for the room.

They all took turns using the bathroom, and she fell into bed next to Sydney. She looked over and saw Asa already lying in bed, the covers halfway up. He had a T-shirt on with a large redwood tree down the front. His arms were behind his head, and he looked deep in thought. Brady was the last one down. He was only wearing a pair of boxers, and she couldn't help but notice his flat stomach and well-defined arms. She blew a frustrated breath out her nose. She was falling for him; she knew it now. She rolled over and faced the ceiling.

"I don't think we have slept in the same bed together since we were in middle school," Brady said, pulling the covers up on his bare chest.

"Who's the big spoon?" Sydney asked. She was the only one who laughed at her joke.

It only made Roxy picture Brady and her lying together, and she kicked the blankets off her feet restlessly.

"What's going on?" Sydney asked, turning her head around to see why she was being so fidgety.

"Sorry, I can't get comfortable." She sounded irritated, even to herself.

"Maybe she wants you to be the big spoon this time," Asa said.

"Funny," Sydney said dryly.

She heard Brady whisper something to Asa, and they both laughed.

When she had finally fallen asleep, she was awoken by Sydney.

She was kicking her arms and legs out.

"Syd?" She gently shook her.

She kicked out again.

"Sydney, it's me. You're okay." Sydney jerked up into a sitting position and looked around.

"Another nightmare," Sydney whispered. "I had the same one on the bus."

Sydney laid back down, and she cuddled closer; she took Sydney's arm, and just like when they were kids, she rested her temple on Sydney's temple.

"The Brotherhood had us, huh?" she asked.

"Yeah," was all Sydney replied.

"Were they hurting you or me?"

"You," she said with a hitch in her voice. "I couldn't get to you. There is, like, this invisible wall I can't break down. But this time I was pounding on the wall, and Cal came up behind me. He had a knife to my throat."

She grew quiet.

"Syd?" she said, making sure she was listening. "I think the four of us are going to make it to Maine, and I believe that we will be safe there. We are going to bring down the Brotherhood and bring Dad's murderer to justice; I just know it."

"I'm just glad we're not alone," Sydney said.

"Yeah," she whispered back. "Me too."

"I was thinking, there is no way that me and you would have made it this far by ourselves. I would be dead at the pawnshop and you at Margie's house."

She felt tears burn her eyes. "I know. But we can trust them. I just know

175

they will get us to Maine safely." She leaned closer to Sydney.

She heard someone roll over in the other bed, then all was quiet.

*

She awoke to the slam of the hotel door. Her eyes flew open, and she sat up. Asa standing by the door.

He cringed. "Sorry. My hands are full."

He was holding three coffees and a brown paper bag.

"What time is it?" She rolled over on her back.

"After ten," he said softly.

"I smell coffee." Sydney sat up against the headboard.

Asa walked over and handed them both the hot drinks. "I got muffins too."

Sydney frowned. "Drip?"

"It's all the lobby had."

"Thank you," Sydney said quickly, taking her coffee.

"We really slept in." She rubbed her eyes. "Where's Brady?"

"He's down in the lobby using the community computer station." Asa sat down on the end of his bed and sipped his coffee.

"Is he being safe? They're watching our accounts. I better go make sure." She swung her leg out from the blanket. She was running all the safeguards needed through her head when Asa held up his hand.

"He's got it, don't worry." He smiled at her.

She paused, her legs still hanging over the bed. "I guess he would." She sat back and swung the blanket over herself.

"So, what's the plan?" Sydney asked. She looked like she was enjoying drinking coffee in bed.

"He's looking at bus ticket sales. If we have to steal some, we want to make sure they go straight to Maine. We are only about eight hours from Granny's house. He's also looking for cars for sale in the area. Cash only sales."

Roxy thought about their situation. The Brotherhood was watching them. They were monitoring technology.

"They know that we're heading to Maine," she realized, not really saying it to anyone.

Asa stood. "Yep. We've been thinking about that too. If they're smart, which we know they are, they will be watching the state lines and watching Granny's house too." He paced. "We'll most likely come across them again." He stopped pacing and looked to them lying in their bed, frowning.

The thought had her stomach in knots, and the coffee she was drinking threatened to come back up. She put it down on the nightstand.

Sydney continued to sip hers. "Then we will have to be ready," she stated simply.

"We're working on it." Asa still wore his frown as he studied Sydney.

The burner phone in his pocket rang, and he pulled it out. "It's Brady."

"What's up?" he answered.

He walked toward the door on the other side of the room, mumbling. She had a hard time hearing.

Sydney patted her hand. "We'll be okay. Remember what you said last night. I believe you're right."

She nodded at her sister, but she was starting to doubt her own words.

"I don't know, man," she heard Asa say into the phone. "I know, I know, no pressure, right?"

She wondered what they were talking about.

"Fine." Asa hung up the phone.

He started to dig in one of the bags and pulled out the third gun. He dropped the clip, checked it, and then slammed it back in. He pulled the slide, making it snap, then handed it toward them handle out.

"I have to go meet Brady. It won't take long. But just in case."

Sydney reached over her and took the gun. "I got this." She placed it on her lap. She did notice that Sydney's hand shook slightly.

"It's loaded and ready," Asa added.

She picked it up and placed it on the nightstand facing the opposite wall.

"I'll text every fifteen minutes on your phone. If you don't answer back, I'll know something is wrong. So, text back." Sydney got up and took the phone out of the front pocket of her bag. She held it up to him to let him know she had it.

"Three knocks before I come in. Please don't shoot me." He grinned. Sydney smiled back. "I won't if you come back with a nonfat, sugar-free vanilla latte." Sydney smiled.

Asa shook his head but had a smile. "Smartass." He turned and left.

The door shut quietly this time.

"I hope everything's okay?" she said.

"Me too." Sydney looked over at the gun.

She hoped Sydney wasn't thinking about yesterday.

"Syd? What do you think of Brady?"

Sydney looked confused. "What do you mean? He's great, they both are."

"Like, I mean…" She didn't really know how to phrase it. "I mean, we kissed." She paused and looked at Sydney who was staring back at her.

"More than once." She smiled. She couldn't help it.

"What? When?" Sydney shuffled in the bed and faced her. "Tell me."

"The night at the motel when we took the garbage out. And then at the rest stop in Tennessee, while you and Asa were practicing self-defense. On the side of the truck."

Sydney smiled. "You harlot. I love it. In fact, I think it's great. You guys are pretty perfect for each other. Computer nerds and all."

Roxy grinned and felt herself blush. "Really? You think so?"

"Yes, now tell me everything."

She did. It felt so good to talk to her sister about it. Sydney asked questions and gave advice. They were laughing and joking.

The burner phone beeped, and Sydney checked it.

She texted him back, and when she was done, she tossed the phone on the bed.

"You know, the night in the motel," Sydney started. "Asa almost kissed me too. We were interrupted by you guys busting through the door."

"You did? What happened?" She leaned forward, eager to continue the girl talk.

Sydney told her what happened.

"I'm sorry," she said. "I had no idea."

Sydney shifted on the bed. "I don't get him. One minute he is hugging and comforting me or flirting, and the next he is so serious and distant."

"How do you feel about him?" she asked.

"He is very good-looking. But I don't know." Sydney pulled her hair out of her ponytail and ran her fingers through it.

She thought about what Asa had told Brady.

"Asa told Brady to be careful when it came to me. He said that we were in a high stress situation and that our feelings can get muddled."

"What did Brady do after?" Sydney asked.

"We made out on the back side of the Suburban." They both laughed.

"Brady said he knew what he wanted." Her heart swelled in her chest.

*

They both took showers and got halfway through a Lifetime movie when they finally heard the three knocks on the door.

"Don't shoot. It's us."

The two of them came in. They were both carrying multiple shopping bags.

"What, you went shopping without us?" Sydney whined.

Roxy was sure she was only half-joking.

Asa dropped several bags on the bed. "These are for you guys."

"What?" Sydney jumped up to check them out. She pulled out a gold dress. "This is beautiful." She held it up and examined it.

"The other one is for Roxy." Asa was looking at Sydney, admiring the dress. He looked pretty pleased with himself. Maybe there was something more going on there than Sydney thought, she considered as she watched them.

"Hey, this was my idea," Brady laughed. "We thought we would all go out to the casino across the street from here."

She began to object. But Brady started again. "I already checked out their security; it's completely an in-house private server. Not hackable. Trust me, I had to prove it to this guy." He pointed his thumb at Asa.

"How did you get this stuff?" Sydney asked, pulling matching gold heels from the bag as well.

"The hotel manager here is dating the dress shop owner down the street. He had her pick out dresses and shoes, and we even had her throw some hair clips and makeup in there." Brady looked equally as pleased as his cousin.

"We got ourselves something too," Asa said. "Plus, another room right next door. "We thought you girls could have more room."

"What about our plans for tomorrow?" she wondered.

"I have a couple leads on people heading to Maine with bus tickets, but nothing close to Granny's house. There is a car for sale on the other side of town. But they can't meet till tomorrow afternoon. We are kind of at a standstill right now. We all need to relax and blow off steam. Yesterday was

179

tense." Brady looked over at Sydney, studying the dress, then he looked at Roxy. "I think we will be safe; they won't expect us to go in public, let alone know we're here."

"Dad always said the best scams were the ones right under your nose," Sydney said. "I think it's great. We can drink and gamble all of Asa's cash."

Brady laughed. "I like your style."

They ordered takeout and had it delivered. Even though Asa and Brady had gotten another room, they all stayed in the girls' room and had a late lunch together. If Brady made a flirty comment, Sydney would smile at her.

She noticed that Asa often side-glanced Sydney and stayed near her. She didn't even think he knew he was doing it.

When it got to be late afternoon and the end of the second Lifetime movie, Asa and Brady left to go get ready.

"We'll be back over in two hours. Is that enough time?" Asa asked.

"It should be," Sydney said.

How long does it take to get ready? she thought.

After they left, Sydney pulled out an old hair straightener from under the bathroom sink.

"This might have lice, but we are going to straighten your hair and curl mine.

"Have you seen the dress they got you?" Sydney walked over to the bag. She pulled out a tight black silk dress. It was long and strapless.

"You're going to look so good," Sydney said as she smiled and laid the dress on the bed.

Sydney

They showered again, and she sat Roxy down on the floor in front of the mirror in the main room. She started to straighten her short, black hair.

"You think we are really going to run across the Brotherhood before we get to Maine?" Roxy watched her in the mirror.

"Most likely." She pulled the straightener down a lock of Roxy's hair.

"Why are you so calm about it? I'm freaking out." Roxy's face was stressed.

"I'm freaking out too. But, just like you said, we're going to make it. We all will play it safe, and we will do what we have to." She thought of yesterday. She was never going to let them touch her or her sister ever again, no matter what.

"We have to finish this," she added.

"What if they find us tonight in the casino? You really think this is a good idea?" Roxy twitched when she accidentally pulled her hair.

"I think it's a great idea. They won't find us here. They don't know where we are. I don't think Asa would agree if he thought that we were in danger. Plus, these dresses are gorgeous, and I haven't dressed up in a long time. No more worrying."

Roxy still had a frown on her face.

"Wait till Brady sees you tonight. You're going to look so hot. It'll drive him crazy." She laughed.

Roxy smiled. "You think so?"

When she finished Roxy's hair and did her make-up, she realized that she had never seen Roxy with eyeliner, and she looked beautiful. She curled her own hair and put a cute gold pin she had found in the bag on one side to hold it back.

After she did a little make-up, since that was all there was, she slipped the dress on. It was soft, and it fit her perfectly. It rested easily on her curves. She ran her hand down her flat stomach and admired the dress. It had thin straps, and the bottom reached to mid-shin. There was a slit that ran all the way up one leg to her mid-thigh. She strapped her foot in the gold stilettos.

They made her feel tall, and her legs looked long; it made her smile.

"Can I get some help?" Roxy was trying to pull up the zipper on the back of her dress.

She walked over to help. Roxy turned around.

"Dang, you look like a supermodel." She spun Roxy around.

She really did. The black strapless dress was tight. It went just pass her knees. It was a dress only Roxy, with her slim, straight figure, could pull off.

"I feel stupid," Roxy huffed out. "We are going to be so overdressed."

"Hey, it's better to be overdressed than underdressed. Besides, you look amazing."

She handed Roxy her shoes. They were black, strappy, and had a wide, low heel. "It's like the lady at the shop knew you couldn't walk in high heels." Roxy slipped them on and started to walk around the room.

She decided they were ready, picked up the flip phone, and texted Asa.

He immediately texted back that they were in the hall at the vending machine.

"Let's go. They're in the hall." She grabbed the room key.

"Are you sure I don't look stupid?" Roxy awkwardly pulled on her dress.

"Only when you do that," she said and opened the door.

She saw them about halfway down the hall. Asa was wearing gray pants with a gray vest and white button-up; he had the sleeves rolled up to his elbows and the collar open. His hair was slicked back, and he had trimmed his beard.

Brady was in black pants with a jacket that looked tailored just for him. His hair was combed to the side, and his face was freshly shaven. With his glasses, he looked like a sexy bookworm.

The guys turned when they heard the door shut, and they both stared. She noticed Brady's eyes never left Roxy, and she smiled. Her sister was beautiful. She watched as Asa slapped Brady on the back and grinned.

He looked to her, his grin turning to a soft smile. She couldn't help it and smiled back.

"Damn, you girls look great," Asa said.

"You guys clean up nice too," she said, looking them up and down.

Brady grabbed Roxy's hand and spun her around. Surprisingly, Roxy spun and blushed. "Beautiful," was all Brady said.

182

They walked out of the hotel and into the street. A sense of panic set in as they made their way to the crosswalk. Standing there, waiting, she found herself close to Asa. Roxy was holding Brady's hand, and she, too, stayed close to him. There were people everywhere. She studied faces as they also stood for the light to change. She found herself looking for the navy-blue suits the Brotherhood all wore.

When the light changed and they started to cross, Asa took her hand, and she was grateful. She didn't let go.

They entered the casino, and they all decided to head to the bar. They sat down in the corner booth. She noticed that the casino was pretty empty, and she was glad. There were mainly older couples and a few younger people milling around. Roxy was right that they were overdressed, but she didn't care. Normally, she would be scoping the place out. If they needed money, this place would be easy picking. The thought of the widow at the bus station popped into her head, and she wondered if she made it to Atlantic City all right. Guilt slipped in until the waitress came over and distracted her from her thoughts. They ordered their drinks. When the waitress placed her hand on Asa's shoulder as she left, she tried to ignore the little bit of jealousy that crept in.

"So, any ideas on how we are going to get to Maine?" Roxy asked, looking around the table.

Brady placed his hand on Roxy's and lightly rested it there. "No talk of Maine, the Brotherhood, or the ring tonight. Just fun." He smiled at her.

Roxy took a deep breath.

"Everything will be okay," Brady said, giving her a reassuring smile.

The waitress showed up and delivered their drinks. When Asa paid, she saw how the waitress's fingers lingered on his. She glared up at her and cocked her head. The waitress glared back and turned to leave.

Asa saw her face, and he put his arm around the back of her seat. He leaned over and whispered in her ear. "Someone just got a little jealous."

"No," she immediately answered, flicking her hair over her shoulder. But Asa just laughed and pulled her in closer.

She caught his familiar forest smell, and her nerves tingled and her shoulders relaxed. She leaned in.

She looked toward Roxy, who had a smug smile as she took a sip from her straw.

She rolled her eyes; just because Roxy was all lusty didn't mean she was too.

"Let's go walk around," she suggested.

They took their drinks and circled the small casino. It was old, but still had some charm.

They came across some slot machines. "I've never played slots before." Brady sat down at one. "Been wondering if these things have a pattern."

Roxy sat next to him. "I hear they have to pay out so much every month. That means the machine most likely has to have some kind of method. It can't be totally random."

Brady put in a hundred dollars and did a small bet. He won a dollar fifty, and he spun again. He was staring at the screen, his eyes darting back and forth.

"Is he trying to memorize the reels?" She leaned in to Asa while she looked toward Brady.

"He'll be here all night." Asa rolled his eyes. "You want to ditch them and head for some cards?"

She nodded, excited to play, or maybe it was to have some alone time with him.

"Brady, we're going to check out the tables."

Brady didn't even look up. "Yep, we will meet up with you guys later."

She looked to her sister. Roxy just nodded and took a hundred-dollar bill that Brady was handing her and put it in the slot machine in front of her.

"Don't leave his side," she said, placing her hand on Roxy's shoulder.

"I won't." Roxy was studying her machine too.

"I bet," she mumbled under her breath as she and Asa turned to leave.

As they walked away, Asa held out his arm, and she took it. They found the card games toward the back and took a seat at a deserted table; it was blackjack. Margie had taught her and Roxy how to play. She thought about how they used to bet with pretzels and popcorn. She smiled to herself.

Asa exchanged cash for chips and handed them to her. "What are you thinking?" he asked. "You've got a smile on your face."

"Margie taught me and Roxy how to play." She put a chip down in front of her. The dealer passed out the cards.

"Margie seems like she was a good lady." Asa tapped the table for a hit.

"She was, and I miss her. I regret the last couple of years, though. I should have called more." She held out her hand to stay. She had a queen showing and an eight face down.

"How come?" Asa busted and he threw his hands up. She laughed. The dealer had seventeen, and she collected her winnings.

"I don't really know. I guess I was angry. I wanted to get out on my own. I kind of ditched Roxy and Margie. Too many bad memories." She stopped and looked over at him. "I think I knew that they wouldn't approve of what I was doing this last year."

Asa only shook his head. He placed another bet.

She placed another one also. *Had she just said that out loud? It was true, too,* she thought. She told herself that she was doing a good thing. But if she was doing a good thing, why did she hide it from the two people she loved? The last year, she went as far as avoiding phone calls and bailing on holidays.

"You want to hit or stay?" She looked up from her thoughts. She had forgotten where she was and what she was doing. She glanced down, saw a five, and quickly checked the other card. It was a two.

"Hit." She brought her thoughts back to the present. When the next card was an ace, she stayed.

When the dealer busted, she held out her hand to Asa for a high five. They slapped hands.

"You want another drink?" he offered.

"Yes, please."

He waved a waitress over and ordered for the both of them.

They played for a good hour. Every time they won, they high-fived. When they lost, they bumped shoulders, saying next time.

When Asa doubled down, she grabbed his arm in anticipation, holding on tight. When he won five hundred dollars, she jumped up in celebration. He grabbed her face and planted a loud, smacking kiss on her mouth. "My lucky girl!"

She tried not to blush.

They played a couple more hands, and he kept winning. She took her chips off the table and instead stood next to him cheering him on. Right before the dealer laid his cards down, Asa would grab her hand and kiss the top for luck. When the dealer busted, he would wrap his arm around her waist and pull her in for a tight squeeze. He finally seemed happy and relaxed.

She noticed that a crowd had formed around the table, and people were joining the game or standing back to watch. The table got loud. Asa hit twenty-one, and everyone cheered.

"That's my favorite number," a low voice behind her said.

She looked over, and standing next to her was a man. He was dressed in black slacks and a black sweater. He had a large grin and he winked.

She shuddered. The image of Cal crossed her mind, and her heart skipped a beat and her skin prickled with fear. She went to sidestep away from him, but in her quick movement, her ankle rolled in the high stilettos, and she stumbled. The man reached his hand out and grabbed her arm. Panic swept through her and she balled her fist, ready to swing. Asa stood up instantly, almost knocking over his stool. He stood behind her and gently pushed her fist down, looking around in confusion. She could feel the heat coming off him against her back and she relaxed.

The man still had her arm. "What's going on?" Asa asked.

She took a step back into him as she tried to tug her arm free.

The man looked up at her and let her arm go. "Hey man, she tripped. I was just helping her."

She turned and faced Asa, burying her face in his chest and trying to forget the image of Cal's wicked grin and the man's sweaty hand on her bare arm. Asa wrapped an arm around her back. "It's cool, man. I got her."

Everyone at the table saw what was going on. Some stared while others backed up, wondering if a fight was going to break out. Asa looked at the crowd nervously. He then turned and grabbed his chips. He slipped a large tip to the dealer and, turning away from the table, he guided her away. He took her hand and pulled her close. "What happened? Are you okay?"

"Sorry." Her heart was still pounding. "That was embarrassing. All he did was smile at me, that's all, and he reminded me of… Cal." She felt like she had to spit out his name. "Am I going crazy?"

"We should go back to the hotel. Maybe this was too much, too soon."

"No," she said, stopping mid-stride. "I was just being stupid. Let's go back to the bar and get another drink."

He gave her a strained look and then he nodded. "Are you sure?"

"I'm fine." He stared into her eyes. Without saying anything, he took her hand, and they headed back to the bar where the four of them had started their night.

When they got there, they stood in line. There was music playing now by a DJ, and people were on the dance floor. It was older music, and the dancers were all of the older generation. She watched as a white-haired man spun a white-haired lady. They came back together fast, and he held her tight as they swayed to the fast pace.

It looked like they were having fun.

Asa had ordered for her as she watched, and he handed over her gin and tonic. They took a seat at a small table in front of the dance floor, and she continued to watch people dance.

After about two songs, the DJ took a break. The room grew quiet except for low conversation.

"Are you sure you're okay?" Asa rolled his glass of whiskey on ice on the table. "You looked pretty scared back there."

"I'm fine." She looked over at him, noting the stress and tension back on his face.

"You know, I was just thinking how good it was to see you smile and relax. Then I have to go and get freaked out, and now you're back to being serious again." She pouted. "I want the happy Asa back."

"You went so pale. That guy had his hand on you and…" His voice trailed off.

"What?" she wanted to know.

"I got scared."

She laughed. "You, scared? I've seen you serious and in fight mode. But you never seem scared."

"It seems ever since I met you, all I have been is scared." He looked down at his glass.

Her heart fluttered a little.

"You seem to always get yourself in trouble." He picked up his glass and took a sip.

She leaned forward over the table. "And you always seem to be there to save my butt." She smiled at him. Her voice softened. "You're like my hero."

He jerked back, surprised or confused; she couldn't tell in the low lighting.

"Just trying to do the right thing." He looked back over to the dance floor, watching the DJ getting ready to start the music again.

She didn't know what to think of his comment, but she had meant hers. He was the only person who had made her truly feel safe, at least since her dad, and that was a long time ago.

"I think you're doing great."

He frowned, not looking away from the DJ. "Like I told you, I took an oath to protect and serve."

Now it was her turn to frown. That wasn't what she wanted to hear. But she let it go. The room filled with music again and the dance floor slowly filled once more. They watched.

The next song started; it was a slow melody. She stood up and walked over to his side of the table. "Would you like to dance?" She held out her hand.

Asa shook his head. This time he did look a little scared. "I don't dance," he said.

"Come on, it's a slow song. You don't have to do much." She kept her hand out.

The man sitting at the table behind Asa leaned over. He was wearing a flowered Hawaiian shirt with the top two buttons open, revealing his white chest hair. "When a pretty girl like that asks a man to dance, he dances."

She smiled a huge grin. "Yeah!" she said, agreeing with the stranger.

Asa threw his arms up. "You're right." He looked from the older man back up at her. "Only an idiot would say no." He got up slowly, taking the last gulp of his drink. She pulled him out to the dance floor, but he looked like a man walking to the gallows.

She faced him. He grabbed her hand and placed the other on her waist. Putting her hand on his shoulder, they started to sway slowly.

After a moment, he spoke.

"Did I tell you how beautiful you look tonight?" He looked down at her.

"I don't think so?" Her stomach fluttered.

"You look absolutely beautiful."

She smiled. It felt amazing to be in his arms. Not because he was comforting her after she shot a man or running for her life. But in a fun, relaxed atmosphere.

"Thank you."

He leaned in. She stilled. Then he dipped her back with one arm. She laughed the whole way back and when he pulled her forward, he slid his free hand down to the slit in the dress and ran his hands up her leg and back to her waist. He leaned in, his mouth close to her ear, and said, "I've wanted to do that since I saw you walk down the hall back at the hotel."

She felt heat run through her body. She turned looked into his smiling face. He was handsome.

"I like it when you smile," she said shyly.

He twirled her and brought her back. His grin grew even bigger, and he pulled her close. She laid her head on his shoulder and he placed his cheek on the side of her forehead. Her heart pounded and she wondered if he could feel it through her chest. They didn't talk; they just swayed to the music. Then the song ended. Everyone was exiting the floor. He pulled back and, to her disappointment, led her off the dance floor.

They sat down and she took a sip of her drink as she watched a group of women shake their butts to fast music. She giggled and started to feel tiredness seep in, though she tried to ignore it. She didn't want the night to end. When it ended, it meant they were back to planning and preparing for their escape to Maine. She looked away from the group of women and saw Asa sitting back in his chair, his legs crossed at the ankle, looking relaxed. He was scanning the crowd.

A man about her age walked up and held his hand out to her. "Would you like to dance?" he asked. He had on tight jeans and an even tighter blue tank top. She didn't want to and, feeling even more drained from this man's unwanted attention, she declined.

"Whatever." He looked over to Asa. "How much did this one cost you?" Asa stood up quickly, his fists balled tight. "What did you just say?"

"Whoa man, chill." The young man jumped back, fear evident in his eyes.

She stood and rushed to Asa. The last thing they needed was Asa going to jail. "Hey, let's go." She placed her hands on his chest and gave him a little shove. He didn't even budge. His stare was on the man. He looked dangerous. She tried to get his attention.

"Don't disrespect her," Asa boomed.

"Come on, Asa, take me back to the room. I'm tired." She ran her hands down his chest. She snagged the V of his vest and pulled him toward her. He finally looked down at her, but then he looked back up at the man who was stupid enough to still be standing there.

"Say you're sorry." Asa leaned forward.

She turned and watched the man back up. "Sorry," he said flatly. He finally walked away.

"Prostitute," she huffed out. Watching him walk away. "He wouldn't even be able to afford me." She heard Asa give a throaty laugh. She turned to face him, ready to tell him she wanted to go back.

"You would be expensive," he said and stepped closer to her. He stared down at her. She felt heat run through her.

He leaned in and softly kissed her shoulder right where it met her neck. Without realizing it, she immediately tilted her head and exposed her neck to him; his breath was warm and she smelled a hint of whiskey, her eyes closing. He kissed her again this time further up her neck, and every nerve in her body lit on fire. He kissed again a little further up, close to her ear. and she all but moaned. He tilted his head up and she felt his beard rub roughly across her skin, igniting another fire. She opened her eyes and saw a smile on his face. He stepped back. She was still trying to catch up.

"Ready to go?" His voice was low.

"Yes," she stammered. He took her hand.

They made their way out of the casino and out to the street. There were more people out after dark.

The cool night air felt good on her overheated skin. When they stopped at the crosswalk, he let go of her hand and placed his arm around her shoulders and pulled her in close. "You smell like warm flowers," he said into her ear.

"That's just hotel shampoo." She was still uneasy after what had just happened. Her body was on high alert, and she was aware of every part of him that was touching her.

They were waiting for the crosswalk to change to green, when she heard a buzz. Asa used his free hand to pull out his phone. "It's a text message from Brady." He flipped it open. "Well, I'll be damned." He gave a short, loud laugh.

"What? Is everything okay?" she asked, worry bringing her out of the Asa-induced coma he seemed to put her into.

"Everything is fine. Brady and Roxy are already back at the room."

Good, she thought and relaxed as they crossed the street.

They walked up to her door. She knocked three times to alert Roxy that it was just them.

"I don't think you need to do that. They're in the other room."

"Oh." She was a little surprised, but she pulled the key card out of her bra and swiped it.

Asa's eyebrows shot up in surprise.

She just smiled up at him and continued into the room, Asa right behind her. He sat down on one of the beds and started to kick off his shoes. "I guess we're roomies tonight," he said.

"What?" She was confused and her stomach clenched.

"Where is Roxy going to sleep?"

He looked over at her, his eyebrows high, his chin low.

It slowly dawned on her, and she gave a laugh. "Go Roxy. That was the text, huh?" She puffed out her chest and did her best man impression. "Hey brother, getting laid tonight, get lost."

Asa laughed. "Pretty much."

She walked over to the table and used it for balance as she slipped her shoes off. She sighed when she set her toes free.

"You know you did the same thing. The first time I saw you?" He was still sitting on the bed when she turned to look at him. His face was tense and he was staring at her.

Her skin flashed hot.

She took a step toward him. "Thank you for the dress."

His eyes darted up to her face. "You're welcome."

He looked nervous and it made her brave.

She took another step closer. "It fits perfectly." She tilted her head and ran her hands down her sides.

Asa went to stand up but she placed her hands on his shoulders. She leaned in and softly kissed his lips. They were warm and tasted of whiskey.

She slowly pulled back. His gray eyes slowly opened. "We shouldn't do this," he whispered.

"Why?" She leaned in again. This time Asa didn't let her kiss him, he kissed her. It was hard and fast. His hands went to her hips and he pulled her onto his lap. She straddled him and wrapped her arms around his neck. He broke away again and this time he moved his face into her neck, kissing a line down.

"I need to keep focused," he whispered against her collarbone. He slowly started to kiss up the other side of her neck. "I need to get you safely to Maine," he lightly said into her ear. Pushing her hair back and gripping it in his fist, he stopped, his mouth hovering over hers. She lost her thoughts and moaned his name.

A growl formed deep in his throat. In a fast and rough single move, he cupped her bottom, and with a firm grip he stood. She wrapped her legs around his mid-section and pulled him in for a deeper kiss. Her body was responding like nothing she had ever experienced. She desperately wanted his hands all over her.

He turned and laid her on the bed. She let her head fall back and she looked up at him. He stood over her. His eyes were tense and clouded, his body rigid. He looked sexy and capable. She smiled; she couldn't help it. She liked that she put that intensity on his face. It made her feel sexy and powerful.

"Come here," she said softly.

He let out a breath he was holding and slowly leaned over her; she reached up for his face and brought her lips to his slowly.

He reached back behind him and without breaking their kiss, he grabbed the bottom of her dress and slid it up, dragging his rough hands up her leg. When he reached her panties, he slipped his finger under the elastic band and started to pull them down. Her breath hitched. She was already unbuttoning his vest. Then he stopped. He pulled his lips away.

She opened her eyes. He was frowning.

"What is it?" Fear sprung into her chest.

He jumped up and looked to the door. Then she heard it too. A light scraping noise outside. She sat up on her elbows and saw shadows moving under the door.

"It could just be Brady or Roxy." She sat fully up.

"They would have knocked." He crept over to the door and looked through the peephole.

"Shit." He took three long strides back from the door and grabbed her arm, pulling her toward the window. He threw back the curtains and tried to pull the window open. It didn't move.

"Shit," he said again. "Get your shoes on." He grabbed the flip phone from his pocket.

She went to the other side of the bed and found her ankle boots. She slipped them on, and when she noticed Roxy's Converse, she grabbed those too.

Asa was pacing back and forth, the phone to his ear. "Come on." His voice was rough and stressed.

"Thank God." He ran a hand through his hair resting on the back side of his head. She heard Brady give a short mumble on the other side of the phone; he didn't sound happy. "They're here."

She heard the door handle lightly turn, but when the person on the other side realized that it was locked, it turned back slowly.

Asa had pulled his gun from the small of his back. With the phone between his ear and shoulder, he raised it with both hands.

"Check your door," he whispered.

The shadows under the door shifted. Not knowing what else to do, she grabbed her backpack and started throwing her and Roxy's belongings into it. Brady said something on the other end and Asa looked to her and just shook his head no. "Leave it."

She started to shake. With nothing else to do, she moved closer to Asa.

"No, that's a horrible idea." He paused. "Thirty seconds." He snapped the phone shut. He looked through the peephole again and turned. "Stay behind me."

"What are you going to do?" Her voice shook.

He held up his finger to his lips, then he looked through the peephole again.

She heard a yell, then Asa swung the door open, stepped into the hallway with his gun raised, and fired.

Roxy

Her body felt completely relaxed and totally alive. She rolled over to face Brady. His arms were wrapped loosely around her waist. He looked over and smiled. He wasn't wearing his glasses, and she found that he looked just as sexy without them. This night was turning into the best night of her life, and it had only just begun.

As soon as Asa and Sydney left them at the slot machines, the attention Brady had been paying to the machines turned and focused on her. He had kissed her desperately, like a man drowning. She had sunk into his arms. Forgetting that they were in public, she moaned on his lips. When he broke the kiss, he didn't pull away but held her close. "You're the most beautiful person I have ever met," he whispered.

She smiled, feeling the blush sweep over her cheeks. He placed his hand behind her head and pulled her face to the side. His mouth close to her ear, his breath warm on her neck, she tried to breathe.

"Will you go back to the room with me?"

"Yes," she breathed out slowly.

He pulled back softly. He wasn't smiling; his face was serious and intense. The hand behind her head moved to her cheek, and the pad of his thumb caressed her there tenderly. He smiled then. Without saying a word, he took her hand and led her to the exit.

*

"What are you thinking about?" Brady asked, bringing her back to the present. "I can hear the gears turning in that wonderful brain of yours."

She smiled. "You," she said simply.

"I like that." He wrapped his arms around her and rolled her onto his chest. Looking down on him, she pushed his light hair from his face.

"Did you really text Asa?" she asked.

"Yep, he will be staying with Sydney tonight. So, it's just you and me all night, alone." He smiled on the last word.

She wondered if that was okay with Sydney. Sydney had mixed feelings when it came to Asa. Brady saw the thoughts on her face.

"Stop worrying about your sister," Brady said. "Asa will be with her. She's safe. Plus, the way I saw the two of them look at each other tonight, they will be having just as much fun as we are."

"You think so? I thought Asa had doubts about getting involved with… you know." She paused, looking for the right word. "Not letting emotions muddle the mind."

He laughed. "I'm pretty sure his mind is muddled tonight."

She smiled. She liked the idea of Sydney and Asa.

"I love it when you smile." Brady leaned in and kissed her. She was excited. She and Brady together alone, all night. She deepened the kiss.

She heard the buzz of the phone on the nightstand. She tried to pull away, but Brady just ignored it, not wanting to stop.

She laughed. "If he's calling, it's probably important. Brady let his head drop back down on the pillow.

He stretched his arm up and grabbed the phone.

"What?"

Brady's face quickly changed from soft and relaxed to the hard soldier, causing fear to slam into her. He moved to get out from under her, and she let him roll away. He grabbed his glasses off the table.

Naked, he ran to the door and looked out the peephole. "I got no one here," he said into the phone.

He turned back and started to pull on his pants. He looked up to her and said, "Get dressed now."

He went to his backpack, pulled on a white T-shirt, and pulled the black pistol from his bag, stuffing it into his belt.

"I'll make a distraction," he said into the phone. "Then come out and shoot them."

She found her dress in a pile on the floor. She was struggling with the zipper in the back but froze when she heard what he said.

"It's all we got." He walked over and zipped the dress the rest of the way.

"Give me thirty seconds. Hey, Asa," he paused and looked down at her, "don't miss."

He hung up and shoved the phone in his pocket. He slipped on the jacket he had been wearing that night.

She followed him to the door. "What's going on?"

"Stay in front of me." He took a deep breath, pulled the gun from his belt, and swung the door open. He jumped out and yelled, "Hey!"

He grabbed her hand and whipped her out the door. He immediately swung her in front of him and down the hall, pushing her to run.

She heard a gunshot. Brady fell on top of her, throwing her to the floor. His weight was crushing her.

Did Brady just get shot? She tried to roll out from under him, but he had her pinned. She heard several more shots. Brady whipped up and spun to look behind him.

She rolled just in time to see Brady hold the gun up and fire. She watched as Asa ducked, and a man in a navy suit behind him fell, his chest spraying blood. She saw two more lying in the hall between them and Asa.

Sydney shot out the door. She looked both ways, her face pale.

She looked to Asa, who only nodded, and she ran toward them. "Roxy, are you okay? Brady?"

Roxy looked to Brady, searching for a gunshot wound. "Are you shot?"

Brady stood quickly and reached down to help her up. "Nah, I knew Asa had them. Are you okay? I took you down pretty hard."

"Fine," she said as Sydney reached them, searching her for wounds. Asa followed.

The door down the hall opened, and a man in a bathrobe stuck his head out. He saw them at the end of the hall. His eyes went wide, and then he quickly shut his door.

"We better move," Asa said.

"Here." Sydney looked down at her bare feet. "I brought these for you. Didn't think you would make it in those heels."

"Thanks." She slipped her feet into her familiar shoes, quickly trying not to stumble while following the rest of them.

They took the back exit and headed for the main strip. They kept their heads down. The air was cool and she shivered. Brady took his jacket off and wrapped it around her shoulders. She gave him a smile of thanks, and he took her hand.

She watched her sister and Asa walk in front of them. Sydney had both arms linked into his one.

They reached the corner and saw a hotel shuttle parked, its doors open, and a few people getting on.

"Let's take this shuttle to wherever." Asa pointed. "We need to figure out what's next."

When they reached it, Brady asked which hotel. The driver was an old man with thick glasses. He leaned forward. He must have been hard of hearing because he started to yell, "You kids heading to the Ocean Casino? 'Cause if you are, that's where I'm headed."

"Yes, sir," Brady said. Then let her on first.

She sat in an empty seat, Brady next to her. Asa and Sydney sat behind them.

Brady gave her an encouraging smile, then turned to the aisle, and he and Asa put their heads together and started to talk in low voices.

Sydney leaned forward. "Your hair is a giant rat's nest back here." Sydney started to run her fingers through the back of her head to get the tangles worked out.

"It's almost like you have pillow hair or something." She heard the giggle in Sydney's voice.

She slowly turned to face her sister, trying not to pull her hair.

Sydney winked. "So, did you?" she whispered.

"Yes." She wanted to scream it. Tell Sydney how amazing it had been. Tell her everything. But she kept her tact and just rolled her eyes back and mouthed, "OMG."

Sydney laughed. "Good. I'm happy for you." Sydney wrapped her arms around her shoulders over the back of the seat.

"What about you? You don't have pillow hair?" She was still keeping her voice low.

Sydney let go. "I would if it wasn't for the damn Brotherhood." Sydney wrinkled up her nose in frustration.

Sydney was about to say something, but Asa and Brady broke up their conversation and sat back in their seats.

Brady looked over. "We're going to head for the restaurant and make some plans."

"What are we going to do?" she asked.

Brady frowned. "I don't know."

When they arrived at the casino, they went straight to the bar and took a dark corner booth.

None of them wanted any drinks and ordered water. Asa ordered an appetizer, if anything to be polite. When the waiter left, they all sat forward.

"Do you think it was just the three of them?" Sydney asked.

"Either way, they know we're here." Asa sat back in the booth and crossed his arms over his wide chest.

"Do we take another bus?" she asked.

"If they know we're here, then they know we took a bus. But we need to get out. We just left three dead bodies in a hotel hallway." Brady pushed his glasses up his nose and took a long drink of his water.

The waiter dropped off the food and refilled their glasses. No one reached for it.

When he left, Brady leaned over the table. "Maybe it's time we called Max. He can bring a car and guns; we could use the backup."

Asa placed his elbows on the table and ran both hands through his hair.

"They'll know to watch Max. An army buddy who works for the family. Plus, the phones are tapped." Asa dropped his hands to the table. "I'm at a loss." Sydney reached over and placed her hand on his arm. He put his hand on top of hers, then turned to Brady, "I don't know what to do, we're back to square one."

"Do you have the ring?" she asked, thinking of their fast getaway.

Asa shook his head yes. "Damn thing. I swear its bad luck."

"No, just cursed," Sydney said, rolling her eyes.

They all went silent for a moment.

Asa broke it. "Maybe we split up?"

They all looked over at him, surprise on everyone's faces. "It will be harder for them to track two groups than one. One group can head to Granny's, the other in the opposite direction. The group that goes to Granny's can gather weapons and Granny's security, bring a plane, and pick the others up. The other group maybe is a little more obvious and lets them track." He paused. "We can meet in a set location on a set day."

"That sounds dangerous." She looked to Asa.

Brady pushed his glasses up and rubbed his eyes. "That plan has a lot of holes in it." He placed his glasses back on his nose. "We need to get out of town. We can think about it as we leave. I say we get a cab and head north. Then go from there. We should probably ditch the phones."

They all agreed.

Asa got out from behind the table and dropped money on the table for the food; he then dropped the burner phone and Brady did the same.

She took Brady's hand.

They waited as Asa helped Sydney out from the back of the booth, then they made their way to the exit.

Sydney

When they got to the street, they hailed a cab.

The cab was small, and Asa sat in front while the three of them crammed into the back.

Roxy sat in the middle, and she and Brady were squeezed against the opposite doors.

Asa told the driver to take the 30 to Absecon.

The driver nodded. He was an older man, skinny and dirty, with shaggy hair that covered his eyes. He pulled out in traffic. She had no idea where they were headed and wondered how Asa knew where that city was. She didn't question it.

"So did you win big?" the cab driver asked, shaking his hair out of his eyes.

"We did all right," was all Asa said. The rest of them didn't answer. She was exhausted. It had been a long night, and she had a feeling it wasn't going to end anytime soon.

"That's good, man. I swear, my wife loses more than she wins. Probably could have bought a big fancy house by now with all the money she's lost." The cab driver chuckled. Asa just smiled at him.

She was relieved she was in the back; she wasn't in the mood to make small talk. She could tell Asa wasn't either.

The driver made a turn, and soon they were on a bridge. She looked in the distance, wondering what their next move was. Where they really going to split up? She was sure that they wouldn't leave her and Roxy by themselves. Would her and Asa go together? She was sure after tonight Brady wouldn't let Roxy out of his sight. She looked over and saw Brady holding Roxy's hand tight. She didn't like the idea of half of them drawing attention to the Brotherhood and the other trying to make it to Maine by themselves. Asa and Brady were sure that the Brotherhood would be waiting for them in Maine. Her stomach ached. The worst part was she was starting to get used to it—the constant fear and worry.

"Hey, man, this isn't the exit," Asa said, sitting straight up in the front seat. She saw Brady jump to attention.

"I know a shortcut," was all the driver said.

"No, get back on the freeway." Asa turned to the driver.

"Trust me, man. Been driving a cab for ten years and lived here my whole life. Just saving you some dough."

She watched as Brady let go of Roxy's hand and pulled his gun from under his shirt and placed it between his knees. Asa quickly eyed Brady over his shoulder. She sat up straight in the seat, and she grabbed Roxy's hand, her nerves on edge. Was this guy really just taking a shortcut?

"I don't care. Get back on the freeway." Asa was fully facing the driver now.

The driver turned suddenly, throwing her against the door, and she felt the weight of both Roxy and Brady holding her there. He made another sharp turn and pulled into an old warehouse parking lot, slammed the brakes, and threw it into park.

Brady righted himself and jammed the barrel of his gun into the driver's head. "Get out of the car," Brady demanded.

Asa pulled his gun from behind him and pointed it at the man also. Roxy squeezed her hand, and she pulled Roxy in close.

"Hey man." The cab driver placed his hands up in surrender, his voice shaking. "Was told to bring you here, gave me good money too. Like I said, wife has a gambling problem."

Just then, her door flung open, and a large, strong hand grabbed her by the hair and pulled her out. Roxy didn't let go of her hand. She screamed in pain as she felt her hair being ripped from her scalp. The hand pulled harder, and she let go of Roxy's, trying to relieve the pull. She was being dragged across the parking lot. She reached up to grab a hold of the hands, trying to stop him as the pavement ripped at her legs.

When he stopped, he grabbed her around the neck and placed her back on her feet. The arm wrapped around her, cutting off her airflow. She pawed at the arm, scratching and twisting, but the hold was strong.

She watched as a man in a navy-blue suit pulled Roxy out of the car, and there were two others, each one in front of the guy's doors, guns drawn and pointing through the window. They weren't letting anyone out.

The cab driver kicked his door open and jumped out.

"Hey man." He placed his hands up like he had done in the car, showing surrender. "I want no part of this." He backed up slowly. "Can I just have my money, and I'll go?"

The man standing in front of Brady's door turned and shot the driver right in the forehead. He dropped to the concrete.

She jumped at the sound of the shot, and a scream stuck in her throat; She was struggling to breathe. She gasped, and the man let up a little, letting her breathe a bit. Thinking of it as an opportunity, she tried to elbow him in the ribs. But she felt the cool metal of a pistol placed at her temple. "Don't even try, honey," he whispered in her ear. "The boss said to keep you alive, but I've lost three of my brothers tonight and won't hesitate putting a bullet in your pretty face."

She stilled. The man's voice was deep and dark. She could tell that he meant it.

The man carrying Roxy came up next to them. She was in a chokehold also, but he wasn't letting up, and her face was turning blue.

"Please," she said in a choked voice. "My sister, she can't breathe." She pulled on the man's scarred hand.

"Bry. Let up. Alive, remember? Her face is blue, man."

The guy named Bry jerked Roxy to the side and looked at her face. He must have loosened his hold because Roxy took in a large gasp of air.

"Sorry, man, I just want this over." He jerked Roxy again. "Bitches," he said with venom.

She felt the man holding her nod in agreement.

Then she heard a gunshot and the shatter of glass. She looked over to the cab. Brady was out and in a full-on brawl with a man in navy slacks and a white, now bloodstained, shirt.

It looked like Asa had shot at the man through the window, his gun held out. The man in the navy suit held his bicep, the gun pointed down. Asa jumped out of the car, his gun pointed at the man. Asa took two steps forward and looked up at them. "Let the girls go now or I put one in his head."

She felt the man holding her shake with laughter. "You can try."

A black SUV came whipping into the parking lot, followed by two more. Their headlights lit the scene. The headlights flashed off Brady's glasses, blinding him for a second, and the man laid a hard right hook to his face. Brady didn't go down, but stumbled backward.

Asa looked behind him panic and pure terror crossed his face. He shot the man in front of him—a head shot, and he fell to the ground. He ran to the side of the cab.

He yelled something, and Brady dropped to the ground. Asa pulled the trigger again, and the man with the bloody shirt hit the ground. Asa ran to Brady to help. But each black SUV held another group of navy-blue-suited men. If they were armed, they didn't pull their guns, but descended on them like a pack of wolves on their prey.

"We want you to watch as our Brotherhood devours your so-called warriors," the man holding her whispered in her ear, his deep voice softening. It sent a chill down her spine. *What the hell was he talking about? Warriors?*

She watched as Asa and Brady were back-to-back fighting. They would take down one only to have another step in. When the Brotherhood had them separated, they came at them from all sides. She watched as they fought tirelessly. Not stopping, not giving up.

"Stop, please," she pleaded, only to feel the laughter of the man holding her.

"I'll go with you peacefully. Just let them go."

Asa threw a punch, hitting one in the nose. She watched as blood literately sprayed, only for him to then be jumped from behind. The man soon had him in a chokehold. Brady, seeing Asa in trouble, turned and punched the man's ribs. The man howled in pain and loosened his grip, giving Asa room to turn and place a punch to his stomach. Where had Asa's and Brady's guns gone?

Another black SUV pulled into the parking lot, and more men in navy suits jumped out.

"Let's go, Bry," the man holding her said. "They got this. They have their orders. The boss will want to see the girls."

The man holding her swung her to the side. He pulled her toward a black SUV, the gun still pressed against her temple.

She screamed Asa's name. As she was being dragged, she kicked and scratched. But the man wouldn't loosen his hold.

The last thing she saw before being thrown into the back seat of the SUV was Asa pushing his way through the sea of navy suits, ignoring the elbow to the stomach. Trying to break through to get to her. His face was full of fear and fury. Someone had grabbed his arms, pulling him back. The door slammed in her face. A man in the backseat was trying to place zip ties around her wrists, and she kept ripping her hands out of his grip, struggling to reach for the door handle. She heard Roxy scream, and she turned. She felt a pinch on her arm, and when she looked over, she saw a syringe in the man's hand. Her head spun, and then everything went black.

Asa

Pain. That's what woke him. Every part of him had white-hot pain. He tried to move, but his hands were bound.

He opened his eyes. Bright light blinded him, and he had to blink several times.

"Sydney?" His voice was raspy, and his throat dry.

The last thing he remembered was hearing Sydney call his name as he watched a man drag her to a car. He remembered fighting. Fighting so many that he couldn't get to her. *They have her*, he thought, and the fear ripped through him.

He struggled to get up. But his hands were tied behind his back, leaving him unsteady. Hot pain shot through him again. His eyes slowly adjusted, and he realized he was in a room. It was all white. White walls and large fluorescent lights were shining down on him from up above.

His head was pounding.

He looked over and saw Brady slumped against the wall. His glasses had a crack in one of the lenses. The same eye was swollen and puffy. He had blood running from his nose.

"Brady?" He leaned closer and almost tipped over, but caught himself. "Wake up."

When Brady didn't move, he panicked. He tried to scoot toward him, but he was hit with a wave of dizziness.

"Brady? Come on, brother? Wake up," he pleaded.

Brady moaned and moved his head to the side. He felt a little relief.

"Brady, man, wake up."

Brady moaned again. Then his eyes snapped open. "Roxy?" he shouted, and tried to stand up. But halfway up, he stumbled and came down to his knees. His hands were bound behind his back, too.

"She isn't here," Asa said. "They have the girls. We have to find them."

Brady sat back on his knees and hung his head.

He, too, hung his head and looked down at his bloodstained shirt. He noticed the top two buttons of his vest were undone. He thought of Sydney.

He knew that going out was a bad idea. But Sydney had been so excited, and the way she looked in that dress, he let his emotions get clouded with her and now look. Just what he feared.

Brady looked up at him. "Man, you look like shit."

"Trust me, brother, you don't look any better. Can you even see?"

Brady slowly tried to stand up, but he gave up when the dizziness hit him. "Yeah, kind of. Where are we?" Brady started to scan the room with his one good eye.

There was nothing in the white room. The floors had white tiles, and there wasn't even a window. There was just one white door at the other end.

"How long have we been out?" He started to feel the panic rise again. "We don't know where we are or how long it's been. It could be days."

He scanned the room again, looking for a way out. He leaned against the wall and slowly slid his body upward to a standing position. He walked over to the door and was thinking of kicking it down. But his head was spinning and he took another moment to get it straight. He started to slowly pace the room. He had to get to Sydney and Roxy. Where were they? Thoughts started to swirl in his head, and he pictured Sydney being dragged off into the black SUV again while she screamed his name. He stopped and was about to rush the door and try to bust through when he noticed Brady take a step forward. Brady must have seen it on his caged animal face. He interrupted his thoughts.

"A, let's get our heads together. Use your training. We have no guns or weapons. We are both tied up and hurting."

Brady was right, and he took a deep breath that hurt his ribs. He wondered if they were broken.

"Why didn't they kill us?" he asked, wincing from the pain shooting up his side.

"I don't know," Brady said. "I hope it means they haven't killed the girls yet either."

"Why does he want them?" He looked down at his pants pocket. The familiar lump wasn't there. "They have the ring." His shoulders slumped.

Brady started to pace the room, slightly wobbling as he did.

"They have the ring and the girls. Why keep us? They wanted the girls for revenge, right? To even the score for their lost friends."

"I think it started that way, but the guys keep saying the boss needs them alive. I think he has plans for them," Asa answered. "For what, I don't know."

Brady looked to him. He wasn't sure if it was fear or determination that was written on his face. Brady took a deep breath and looked him right in the eyes.

"You ready, man? We're going to have to fight our way out, find the girls, and run. This isn't going to be easy."

"We just took on twenty or more guys, and we're still standing." He paused, then added, "Barely. What are a few more?" Asa forced a smile.

He knew what Brady was saying. This wasn't going to be easy. They could die, and the girls would die too, but not before God knows what might happen first. Fear banded his chest. He saw Sydney's beautiful face and raven black hair. And then thought of how she could be stubborn and a smartass. He pictured her face bloody and beaten. Rage built inside of him. He was ready; he would kill every one of those Brotherhood assholes.

"I'm in."

Brady rolled his neck and shoulders. "We need a plan."

He was about to answer when the door to the small room flung open.

"Good, you boys are awake. This will make it way more fun."

Three men in navy suits stood at the door. They all had guns and smirks on their faces. The man in the back stepped forward. "Hey, big guy. Remember me?"

He looked over, assuming the man was talking to him and not Brady. He studied his face and recognition hit his brain. He remembered him from the pawnshop. His mind flashed back to the man Sydney had called Cal.

He had been dragging her to the back room in the pawnshop. He had threatened to rape her. The fear on Sydney's face flashed through his mind.

"Yeah," he said calmly. "I remember you, and I remember beating your ass."

Anger spread across Cal's face, and he took a step forward. The man to his right, a large older man with thick black hair entwined with gray, put his arm out and stopped him. "Easy, Cal. You'll get your chance." His voice was deep and slow.

Cal shifted on his feet and pointed a finger at him. "You're mine," he said softly, though his face looked hard.

Any other time, Asa might have felt fear, but he was in survival mode now, and his training was kicking in; he was ready for this. He was going to finish this today. No more running.

"Hey, four eyes," a skinny, tall man with a southern accent said as he looked at Brady. "Sorry about the glasses. I hope you can still see, because we're going to give you front-row seats. We're going to let you watch what we do to your girl right before we bleed you dry." The man gave a wide, toothy smile.

He looked over and saw Brady's shoulders go up. He also noticed that he had his war face on.

Before all this happened, he had only seen that face one time before on his cousin. They had been on vacation in Mexico, and a man had grabbed Haley in a large bear hug from behind. It was a mistake on the man's part; he had mistaken Haley for his wife, but he had thought that Brady could have killed the poor man. It had scared him back then, but he was glad to see it now. He had seen it several times now since they had met Sydney and Roxy. Brady was ready.

He looked at Brady and gave a small nod. They had been raised together and played team sports together. The only time they were separated was when Brady was in the army. They knew each other better than anyone, and they didn't need words to know what the other was thinking. The nod they shared was the signal to say that it was on.

They both stood, waiting for the enemy to make the move.

The three men stepped forward, their guns out.

He noticed that all three had scars on their hands, just like the man in the alley. Was it a Brotherhood thing?

"Don't try anything," the older man in the front said. "We're going to take you to watch. Then it will be your turn."

His first instinct was to fight, but if they were going to bring them to the girls, he was going to let them. When the skinny one grabbed Brady and he didn't fight back, he knew Brady was thinking the same thing.

Cal walked up to him, a wicked grin on his face. He could see why Sydney was scared of him; he looked evil. Like there was a twisted darkness inside trying to escape.

Cal kept his gun level to his chest. Cal grabbed him by the shoulder and spun him around, causing the pain in his back and ribs to heighten.

He watched as the other man pushed Brady out the door, and Cal shoved him hard. "Follow," Cal said simply, grinding the barrel of his gun into the middle of his back. They passed the older man. He looked bored but turned to follow.

The hall was wide, and yet, they still walked in a straight line. The hall's walls were covered in expensive art from different time periods, and the floor was carpeted in red and gold rugs. It was a house owned by a man with influence and money.

They passed several big oak doors and one was open. He watched as Brady walked past, and something caught his one good eye. He stumbled past the room, staring into it as best he could as he was pushed, his head craning to get a better look. Asa was interested. What had Brady's attention?

He wanted to see in the room, too, thinking maybe Brady saw the girls. But the older man stepped up and closed the door before he was able to walk by.

He was hoping Brady would give him a signal of an action if the girls were in there or a way to escape presented itself, but instead Brady kept on walking.

They were led to a narrow staircase. It was designed to be a servants' staircase kept in the back of large, old mansions. So, the servants could move without bothering the master of the house. He remembered one of his clients having a staircase like this in their old southern mansion.

"Go." The older man made a sweeping motion with his gun toward the stairs.

Brady went first. The others followed.

He took a step to follow when Cal grabbed his shoulder and pushed him against the wall, knocking a large picture frame askew.

Cal stepped up to his face. "You broke my nose."

He looked at Cal's face, and there was a lingering bruise under his eyes.

"You jumped my brother and then took a cheap shot. You're lucky my boss wants you alive; otherwise, I would kill you right now." Cal held his gun up to Asa's head, and his hand shook with anger. His face twisted in frustration.

He just stared Cal in the eyes, daring him to pull the trigger. Cal snapped his hand back, pulling the gun away.

"You were going to rape an innocent woman." Asa's voice was low and disgusted.

Cal laughed. "Innocent? She's a dirty witch and deserves it."

Cal stared at him, his face calculating, then his shoulders lowered and his intense posture relaxed. He tilted his head to the side. "She has you bewitched. She has you doing her dirty work." Cal's eyes had a far-off, dreamy look. "Just like before."

What the hell? he thought. *What is this crazy talk?* It wouldn't have surprised him to learn that Cal was insane.

Cal pulled him to face the stairs and pushed him hard. He stumbled. He tried to catch his step, but he missed the stairs and with his hands bound, he fell. He hit the stairs hard. He was able to turn to his side and protect his head. The pain shot through his body. If his ribs weren't broken before, they were now. He rolled down and hit the landing on his back with a thud. The force had his head whipping back, and he smashed it on the floor. He felt his mouth fill with blood and his tongue ache. He rolled over and saw Cal at the top of the stairs, his smile large and stretching from ear to ear. He looked Cal right in the eyes and spit his mouthful of blood on the floor. It pooled on the step.

He turned and looked down the rest of the staircase and saw Brady struggling to get to him. But one of the men punched him in the stomach. He bent in pain, gasping for breath.

He shook his head with a moan, trying to tell Brady to stop, that he was okay.

He rolled, and by the time Cal reached him, he was on his knees. Cal yanked him up to his feet and pushed him toward the others. He walked the rest of the stairs with a limp. They reached a door, and the man in front of Brady swung it open. He dragged Brady out by his shoulder, and Asa followed with Cal close behind. They were on a large, sprawling lawn that backed to a tree line. The sun was just setting behind the trees, giving the day a yellow and orange haze.

They were escorted to a black four-door jeep. They pushed him and Brady into the back seat. The older man got behind the wheel. Cal got in the passenger side, and the tall, skinny man jumped into the back cargo. He leaned on the seat's back and held his gun between them, a wide smile on his face.

The older man placed the jeep in four-wheel drive and drove right over the well-manicured lawn. He headed straight for the tree line. As they got closer, he saw an overgrown dirt road, and the jeep headed straight for it. The dirt road was rocky and full of potholes. The older man didn't seem to care and didn't try to avoid the holes. Every bump made his body scream with pain. He tried not to let it show on his face, but he saw Brady wince too.

The skinny man also noticed. "You ladies having fun yet?"

The skinny man placed his gun to Asa's head and rubbed it through his hair. Asa stiffened. When he pulled the muzzle away, he shoved it in Asa's face.

"Looks like your head's bleedin' some." The man did a quick, high-pitched laugh.

"Took quite the beating, you two did. Tell ya the truth, I was pretty impressed." He let the gun drop down, pointing it to the seat. He scratched his chin. "Still lost, though." He sounded disappointed.

They hit a large pothole, and the man hit his head on the ceiling.

"Damn! Jim. Take it easy, will ya? I'm not in a seat." He rubbed his head.

"I will when you shut your loud mouth," the older man named Jim replied. "We're almost there."

The forest was growing dark, and the jeep grew quiet. Jim turned the headlights on, lighting the road. Trees scraped the side of the jeep, giving off an eerie whine.

He thought of Sydney. He was growing edgy. He wanted to see her, get her away from here, and away from these people. He didn't know what he was walking into—unarmed and bound.

He thought of the other night. How she had danced with him. Her body pressed against his, how she had felt so right in his arms. He had tried to control himself. She had made it too damn hard.

He wanted nothing but to keep her safe and kill anyone that had her. He thought of her beautiful face. When she smiled, her big blue eyes lit up.

Then the image of her eyes full of fear when they had dragged her away. She had reached out for him and yelled his name, and now he was captured, beaten. She was God knows where. He had failed.

His chest tightened. Fear ripped through him. He couldn't fail. Not now. Not when she and Roxy were only in the whole mess because of his family and their crazy superstitions. This was all his fault. He shouldn't have played along with his granny's crazy stories and dreams.

He felt Brady stir next to him and looked over. Brady was staring out the window. He was probably studying the area. His face looked hard and determined. Brady was getting ready. He was planning. Asa knew that Brady was in love with Roxy. He knew from the beginning, and no matter what his opinion was or what he said, Brady wasn't listening. He was going to save Roxy; there was no doubt in his mind.

If they made it out alive, Granny was going to push harder for the ring more than ever.

He pushed that out of his head. *Screw that ring,* he thought.

Brady stirred again; he was in pain, too, but his face didn't show it. He was glad that Brady was with him. There was no one he would rather have by his side in a life-or-death situation than this man. Brady didn't give up. He was feeling sorry for himself while his cousin was planning and preparing. Asa sat up straighter in the seat. He started to scanning the area also. He was going to fight. He was going to back up his cousin, and the four of them were going to walk out alive.

The jeep stopped in front of a small, rundown cabin that was sitting in a small clearing in the trees. The roof was covered in moss and the wood was rotting. There was a small stack of firewood under the dust-covered windows. A small cloud of smoke streamed from the chimney.

Jim, the driver, got out first and went to the back of the jeep and opened the hatch. Cal stepped out and opened Asa's door. The skinny guy in the back pointed his gun back and forth between him and Brady. "Don't start anything. We have permission to kill you boys if you start anything." He slipped out the back, still pointing the gun.

Cal grabbed him and pulled him out of the seat. He stumbled but didn't go down. He was hit with a wave of dizziness that had him wondering if he had a concussion on top of broken ribs.

The three men walked him and Brady over to the windows. Brady was on one side and he was on the other. Each was guarded by one navy-suited guy. Jim stayed back, mumbling, "I can't watch this shit." He lit a cigarette and leaned against the back of the jeep.

Cal took the sleeve of his suit and wiped the window. "You're going to want to see this," he said, his smile grizzly. He pushed him up closer to the window, and he racked his knees on the firewood. Pain shot up his legs.

What he saw had him gasping for air, pain forgotten.

The cabin was just one room. It was dark, lit by the small fire in the fireplace and a few candles spread out along a table on the other side of the room.

In the middle were two tables, each one holding one of the girls. They were naked except for a pair of white panties. Their arms were spread out to the sides, tied down with large, thick, leather straps. There was another leather strap across their chests, covering their breasts, and their feet were bound at the bottom.

Both were bleeding from their chests. Blood dripped down their sides and into their armpits. Blood pooled on the side of the table. He saw Sydney's long black hair soaking in a pool of her own blood. His vision went red around the edges and fear filled every inch of his body.

"If they're dead...' he started to say as he turned to Cal. It was then when he saw Brady struggle with his bindings, trying to twist out of them, arms flexing and pulling. His face was white with fear. The skinny man only laughed and pushed Brady back to the window. "They ain't dead. Check this out."

Brady froze and stared into the window, and Asa swung his head to look.

Walking into the cabin was a man. What was the size of a man, anyway. It was wearing a black hooded robe. The face wasn't human but a deer skull, a mask. The eyes were black and hollow, the tip of the nose chipped and splintered. The white of the skull glowed in the firelight, seeming brighter in contrast to the black robe. The robe was tied around his waist with a gold rope. Two gold-sheathed knives hung from it, and hanging from his neck, on a glimmer of silver, was the ring. It had been laced through a silver chain and danced with the firelight.

He went lightheaded. Was the thing going to kill the girls? Skinny guy had said they weren't dead.

He watched in fear as the robed deer walked in between the girls, laying his black gloved hand on their heads and petting back their hair. He stared at both, moving his head side to side and keeping his hand on their foreheads. He watched as the man/creature ran his hand down the side of Sydney's face and down to her neck. The skull looked right up at him, staring as he stroked his thumb over her throat, smearing blood.

He lost it.

"Don't you touch her!" he yelled, still staring at the deer skull.

He felt Cal press the pistol to his back. In a fit of rage, he swung around and shoulder checked him. Cal stumbled back, surprise on his face. But it gave him the opening he needed. Digging back to his football days, he ran straight at him, head down and shoulders out. Cal went down. Knocking his head hard on the ground, Cal gave a weak moan but didn't get up, his gun laying on the ground. Asa kicked it away. He looked over and saw Jim throw his cigarette down and scramble to pull his gun from his coat. He watched as Brady head-butted the skinny man hard in the face, causing blood to splatter.

He turned to Jim.

Jim was running, gun drawn. Asa rushed him. Jim fired. But Jim's aim was off and missed. Asa kept at him, too blinded by fear to care.

Jim's face turned to panic, and Asa continued to rush him. Jim tripped on the uneven ground and sent another shot. Asa reached him and hit him hard. They both went down in a tangle of limbs. Following Brady's lead, he head-butted Jim straight in the face. A sharp lightning bolt of pain shot through his own head, leaving him dizzy and disoriented. He shook his head and looked down at Jim. He was still on the ground; his gun had flown from his hands, and he rolled to the side to whip out a knife from his belt. It was a small, three-inch utility knife. Jim was struggling to get up when Asa jumped to his feet. He took the three steps and kicked out his foot as hard as he could, connecting with the side of Jim's face. He heard the crunch and watched as Jim grunted, then his head rolled to the side. He didn't know if he was dead or not and he didn't care. He wasn't stopping. He got down next to Jim and hesitantly put his back to him. With his hands still bound, he reached behind him and tried to grab the knife from Jim's hand. He positioned the knife in his hands and started to saw at the zip tie. It was awkward.

He looked up to see Brady battling it out with the skinny guy. Brady had knocked the gun away, but he watched as a punch connected with Brady's face. He looked over to see Cal start to rise on all fours, shaking his head.

He needed to move.

When he finally felt the tie snap, he jumped up and grabbed Jim's gun. He aimed to take out Cal, but he had already gotten up and was just rounding the corner of the cabin and was out of aim. The coward.

He turned to Brady. Brady was on the ground, and the tall, skinny man was throwing kicks at his chest and stomach. He fired again, hitting the man in the shoulder. The shot threw him back. Brady rolled over, trying to get up. Asa watched as the man turned to him, his eyes alight with spite. Asa pulled the trigger and the man dropped. He ran to Brady and, using the knife, he cut his hands free.

Neither one stopped but raced to the door of the old cabin. He pushed the door, and when it didn't open, he stepped back and kicked it hard. The door jamb splintered, and the old door fell forward, hitting the floor. Brady rushed in. The deer-headed man was gone. There was an open door to the side, letting in a breeze that had the candle flames dancing.

"Coward heard the gunshots and ran," Brady said. He headed straight to Roxy. Asa followed and looked down at Sydney.

There was blood pooled around her neck and in her hair. Asa's body vibrated, and his ears buzzed with fear when he saw what was carved into her chest. It was a perfect V with two slashes above the ends. It was deep; it went from her cleavage to her collarbone, and it was going to leave a scar. The wound was slowly leaking blood. He looked over at Brady who was studying Roxy.

"It's the same mark that they have on their hands."

Brady only nodded, his face white. He looked back down at Sydney.

"Sydney? Can you hear me?" he whispered in her ear as he tried to keep his emotions in check.

He reached over and felt for a pulse in her neck. He found one but it was weak. He started to unstrap her hands.

"Sydney, baby." He leaned over her and whispered in her ear, "I need you to wake up."

When she didn't respond, he looked to Brady again. His face still white, he was talking to Roxy as well and unstrapping her ties.

"Is she awake?" he asked Brady. Brady just shook his head no and continued to unstrap her, a frown deep on his face.

Asa heard a soft whisper and looked down to see Sydney move her head slightly as her eyes fluttered.

"Sydney. It's me. Open your eyes."

Sydney moaned and rolled her head. He ran his hand over her cheek lightly, and her eyes flew open. She started to scream. "No! Don't!"

"It's okay," he cooed. "It's me. I got you."

She stopped and stared. "Asa?"

He smiled at her, and she dropped her head back on the table. "Where am I?" She started to scan the room. "Where is Roxy?"

"She's here. Brady's with her." He started to unclasp her chest strap. When he pulled it off, he averted his eyes. She was still scanning the room and didn't even seem to notice.

Not knowing what else to do, he unbuttoned his vest and went to hand it to her, but realizing it would do her no good, he tossed it down and unbuttoned his shirt. He draped it over her. It was dirty and had his and others' blood on it, but it was all he could do. The undershirt he had on was soaked with blood as well.

He freed her other arm and her feet. He helped her up, and she pulled the shirt on, all the while wincing with pain. He watched as she looked down at her own chest. Her face turned white. "Oh my god."

Not caring that she was bare-chested, she ripped the shirt open. "What the hell did they do?" She looked up at him, her eyes full of tears.

"They cut something into your chest," he said weakly, taking a step closer. He gently pulled the shirt closed, covering her breasts, ignoring the small burn of lust forming in his chest. "It will be okay," he continued softly. "It needs to be cleaned, though."

A tear ran down her cheek, and she looked up at him, her eyes scared. "What's going on?"

He reached forward and pulled her into a hug. "I'm so sorry." It was all he could get out, guilt-tripping his words.

She sobbed. "What is happening to us?" She jerked her head back. "Does Roxy have it too?"

He nodded. He looked over at Brady; he was now bare-chested. Roxy hadn't woken up, and he had gotten all her straps off. He was gently pulling his shirt over her head as she lay there.

"Roxy!" Sydney yelped, and she went to jump down off the table. When she stumbled, Asa reached over and steadied her. Together, they walked to Roxy's table.

"She isn't waking up," Brady said, his voice low and unsteady.

Sydney helped pull Roxy's arm through the white T-shirt, being mindful of the wound.

The realization of where they were and what just happened jumped into his mind.

"We need to get out of here. That creepy asshole could come back with more of the Brotherhood."

Brady nodded. "We need to go back to that main house first."

"What? Why?" Asa was confused. "We all need medical care."

"I saw a room in the main house. It was full of computers."

Asa was about to jump in and tell him it was no time to play his computer games when Brady cut him off.

"I can use them to find out where we are. I can also contact Max, and depending on where we are, I can have him send a plane or helicopter or even a car. Tell him to bring backup."

Brady looked up at him, his eye still swollen shut and the other stressed. There were bruises and cuts across his bare chest. Brady didn't have jokes or a goofy grin right now. He didn't even have his war face on. This was different. "We need help," he said flatly.

Sydney

Her chest was on fire, and she felt the blood drip down her stomach. Her head was foggy from what she assumed was the drugs. She had no memory of how they got there or what had happened. The last thing she remembered was being pulled by her hair out of the taxi.

She looked over at Asa; he had been beaten badly. His face was swollen and puffy; there was blood coming from his hairline, and he was favoring his right side. Brady was no better. He had a long cut on his arms and his eye was swollen shut, and his glasses were broken. She watched as Brady picked her unconscious sister up and cradled her in his arms. She prayed that Roxy would wake up. What had they drugged them with? Did they give Roxy too much? She noticed the blood seeping from Roxy's chest, staining the white shirt she wore.

Asa went to the front door, a gun held close; he was scanning the area. It was dark, and she saw no lights outside.

"Is the jeep still there?" Brady asked, shifting Roxy in his arms.

"Yeah. Let's move." Asa went first and she followed, staying close to Asa's back. She noticed that he was doing quick head shakes.

"You all right?" she whispered to his backside.

"I'm fine." He had the gun pointed down and he was scanning the area.

She just nodded, accepting his answer. Now wasn't the time to press him for more information. She looked behind her and saw Brady close behind, her sister limp in his arms.

They made it to the jeep. She ignored the two dead bodies on the lawn. Brady slid Roxy in the backseat. She was ready to jump in back with her when Brady placed his hand on her shoulder.

"Here." He handed her his gun. "Sit in front with Asa."

She watched as he pulled another from behind his back.

Brady got in the back and gently cradled Roxy's head in his lap. His one good eye was full of worry and stress. She knew in that instant that this man was in love with her sister.

She felt relief, and even in this horrible situation with her chest on fire and blood running down her body, she knew that her sister was safe with him.

Asa took the narrow dirt road slow. He tried to avoid potholes, and she noticed his winces when he hit one. He only had the parking lights on, trying not to draw attention. She scanned the passenger-side window, looking for any movement as Asa and Brady described the crazy, skull-faced freak to her, and it made her shudder. "Do you think he's the leader?" she asked.

"Most likely. He was doing some kind of ritual. They keep saying the boss had plans," Brady said from the back.

The thought of a crazy man playing dress up and cutting into her and her sister's chests while they were out cold and naked had her head spinning. Why? What kind of psycho were they dealing with? She started to shake with fear. She gripped the armrest on the door, trying to steady her hands. *This is crazy,* she thought. *What had her dad gotten her and Roxy into with this ring?*

She was half-naked, her chest burning and carved up, out in the middle of nowhere, being chased by a man in a robe with a large army.

Was it really just a few weeks ago that she had broken in to that senator son's hotel room in New York and robbed him? That felt like a million years ago. Then, that morning, she had gotten the call about Margie. Sadness started to sink in along with fear and anxiety. Her thoughts were spiraling.

"Get it together," she whispered to herself and took a deep breath. She had to be strong. Roxy was out, Asa and Brady were beaten to hell, and she needed to be strong. She needed to pull herself together and make it out of this alive.

They hit the tree line, and Asa stopped and turned the lights off. They all sat there in silence, watching and waiting. She saw a large house about thirty yards away. There were no lights on inside, and it looked like no one was home.

"That's where they took you guys?" she asked.

"Yeah," Asa said, leaning forward to look. "It's a newer house, and the owner has money. Lots of pricey furniture and art."

Brady leaned forward between their seats. "I need to get in there and find out where we are."

Asa crept the jeep forward. "I think we should leave the jeep here and walk."

"I don't want to walk that far with Roxy passed out," Brady said. "We either drive up or leave Roxy here."

"We can't leave her here alone," she said quickly. "Leave me a gun, and you two run in."

"No," Asa said. "Not with that freak looking for you both."

"I have to go," Brady said. "I sneak in by myself, and you two stay with Roxy."

Asa rubbed his chin and pulled on his beard. "I don't like you going in by yourself. Your back won't be covered when you're on the computers."

They sat there.

"I'll go with Brady," she finally said. "I'll watch his back when he's on the computers and you stay here with Roxy. When we're done, you drive up and pick us up, and we get the hell out of here."

Asa looked in the rearview mirror at Brady. "I don't know."

Brady gave a shrug. "Best we can do." He adjusted Roxy's head and opened the door.

Asa turned, reached over, and grabbed her hand. Looking down, he brushed his thumb over the back of it. She felt the warmth, not just from his touch but deep inside her chest.

"I'll be fine." She looked up at him. He gave her a weak smile.

In the back, Brady slid Roxy's head from his lap. "We need to hurry," was all he said as he stepped out the door.

She opened her door, but Asa didn't let go of her hand. She turned to him. "I'll take care of him." She smiled.

"I know. Take care of yourself." He pulled her closer and leaned in. He brushed his lips to hers softly, slowly. She felt everything in that moment. Happiness, lust, fear, loss, and trust. She opened her eyes and looked at him. Blood on his face, his eyes bruised and puffy. She felt warm and tense all at the same time. Was this what love felt like? She looked up into his eyes. They were staring at her with intensity. She could feel the blush rise on her cheeks. The memory of waking up tied to the table and seeing his face. The flood of relief that overwhelmed her, knowing she was going to be okay again. Her heart squeezed. He let go of her hand and broke their eye contact. She slid out of the car.

Brady was waiting by the door, antsy, ready to go. She pulled her shirt down.

Brady stepped up to the door. "Don't worry, man, no one will touch her."

"Same," Asa replied, and their fist bumped. Brady shut the door.

She was carrying the gun Brady gave her, and he had one also. She wondered if it was enough.

She followed Brady over to the edge of the trees, and together they scanned the large, manicured lawn. It was dark and hard to see. The house was dark, too, expect for a small porch light. She wasn't sure if this was a good thing or a bad thing.

Brady interrupted her thoughts. "Ready?" he asked. "We'll follow the tree line till we get to the side of the house where the trees are." He pointed to a shadowy swell in the trees that came close to the house. She nodded. He scanned the yard one more time.

"Brady, this doesn't seem right. That creepy guy left; don't you think he would have called for backup by now?"

Brady looked at her. "We don't have a choice. Those two back there are in bad shape." She thought of Asa and the way he kept shaking his head to focus.

"Asa is trying to hide it, but he's hurting," he said and looked back at the jeep.

She agreed. She felt the weight of the gun in her hand. She tried to remember everything that they had taught her about self-defense and tried to mimic what she had seen them do. The way they held and ran with guns, how they shot.

"Ready?" he asked. He looked at her gun, then back up at her. "Aim for center mass."

"What?"

Brady tapped his chest. "Center mass, aim for the chest. Better odds."

She nodded. "Center mass," she whispered.

She looked over at Brady. He was staring up at the house. Even in the low light, she watched as his eyes glossed over and his face went hard.

She thought of her sister passed out and Asa's soft kiss. She felt her muscles contract and her heartbeat start to punch in her chest. She was going to do this. It was her turn to protect.

She wondered if her face looked like Brady's.

They stayed low as they ran along the tree line. They stayed on the grass line, which she was grateful for considering she was barefoot. When they hit the trees that Brady had pointed to, they crouched down and scanned the yard again.

Nothing moved, and there was no sound—not even a common forest noise. There were no animals or rustling bushes.

It made her uncomfortable and had her wondering if the skull-faced guy was going to jump out at them. She quickly looked behind her, expecting to see him standing right behind her. Her adrenaline started to pump hard. She didn't have much time to talk herself down when Brady interrupted her thoughts.

"Head straight to the back porch and wait for me. Stay low. I'll cover you." He paused, then scanned the yard. "Go."

She didn't even think or question. She just got up and, hunched over, ran for the house. She waited for the sound of gunshots, but when she stopped at the porch and spun around, she realized that she made it and she took a deep breath. She watched Brady. He didn't hunch over but instead walked fast and with purpose, with his gun pointed. He swung it back and forth, like he was just waiting for someone to jump out at him. She had a moment of envy, watching how cool and collected he looked, ready for action. She probably looked like a frightened animal running for its life, tail tucked between its legs.

When he reached her, he immediately reached for the door handle. She was expecting it to be locked, but it opened. She gave him a suspicious look. "Too easy."

"Me first. Stay close," was all he said.

She watched as he swept both sides of the entrance, then waved her in. She followed.

They were in a small entrance with a set of stairs. The walls were white and plain. There were no windows, and the stairway was dimly lit. Brady started up the stairs, and she stayed close. When they got to a landing, she noticed a small pool of blood splattered on the floor. The crimson color was stark in the white, sterile hall. It gave her a chill. She looked up at Brady, but he just ignored it and continued on.

When they reached the top, the door was open, and Brady scanned the hall then stepped out. He waved her in. The difference of this hall with its huge oak doors and deep red carpet had her pausing to let her eyes adjust.

She stayed close to Brady but she was distracted by the art on the walls. She noticed a few famous artists, all very expensive. But there was a lot of strange work. There was a huge painting of a cliff with waves breaking in a storm. It was beautiful. Underneath on a small table was a statue of a dragon. It was white and extremely detailed. You could see the scales perfectly, even though the statue was no bigger than a man's shoe. The eyes were black, and the nostrils flared. But what was weird was that the small wings were broken off. *It could be an accident*, she thought, *but why would it still be on display?*

She was about to walk over and study it more, but Brady stopped in front of a door, and she almost bumped into him.

Brady slowly opened the door, gun drawn. The room was dark, and there was a low hum coming from within.

She had her gun ready as well. She had a flashback of the alley. Could she really kill again?

Yes, she thought, *after everything that has happened and what those creeps did to me and Roxy, the way they beat Asa and Brady*. She was done and ready to pull the trigger.

Brady flipped the lights on, and the room came into view. There were several computers spread out on a desk, along with huge computer box things in the corners. *Servers?* she wondered.

Brady immediately made his way to the desk chair and started to boot up the computers. She stayed by the door and kept watch. She looked around the room. It had plain white walls, no art or statues. There was a closet, the doors shut. She checked the hall again and listened. There was no sound or movement. She looked over at Brady, and he was typing fast and pulling files up. No wonder Asa wanted someone to watch his back; Brady was in the zone.

She watched as his shoulder blades moved as he swiped the mouse around; he had bruises and cuts along his back and around his rib cage. Sadness filled her heart. These guys were helping them and were getting hurt all because her dad was trying to give her and Roxy a better life. She pushed the thought away and checked the hall again. This wasn't the time for a guilt session; she had a job to do, and she was going to make sure she did it.

A few minutes passed, and her adrenaline must have started to wear off. Her chest stung. Her sweat had dripped into her wound, and it burned. She unbuttoned the top button of the shirt and looked down. The cuts were slowly oozing blood. This was the mark that the Brotherhood had on their hands. They marked her like they marked each other. They kidnapped her and cut her, branded her. Her eyes filled with tears. She wanted to scream. She wanted to cry. But instead, she took a deep breath and wiped her eyes. She looked at the closet again.

Maybe there was something she could use to wipe the blood and sweat from her cuts? Or if she was lucky, some shoes or a shirt for Brady.

She checked the hall again. When nothing moved, she walked over and slowly opened the door. She gasped.

With the little light coming in from the room, she saw nothing but pictures. Hundreds of pictures, and they were all over the place. Some were taped to the walls and others were laying on the floor. She stepped in, chest pain forgotten, and saw herself and Roxy, everywhere. They were in all of them. There were pictures of them in their high school uniforms walking to class. Pictures of them at the mall in the food court, their normal weekend hangout when they were teenagers. She bent over and picked one up off the floor. It was them, at their father's funeral. They were standing at the grave site, huddled close. Roxy had just dropped a rose in, and she had tears falling from her cheeks.

"We were only twelve," she whispered.

She looked up, and Brady was standing next to her. She hadn't even noticed him coming up behind her.

"What the hell?" he said.

She handed him the photo she was holding. "This was at our father's funeral."

She grabbed another off the wall. It was a picture of Roxy sitting at a bar with a man. She was laughing. She wondered if it was David, the man she had lost her virginity to.

"This can't be more than two years ago," she said, thinking of their conversation at Margie's house. She handed it to Brady.

She picked another, and it was her in a blue dress outside an art gallery in New York. She remembered the night she was attending a charity dinner, held by a woman who kept the cash donations instead of donating them to the wildlife preserve. She had stolen the cash and donated it in the woman's name.

"This was six months ago."

Brady reached in and pulled out another; it was Roxy walking in to her apartment building holding a bag of takeout.

"Brady," she said, realization hitting her. "They have been watching us since our dad died."

A sense of dread sank in. They had been following them for years. Knowing where they were this whole time. They could have grabbed them or killed them at any time.

"Why now?" she asked.

Brady looked up. "They've been waiting for you to find the ring or show that you had it. Wear it or sell it, maybe?" He looked over at her. "They figured you guys would end up with it or find it eventually. Considering your father had it last." He turned and went back to the computer.

"They've been very patient." He started going through the drawers of the desk. "When you tried to pawn it, their patience paid off and they made their move."

He pulled something small out of the drawer and plugged into the computer.

"We're in Louisiana," Brady said and started to type. "Leave the pictures, check the hall," he said, not looking up from the computer.

She threw the pictures in the closet and slammed the door in disgust. She went over to the hall and peered out. There was no sound, nothing.

"Louisiana? How long have we been out?"

"Two days."

"Shit," she said in disbelief.

Brady unplugged the small device from the computer.

"Max and a couple of guys from Granny's security team are meeting us at the airport in six hours. Unless we contact them otherwise." He shoved the device in his pocket. "We have to move. We're in the middle of some swamp and have a long ways to go."

"What about the pictures?" she asked.

Before Brady could say anything, there was the now-familiar sound of gunfire. It was coming from outside. Then a loud crash causing her to jump.

Brady didn't hesitate. "Come on. That was out back."

Her heart skipped a beat and she followed Brady.

He checked the hall and then turned back the way they had come.

They ran, her chest burning and fear ripping through her body.

They made it to the end of the hall, and Brady threw the door open. But before she could even stop, he was turning and spinning, pinning her to the wall. She heard the deafening crack of gunfire and heard the drywall explode across from them.

Brady rolled over toward the door. "Stay here."

He put his back to the wall and held the gun with both hands. She copied his stance next to him, prepared to fire.

He turned the corner and fired two shots down the staircase.

She heard the thump of a body falling to the ground. Brady didn't hesitate and went down the stairs. She hesitated for a second, told herself to stop being a chicken, and followed.

He took the stairs faster than she thought was safe, but the worry for the rest of their group had her staying close and ready.

As they thundered down the stairs, there was more gunfire outside, and she heard the rev of an engine. *Several engines*, she thought, as the noise grew louder.

The Brotherhood had arrived, and it sounded like they brought backup.

Roxy

She was lost in the fog and she heard yelling. It was her dad. She tried to follow the screams. She ran through the fog, searching. She came to a forest. Another yell. Her father came running out. He was wearing his signature white, greased, stained T-shirt, and blue jeans, and his hair was ruffled by the wind. He was running through the fog being chased by a large deer, its hooves thumping. The deer was trying to run him through with his bleached white antlers, swiping its head back and forth, the sharp tips just missing his back.

"Dad, I'm over here! We can help!" she yelled.

But then Margie stepped up next to her. She held a pistol in her hands. But she didn't hold it up to save her father; instead, she looked down on her. "It won't help. I've tried."

Just then, the deer rammed his head into her father's back, the antlers coming out of his chest. It swung him up off the ground.

"No!" she yelled and tried to run to him. But her movements were slow, and the fog was thick, keeping her from him.

The deer dropped her father's body and turned to face her, blood dripping from its antlers and running down its nose.

Its black, glossy eyes stared her down, unblinking. She felt fear ripple through her body, but she didn't stop. She pushed through the fog, running straight for the deer.

Right when she was nearly there, it disappeared, leaving her father's broken and bleeding body on the ground. She dropped to her knees and flipped him over. But it wasn't her father; it was Brady. He was covered in blood, eyes staring out into the fog.

She tried to scream, but there was no sound. All of a sudden, Brady's broken body started to slide away from her. "No!" she tried to scream, but again it came out silent. The fog circled her, sweeping Brady from her. It was dark. She felt a burning sensation in her chest. It stung, burning hot. She felt wet, warm liquid running down her stomach. She rolled her head side to side, her breath coming short and quick.

"Roxy?" She heard a deep voice and thought for a second that it was her father's.

"Roxy, can you hear me?" the voice said again.

It wasn't her father's, but it was familiar.

"Open your eyes, Roxy," he said again. She tried.

Everything was dark, and her head was spinning. Her eyelids felt like they weighed a ton. It took all of her effort to open them. She wanted to keep them closed.

"Come on, Roxy, I need you to wake up." The voice had a sound of desperation.

The voice brought her back. The images of Brady, of Sydney, and of Asa. The last week flew through her mind, and she remembered.

She sat straight up. Dizziness swept through her body, and she grabbed the headrest in front of her and focused on the voice.

"It's me, Asa. How do you feel?"

"Dizzy," was all she could muster.

She looked around. It was night, and they were in a car. Asa was sitting in the driver's seat alone.

"Where are we? Where are Brady and Sydney?"

"Everything is fine," he started. "Brady and Sydney are finding out where we are, and then we are getting out of here." He looked away from her and back out the front window.

She adjusted herself in the back seat. She felt the sting in her chest again and looked down. She was wearing nothing but a large white T-shirt covered in blood. She panicked, thinking of her dream, and pulled the T-shirt up and saw more blood. When she looked at her chest, she gasped. There was a large V cut on her chest; it was deep and leaking blood down her front. The two smaller slashes above it were also leaking blood with every rise of her chest.

"What the hell?" she stammered.

"They cut you and Sydney pretty bad." Asa said quietly, keeping his eyes forward. "You girls were tied to the table when me and Brady finally got to you."

She looked up at Asa, and even in the dark night, she could see blood running down the side of his face and the bruises around his eyes.

"Are you okay?" she asked and reached across to the front seat.

"I'm fine," he said, ignoring her hand. He looked out the front windshield.

They sat there in silence for a few seconds until it all came rushing back.

"I woke up," she started, her voice low. "I woke up and saw a deer skull. But a man's body and hands. He had a large gold knife, and he was raking it across Sydney's body." She looked down at her chest again, the memories flooding back. "I screamed for them to stop. I thought they were killing her. Then the deer turned. He had a syringe in his hand."

She looked down at her arm. It was too dark to see anything, and she looked back up to Asa. His face was tired, and he shook his head, like he was having trouble thinking or seeing.

"Are you sure you're all right?" she asked again, but all Asa did was look up at her. "I'm sorry we couldn't get to you guys sooner. They had us locked in a room, in that house. He pointed at a large white house across a lawn. They took us to you, to watch you guys be tortured by the man with the skull face."

"It's not your fault," she said and scooted up in the seat. "What matters is that we are all back together and getting the hell out of here."

"That's not the point," he paused. "Besides, we aren't all together yet." Asa pointed out, scanning again.

"We will be," she said.

She sat back, willing the dizziness to relent. She took deep breaths and tried not to think of her dream. She wanted Sydney and Brady back safe. Then the four of them needed to get out.

"How long have they been in there?" she asked.

But before Asa could answer, she heard the roar of an engine. She shuffled over to the middle of the back seat and stared out the front window, where Asa's gaze was already fixed.

A large black SUV, headlights bouncing, skidded through the grass and stopped. Four men jumped out and headed for the house.

"Shit." Asa started the car and threw it into drive. He looked back at her. "Hold on."

He punched the gas, and the jeep spun its tires in the soft ground. When it finally caught, she was thrown back in the seat, and she reached over to put her seat belt on. Asa headed straight out onto the lawn. He held the gun out the window and fired shots at the men running for the door. Three of the men made it in but Asa hit another in the back, and he fell to the ground.

227

She looked over and saw another pair of headlights coming around from the other side of the house.

"Asa!" she shouted, trying to warn him of the incoming car.

Asa looked and turned the jeep, heading straight for it.

"Hang on, I'm going to cut him off."

But instead of stopping or turning away, the SUV didn't slow; instead, it sped up. A man on the passenger side hung his body out the window, his long blond hair blowing straight back from the speed of the vehicle, and the huge demonic smile, lite by another pair of headlights, had her ducking behind the seat. She heard three gunshots before the SUV slammed into the side of the jeep. It hit on the front passenger door and had the jeep spinning sideways. She was thrown to the side, but the seat belt kept her upright. When the jeep stopped, they were facing the way they had come. She looked over to Asa, and he was leaning over the steering wheel, breathing hard.

"Get out of the car." He breathed through gritted teeth.

"You're hurt?" she said, struggling with the seat belt.

"Fine." He threw open his door and twisted out.

She slid over to the opposite door to meet him. When her feet hit the cold, wet grass, she realized that she was barefoot. She looked to Asa and saw a small red hole in his chest. Blood poured down his stained white undershirt. She reached for him as he stumbled toward her.

"Oh my god, Asa." She hurried to his side and pressed her hand to his wound, trying to stop the blood flow.

He grabbed her and spun her behind him as he took another shot to the shoulder. With his good arm, he held out his pistol and fired three times, hitting the man with the hair and evil smile every time in the chest.

"Get his rifle," he ordered her.

She ran toward him. When she reached him, she slipped in the wet grass and fell to her knees. The jolt had her head spinning. She pulled the large rifle from the man's hands. She ignored the blood and his cold, dead eyes.

She stood and took two steps before she stumbled. The wave of dizziness gripped her head, and she almost fell. She looked to her side to get her bearings and noticed the SUV that had hit them. She saw that the driver was slumped over the wheel, either dead or unconscious.

She made it back to the jeep. Asa's shoulder wound had his arm dangling at his side and, using the jeep hood for cover, he was shooting with his good hand.

She ran up next to him and handed him the gun. She peeked over the hood and watched as a man came running from the side of the house. More were coming. Asa fired the rifle but he couldn't get a good shot. Shooting with one hand and the gun's recoil had him grimacing with pain.

"Roxy," he said. "I'm going to need you to shoot."

She took a step back. "Me?"

Asa ducked down behind the jeep, his face slack with pain. Blood was seeping fast out of his chest wound. Her heart fell to her feet. Asa was hurt bad. How many times had he stepped up for her and her sister? This man was one of only two reasons she was still alive.

She stepped up and took the gun from him.

"Keep the butt of the gun tight to your shoulder."

She nodded and stood, doing what he said. She fired round after round into the group of navy-blue-suited men. She watched one fall to the ground while holding his leg and another jump behind the other SUV for cover.

From the corner of her eye, she saw the back porch door swing open, and Brady stepped out. Her heart jumped; relief filled her until she realized that he was shirtless, bleeding, and bruised. She saw a man head straight for him, and she shot several rounds at him. The man fell to the ground in front of Brady. He swung his head over and saw her. His face relaxed just for a second, then turned hard again as he fired shots into the crowd. He, too, had a rifle, and she wondered where he got it from.

Brady stepped forward, and Sydney stepped out, pistol raised; she was also taking shots. Roxy was taken aback by her sister's appearance. She, too, was covered in blood, wearing only a white button-up shirt that clung wet and red to her chest.

She fired more rounds into the group of men. She was trying to cover for Brady; they were slowly making their way back to her.

They were about ten feet away when another black SUV came swerving around the house and through the lawn. This time the back seat window was down, and a dome light showed a robed man with an animal skull for a face drove by. He had a rifle, like the others and was shooting into the crowd. He didn't care who he hit; he was swinging the rifle left and right, showering the lawn with bullets. The spray of bullets came like rain. She watched as Brady pulled Sydney down to the ground.

She dropped her gun and ducked down and covered Asa's body with her own. He couldn't take another bullet.

The sound of bullets whizzing by and shattering glass had her holding tight to Asa.

"We're going to be okay," she whispered over and over. "We're going to be okay."

Sydney

The bullets were never-ending. She was on the ground, and Brady was next to her, pulling her into his side. She saw the SUV coming and saw Cal driving, his devilish grin wide. When the back window came down and the skull face appeared with a gun, she froze with fear. Brady had pulled her down, and she racked her jaw on the ground. The pain had shot through her head. She laid there, head throbbing, bullets whizzing by, and she thought that this was it. But Brady had demanded that she crawl to the jeep, and that's what she did.

They rounded the side of the jeep just as the bullets stopped, and Cal and the freak disappeared around the other side of the house.

What she saw shattered her heart.

Roxy and Asa were huddled together. Lite by the headlights of a smashed SUV a few feet away, Asa was up against the jeep, his head slumped to the side. Roxy's small body was trying to cover him, protecting him. Her sweet, shy sister had her eyes tightly shut, and she was whispering in Asa's ear.

Both her and Brady crawled to them. Brady slowly peeled Roxy from Asa's body.

"Are you okay?" Brady ran his hands all over her, checking for bullet wounds.

She looked to Asa as Brady checked Roxy. Asa was bleeding from two bullet wounds, one in his shoulder and the other in his chest.

"Asa, oh my god." She crawled as fast as she could and grabbed Asa's face. He moaned.

"Brady! Asa's been shot." She all but screamed. Brady whipped his head from Roxy and saw his cousin's condition.

Brady's body sagged as he took in Asa's limp form and pale skin. "He's going to be okay," Brady said to himself. He stood slowly, his rifle held up. He scanned over the jeep's hood and took two shots.

He ducked back down. "There's an empty SUV still in good condition. We need to get to it."

He looked to her and Roxy, then at Asa.

"I'm going to have to carry Asa. Sydney, you still have ammo left?"

She popped the clip like she had seen them do before. "Only three shots left," she counted.

He handed her the rifle he had taken from the man in the stairwell. She handed him her pistol, and he placed it in the small of his back. "Roxy, you have ammo left?'

She nodded and reached for the rifle, where she had dropped it.

Brady stood and scanned the yard. It was quiet. "I don't know if they are all dead or if they retreated, but we make our move now." He bent and shifted Asa onto his shoulders into a fireman's hold. When he stood, his face strained with effort and pain. She remembered his bruised ribs.

She looked to Roxy. "Ready?"

Roxy held the gun to her shoulder, looking way more dangerous than she ever thought possible. "Ready." To her surprise, Roxy took the lead, and Brady followed. She took the rear, holding the rifle to her shoulder, and going with instinct, she turned as she moved, covering their backs and sides.

They made it halfway there when a man came bursting through the porch door. She whipped her gun toward him, but before she could pull the trigger, Roxy took a shot. It missed and hit above his head. The door frame burst into splinters. The man ducked his head but recovered fast and aimed his pistol.

Sydney didn't hesitate. Center mass ran through her head, and she pulled the trigger. The shot hit him square in the chest, and the man fell.

She had no time to process if she was happy she hit her target or dread that she just took another human life. Again. Brady picked up his pace, and she scrambled to catch up. Just then, three others came around the side of the house.

"Hit the light!" Brady yelled. They were almost to the SUV.

She took aim for the porch light but missed and put a hole in the door.

She heard Roxy shoot again and watched as one of the men fall to the ground. She took aim again for the light but was distracted when a bullet whizzed by her ear.

"Shit," she said simply and just opened fire at the light. After about three quick shots, the bulb popped, and the light went out. They were in complete darkness now.

"Quick!" Brady said, breathing hard.

She aimed her gun down and started to jog. She kept her ears open, trying to focus on the dark mass in front of her that was Brady and Asa, and trying to listen for the other two men out there.

Roxy hit the car first, and when she opened the door, the dome light came on, giving off little light. Brady gently dumped Asa in the back seat and took Roxy's gun. Roxy jumped in the front seat as Brady took point, and she started the rig. They hadn't taken the keys out, and for that, she was grateful. She watched as Roxy slid over the center console and into the passenger seat.

Brady was firing at the corner of the house, where she assumed the men were holed up.

Asa was lying in the back, blood dripping from his wounds; he was out cold. She arranged his feet and arms so that he was in a more comfortable position and then slid in under his legs.

"Roxy, I need napkins or a blanket. Something I can use to place pressure on his wounds."

Roxy immediately started searching the glove box. Sydney looked in the back cargo, but in the dark, she couldn't make anything out.

She realized the shirt that she was wearing had long sleeves rolled up and she started to pull, trying to tear them.

"Here, this was in the glove box." Roxy handed her a small pocket knife.

Just then, Brady jumped in behind the wheel, slamming the door and cutting off the light. He threw it in drive and gunned it. She was thrown back in the seat. Glad they were getting out of there; she breathed a sigh of relief. She started to cut her sleeves.

"Roxy, have that gun ready," Brady stated as he pulled around to the front of the house.

She had cut one sleeve and folded it up and placed it on the chest wound. It was bleeding more than the other, and she was hoping that it hadn't hit something important. She just started to cut the second when they came around the front of the house.

The SUV lit up. Surprised, she looked up to see a row of black SUVs lining the driveway. They formed a wall, their headlights spotlighting and blinding them. It made her feel like she was caught in the act. The large trees that lined the driveway behind the SUV were lit by red brake lights, giving their exit an eerie, bloody look.

Roxy

She was blinded. She raised her hand to her forehead to try to see. There were at least twenty black SUVs lining the driveway and the yard, completely blocking their exit.

She looked to Brady. They were outnumbered and trapped; there was no way out.

His hands clutched the wheel, his knuckles white. She saw blood covering his bare chest, most likely from Asa's gunshot wounds. His glasses were broken and his face looked hard. He turned to her, and his face softened, and he smiled. He leaned forward. Understanding what he wanted, she leaned forward and kissed him. She ran her hand down the side of his face. When their lips parted, he rested his forehead on hers. "I love you," he said quietly.

"I love you, too," she said back. She knew what this meant; he was saying goodbye. Her eyes filled with tears.

She turned to the back seat and saw Sydney. Her sleeves were cut off her shirt and covered in blood, and both hands were applying pressure to Asa's bullet wounds. Sydney was staring at Asa. She lifted her hand from the shoulder wound and took Asa's; she kissed his palm. "Now it's my turn to keep you safe." She gently laid it on his chest. She applied pressure back on his wound and looked up at her.

"We can do this," Sydney said.

"We're not going down without a fight," she said in response to Sydney, then turned to Brady. Brady smiled and nodded.

"That's my girls." He put the SUV into neutral and revved the engine.

He placed his hands on the shifter to put it in drive when headlights appeared, coming up the driveway behind the SUVs. They were going so fast that the truck drifted around a corner, the turn spraying gravel everywhere. There were four pickup trucks. Two were old, dented, and rusty, and the other two were brand new.

She watched as men jumped out of the beds and cabs of the trucks; there were at least twenty, all armed with large rifles. They were decked out in military gear from head to toe.

She was just relieved they weren't in navy suits.

They started to fire on the SUVs that were blocking their path. The Brotherhood, suddenly under attack, turned their attention to the newcomers.

"No way," Brady said quietly, and he squinted through the windshield. "That's Chess."

A bullet hit the front end of the SUV, giving off a loud, tinkling noise. Brady threw the SUV into reverse and swung the vehicle into the back yard. He pulled all the way back to the small dirt road that led to the cabin, and parked, hidden in the tree line.

"Stay here." He reached for the guns that she had placed on the floorboards.

"Wait," she said, grabbing his arm. "Where are you going? Who are those people?"

"It's an old army buddy. Max must have called him in. I'm going to help. Can't have Chess cleaning up my mess." Brady was half smiling when he said it.

When he looked up into her eyes, he placed his hand on her face. "Stay here and help Sydney take care of Asa. I'll be back soon. Then we're getting out of here."

Fear gripped her. He pulled her face in for a kiss. "We are going to be okay now," he said. "I meant what I said. I love you."

It almost made her feel better, and she gave a smile. "Me too."

His smile grew, and it was nice to see the old Brady again.

He shoved the pistol into his belt and grabbed a rifle. He handed her the other. "Take care of our family."

She took the gun and smiled. She was going to protect their family.

*

The sound of gunfire went on for what seem like forever. She watched out the window for anyone or anything that moved.

"How's Asa?" she asked, not taking her eyes off the yard.

"I don't know. His pulse is still weak. He's so pale," Sydney's voice cracked. "I don't know how much longer he has."

"He'll make it." She paused, then added, "Just listen. The gunfire has

235

pretty much stopped."

They both listened. There was a shot here and there, but the majority of them had ceased.

"Look," Sydney said, pointing through the seats out the front window.

There were two shadows jogging their way. They were highlighted by the glow of headlights coming from the side yard. But shadows covered their faces.

She gripped the gun. What if they were from the Brotherhood? What if they won and Brady and his friend were dead?

She slowly opened the door and stepped out, gun held up.

"Stop right there," she said in a stern voice. Only to her, it sounded weak and scared, just like she felt. If this was the Brotherhood, she was going to have to kill them and then try to drive them out. Her knees started to shake.

"Whoa, whoa." It was Brady's voice. "It's me. Don't shoot. It's done." She dropped her gun and ran to him. She jumped into his arms and buried her face in his shoulder. "It's okay." He kissed the top of her head. She let go of him but only stepped to the side and took his hand. At that moment, she never wanted to leave his side.

They continued to walk to the SUV.

"Meet Chester Rodriguez, or we call him Chess," Brady said, gesturing to the man standing next to him. He was a couple inches shorter than Brady. He had dark hair and dark eyes. He gave a short nod. "Nice to meet you. Glad we could come help—me and the boys have been looking for something to do. Plus, I'm used to saving this guy's ass." He slapped Brady on the back, making Brady wince.

They reached the SUV, and Chess looked in the window. Sydney gave a yelp and jumped. Chess threw his hands up in surrender. "Sorry, Miss. Just checking on Asa."

Brady came up behind him. "It's okay, Sydney, this is Chess. He was a field medic. He can help."

Sydney shuffled over and let Chess open the door. His face grew serious, losing the playful manner he had with Brady.

"It's bad. We need to get you to that plane now and him to the hospital."

Chess slid in into the third row and leaned over the back of the seat. He started taking Asa's pulse and checking his pupils. He caught Sydney watching him.

"You're doing good. Keep pressure on the wounds."

Brady pulled the SUV out of the tree line and through the yard back out to the front. She looked around the driveway. There were men driving the SUVs out of the way, giving them a path through.

"Stop here," Chess said. He leaned forward, rolled the window down, and spoke Spanish to a man. He, too, looked and acted military, and when Chess was done giving his orders, the man whistled, and all the others ran back to their trucks.

Chess rolled his window up. "The guys are going to give us an escort to the airport. Where Max should be by the time we get there."

"So, how did you know?" Brady asked, turning out onto the main road.

She still hadn't let go of Brady's hand, and he didn't seem to mind driving with only one.

"Max told Clint that you were sending files. Clint jumped on it. Then, a new email came in saying that they needed all available brothers to this address. That the orders were to kill the two males and bring the females in alive. Clint figured you were going to need help. Max knew I was in New Orleans and called to see if I could help. So, I said, 'The boys and I, we're bored. Let's go save Sinclair's ass again.'" Chess chuckled. "Good thing, too. You guys were outnumbered. Looked like you were ready to give them hell, though." Roxy looked back at him. He looked up at her and smiled.

"Thank you," she said.

He just nodded and started to take Asa's vitals again.

"So, how did you get into this mess?" Chess asked, looking down at Asa.

She looked over at Brady; she leaned her head back on the headrest of the seat. She turned to look out the window and watch the trees fly by outside as she listened to Brady tell the story.

It took two hours to get to the airport. She was drifting in and out of sleep. She picked up parts of the conversation between Chess and Brady. Chess had a lot questions about the Brotherhood and agreed also that deer mask guy was most likely the leader. She heard Brady say he wanted a deeper dive into the files he sent Clint, along with the ones he downloaded on a USB drive. She wanted to study them too, and tried to listen more, but she drifted off again. Images of the deer came back. It was chasing her through the woods. She awoke with a jump when Brady said that they had arrived.

She sat up and looked out the window. It was a small airfield, and a small personal jet sat on the runway. She watched as four men in military gear jogged out, guns drawn. Chess's group pulled up behind in their trucks and were quickly given friendly greetings.

A doctor in a white lab coat ran out, followed by a stretcher. Seeing that got her moving, and she exited the car.

Chess, the doctor, and two nurses lifted Asa onto it, and they immediately wheeled him to the plane. Sydney followed close by.

"Ready?" Brady asked, walking to her. "A nurse is going to check your cuts. I'm going to thank Chess's crew, then head in. I'll be right behind you."

She only nodded. Her chest ached and felt tight. He kissed her forehead. "We're safe now."

He walked toward the pickup trucks.

When she stepped on the plane, it was small. Asa was in the middle, surrounded by the doctor and two nurses. They were putting him on an IV. Sydney was standing back, watching tears running down her face. She went to her.

"He's with a doctor now." She went to put her arm around Sydney but winced with pain. The cuts on her chest reopened, and she felt warm blood run down her front.

A nurse stepped up to them. She was an older, skinny woman with blonde hair. "Come; let's go to the back room. I was told you girls have large cuts on your chests."

"What about Brady?" she asked. "He's hurt too."

"Chess already agreed to look him over till the doctor can. Now let me see." She shut the door of the back room behind her.

She looked to Sydney and they shrugged. Sydney started to unbutton her shirt. But she wanted out of the dirty, blood-soaked rag, so she just tore it over her head.

The nurse gasped. She looked from her to Sydney and then back. She signed the cross over her chest and kissed her hand. "Mother Mary," she said, and with shaky hands, she got the gauze from the cupboard.

Sydney

The nurse cleaned both their cuts then called the other nurse in to help stitch. When the other nurse came in, she couldn't help it. "Is Asa okay?" she asked, sitting up straighter in the chair.

The nurse smiled. "He's lost a lot of blood. The doctor was able to get the two bullets, but he needs surgery."

The nurse went to the small bathroom, and she heard the water run. When she came back, she was drying her hands on a white towel, and she sat down in front of her. She started to examine her wounds when a frown appeared on her face.

She started to stitch. "Is he going to live?" she asked quietly.

The nurse didn't look up but instead shot her with more numbing agent.

"Mary Sinclair has some of the best doctors waiting for us to land. Now, lie back and let me work."

Her answer was not too convincing, but she leaned back in the chair and let the nurse stitch.

An hour later, they were stitched and bandaged.

She was feeling tired but wanted out of the small room to check on Asa. One of the nurses found two bathrobes; they were black with a gold S embroidered on them. She slipped it on and noticed how dirty her feet were. She thought how badly she needed a shower.

They exited the small room; Roxy went straight to Brady. He and Chess were talking while sitting on the small recliners. Brady still had no shirt, but his ribs were wrapped, along with several bandages on his arms. They had washed most of the blood off, and he had new glasses. They were talking low, heads close.

Asa was still on the stretcher; he had been wheeled to the side. His head was wrapped, along with his chest. There were tubes coming from his arms, and he had been hooked up to a monitor of some sort. She went to him. She grabbed his hand and held it. She looked down at his face. He looked ten years older; his beard was scruffy and his face pale.

Roxy, leaving Brady, came to her side and put her arm around her shoulder. "He will pull through; he's a fighter. He took that shoulder wound for me. Pulled me out of the way at the last second. I'll be forever thankful." Roxy wiped a tear from her eye, then rested her cheek on her shoulder. "Are you okay?"

She just nodded her head. She had no words in that moment.

Brady stepped up. He looked down at his cousin but said nothing. He pulled both girls into a hug. "We'll be safe in Maine. Granny has twenty-four-hour guards along with the best security system I could design. We'll get Asa better, and then we take those bastards down."

*

When the plane finally landed, the doctor and nurses ordered Asa off first. Sydney looked out the small window and saw that there was an ambulance and several cars on the airfield. She stood up as they carried the stretcher out the door. "I'm going with Asa," she said and tried to exit the plane.

Brady stood. "You can't. It's not safe. You need to come with us and get to Granny's."

"No. Asa will be by himself, unprotected." She felt hysteria rising in her chest, which had her cuts screaming in pain.

"He will be protected. The doctor understands the situation, and we are sending armed guards with him. As soon as he is stable, he will be coming to Granny's to be watched over by an in-home doctor." Brady took her hand.

"But what if he doesn't make it?" she asked.

He looked her in the eyes. "We have to believe he will."

She exited the plane and watched as Asa was slid into the back of the ambulance, and with four large white trucks and SUVs following, he was escorted off the runway.

Panic set in. They hadn't been separated since this whole thing started, and she was getting used to him being around. She felt exposed without him nearby.

That thought had her feeling weak. What was wrong with her? She had always been independent. She was a thief, a good one too. She always worked alone and had never needed anyone. But watching Asa drive away hurt, beaten, and shot made her feel vulnerable. *Maybe it was better that he was somewhere else*, she thought. She hated herself for it.

Her self-loathing ended when a large, gruff voice broke her thoughts.

"What's this I hear? You having all the fun without me?" She turned and saw a large man walking toward them. He looked like he spent all his free time in the gym. He had dark hair and skin, and his arms were covered in tattoos.

Brady walked up, grabbed his hand, and pulled the man in for a short hug. "Max, it's good to see you," Brady said with a smile.

"I'll fill you in in the car. We're too exposed out here. They're everywhere, man." Brady waved her and Roxy over to get in a white four-door truck.

They pulled out, and she noticed three other white vehicles pull in behind them.

She watched as Brady scanned their surroundings and watched the vehicles behind them.

"Max, this is Roxy and Sydney Wright," he said. She watched as Max eyed them through the rearview mirror.

"I get it now," Max said with a laugh. Brady only glared at Max. Max's eyes went up with surprise.

"This is Max. The head of Granny's security," he said. "We were in the army together also."

"Yeah, saved this guy's butt many times," Max added.

"Please," Brady said, rolling his eyes. "If it wasn't for me, you wouldn't have made it out alive."

"True." Max held his fist up, and Brady bumped it with his own.

She wasn't up for the banter. She was too worried for Asa's future and her own thoughts. She slumped in the seat and let sleep take her.

She dreamed that she was running down the hall of the house. The red carpet was wet and splashed under her bare feet. The dragon statue with the broken wings was chasing her. It was as big as the hall and was blowing fire. The curtains next to her burst into flames. Fear had her running faster. There was a door at the end of the hall. But it seemed to only get further and further away. She heard the dragon blow fire again, and she expected to feel the heat, but she awoke with a small yelp.

Roxy looked over at her.

"Nightmare?" Roxy asked quietly.

She shook her head yes.

"I've been getting them too." Roxy reached over and took her hand.

Finding comfort, she leaned back in the seat.

A few minutes later, they turned down a one-lane road buried deep in trees. They came to a gate with a guard station. After a few minutes of talk and what sounded like more banter, the guard opened the gate and let them drive through. The one-lane road was surrounded by trees, and the forest was thick with its dark green and brown colors. She found it soothing and watched as the trees widened and came to a large concrete fence.

It, too, had a guard tower, and she watched as armed men patrolled the fence line. The gate opened, and they drove in. The lawn was huge; it sprawled for acres. The huge house looked like a southern plantation, and roses surrounded the porch. The large circular driveway was gravel and had a fountain in the middle.

When they finally stopped, the big front doors opened, and a thin, older woman stepped out. She had a blonde cap of hair. She was dressed in an expensive looking coral suit. Pearls hung at her neck.

When they all stepped out of the truck, her hands went to her mouth, the rising sun glittering off her large rings.

We must look horrible, she thought. She looked to Roxy still in the black robe, her feet dirty and bare like her own. Brady still had no shirt and was covered in bandages and bruises.

"Oh my!" she said. "It's worse than they told me."

Brady quickly jogged up the stairs and met her on the porch. He bent down and gave her a big hug.

He turned and introduced them. "This is Roxy and Sydney Wright." He put his arm around the woman. "This is Mary Sinclair, my grandmother."

They both gave weak smiles.

"Please, come in." She gestured to the door. "I had Ann make soup and sandwiches. I figured you all would be hungry."

They started up the stairs. Even though she couldn't remember the last time she ate, the sound of food made her sick to her stomach. Mary must have seen the look. "A shower might be better first?" she said.

"Any word about Asa?" Brady asked as they entered the house. She perked at the question, eager for an answer.

"Not yet," Mary said with a frown. "But they promised to update me as soon as they can."

Brady nodded. "I need to get to my computer. The brotherhood has the ring now; I have research to do. Can you send my food up?"

"Of course." Mary said. This was obviously a regular request.

Brady turned to Roxy. "You need to eat and shower."

"I want to check out the research too," Roxy started. "I would like to get my hands on a computer again." She smiled.

"You come up after you eat. I'll have it all ready for you by then."

Brady pulled her in for a soft hug and kissed her on the mouth. Sydney couldn't help but see the large grin Mary sported at the public display of affection.

Brady turned. "Good to see you, Granny." He turned and started for the large staircase next to the entrance.

"Come, girls, I'll show you to your rooms."

The foyer was huge with high ceilings. The floors were hardwood and polished to a shine. There was art and family pictures tastefully hanging from walls and set on tables. The colors of the room were light but subtle. She liked it. It felt homey but also full of class at the same time. The rooms were spacious, and there was little furniture. Their rooms were on the first floor.

"These two are for you girls. They each have a bathroom, and I had some clothes brought in for you too." She looked at both girls. Her face was soft, and the wrinkles in the corner of her eyes deepened as she gave a weak smile. She lowered her head. "I'm so very sorry for all of this. I want to explain everything. Will you girls give me the chance?"

She stayed silent. After all, it had all started with this woman.

Roxy answered for her. "Yes."

Mary nodded. "Get cleaned up, then we talk." With that, she turned and left.

She entered the room. It was white-walled, and the bed was made with a blue comforter. Little pictures of ocean landscapes hung on the wall. There was a small dresser and mirror. On the dresser was a pile of clothes. There were bras and underwear still with tags. She also saw her favorite—yoga pants along with a tank top, hoodie, and a pair of running shoes.

She looked into the bathroom and saw the basics—soaps and shampoos. There were big, fluffy towels. She picked one up. It had been a while since she showered. She looked up in the mirror over the sink. Her black hair was matted and crusted with blood. She had dark circles under her eyes and a fading bruise along her jawbone.

She opened the bathrobe and saw the white bandage was starting to bloom red. She unwrapped the Ace bandage around her chest and peeled the tape off the gauze. When it was off, she stared at her chest. The stitches were dark against her pale skin. The bottom half was oozing blood. The cuts showed bright and red. She looked like a monster, Frankenstein, all stitched together. She started to cry and dropped to the floor of the bathroom.

Roxy

She found the clothes that Mary left for her on the dresser. The black T-shirt and hoodie, the jeans and Converse—it seemed Mary knew her. She caught her reflection in the mirror above the dresser. Her skin was pale, and her cheeks looked hollow. She tried patting her hair down, but it was crusted up in the back. She turned and looked around the room. A sense of panic ran through her; she didn't want to be in this room alone. She grabbed the clothes off the dresser and she whipped the door open and turned to Sydney's. She didn't even knock, but just entered. She dumped the clothes on the bed and called for Sydney. When she didn't answer, she made her way to the bathroom. She found Sydney on the floor, tears streaming down her face, her bathrobe open, and her wound uncovered.

She fell to the ground with her sister and, together, they wept.

When they finally pulled themselves together, they realized that taking a shower wasn't going to work because they needed to keep their stitches dry. They ended up washing each other's hair in the sink and took turns taking a bath. Sydney never asked her why she was in her room; she must have understood the need to not be alone.

After Sydney took a bath, she rinsed the tub and let it fill back up. She watched as the tub slowly filled and watched the steam smoke upward. She wasn't really thinking of anything when she slipped into the water. She immediately sighed from the warm water and let her muscles relax. She took her time washing and paid special attention to her feet.

When she got out, she noticed the water was a combination of blood and mud. The memory of waking strapped to the table and seeing the man dressed in the robe and deer skull cutting Sydney's chest came flashing through her mind. She closed her eyes and gripped the sink counter while trying not to cry out.

Brady flashed through her mind. The way he looked the first time she met him. He had her tackled to the ground in the mud. She remembered him standing up and reaching his hand down to help her up. She opened her eyes.

She looked in the mirror and focused. The bath had improved her appearance some. She had a little more color. She brushed her hair, and it went down in its natural straight style. *She needed a haircut*, she thought her normally short, bob haircut was almost touching her shoulders. She dressed slowly, paying close attention not to tear her stitches.

Sydney jerked the door open. "Good, you're ready," she said. "I have some questions for Mary, and I want to know any updates on Asa. Plus, I bet you're chomping at the bit to get your hands on Brady's computer." She smiled after the last bit and gave a little laugh. The bath must have done some good for Sydney too.

A knock on the door sounded as she was zipping up her hoodie.

Sydney answered, and it was a short Italian woman, probably in her sixties.

"I'm Ann, and Ms. Sinclair wanted me to check on you girls. Food is ready." She gave a slight bow.

"We were just on our way down." Sydney turned to her. "Ready?"

She nodded and followed them out the door.

*

Ann led them to a small room. Immediately to the left of the door was a small bar with stools; there was an average fridge and sink with a small countertop. There were shelves lined with martini glasses and tumblers. The room stepped down into another area. It had a short table with four chairs and one whole side of the room were windows overlooking the well-manicured lawn and off into the tree line. The sun was high in the sky, and she wondered what time it was. Besides some large plants in the corners, there was nothing else.

Mary walked in right behind them. "There you girls are. Ann, can you bring the food, please?"

Ann just gave a little nod, then left silently.

Mary pulled three bottles of water out of the fridge and took down some glasses.

Roxy eyed the glass and when Mary handed it to her, she couldn't help herself. She took big gulps till she realized that Mary and Sydney were staring. "Sorry," she said, wiping her mouth. "I just can't remember the last time I had a cool glass of water."

Mary smiled. "Don't mind me, you drink as much water as you want."

Even though Sydney wasn't gulping it down, she noticed that she was also drinking more than normal.

Just then, Ann came in holding a tray; it held steaming bowls, and she placed them on the table.

"Please, come sit," Mary said. "Knowing my boys, I'm sure you girls have probably been living off of takeout and junk food."

They both smiled. It was pretty much what they lived off of before all this anyway, but neither commented.

"Any word on Asa?" Sydney asked. She was seated in front of the soup, but her hands were in her lap.

"The doctor called and said that he is still in surgery, but it's going well." Mary picked up her spoon. "Don't worry, Sydney," Mary said. "I have the best doctors. My grandson will be coming home to us." Mary's face was full of determination. This woman was used to getting what she wanted. It made her smile.

"But I would like to ask for a moment of your time." Mary took a deep breath. "I would like to explain myself to you girls and give you an apology."

She looked up at them.

"That's not necessary," she said, looking to Sydney, who nodded in agreement.

"It is." Mary sat up in her chair. She put her spoon down on the napkin next to her bowl and took a deep breath.

"I want to start by saying I'm sorry for what happened to your father. I had no idea anyone even knew about this stone, let alone wanted it." Mary took a deep breath. "At first, I didn't really believe in the curse. I figured it was just a family legend. But when my husband died in a plane crash in good weather and with an experienced pilot, I started to believe. Then, when Brady and Haley's mother died and I watched my son and grandchildren mourn her death, I knew that something had to be done. That it was real.

That night, I had a dream. Henry, my ancestor—the one who found the ring in the first place—came to me. He said that our family and others had suffered enough and that it was time to end it. To find the ring and bury it in the grave of his one true love, Abby. By doing that, they could finally be together, and the curse he started could finally be broken. I awoke that morning with a new purpose. So, I hired investigators and started research

247

myself. I looked in all of our family history and old folklore from England, which is where my family originated. I also researched rare stones, white stones, stones with legends. After years, one of my investigators found an estate in Japan that had a ring with a white stone. I immediately bid on the estate. But I was outbid by an anonymous buyer. I found out that the estate was being shipped to Seattle. I had my investigator hire a low-level thief from the area that could get a job unloading the cargo, find the ring, and bring it to me."

Mary took a sip of water and looked up at them.

Roxy was listening and stirring her soup, whereas Sydney had been listening intently, her soup untouched.

Her father's murder was finally going to make sense.

"I really didn't think the buyer was even interested in a worthless ring; it had no value. The shipment contained thousands of dollars' worth of art and jewelry." Mary paused. "I met with your father."

That got her to look up from her soup.

"I told him the whole story. I think your father was a romantic. He liked it." Mary smiled. "He asked millions of questions. What did Henry find in the caves in Ireland? What was the story with the loss of his thumb? How did he curse the stone?"

It sounded just like her father; he loved stories and adventures. Her heart ached thinking about him.

"Of course, I had no answers for him, and I think he was a little disappointed. But he agreed to help. I think losing your mother early also had him wanting to help. He told me about her." She paused. "She sounded like a wonderful woman and your father truly loved her."

She had no memories of her mother. Not even a picture. Everything burned down in the fire. Anger welled in her. The Brotherhood burned her house down, taking not only her father but the memory of her mother as well. She pushed her bowl away; she couldn't stomach it.

Mary continued, "I promised your father cash and that I would help him move to Maine. I think your father felt this was an opportunity to start over. He took it. He called me the morning after; he said he had the ring hidden and the plane tickets. He was going to leave in a few days, and I arranged to have a car pick you guys up at the airport. The morning you were supposed to arrive, my driver called to tell me Gabe hadn't been on the flight. I got nervous. I called and called but couldn't get a hold of him.

I had my investigator look for him. It didn't take long to find out what happened.

"He was murdered, his daughters orphaned, and his house burned down. I panicked. My investigator told me you girls were staying with your neighbor, Margie Simms. He also told me that a group that called themselves the Brotherhood were suspected of being involved, but there was no proof. I contacted Margie. Told her everything. I was scared for you, girls, and I paid for you two to go to an all-girls' home in Oregon. I had all your records sealed. I offered to relocate Margie as well, but she didn't want to leave her house and said that not even the Brotherhood could make her move away from her home. The next few months, I was so riddled with anxiety and fear that I told myself to take a break from the ring. I had upgraded my security, and I threw myself into work and taking care of my family. The Brotherhood was quiet. I figured they couldn't find you and considered you guys a non-threat. I never forgot, but the anxiety subsided and I started to feel normal again."

Mary picked up her spoon and, looking down, started to stir her soup.

"When Haley and Marcus came to me with their engagement announcement last year, the fear came back. I knew what I had to do. Asa was already an independent investigator, and Brady a tech genius. It was almost like fate. I just knew that this time it would end."

Mary looked up at them. "I had no idea it was going to be like this. I'm so sorry that I involved you and your father, plus my grandsons are now in trouble too. Everything has spiraled out of control."

She put her face into her hands and started to weep.

Both Roxy and Sydney were silent, not knowing what to do. But Mary pulled herself together quickly. Taking her napkin, she wiped her eyes.

"I found pictures," Sydney said. Both she and Mary turned to stare. "When I was with Brady in the house. There was a whole closet full. Pictures from when we were kids all the way up to the present. I think they have been watching us since the day Dad died."

Roxy was stunned. "Seriously?"

Mary just stared. Sydney described a few of the pictures she found. Mary stood suddenly and turned to the window, looking out. "I thought I was keeping you safe. Hiding you out in Oregon and sealing your records. But this whole time, they knew where you were." Mary turned, her arms crossed over her chest. "Why didn't they come for you sooner?"

"Brady believes that they were waiting for the ring to appear. Give proof that we had it."

Roxy felt a shiver running up her spine. They had been watching the whole time. She felt violated. She had tried hard to keep her life private.

Roxy stood. She needed to get out of there and behind a computer. She was going to get these murderers, and there was only one way she knew how. "Where are Brady's computers?"

"Wait." Mary sounded desperate. "I'll have Ann take you, but please, first, I want to say I'm sorry to both of you." She looked back and forth between them, tears welling in her eyes.

They both just looked at her, unsure of what to do. Her stomach turned. Could she forgive the woman who started this whole thing? Forgive Mary for everything she lost?

Mary took a deep breath. "I'm sorry." Tears started to fall down her cheeks. "If I could go back, I would. I would have done it different."

"How?" Sydney asked.

Roxy looked over at her sister with surprise.

Mary looked up at Sydney.

"I don't know how, but I would have done better by you girls and your father. I would have shut my fear down. I would have stopped hiding and been strong for your family. I'm sorry for my weakness." Mary dropped her arms to her side in defeat.

"I forgive you," Sydney said. "I believe you."

Roxy felt a lightness come across her chest as the words spilled from her mouth. "I forgive you, too. No one could have predicted this would turn out this way." Tears filled her eyes. "I can't be mad at you. This isn't your fault. Our father agreed to this."

Sydney shook her head in agreement.

Mary gasped. She brought her hands to her face and wept. "Thank you," she sobbed.

*

Ann took her to Brady's room. Once inside, she was impressed. There were computer screens everywhere. They were all lit up; she watched as newscasters reported the latest news on the two of them; one had a program running, and she watched as letters, numbers, and words streamed across the screen. One had what looked like important scanned legal documents. The hum of the room was hypnotic, and she couldn't wait to get in there. Brady looked up from his screen. "Hey, how are you?" he asked, standing and pulling her in for a hug. She flinched when their chests bumped, and he let go immediately.

"I'm ready to get behind a computer," she said, ignoring the pain. She sat in the empty desk chair next to him. He frowned. "Well, I'm ready to see your brain in action."

She started to dive into the USB drive that Brady had downloaded. She scanned emails and files. There were a couple photos of her and Sydney on one file and it creeped her out. She tried to connect places and people. Some of them were under short, odd names, and what she thought might be nicknames. She found some mentions of properties and started to research them. Brady was over her shoulder, watching and commenting. Not used to the company when working, she convinced him to finally take a shower, explaining that even though she still loved him, he was stinking up the room. He got the hint and left her to it. Her fingers flew over the keyboard, trying to make connections. When she kept hitting dead ends, she blew out a breath. It was going to be a long night.

Sydney

After Roxy left to find a computer, she made the excuse that she was tired and needed to lie down. But she made Mary promise to wake her with any news from Asa.

Back in her room with nothing to do, she laid down on the bed. She didn't think she was tired, but the next thing she knew, she was waking up to a dark sky outside her window. She looked up to the bedside clock and saw that it was nine p.m. She wondered what day it was. Surely Asa was out of surgery by now.

She got up, went to the bathroom, and splashed water on her face. Her eyes were puffy from the sleep, and she ran a comb through her hair.

She slowly opened her door and checked the hall. No one was around, and she started to wander around. She took a right that led to another hall. She saw pictures hanging on the wall. It wasn't art, but family photos all in nice frames. She saw pictures of Mary and who she assumed was her husband, as they were holding each other. It looked like they were at a wedding. She scanned another. It was Asa and Brady when they were teenagers; they had on basketball jerseys, and there was a hoop in the background. Asa was holding the ball under his arm. Brady had his signature black-framed glasses, his blond hair a mess. Asa's jersey was sweat-stained, but they both had cheesy smiles. They looked young and happy.

"That's one of my favorites." She turned and saw Mary. She was standing at the end of the hall. She was still in her coral suit. There were dark circles under her eyes. But she stood straight, and her arms were crossed in front of her.

"They won that game." Mary started to walk to the photo and stood next to her. "It was the first time Brady played on the team. It took Asa a month to convince him to play." Mary's smile was sad.

"This one here is Haley and Brady." She pointed to an eight by ten photo in a black frame. Brady was standing next to a blonde-haired girl in a prom dress. He was in a T-shirt and jeans. They had the same green eyes and goofy smiles.

"That was Haley's senior prom."

She studied the photo. "Brady didn't go to prom?"

"No, he was already at MIT by then." Mary sported a smile full of pride for her grandson. "He came down that weekend just for Haley. She wanted a picture of them together. Really, I think Brady came down to meet Marcus. Asa had told Brady that a boy was hanging around Haley. But Brady and Asa made it clear to Marcus that Haley was to be respected." Mary smiled warmly.

"Where is Haley?" She looked over at Mary.

"After Brady called and I realized you guys were in trouble, I sent her to Paris. Marcus manages his family's hotels. He was there on business. I sent guards with her. Both Marcus and Haley know what's going on. Haley calls me every day." Mary frowned. "She worries for her brother and Asa."

Mary looked away from the wall. "Come. I was just going to the parlor to have a drink. Will you join me?"

She followed Mary down the hall and into a small room. It had a low-burning fire in the fireplace. The room was dark and gave off a sort of quiet dignity. There were shelves of books along one wall. The other wall was large windows, the dark curtains pulled tightly closed. There were two huge chairs in deep dark red, almost brown in coloring from the low light, next to each other, facing the fire.

Mary walked to a small drink cart and took two glasses and filled them with an amber-colored liquid. She handed one to her and gestured for her to sit.

She sat and took a sip. It burned her throat, and she tried not to gasp for air.

"It's strong, I know. But I feel the circumstances call for it." Mary took a sip. She didn't even flinch but leaned back in the chair.

"This is actually Asa's favorite room. When he visits, I often find him in here at night reading a book and drinking my Scotch." Mary laughed and rolled the glass in her hand.

She pictured Asa in the room, the firelight flickering across his handsome face, a book in his lap. She could see him in the warmth and the low lighting, looking relaxed and content. Her stomach clenched. "Any word?"

"Yes, the surgery went well, and they will be sending him here tomorrow night." Sydney relaxed and breathed a sigh of relief.

"But he isn't conscious, and they don't know when he will wake up. It will be a long road to recover." Mary's voice dropped. "If he will." Her eyes filled with tears, and she looked toward the fire. Sydney did the same.

"I see you worry about him," Mary said a few minutes later, having gotten her composure back.

She looked up to see Mary studying her.

"I owe him everything," she said.

Mary gave a smile. "He's a very serious man when he needs to be, my Asa. He always tries to do the right thing, no matter the cost. He puts a lot of his self-worth into his actions."

"He's a good man. They both are," she said quietly.

"Yes, Brady is too." Mary looked to the fire. "I think my Brady is in love with your sister."

She looked up, shocked by Mary's boldness. "I know that they are," The image of her sister and Brady in the front seats of the SUV, Brady's final good-bye. Her heart had squeezed at the private moment.

"You know Brady is a direct bloodline with Henry Slate?" Mary said, taking another sip and watching her over the top of her glass.

"You believe this curse will get my sister." It wasn't so much of a question but a statement.

Mary nodded. "You know I do, or we wouldn't be in this situation. Your father believed it too."

Sydney sat there for a second, letting it all come down on her. A new determination and fear filled her.

"Well, we're just going to have to get this ring back."

Mary smiled and took another sip.

Sydney turned to the low fire, staring at the flames, thinking of taking the Brotherhood down.

*

That night, she tossed and turned. She struggled with the whole idea of a curse. Was it real? Could she chance her sister's life on it? Or is she just believing in fairytales? Curses aren't real. But men don't dress in deer skulls and carve symbols into people's chests either, or have large armies doing their bidding, traveling around the country killing and looking for a stone.

What had her life come to?

She finally couldn't take it anymore and crawled out of bed at five a.m.

The one thing she did know was that she needed to learn how to shoot a gun and she wanted more self-defense moves. She was going to go see if Roxy and Brady were up. Knowing Roxy, she probably hadn't even gone to bed yet.

She wandered the halls, looking for them. She took a corner when she saw Ann backing out of a door with a laundry basket.

"Hey Ann," she said quietly, afraid she might wake someone.

Ann jumped two feet and grabbed her chest. When she looked at her, she mumbled something in Italian. "You scared ten years off my life. What are you doing wandering the halls this early in the morning?"

"I'm looking for Roxy. Do you know where she is?"

"I know where everything and everyone is all the time. Come, follow me." They started toward the end of a hall that brought them to a different staircase. It wasn't as grand as the one in the foyer but still nice.

Ann turned to her. "I've been working for Ms. Sinclair for almost forty years. Watched her children grow and her children's children grow. This house is just as much mine as it is hers. I know about everything that happens in these walls."

"What about your family?" she asked, following her up the stairs.

"My family lives in Italy. I came to America with my husband. He died in a car accident when I was barely twenty. I had no money and was losing my small apartment. Ms. Sinclair took me as a nanny and housekeeper. Been here ever since."

"You know about the family curse?"

"Yes." Ann did the sign of a cross across her chest. "I have seen it in action, and felt the consequences of it too."

Ann stopped at a door at the top of the stairs. "Your sister is in there." She pointed to the door. She turned to go back down the stairs but stopped and turned, adjusting the basket on her hip. "I worry for your sister too."

Ann turned and went back down. All Sydney could do was stare.

When she opened the door, she saw exactly what she thought she would. Roxy with her hair back in a stubby ponytail, dark circles under eyes that were glued to a computer screen. Brady was standing at a printer, pulling a paper out of the tray. There were notes pinned all over the walls, along with maps and printouts of buildings.

"Have you guys even taken a break yet?"

"Yep, not too long ago," Brady said, then looked up at her and winked. Even with the blue light from the computer screen, she saw Roxy's cheeks blush.

She realized what he meant. She looked over at the only table without a computer on it. *"Ew."*

Brady gave a short laugh, and Roxy kept typing, oblivious to what was going on.

"Anyway," she said, trying to change the subject. "Making progress?"

"We're slowly getting there," Brady said, sitting back down at his computer and starting to type again.

The room fell silent again, except for the clatter of the keyboards.

She sighed, remembering this was often how Roxy was growing up.

"Brady, I want to learn how to shoot. Who can I ask for help?"

Brady spun in his chair and faced her. "I think that's a great idea. Roxy needs to learn too." Roxy just grunted and continued. Brady looked over at her with a smile. "Isn't she great?"

Sydney laughed. Then her chest tightened. He loved her. That meant Roxy was in danger.

"Brady," she said, bringing his attention back.

"Right, I'll call Max. He'll take you to the range and teach you. He's a great teacher."

Brady made the call, and a half hour later, she was in a golf cart, next to a large, scary man, driving to the gun range at the back of the Sinclair property.

*

That night, they brought Asa home. He was on all kinds of machines and under doctor's watch twenty-four seven. She sat with him every night, holding his hand and talking to him. She found, which she thought was fitting, a Lord of the Rings book in the side table, and she read to him till her eyes grew heavy and she fell asleep in the chair.

With the Brotherhood still out there, Brady wasn't sure if calling Bev was such a good idea. So, she sat down and wrote her a letter and told her the whole story. It was going snail mail, but it was the safest way. She promised Bev when everything was done, they would come visit.

Her mornings were spent with Max at the range. She was getting better, and Max said she was making good progress. After the range, she tried jogging, but she ended up breaking several stitches. The in-home doctor wasn't happy, and instead, she took walks around the Sinclair estate. Max often followed her, saying that she shouldn't be walking by herself and that Asa would have his ass if he knew she was out wandering alone.

On their walks, they talked mostly about Asa. She found out Asa and Max became good friends when Max moved to the estate and took the head security position.

When she asked how he got the job, he would often clam up. But on the fifth day, she got him to spill.

It turned out that after his tour, Max came home to find he had PTSD. He was having trouble functioning in a society that wasn't at war. He lost his temper and started fights. Loud noises had him jumping and reaching for his gun. He couldn't find a job because of his background, and when he did, he often lost it because of his temper. He made friends with some bad people and turned to selling drugs and stealing to pay his rent. He was arrested and thrown in jail. Chess had bailed him out.

Pissed at the country he fought for and breaking his own moral code just to survive, he tried to commit suicide. After Brady received a phone call from a worried Chess, Brady had come over to his small apartment to offer the security position to him.

Brady stopped him from putting the gun to his mouth and took him to the hospital. Mary came with Brady to visit him, and she grew fond of Max, stating that a war hero should be celebrated and honored, not shoved to the dark side, left to the streets. Mary got him the best doctors and psychologists. He worked the estate and came to enjoy it. He still had relapses, but he had better control. He found peace with the Sinclairs and began to consider them family.

"I owe my life to them," he said finally.

Sydney was speechless. The story had opened her eyes a little to the people Asa surrounded himself with. She was starting to get a whole new respect for the Sinclair/Hallows family.

The next day, right before their walk ended at the front porch, she asked him about the curse. He just shrugged. "Families have their stories."

"But do you think it could be real?"

"Sometimes things are only real because we believe they are."

She paused, taken aback by his answer.

"I got to go check on my guys. See you tomorrow morning."

She waved bye as he jogged away.

When she walked through the door, Ann was waiting for her.

"There you are. I was getting ready to send someone out to get you." Ann grabbed her arm and started to pull her toward the back of the house.

"What's going on?" Fear filled her head. "Is it Asa?"

"Yes. Come quick. He's awake!"

When the words she had been wanting to hear for days finally filled her ears, she ran right past Ann and straight to Asa's door. She pushed past the nurse and to his bedside.

"Asa?" She reached for his hand.

He slowly rolled his head toward her. He looked her in the eyes, then a smile spread across his face.

A slurred "Hey" was all he could manage. Tears filled her eyes and she held his hand. "I knew you would come back."

He squeezed her hand softly; he then closed his eyes again.

She looked to the doctor, scared that he was gone again.

"It's okay; he's sleeping. He'll be in and out of it for a while. His body has a lot of healing to do."

She stayed the rest of the night in his room, taking her dinner there. He hadn't woken up. But when she started to read the book, he rolled his head her way, eyes still shut. "This is my favorite part," he whispered, and she read to him with a smile across her face.

The next morning, she canceled her training session with Max and stayed with Asa. The doctor was in and out throughout the day. So was Asa. That afternoon, she left so the nurse could give him a sponge bath. When she returned, he was awake.

"So, tell me what's going on," Asa said, his voice rough.

"Well," she sat down in her chair. "Brady and Roxy have been nonstop on the computer researching. Among other things." She rolled her eyes.

Asa softly chuckled.

"They say they're making progress. But nothing yet on who the leader is. Max has been showing me how to shoot. We have been going to the range in the back of the estate."

Asa frowned. "Max has been taking you?"

She nodded. "Yeah, he says I've improved. Turns out I'm not that bad of a shot."

"That's good. I'm glad you're learning, but I don't think you'll need it now that we're here."

"Asa, this isn't over for any of us yet. The Brotherhood still has the ring. I want to be able to defend myself and others."

He smiled and squeezed her hand.

Asa rolled his head and looked to the ceiling. "How did we get out? I don't remember much."

She told him everything, from when he took the bullet for Roxy to the man with the skull mask shooting everyone, to Chess showing up.

"I met Chess once," he said. "Seemed nice. I hear he's a good field medic and likes his fights. Always wondered why he never did another tour; war seem to be what he liked."

She scooted her seat closer and rubbed her hand down the side of his face. The bruises were healing and were fading to green. The doctor took his head bandage off, and he looked less beat up.

"It hasn't been the same without you," she said, brushing his hair out of his eyes. It was true. She watched Roxy and Brady together, and it made her feel lonely. She had gotten used to the four of them together, and she missed their little group.

He took her hand from his face and lightly kissed her fingertips. "I'm here. I'm not going anywhere." He let her hand go. "I'm tired. Will you read to me?"

She smiled and reached for the book.

*

She stayed in his room for the next couple of days. Brady and Roxy worked on finding the leader on the computer, and she tried to get Asa better. At night, when he was asleep and the house was quiet, she thought about her life.

She thought about stealing. Then about how Max was disgusted with himself for doing it. She wondered if he knew she did it, if it would change their new friendship? She thought about the lady at the bus station, how she stole the tickets and ruined her trip to Atlantic City. Was she no better than this leader they were searching for? He had tried to steal the ring from them. The whole mess started with her dad stealing it first. Anger flashed in her.

259

Why couldn't her dad just be a normal dad? She thought about how they grew up and the things he taught her, how to pick a lock, how to pick pockets, and how to con.

Her thoughts went to the bank account Roxy set up for her; that was stealing too. They were sisters born to the same dad, and Roxy chose to work and earn money; the only stealing Roxy was doing was keeping Sydney's bank account full. Why did she choose this path?

She thought she was doing good, punishing the evil, but wasn't she just as bad as they were? Maybe it was her turn to be punished.

Maybe it's time to stop, she thought. *Maybe I need to live my own life and not Dad's.*

She also thought of the leader of the Brotherhood, whoever he was. How had he built an army? How had he gotten followers? And why was the ring so damn important?

Roxy

"This has to be him," Brady said, holding up the printout.

"We have to be sure," she said. "This isn't any ordinary man. If we go after him, there will be consequences."

"We need to gather everyone and show them what we found." Brady put the paper down and checked the time. She looked to the bottom of the computer screen and saw that it was six a.m. *What day is it?* she thought. Their naps had been sporadic and only for a few hours. Their so-called breaks had been the best. They had taken several in the office chairs and on the table. She would never look at a desk chair the same again.

He caught her staring at the chair. He smiled. "As much as I would love to, we need to get rolling on this; it's been long enough. Most everyone should be awake by now."

She blushed. "I don't know what you're talking about." She stood up and went to grab another printout. But not before he gave her butt a quick pat and pulled his phone out to call everyone in.

Twenty minutes later, the small room was filled with people. Sydney and Mary were sitting at the small table, both with mugs of coffee. Max and Chess were leaning on the wall. Clint, who was a skinny man but had toughness about him that was easily recognizable, stood with tense posture and his eyes were hard. She had only met him a couple times. He was hanging by the door. Asa was asleep, and everyone thought it best they left him out. She didn't feel right about leaving him out; after all, this was about him just as much as the rest, but there was nothing she could do. The few times she came to visit him, he had been pretty out of it.

Ann walked in with a tray of coffee mugs and handed them out.

Clint took his and smiled at Ann. He took a sip, and them moaned in ecstasy. "I love you, Ann. When are you going to run away with me?"

Ann smiled and lightly hit Clint on the arm. "You need a girlfriend," she said and went to hand out the rest.

Maybe Clint wasn't such a hard ass after all, she thought with a smile.

When the tray was empty, she expected Ann to leave, but instead, she held the tray in front of her and leaned against the wall.

No one questioned it.

Brady grabbed the paper off the desk, and the room went silent, all attention on him.

"We think we know who the leader is," he started. He held up a printout of a picture. It was a man with gray hair combed perfectly to the side. He was thin and had bright brown eyes. He was wearing a navy-colored suit, an American flag pinned to the lapel of his jacket. She was now familiar with the picture since she had been studying it for the last three hours.

"This is Congressman Ray E. Jackson."

The room was silent as everyone stared.

"Shit." Max broke the silence.

Clint shook his head in agreement.

"That can't be," Mary said. "I was at a function not two months ago with him and other congressmen."

"Before we all freak out," Chess started, pushing himself from the wall. "Tell us how you know that."

Brady sat down on the edge of the table.

"We started with the shipment that the ring came to Seattle in. The one in 2012. The buyer bought it through a trust. It was difficult. He covered his tracks well, and we were jumping around a lot. We found properties owned by the trust all along both the east and west coasts. We followed the money. The congressman has quite the interest in antique auctions and estate sales. Among other things." Brady rolled his eyes.

She had seen the other things. He liked to keep his Brotherhood men in young women.

"He has weak connections with a lot of shady businesses and businessmen. But nothing solid that we can find. He covers his tracks well."

"But what really cements it is the medical records. Back in the eighties, Mr. Congressman spent some time in a mental institution. He had a doctor named T. Hunt. He diagnosed Mr. Jackson with obsessive-compulsive disorder and schizophrenia along with psychosis. Roxy was able to find a transcript from one of his sessions with Dr. Hunt." Brady looked at the papers in his hand. It was twenty pages long. "In short, it says that Ray Jackson, or his real name, Raymond Ernest Jackson, from the swamps of Louisiana, thinks he is a wizard.

With his magic, he can travel through different realms. He befriended a white dragon, who promised power and money only if he brought the dragon a magical stone. That stone was stolen many years ago."

Brady paused and frowned. "He said that two black-haired witches stole the stone from the dragon and had their bewitched warriors cut off the dragon's wings, leaving him stuck in the cave. The dragon told him to find the black-haired witches, and they would lead him to the stone." Brady tossed the papers on the table.

"Black-haired witches." Sydney sat straight up in her chair. "That's what they keep calling us. They called Asa and Brady warriors, too." Sydney looked to her for confirmation, and she nodded back. Sydney turned back to the room. "It could be why he has been watching us and taking pictures. If he thinks we're the black-haired witches."

Brady turned to his computer. "We found a clip from one of his sessions with Dr. Hunt. It was buried really deep. We had to go the dark web to find it. He tapped the mouse, and the video started.

Ray was young, in his twenties. His hair was dark blond and shaggy. He was in a white T-shirt, sitting at a table, and smoking a cigarette. The smoke made the room look foggy and dark.

"So, tell me, Raymond," Dr. Hunt started but was interrupted.

"It's Ray," Ray said, flicking ashes into a brown plastic ashtray. His eye twitched. "My mother was the only one who called me Raymond."

"Ray. Tell me about this dragon." Dr. Hunt was hidden behind the camera. His voice was smooth and low.

"I already told you," Ray said without making eye contact. "The bewitched warriors cut off his wings. He's trapped in the cave, and only I can save him."

"How did you meet this dragon?"

"I met him in the swamps, behind my mother's house."

"There is a dragon living behind your mother's house?"

Ray placed his cigarette down on the ashtray and sat up straight. He folded his hands on the table. He looked right at the doctor. "Don't treat me like I'm crazy. I'm not like the others you have here. I have a destiny. A purpose. And I will be powerful. You'll see."

He picked his cigarette back up and drew on it hard. The tip glowed red.

"Okay, Ray," the doctor said. Keeping his voice calm, he continued, "Back to the dragon. You said that the dragon will reward you for saving him from the cave?"

"With power and magic," Ray said, looking at the glowing end of his cigarette.

"What do you have to do to save him?" said Dr. Hunt.

"Get the stone."

"Just any stone?"

"The white stone, the stone of prosperity." Ray looked up. His eyes were hard, and dark. "Then I bathe the stone in the black-haired witches' blood. In a special ceremony. It will set the dragon free." He cocked his head to the side. "But I cannot show my face. I must mask it with nature and death." He stared up at the camera, a smile forming on his lips.

"Who are the black-haired witches?"

"I don't know yet." The question seemed to wipe the smile off his face. "The dragon said to be patient. They'll show up."

"Do you think you will find them?"

"Yes, and my army will bring them to me." He took a drag of his cigarette and looked to the ceiling. He blew a smoke ring.

"What army?" asked Dr. Hunt.

Ray looked at the doctor; smoke curled from his nostrils. "The one I will build."

"Ray, can you tell me what this means?" Dr. Hunt slid a notebook across the table.

She wasn't as surprised this time as she was the first time she saw it, but she heard Sydney gasp. The paper on the top was covered in a symbol—the same symbol that was now carved into their chests. The same symbol that scarred the hands of those in the Brotherhood. The large V and the two smaller slashes at the top.

"It's the mark of the dragon," Ray said. He looked up at the camera, and a smile crept across his face, his eyes dark. The video went fuzzy, then stopped.

She looked around the room at everyone.

"El Diablo," Chess whispered.

"He wants to bathe the stone in our blood?" Sydney croaked. Fear all over her face, she touched her chest.

"He sounds crazy," Mary said. "I can't believe it; I've been in the same room as this man."

"He lived in that cabin that he had us in," Roxy said. When all eyes

264

looked toward her, she started to sweat. She grabbed her research about Ray off the table and started to read.

"He lived there when he was a child with his abusive, alcoholic mother. His father left when he was a baby, and his mother blamed him. She would beat him and belittle him. Afterward, he would run into the swamp. The doctors think he made up the story to give him purpose and a place to hide from his mother."

She stopped; everyone was still looking at her. She pushed her nervousness away and continued. "I looked into his school records, and he was constantly bullied and was in a lot of fights. He had no real friends. But somehow, he rose up in the small town and became mayor." She looked up and shrugged when she saw all the confused faces. She still doesn't understand that one either. "His term was cut short; that's when his public record becomes spotty, and it starts back up six years later, as Ray E. Jackson instead of Raymond Ernest. My guess is that was when he was in the hospital. His mother died right before he became mayor of their small town, and he inherited the land. He had that large house built out front when his career started to take off, and that's his primary residence."

The room was quiet.

"Well, I think you guys found him," Mary said, taking a sip of her coffee. Her hands were shaking.

"This guy is a damn psycho," Max said, still leaning on the wall.

"His doctor committed suicide two weeks before Ray ran for Congress." Brady stood up. "My guess, Ray didn't want anything coming up during elections."

The room was quiet again.

"So, he's after the girls' blood." Chess pushed away from the wall. "He has the stone. My guess is he never finished his little ritual. He'll want to try again. What's the next move? We can't keep the girls in lockdown forever, and Mary wants the stone."

"We have enough information here, plus everything that's happened in the last weeks to build a solid case against him. Asa has some trustworthy friends on the force. Even that might be hard. We don't know how far his reach is. The ring?" Brady just shrugged.

Everyone was silent.

"We steal it," Sydney said.

Everyone's heads whipped to Sydney. "We steal it, then get him arrested."

"I don't think it will be that easy," Max said.

"It is," Sydney said, standing up. "You guys already know what I did before all this." Sydney looked to Max then lowered her eyes. If he didn't know before he would now. She thought and continued, "This is a walk in the park for me. It's the only thing I'm good at."

"No," Brady broke in. "No way, I'm not sending you in there. You're half of what he needs for his crazy ritual. No way."

Roxy sighed in relief. She did not want her sister going anywhere near him.

"We figure out his next social engagement." Sydney ignored Brady. She looked to Mary. "You said you just saw him."

Sydney turned back to the room. "I'm sure he will have the ring on him or near him. He won't be letting it out of his sight. I'll go in disguise and take it."

When no one said anything, she looked around. Softly, she said, "I have done it a million times. He won't be the first politician I've stolen from."

"I've seen her in action," Brady said. His face was turned up; he looked like it disgusted him for even saying it.

"I'll go with and stay in the background," Chess volunteered.

Roxy's head spun. Was this really going to happen?

"No, she's not going." Roxy surprised herself. She all but yelled it. Everyone stared at her again, but this time she wasn't going to shy away. She looked to Sydney who was still standing.

"Syd, you can't go. You saw how crazy he is." She pointed to the now black computer screen. Her voice got higher. "He wants to bathe a stone in our witches' blood, for Christ's sake!" She placed her hand to her cheeks and felt their warmth. She stood and looked at Brady. "Please don't do this."

Brady's face filled with sorrow. He walked to her and wrapped her in a hug. "I don't want to do this either."

Roxy closed her eyes and leaned in to his shoulder. Tears threatened to flow from the corners. *This is all too much*, she thought.

"It's the simplest plan." Sydney walked to them, and she leaned into their embrace. "It will be fast, in and out. He won't even know. Then we take down his whole operation from the comfort of this room. Of all the people in this room, Rox, you know I can do this." Sydney paused. "Then I'm done. No more stealing, for good." Roxy lifted her head from Brady's shoulder.

"Really?" Her voice sounded too hopeful, and she was slightly embarrassed. Sydney's face softened. "My last job will be stealing from the leader of the Brotherhood." Sydney smiled a sad smile. "We can't go to war with them. They outnumber us, and I don't want anyone else to get hurt or die."

Roxy didn't say anything but laid her head down back on Brady's shoulder. She let her mind try to conceive the fear that this was going to bring. She felt Sydney place her hand on her shoulder and lightly pushed her back, making her look at her. "Fine," Roxy said. "Last time."

Sydney smiled. "Last time."

Brady took a step back, his face serious. "Let's get to work."

The quiet room broke up and started to plan. Max and Clint had to leave to do patrols. Ann had her household duties to do. But Chess and Mary stayed and helped.

They all worked for another half hour when Brady asked the room to watch an old interview of the congressman. It was of his campaign, and Brady turned it up. Ray Jackson had cleaned up since his stay in the hospital. He was a handsome man when he was younger, and he had a striking appearance on stage. *His voice was confident and strong—very compelling*, she thought. He spoke of justice and loyalty to his country. His movements were smooth and sure-footed. He had a strong presence. She could see why his followers—the Brotherhood—could be swayed by him. He spoke with passion. She remembered her research.

"He speaks well." Roxy turned to her new laptop and pulled up a file. She looked over at the others; they were waiting to hear what she was thinking. "He donates a lot of money and time to programs that help and support inter-city children's programs and high-risk youth, along with struggling veteran's organizations. Do you think he recruits from these places?" Brady looked up at her thoughtfully.

Mary nodded her head. "Yes, he does. He sends lots of support and money to the cities with the biggest gang populations and drug issues. Along with veteran hospitals and support organizations."

Roxy turned and faced the room. "So, he's a passionate speaker, and where better to find members for his Brotherhood than places with young adults and teenagers who are looking for family, kids who need structure. Then there are the veterans, soldiers struggling with PTSD, and not to mention his connection to the mental health community." Roxy sat back in her chair.

"It makes sense," Sydney said.

Roxy started to add to her notes when a loud voice boomed into the room.

"What's going on?" They all turned to the door. It was Asa; he was in a wheelchair, being pushed by a nurse. "Sydney is not going anywhere near the congressman. She's not going in alone."

Asa's face was red with anger, and the nurse looked embarrassed. She stammered, "Sorry, Ms. Sinclair, but he wanted to go for a walk."

Mary just waved the nurse off. "Asa, what are you doing out of bed?" Mary rose from her chair.

Asa ignored her and wheeled his chair awkwardly forward with one hand. "Why am I hearing this in passing from Clint? Why am I not in here helping make plans? I'm part of this too. I have a say. Sydney will not go in alone."

Brady stepped forward, but Asa just turned his head toward Sydney.

Sydney stepped forward. "It's the easiest way, Asa. I don't want anyone else getting hurt. I can do this."

"No," he said, this time quietly, and shook his head. "You'll get hurt, and I can't be there."

Sydney stepped toward him. "I've done this before. I work better alone."

"No," he repeated, his eyes softening.

She paused and tilted her chin up and straightened her back. "I did this before I met you and have been fine. I can do this without you. You can't tell me what to do."

Asa's face fell, and he went silent for a minute. His eyes never left her face.

"This is how it's going to be, isn't it? You're going to run off in the middle of the night to steal and put yourself in danger, and I'll just have to sit back and hope you will make it home. I won't stand for that."

He tried to roll the wheelchair back with his one good arm, but the nurse stopped him and pulled his chair back toward the hallway.

"Asa, wait." Sydney ran toward him. He held up his hand, stopping her. "Don't. You're right. I can't tell you what to do all the time, so do what you want. I'm done." He looked to the nurse and waved her forward.

Sydney stood there, staring at the empty hall. Sydney turned to face the silent room. Her eyes were full of tears. "Find the congressman's next social engagement. I'm getting that ring back." Sydney then walked out and went the opposite way down the hall.

Roxy looked to Brady, and he nodded, knowing what they both needed to do.

He turned to Chess. "Find where our congressman is going to be in the next week or so."

Then she and Brady went to the door and, with a quick kiss, they went their separate ways down the hall.

Sydney

She went straight to her room. She didn't know where else to go, but she knew she had to be alone. She paced. *What the hell?* she thought. Who in the hell did he think he was? She paused. They weren't officially together, were they? They were strangers who had been thrown into a scary, life-threatening situation.

Atlantic City filled her head. She remembered their dance and how good it had felt to be close to him. The hotel room when he kissed her. His hands on her. Her heart broke, and she thought about how he said he was done. What did that even mean?

There was a knock on the door. She was about to tell them to get lost, but the door opened, and Roxy poked her head in. "Can I come in?"

She felt defeated and embarrassed. They made a scene in front of everyone. She dropped on the bed.

Roxy came in and sat next to her. "Are you okay?" She placed her hand on her back.

"I'm fine," she said coldly.

After Roxy didn't say anything, she looked up. Roxy had a frown.

"You agree with Asa?"

Roxy huffed out a sigh. "In a way."

Sydney stood, anger and hurt making her feel hot. She grabbed a hair tie off of the dresser and started to pull her hair back.

"It's dangerous," Roxy said. "This isn't like your other marks. This guy knows you. He wants to kill you. He knows that we want the ring, and we've pissed him off. He's crazy."

Sydney turned to the window. She looked out at the morning; the sky was gray, and it looked like it was going to rain. "I know. But I don't think I can stand any more people dying. I want to finish what Dad started. I want to break this curse, Roxy." She turned and looked at her sister sitting on the bed. Her hair was pulled back in a ponytail, and she had dark circles under her eyes. "I want to know that you and Brady can be together. I'm scared for you and this stupid curse."

Roxy's face registered surprise.

"That's what you're worried about? That curse? It's not real." Roxy stood and walked to her sister. "Don't worry about me. Everything is going to be okay." She placed her arm around Sydney's shoulders.

"I can't lose you." Sydney turned and buried her face in Roxy's shoulder. "You're all I have left."

Roxy let her cry. When Sydney pulled away, she could feel her eyes were swollen. "I think I just lost Asa too." She sobbed.

"Asa's just frustrated with his situation. He wants to be involved and he can't. He's afraid he can't be there to protect you. Like he has been." Roxy looked her in the eyes. "He's scared, and I don't blame him either." She paused. Sydney had tears rolling down her cheeks.

"Do you really mean this will be your last job?"

Sydney shook her head. "Yes."

"What will you do?"

"I've been thinking about maybe going back to school. Something like criminal psychology. Congressman Jackson is scary, for sure. But why? Why is he like this, and how come he has so many people believing and following him. I can help put bad guys away."

Roxy smiled. "I think that sounds amazing, and I think you would be very good at it. You should tell Asa. Let him know this is your last job."

"I don't know. It seems like he's done with me."

Roxy smiled. "I doubt he's done. Go take a shower. We have a lot planning to do."

They found a fundraiser in San Francisco, California, two weeks later that Congressman Jackson was attending. They started planning. She decided to give Asa some time to cool down, and for the rest of the day, she threw herself into planning with the others. Brady had gone and talked to Asa, but he said nothing to her of their conversation.

The plan was simple. She was going in as a guest with a wig and would move along the party till she found the right opportunity to take the ring, if he had it on him. Roxy and Brady would have surveillance, and their first job was to see if he was wearing it. If not, then they would pull out of the party and search his hotel room. Chess was going to go in as a guest. He was to mingle and survey the room. They would both be carrying guns.

Mary's job was to get her a dress and wig. She also had to get tickets to the fundraiser for her and Chess. Brady was ordering a van with all the equipment that he and Roxy were going to need. Max was going also as backup and to drive the van. Clint was to stay and watch the Sinclair house.

Mary tried to convince Brady to let her go with Chess. She would attend the party and help. But Brady was firm on his no; he didn't want to worry about both her and Sydney. Mary wasn't happy.

The day wore on, and Asa kept entering her mind. Maybe if she just explained to him this was her last job, he would understand and accept her apology, and they could move on. She thought about crawling up in his bed with him, how good that sounded after the long, stressful day. His arms would be around her, melting the stress, and she could just be for the night. The fantasy had her feeling confident, and she broke loose from the others that evening with high hopes.

She walked to his room, her mind full of everything she was going to say, how she was going to say it, and she imagined his handsome face accepting her.

She reached his door, and it was closed. She knocked, and when no one answered, she slowly opened it. The room was empty. The bed's sheets were gone, and the blankets were folded up at the end. She kept the panic down. *Maybe they just moved him to another room*, she thought, and went to find a nurse. She ran into Ann at the end of the hall.

"Ann!" she yelled and jogged toward her. Ann turned. When she saw Sydney, her smile grew sad.

"Where's Asa?" she asked, fear knotting in her stomach. "Is he okay?"

"Yes, dear," Ann said and placed the rag she was using to dust down on the antique table. "Asa asked to be moved to a rehabilitation center upstate. He wasn't scheduled for another couple of weeks, but he insisted on going today."

Sydney's heartbeat sped up. "Oh, I didn't know he was being moved." She was stunned. "When will he be back?" she asked.

"Not sure, dear." Ann looked defeated at having to be the one to tell her.

"Did he leave a number?" Ann just shook her head.

"Why didn't he tell me?" she whispered.

Ann didn't say anything.

Tears welled in her eyes, and she ran for her room again.

Asa

"You're doing great," the perky physical therapist praised. Her blonde hair was pulled in a bouncy ponytail. "It's hard to believe you have only been here for a week."

Asa pulled the weight back up in a swinging motion. He was in no mood to deal with Marisa today. Her positive attitude was getting on his nerves.

He had been short-tempered and irritated ever since he arrived.

"I think I want to start to use the bag now," he said, pointing to the punching bag in the corner. He wanted to use it to get his frustration out, but she kept holding him back.

"I don't think so, not yet. We need to wait for your wounds to fully heal."

He turned to Marisa, and in the nicest voice, he could muster, said, "I'm pretty tired. I think I'm done for the morning." He placed the weights on the floor and headed for the door, ignoring Marisa's surprised goodbye.

Instead of heading to his room, he made his way outside. He needed to get his pent-up frustration out and he decided to go for a run. It had been raining, and the cool air felt good on his hot skin.

He had talked to Brady that morning. Their plans were in full swing, and they were flying out to California the next day. The fundraiser was still a week away, but they wanted to get set up. They were really going through with it. He was angry with Brady for agreeing. He didn't care how convinced Brady was that Sydney could do it. He didn't care that Chess was going in with her or that Max and Brady were going to be right outside. He needed to be there with her and hated that he couldn't finish what they started. His injuries were holding him back. Not being able to go in with Sydney, to watch her back, was too much for him.

His gut twisted. What if Cal got his hands on her? He shook his head and picked up his pace. Brady said he would take care of her. He promised. Brady told him that Sydney had said that this was her last job. Was it, though? Could she give it up? How would she fill her time?

Sydney flashed in his mind. Her long black hair and blue eyes. Her curvy, slim body, and the way it melted in his hands. Why wouldn't she listen to him? He just wanted to keep her safe. He knew that he couldn't, though, not forever. They could never have a life together. She would be running off in the middle of the night to God knows where to steal from whoever she determined was corrupt. And what was he supposed to do? Wait up all night wondering if she was coming home? Would he have to bail her out of jail one night? What if a client came to him and asked him to investigate a thief? Would he wonder if it was her? He would have to lie and turn down jobs, go against everything he believed in.

He pushed himself faster.

Thoughts of her walking down the hall in Atlantic City in that gold dress with a sly smile on her face. The way she hugged him in the hotel room in Texas, she held on to him like she hadn't been hugged in years. Her quick comebacks. The softness of her full lips on his. The thoughts of her chased him. He ran till his ribs screamed.

Roxy

It was early morning, and she rolled over in bed and felt for Brady. They had rented a large cabin in Yosemite National Park for the last week. They were all ready. They had all gone to bed early last night, worry and anticipation high.

Brady rolled over and pulled her in. His skin was warm against hers and she breathed in his fresh smell.

"Do you think our plan will work?" she whispered it, her voice low from sleep.

"I know it will." He kissed the top of her head. "Just think. By the end of tonight, this will all be over."

She wanted to believe it so bad that it hurt. "I hope so."

He rolled over on top of her, his upper body resting on his elbows. He kissed her nose, then her mouth, then her neck. "This will end tonight, then me and you, we can start a life together."

She stiffened. He stopped kissing her neck. "If that's what you want?" he said quickly. "I mean, if…"

She cut him off. "That's exactly what I want." She smiled and kissed his mouth. She felt truly happy, and for the first time in a long time, she felt excited for her future.

"You scared me; you kind of froze there for a second," he said it against her lips.

"*Shhh,*" she whispered, and he let her roll him over. She sat up and let the blanket fall from her shoulders, letting her bare body feel the chill in the air. "Besides my sister, you're the only other person I can be myself around. I don't feel shy or unsure. You make me feel strong and confident."

"You are strong." Brady touched her scabbed chest lightly and frowned. He then ran his hands down her stomach. "You're also the most beautiful and smartest person I have ever met." His eyes were intense as he took in the sight of her.

Feeling powerful, she tilted her hips. She watched as his eyes, still on hers, glazed over with pleasure, and she smiled to herself. Was this what it felt like to be confident? To be in love? Whatever it was, she liked it.

A few hours later, after a long shower together, they made their way downstairs. The cabin was in full swing. Max had several AR-15s and pistols laid out on the kitchen table and was loading magazines. Sydney was next to him, eating toast and scrolling through the local news on her computer.

Chess was at the stove cooking; he turned. "Well, look who finally decided to join us." He was smiling and flipped a pancake.

"I'm starved," Brady said and reached for a plate that he piled high and handed to her.

She was starving too, and the smell had her stomach grumbling. She took the plate and sat on a stool at the bar. She dripped syrup on her pancakes and started to eat.

Sydney came over and gave her the laptop.

"Looks like Congressman Jackson is still attending the fundraiser, and it starts at seven p.m."

She nodded and closed the article Sydney had been looking at. She pulled up her surveillance feed that she had hacked in the hotel and watched as caterers and others started to set up in the banquet room.

*

The day went off with them going over their plan several times. They tried to play out different scenarios so that they would be ready for anything. They got used to their earpieces that everyone was going to wear. That afternoon, she and Brady set up the van. They made sure everything worked and it was arranged efficiently. Brady tried to call Asa, but there was no answer.

"That's unusual," he said to Roxy as he stared at the phone.

"He just might be in therapy or in the shower. I'm sure he'll call you back."

"He knows we're going in tonight. Honestly, I'm surprised he hasn't been blowing up my phone."

She looked at her monitor. "Hey, I'm getting a weak signal over here on the feed for the entrance. Help me out."

*

At six p.m., they were getting ready to leave. They wanted to show up with the party in full swing. She made her way to Sydney's room to see if she was ready.

She knocked.

When she heard Sydney's soft, "Come in," she opened the door.

Sydney was wearing a long black dress. It had a high collar to cover her chest and was sleeveless. It hugged her curves and looked very elegant.

She was just finishing up by pinning the last of her hair.

"Here, let me get that." She reached for the last few hairs in the back and grabbed a pin.

"The dress looks really good on you," she told Sydney.

"Thanks. Wait till you see me as a blonde," Sydney laughed.

The wig was sitting on a Styrofoam head next to the bed. Roxy walked over and picked it up.

"It's heavy," she said as she placed it on Sydney's head. The wig was long and curly, and it was parted down the middle. "You look like Barbie," she laughed.

Sydney studied herself in the mirror. "I don't like it."

"Me neither," she agreed. "But you do look different."

"Hopefully it's dark enough in there."

Sydney took a deep breath and patted her dress down. "I've never been this nervous before a job before."

"This one is different. We have a lot riding on it." She sat down on the bed. "You're going to be safe, right? I mean, if anything feels off, you just walk away. We can always get the ring a different way."

"I will." Sydney smiled. "I got this, sis."

"I know," Roxy replied before standing up, a sense of dread brewing in her gut.

Sydney

They parked the van in a dark alley a few miles from the hotel. There was a small light hanging off the side of the building, giving off a low, eerie light. Roxy handed out the earpieces. When everyone went through their checks, the group went silent.

"Well, let's get this started," Chess said. He was in a black suit and his hair was combed back. It was a big difference from his usual army green cargo pants and black T-shirt.

"You look very dashing," Sydney said.

Chess pulled the suit lapels. "Thanks. I hope I don't get any blood on it."

The plan was for Chess to grab a cab and show up first. Then Sydney would take a cab and show up after the all-clear sign.

Chess walked to the street, and they all watched as he hailed a cab and left.

Brady and Roxy slipped back into the van and watched for Chess's arrival. Max leaned against the van, silently watching the alley.

She paced the outside of the van, her heels clicking and her chest itching, reminding her of what she could be stepping into.

"It's going to be okay," Max said, eyeing her from the side of the van. "You got the pistol on you?"

Sydney patted her thigh where the small .22 he gave her was strapped in the inside.

Max nodded his approval.

Her earpiece came to life. "I'm in." It was Chess.

"We see you." Brady said in her ear. "Any sign of Congressman Jackson?"

"Not yet."

She started to pace again. She suddenly wanted Asa with her. Her chest tightened. She inhaled loudly and pushed her feelings aside. "Keep your mind on the job," she chanted to herself. She hadn't talked to him or seen him in nearly two weeks. She had cried herself to sleep almost every night.

Her heart was heavy.

Brady had tried to call him before they left and he wasn't picking up their calls.

The van's back door opened and Brady stuck his head out. "You ready?"

She took a deep breath. "Ready."

She turned and walked to the end of the alley.

She made it out to the street and walked to the curb. There were people everywhere, and she started to sweat. She hadn't been around so many people in a long time. They were walking down the street, the shop and restaurant lights illuminating them, while the people inside ate and laughed. They had no clue that a large army of the Brotherhood was just down the street, ready to bathe a stone in witches' blood for a dragon. Her chest itched more.

She stepped forward to hail an oncoming cab when the man next to her bumped her and raised his arm. She stumbled back, bumping a woman, who gave her a nasty growl in the dark. The man took the cab. Paranoia crept in; they could be anywhere, they'd gotten her before, and they had been watching her for years, so they could easily be doing it now. She took a step back from the curb, ready to bolt.

"Everything is okay," Roxy's voice came through in her ear.

"I don't know if I can do this," she whispered.

"This is how it ends," Brady said.

She looked back at the shop front and saw a group of people having drinks, laughing at each other's jokes. *That could be us*, she thought. She ached to be with those people living a normal life. *This is how we get to be like them,* she thought.

She raised her arm and hailed a cab. It zipped up to the curb. She opened the door and got in.

On a job, she never went in the front door, but Mary had given her a fake name and ticket. When she entered the banquet hall, the room was dim, slow music was playing, and people were standing around talking in small groups or sitting at tables eating. There was a small dance floor where one couple was slowly swaying.

She scanned the room and saw Chess standing in the corner with a drink in his hand. He was talking to an older woman. He looked up and gave her a slight nod.

"Any sign of Congressman Jackson?" she whispered softly.

"Not yet," Brady said. "Looks like he likes to make an entrance."

She walked over to a table and grabbed a glass of champagne. She saw the same boring people who always attended these things. People with money looking to buy a politician, or maybe just getting out to make connections or merely be seen. All were dressed in designer clothes and flashing their most expensive jewelry.

She watched as a woman laughed, placing her hand on her chest. A large diamond ring glittered in the light. Just a couple months ago, she would have stolen it. Then, on her way home, she would have sold it and donated it to some charity. The thought held no appeal to her anymore.

Just then, the lights dimmed, and a man stepped out on the stage. People hushed and took seats at the tables.

The man thanked everyone for being there and started an introduction.

She put her glass down and moved to the corner of the room where it was dark. She scanned, looking for Chess, but she couldn't find him.

"Everybody, Congressman Ray Jackson."

She looked up at the stage. There he was, walking out to the center stage, smiling and waving. He looked just like the photo she had been studying for the last week. His gray hair was in a clean cut. He wore a navy-blue suit, an American flag pin on the front. He was tall, and skinnier than she thought. Her chest burned. It took all her willpower not to rub it.

He stood behind the mic, and she saw that smile she was now familiar with come across his face. She wanted to scream; she wanted to pull the gun from her leg and shoot every last bullet she had into his chest, just like he had done to Asa.

But then she saw it. The glint of silver around his neck. The ring. She saw the slight bump on his chest where the ring was hanging under his shirt.

"He's wearing the ring on the chain around his neck," she whispered.

"Confirmed," Brady said back. "We have it on camera."

She couldn't concentrate on the speech. Flashes of the cabin in the woods screamed through her head. She saw Roxy laying on the table, bound, and bloody. Her own chest felt hot and tight. She went lightheaded. She grabbed a champagne from a passing waiter and gulped it down. She just watched him. His smile, his hand gestures, everything about him made her angry.

When he was done, everyone clapped, and he made his way down. He shook hands as he passed people. She noticed that several couples had started dancing.

She thought of all the ways she could get to him. Necklaces were harder to steal, though it was not impossible, but when they were under shirts, it made it even trickier.

She made her way toward him as he remained standing in front of the stage. She stood next to a man who was leaning in toward the congressman's ear. When the man was finished, she watched Congressman Jackson smile and pat him on the back before he turned right to her.

"Congressman," she said with a little bow of her head. She held her hand out, keeping her head low.

"Good evening," he said as he took her hand. He didn't look at her but over her head and nodded to another couple walking by.

"Congressman, I was wondering if I could have a dance?" she said in a shy, timid voice.

The congressman finally looked down at her. She watched as his eyes ran up and down her body.

"I would love to," he answered, and still holding hands, she let him walk her to the dance floor.

He pulled her close, and she tried not to shiver in disgust. She placed her hands around his neck.

He leaned his head in close to her ear. "It's not every day a pretty girl asks me to dance."

"Really?" she said sweetly. "I don't know why? Who wouldn't want to dance with a congressman?"

He laughed and then reached up, took her right hand off his shoulder, and held it in his hand. He used it to turn her in a quick spin, then pulled her back in tight—a little too tight. His body was pushed against hers, his mouth close to her ear.

"Now, Sydney, you don't have to flatter me."

She froze.

She heard Brady cuss in her ear.

He put his cheek to her cheek. She smelled expensive spicy aftershave.

"You really think a wig would hide you from me? That I don't know everything about you? That I haven't been watching you for years? Since your daddy stole from me."

She tried to pull away, but he was a lot stronger than he looked. He kept her close.

"Don't fight me, Sydney. I know you think I'm the bad guy. But I don't feel like a bad guy. I'm simply helping a longtime friend. Someone who helped me a long time ago. I'm simply repaying the favor."

"You're crazy," she bit out.

He spun them in a circle, and she had no choice but to follow.

He rubbed his smooth cheek on hers.

"But really, who is the bad guy? I mean, we all are to someone. Look at you; you think the people you steal from don't consider you the bad guy. That poor woman at the bus stop. I'm sure if we asked her, she would agree. Don't you?"

She pulled her face back and looked him in the eyes. She wasn't surprised that he knew she was a thief. But bringing up the lady at the bus stop made her stomach turn. He only smiled back.

Brady was in her ear. "Max is coming in."

"Let's not forget Granny Mary." He didn't miss a beat. "She had no problem sacrificing your father for this stone."

Sydney's back stiffened, and she looked him in his dark, smiling eyes.

Then they softened. "I didn't involve your father, Sydney, Mary did. I'm just lucky that she brought me the black-haired witches. It happened just like he said it would."

He looked away, smiling, and he spun her again.

"And now," he said, pulling her in close as he squeezed her hand, and she tried to pull it free to no avail. "She throws her two grandsons into danger. By the way, how is Asa doing?"

He laughed as he studied her shocked face. He stepped forward. He pulled her in closer. "I guess the question is, what do we do? Do I keep helping my friend that saved my life and fulfill my destiny? Do you keep stealing from the rich and donating to the needy? Does Mary keep trying to save her family? Does Brady keep being a deadly soldier?" The questions had her mind spinning. Was he speaking the truth?

She looked up at him. "I guess we're all bad guys, fighting over our own good intentions."

He smiled down at her. "You know the saying." He laughed.

"Well, thank you for the dance." He held her out at arm's length. "But I have more guests to attend to. So, I'm going to hand you over to a most trusted colleague. He'll take good care of you."

He had maneuvered her over to the corner of the dance floor, and when he stepped aside, Cal stood there. She froze. Fear ripped through her body at the sight of his smile, his gold tooth catching the light.

She tried to take a step back, but Cal reached out and gripped her arm hard, and the congressman turned to leave.

"No!" she started to yell, but Cal placed his hand over her mouth—hard—and turned her toward the exit door in the dark corner of the dance floor. Her eyes searched out into the dance floor, but no one was paying attention. They were all consumed in their own personal party, and they exited so quickly that in seconds they were in a long hall. He pulled her toward an elevator at the end.

"Where are we going?" she asked loudly when Cal removed his hand, hoping Brady and Roxy could hear. "In the elevator?"

He pushed the button for up and spun her face first into the doors. Pain shot in her forehead, the elevator door cool on her face. Leaning with all his body weight on her, he pulled a knife from his belt and, with the tip, he pressed it against her face. Lightly, without cutting her, he ran it down her cheek. He stuck it next to her ear, and with the tip, he popped out her earpiece. She felt a light burn and felt blood drip down into her ear.

"Oops, usually I'm better than that with a knife. Found the same one in your buddy back there too."

"What did you do?"

"Don't worry; he's not a problem for anyone anymore." She tried to buck him off. But he only pushed her harder against the doors.

"I like it when they fight." She froze as he ran the knife down the side of her neck.

"The door to the elevator dinged. When it started to open, he pulled her up then pushed her in, causing her to fall to her knees.

The doors closed and he looked down at her.

"I like the blonde hair. They say blondes have more fun." He looked her up and down and bit his lip. "Guess I'll find out."

She grabbed a handful of the wig and tore it off her head, taking half the pins with it.

. Cal laughed. "Bummer, guess I won't find out. It's okay. Now I have the black-haired witch to punish."

The elevator dinged again, and he pulled her out the door. They went down a long hall. She fought, but he held on; when she tried to dig her nails into his wrist, he only laughed. When they reached the end, he pulled a key card out and opened the door, pushing her in.

She tried to stay calm, checking her surroundings. The room was dim. The bathroom light was on, casting little light. Other than the bed, there was nothing else. She was on her own.

She watched him as he slipped off his navy jacket and placed it neatly on the bed.

She stood at the opposite side of the room, thinking of the small gun strapped to her leg. She started to pull the side of her dress up. He watched, a smile forming on his lips. "I said I like a fighter, but if you're willing?" He stepped forward.

She reached down and pulled the small gun from under her dress. She pointed it right at him.

"That's cute," he said and took another step.

She stepped back and fired. The bullet whizzed by his head, but he didn't stop. She shot again, and the bullet hit the top of his shoulder.

"You're just pissing me off," he said with a growl.

She held the gun up, this time taking her time. But he rushed her. He hit her hand with enough force that the gun flew from her, and it hit the floor with a thud. He reached forward and brought his open hand down on her face. The smack was loud, and the pain shot through her face and down her neck. But she stayed on her feet. Her face screaming in pain, she looked up to see his wicked smile, gold tooth, and all. "This will be fun."

He pulled his sleeves up and stepped toward her. She put her hands up like she was taught, ready to go down swinging. She threw out a punch, and it hit him square in the cheek; his head whipped to the side, but he just brought it back. His eyes looked darker than before. He jumped forward and threw her down on the bed. He reached down and placed his hand tightly around her neck. She started to twist out of his grip and pulled on his hands, desperate to breathe. "You're going to pay," he said through gritted teeth.

Then there was light, casting a shadow across the room. Cal noticed also and turned his head. There was a loud shot, and Cal let go of her throat and fell to the side. She scrambled of the bed. She quickly looked down and saw that Cal had taken a bullet to the head, his head twisting to the side.

The large figure stepped in. Her heart leaped.

"Asa!" Pain forgotten, she ran to him. He took two steps and caught her mid-jump. She held on tight.

"Oh my god, Asa, what are you doing here? How did you find me?" She buried her face in his neck, breathing in his scent.

She didn't want to let go. All her fear and anxiety whooshed out of her like air out of a balloon. He sat down on the bed with her in his lap.

"Sorry, not completely healed yet." He said, his voice pained.

"Sorry." She scooted out of his lap. She noticed that he held his arm close to his body.

"What are you doing here?"

"Couldn't let you guys finish this without me. I saw you dancing with the congressman and then saw Cal take you in the elevator."

"Thank God." She wrapped her arms around his neck and pulled him in; he rested his head on her chest. She didn't want to let him go; everything felt right again.

"Asa?" She pulled back. She needed to say it. "I'm sorry. I'm sorry for everything." Tears welled in her eyes. "This is my last job, I swear. I have been wanting to tell you."

He looked up at her and rested his hand on her sore cheek. He frowned.

"I just want a future with you, and it scares me to think I might not be able to have one. I thought if I left, it would be easier for my feelings to fade, if I wasn't near you." He paused and looked up into her eyes. "But you consumed my every thought."

She took his hand from her cheek and held it. "Me and you forever?"

He smiled. "Me and you forever."

He stood and pulled her in and kissed her, long and deep.

He pushed his fingers into her hair, and when he pulled back, he rested his forehead against hers. "Let's get the stone and finish this tonight."

She smiled. "Tonight."

She stood up and grabbed her gun off the floor.

"Who gave you that pea shooter?" he asked, taking the small gun.

"Max did," she said, looking at it in his hand.

Asa frowned. "He should have known that gun wouldn't do shit."

The sound of a door slamming out in the hall took Asa's attention from the gun. He handed it to her. "Come on." He grabbed her hand, and they made their way to the door.

Asa peeked his head out.

"Max."

"Asa, what the hell, man? What are you doing here?" He gave Asa a fist bump and eyed her.

"Can't let you guys have all the fun," Asa said. "Brady and Roxy still in the van?"

"Yeah, and freaking out, lost contact with both Chess and Syd."

Max put his hand to his ear. "Yeah, found Sydney, she's okay. Found Asa, too."

Max paused as he listened to the other end of his earpiece. "I don't know. You'll have to ask your cousin."

Max looked back at Asa. "Come on, let's get you guys back to the van."

"No," Sydney said. "He's here, with the ring. This is our chance. This ends tonight."

"I agree," Asa said. "Have Brady find where Congressman Jackson is."

Max put his hand to his ear again.

"He's heading for the kitchen. He's trying to make an escape."

They took the stairs as fast as they could. She couldn't help noticing that Asa was holding his side and keeping his arm tucked close.

Guilt crept in. As much as she was relieved that he was with her, she knew he shouldn't be. He was still hurting.

They made it to the bottom and headed for the kitchen.

Asa went in first, gun drawn, and she went in right behind him, Max followed. The lights were off, and she flipped the nearest switch. The kitchen lit up. She had to let her eyes adjust from the blinding white and chrome interior. It was empty. Asa moved forward slowly, gun still drawn. She made her way around the counter, her small gun ready, and saw Chess lying on the floor. Blood pooled around him from a bullet hole in his head.

"Oh my god." She bent down and felt for a pulse. She knew it was hopeless, but she had to see. This man had come to their rescue in Louisiana. He had helped take care of Asa.

Tears fell from her eyes as she realized that he was gone.

"What happened?" she stammered.

"Sometimes you just trust the wrong people."

She looked up upon hearing Max's voice to find that he was standing in front of the door. He pulled his pistol up and aimed it at them.

"What the hell?" Asa grabbed her and pulled her behind him.

"Max, I don't understand," Asa said, his gun raised, confusion written on his face.

"I could only cover your asses for so long." Max's face looked pained. "I owed the Brotherhood."

"What?" She stepped out from behind Asa. "You said you owed Mary your life. Their family helped you; they trusted you."

"When I told you I started stealing and dealing drugs, it was for the Brotherhood." Max took a step forward. His eyes were full of tears, and his face pulled up in pain. "I tried to get away. But you don't leave the Brotherhood."

He pulled the gun away and placed both of his hands to his head as if he was fighting the demons in there. "I'm the only reason Mary is still alive." He pointed the gun at them again. "I fought them off as long as I could. I made a deal with them." He made eye contact with Asa.

"Just give Ray the girls, and he promises he'll leave the rest of you alone. We can go back to our normal lives. I'll be out of the Brotherhood, and you can go back to your business, and Brady can go back to his computers. Ms. Mary will be safe."

Asa stepped forward. "You know I can't do that."

"Yes, you can!" Max screamed. "Just give me the girl."

The door behind Max opened.

"Yes, Asa, just give me the girl." It was Congressman Jackson.

Her breath caught in her throat. Jackson walked around Max; he was cool and calm.

"You can't win. This is fate. I will save the white dragon." He let out a slow breath, looking at Asa and Sydney. "It's time to stop running."

She heard a door swing open behind her, and she turned. Five more navy-suited men walked in, guns drawn.

Roxy

"What the hell is Max talking about?" Brady typed furiously on the keyboard. "He's not in the kitchen. I have him on the screen right now in the banquet room."

She studied the congressman on the screen. She watched as a man in a navy suit walked up and whispered into the congressman's ear. With a nod, Jackson followed the man out of the camera's sight.

"He's on the move." She searched the surrounding cameras to find him.

She was relieved that Asa was with her sister. When they lost contact with her, she about had a heart attack. She hadn't been able to find her on the cameras.

Brady broke into her thoughts. "What is Max doing? This can't be." He sounded stressed and she looked up. He was running his hands through his hair. "Do you have any surveillance in the kitchen?"

She went in the security cameras but was immediately kicked out. "What the hell?" She tried again.

"Someone's in our system." She tried another angle. "The screen went black. "What the…"

She looked over and saw Brady's screen was dark too. "They know we're here." He pushed back from the screen and looked out the front window of the van. "Shit." He jumped up.

She looked up to see three men in navy suits standing at the end of the alley. One gave a little wave, and her blood ran cold.

She turned to the back of the van and looked out the small, tinted windows. There were two more coming up from behind them. "Lock the doors. There's more behind us."

She heard the click of the locks as Brady started the engine. "Hold on." He threw the van in reverse, and it had her falling back. She heard a thud. She sat up and looked out the back. One man had jumped to the side while the other was gone. Brady put the van in drive and took off. She watched as the man jumped over his fallen friend and chased after them.

She looked out the front and watched as the three men nervously raised their guns. "Get down," Brady yelled.

She ducked down. She reached under the desk and pulled out the pistol she knew was hidden there. She started to crawl to the front of the van when she heard the shots. They dinged off the side of the van, and she heard the windshield crack. She looked up to see a bullet hole on the passenger side of the window. She handed the gun to Brady, and he placed it in his lap. It reminded her of the first time they met. She caught herself smiling. She shook her head, realizing how morbid it was. There was another shot that had Brady ducking.

When they hit the entrance of the alley, all three men jumped out of the way and Brady swerved the van out to the main road. Cars honked, and she heard some yells. He sped down the road and took a right as he circled around the hotel.

"We've got to ditch the van." He took another turn.

She looked out the back, checking to see if anyone was following them. She couldn't tell; it was dark and there was a lot of traffic.

Brady ran through a red light and took the next turn.

She held on to the back of his seat. "How did they get in our system? How did they know where we were? We used your system."

Brady slammed hard on the brakes to avoid a cab. "I don't know. Their tech is better," he said, softly gripping the wheel.

"This isn't going to plan." He ran another red light.

He pulled into an underground parking garage. He went down two levels, then parked. He turned to her.

"We have to leave the rifle. We can't be walking through town with it. We need to head back. We need to help Asa and Sydney. Don't trust Max. Stay close." He opened the glove box, pulled out another pistol, and handed it to her. He then pulled out a silencer and screwed it on the end of his gun. "Keep it hidden."

Out on the street, it was cold. She zipped her hoodie up all the way and put her hood on. The gun was in her front pocket, her hand tightly clasping it. The chill didn't seem to bother Brady. He held her other hand as they walked quickly back to the hotel.

They kept their heads down and hustled through the dark and busy streets.

When they arrived at the hotel, they planned on going to the side door. It was guarded by two men in navy suits. They hid behind a dumpster. Brady

289

pulled the gun from under his shirt and checked the clip. "Stay here till I signal for you to come." She only shook her head in agreement. "What if they don't work for the congressman? What if they are employees of the hotel?" she asked as he slapped the clip in to his gun.

"Employees won't try to kill me." He studied the back entrance.

He stood up and, with the pistol down close to his side, he walked toward the guards by the door. She watched as one guard smacked the other and pointed at Brady.

Brady walked right up to them. They were talking, and then, in one smooth motion, Brady lifted the gun and shot the man right in the head. His elbow struck the other across the face, and then he shot him in the chest. Apparently, they worked for the congressman.

He waved her over.

Brady

They made it to a side entrance to the kitchen. He slowly opened the door, checking behind him to make sure Roxy was still close. She had her gun out and pointed to the ground; she almost looked like she knew what she was doing. He wanted to smile. They crept around the corner to see Asa and Sydney surrounded. Max was next to the congressman, confirming his suspicion. Half the men had their backs to him, and that, he decided, was going to be how it went down.

He took a deep breath; his first shot took the man straight in front of him down. His shot was quiet but not quiet enough. They all whipped their heads around to look at him. He took out two more easy enough. He saw from the corner of his eye that Asa took Sydney to the ground. It distracted him enough that Roxy took a shot at the man to his left, taking him down to his knees. He put a bullet in that man's head. A bullet whizzed by his head, and it had him ducking and pushing Roxy back around the corner. He heard a couple more shots and looked up to see Asa taking a shot at Ray. Max jumped in front and took the shot in the arm. He barely grimaced.

The congressman said something to Max, and he nodded and turned. Max headed toward Sydney.

He went forward to try to help Asa, but a man jumped out and swung his fist; it connected with the side of his face. It hit hard, and his head was spinning. He didn't have time to shake it off before the man tackled him.

The man grabbed his wrist, beating it on the ground, trying to make him drop his gun. He tried to swing with his other arm, but the man brought his knee down and pinned it to the ground. Then, all of a sudden, the man's head exploded, and blood rained down on his face. He pushed him over and found Roxy standing over him.

She reached down to help him up. "You okay?"

"Yeah, I'll be fine." He looked up. He watched as Max grabbed Sydney. Asa pulled his gun.

But another man jumped out, grabbed Asa by his bad shoulder, and yanked him down. Asa growled in pain and Sydney screamed.

He trained his gun on the man holding Asa down.

"Let him up," he yelled.

"Max," Congressman Jackson said, drawing his attention. Jackson grabbed Sydney from Max's arms and swung her in front of him. "Grab the other girl."

Brady immediately swung the gun at Max.

Max took a step forward.

"Don't do this, brother," Brady said, fear ripping through him. He could feel the emotions run through him.

"Come on, Brady," Max gestured with his hand. "Just give me the girl. I made a deal. We can go back to the way things were before all this happened. You can go back to your IT. I'll be officially out of the Brotherhood."

"What?" Brady couldn't believe it.

"Help me out, man." Max took another step forward.

"You get near her; I'll take you down." Brady watched his hand holding the gun slightly shake. He looked back up at Max. "How could you do this, man? We fought side by side together. We pulled each other out of some deep shit. You're my brother in arms."

"That's why I made the deal. I'm saving you and your cousin. Ray said he'd leave you guys out, and Mary too. Just hand over the girl."

He couldn't think straight. Max was in the Brotherhood? He had betrayed him, betrayed their family. He had trusted Max with his life.

Max took another step forward. "Sorry, Brady, but this is how it ends."

Brady held his gun higher. "No, Max, I can't do this." He felt tears forming in his eyes. "You betrayed me."

Then a shot went off, and Max fell to the ground. He hadn't pulled the trigger; he looked to Roxy in confusion, but she was just as surprised.

Ray stepped forward, where Max had stood, his arm out, and a small silver pistol pointed at them. Sydney struggled to breathe, his arm tight around her neck. Tears were falling down her face.

"I'm done with this." Ray looked out at the room. "I wasn't going to keep my promise anyway. You think I would let you guys live? You're under the spell of these witches. Bewitched is what you are. The warriors that cut the dragon's wings off, damning him to his cave."

Congressman Jackson's face dropped, and his eyes clouded. "He said it was going to be hard, that you warriors would be tough." He looked up with a smile. "You guys are fighters." He laughed. "But that's okay." He said it under his breath and looked off. He shook his head and refocused.

It reminded Brady of the video they saw of Ray and the doctor. Ray's eyes were glossed over, and he was sliding into insanity.

Brady looked over at Asa.

Asa only nodded; they both knew without words that Ray was going to have to go down. Asa turned to the man holding him down, pulled his good arm out, and pushed the man's head up as far as he could. Brady took the shot and hit the man square in the temple. Asa stood, his gun aimed at Ray.

Sydney stamped Ray's foot in an attempt to escape, but Ray just laughed. "Sorry, honey, but you'll have to do better than that. You think you're the first woman to try to hurt me? In fact, my mother hit harder than that, and she was twice your age." He lifted his face and looked out at them.

"I remember the last time my mother hit me. She used her tea kettle and smacked me right across the face. See…" He turned and put his face next to Sydney's. Asa aimed his gun, his face full of pain, and he was sweating. Brady knew his cousin wasn't fully healed yet. But honestly, he was glad Asa had come, as he was his true brother in arms, the one man he wanted by his side. He didn't know if he could do this without him.

Congressman Jackson continued, "It was full of water. Lucky for me it wasn't hot yet. I was so angry that night, I ran to the white dragon. The white dragon said it was time. The dragon left his cave for the first time. He walked all the way to my house and killed my mother for me." Ray laughed. "The dragon saved my life. I owe the dragon everything, and all I have to do is free him. Then I will be a powerful wizard, and together the world will be ours." Jackson's laugh was sharp and loud. He then looked off to the side, his eyes wandering around the room, looking at nothing. "The first part of the ritual is done. You both have the mark of the dragon. I need more blood." Ray looked up, then down at Sydney's chest. He jerked his head up and stared out at Roxy.

Instinct had Brady grabbing Roxy and pulling her in close. Ray's eyes were crazy. Rage started to build; the old feeling was coming back. This was it; he was done listening to this crazy man talking about the girls this way. He held his gun up and waited for the opportunity.

Asa

His shoulder was screaming. He was done listening to Ray's crazy talk and again he had to watch a man choke his girl. He saw Brady raise his gun; his eyes going hard, he knew it was time.

Memories of the alley crossed his mind. He hadn't taken the shot then, and Sydney had to take her first life. It was something that he would regret for the rest of his life.

He saw Roxy raise her gun, too.

"Well, look here, seems the odds are a little off." Jackson shifted Sydney further in front of him and tightened his arm around her throat.

"Where's your army now?" Brady asked. "No one left to do your dirty work?"

Jackson shifted slightly, making Sydney gasp. She reached up, tried to pull his arm away.

He stepped forward. "Let her go!" He could feel his body shake.

He wanted to take the shot. He pointed the gun at the corner of Ray's head.

"This won't end," Jackson said. "Just because I die doesn't mean my followers won't take over where I left off. The white dragon will come." He laughed loudly.

Sydney struggled in his arms. He lost his grip a little, causing Sydney to slip down; there was his opening.

He fired.

The bullet entered the side of his forehead. It sprayed Sydney's stunned face with blood. He fell, taking her with him.

He ran to her. He ripped the congressman's arm from her throat and pulled her up. Ignoring the burning pain running through his shoulder, he searched her face for any wounds. "You okay?" he asked.

She nodded her head and stood, her face hard.

Roxy and Brady ran up.

"It's over," Roxy said, and she bent over Jackson. She reached under his collar and pulled out the chain holding the ring. She ripped it from his neck and held it up.

They all stared for a moment.

"We should leave," Brady said. "Someone is going to see this, and we'll be arrested for murder of a United States congressman."

Brady walked over to Chess laying on the white tiled floor. He used his fingers to close his eyes. "Rest in peace, brother." Brady stepped back.

"What about his body?" Sydney said.

"We'll tell his men; they'll get his body," he said and turned to leave.

Brady took Roxy's hand, and the four of them walked out.

Sydney

The next few weeks were a whirlwind. Roxy and Brady spent hours on the computers. They sent every prosecutor, investigative reporter, police station, and judge the evidence they had on the Brotherhood and the congressman. They set up an untraceable website where they published all the evidence and stories they could find that were linked to them. People who had bad experiences with the Brotherhood in the past started to leave anonymous tips; it led to more leads and linked more players in the Brotherhood army. There were many arrests including some high-ranking political figures.

Asa had to go back to bed rest and possibly more surgery for his shoulder.

When they presented the ring to Mary, she wept. She thanked them all and immediately started to plan their trip to England. They were leaving as soon as Asa was able to fly. She wanted them all to go. She felt it was the only way to end the curse.

When Brady told her about Max, Mary wept again. The security team, including Clint, were shocked. There was no funeral for Max. But there was one for Chess. It seemed everyone in Louisiana showed. They had flown out for the day and paid their respects. It was quite the party.

When Asa was asleep, she laid in bed, thinking of everything. She worried about the curse and often found herself bombarding Mary with questions later the next day. Was this really going to break it? Was Roxy safe? How was she so sure? Mary just insisted that it would.

She thought about her future also. She started to apply to colleges that had good psychology programs. When Mary found out, she insisted that she pay for her college education as a thank you for everything.

She tried to say it wasn't necessary, but Asa assured her that it would happen whether she wanted it to or not.

They called Bev and told her everything. She had received Sydney's letter and was thrilled to hear Asa was better. They made plans to come down and visit after traveling to England.

*

They left for England on a cold and chilly morning, four weeks after San Francisco.

They arrived late that night and stayed in a hotel; their plans were to leave for the graveyard in the morning.

She woke up in a large, comfortable bed to warm kisses on the back of her neck. "What time is it?" she asked softly and pressed her back side to Asa's warm body.

"It's early," he whispered against her neck.

"Remember you said you would take me shopping in London today, among other tourist things?"

He pulled her closer. "I remember."

She smiled and snuggled deeper into his arms. She had never felt as warm and safe as she did right at that moment. He rolled on top of her and looked down at her. His eyes were half closed from sleep, and his face was soft. He was warm and heavy. "I love you." He bent his head down and kissed her neck.

Her heart swam. "I love you, too." She turned her head and found his mouth.

They were late to meet the rest of the group. But no one seemed to care. Everybody seemed to be happy and excited. They were all smiles and headed for the rental car.

She wore skinny jeans and a pair of Hunter boots that Mary had bought her. She was excited to wear nice clothes again and was eager to get more in London. Asa was dressed in designer jeans paired with a gray blazer. She couldn't wait to shop with him.

The drive was long but scenic. The green rolling hills looked beautiful in the morning sun, and everything had a wet shine to it.

Asa pulled the SUV onto a small dirt path, and they followed it to an old cemetery on top of a hill. It was overgrown and had a short iron fence around it that was also falling apart. The view from the top was beautiful. It was surrounded by more rolling green hills and wild flowers. The five of them entered and started the search for Abby's grave marker.

She wandered around reading the headstones when Roxy came up next to her, taking her arm.

Roxy was staring at the small gravestone in front of them.

It read, *"Marie Batty, 1842–1843, Lung Fever."*

"What do you think lung fever is?" she asked.

"Most likely pneumonia," Roxy said. "She was just a baby."

They turned together and continued to look.

"Did you ever visit Dad's gravestone?" She looked to Roxy.

She just shook her head no. "Not since the funeral."

"You know, when we go back to Fuller, we should visit Dad."

"I think so, too. It's weird to think he tried to move us to Maine all those years ago. Our life would have been so different." Roxy stopped at another headstone. When she read the name and it wasn't Abby, she continued.

"We would have met Asa and Brady and Mary a long time ago. Maybe would have been friends with Haley also."

"Maybe. It's weird to think, isn't it?" All the possibilities swam through her head. She watched Roxy bend down to move some leaves from a headstone.

"Abby Williams. Daughter, mother, wife. I found it."

She watched as Mary and the others ran to Roxy's side. Mary dropped to her knees in her designer suit.

"It's here, and it's just like in my dream." She pulled out a small, shiny new shovel from her purse and started to dig a small hole.

"Here, Granny, let me," Asa said and squatted down to help. Brady stepped forward also.

"No, no." She swatted his hand away.

Asa just smiled. He walked over to Sydney and put his arm around her shoulders. He kissed her head, and the four of them watched Granny Mary dig a hole in a cream-colored suit.

When the small hole was dug, Mary sat back on her heels. She pulled the ring out and cupped it in her hands. She looked up to the blue sky.

"Henry. This is for you. I hope you can find peace now. Be with Abby and break our family curse."

Mary closed her eyes and held the ring.

"Come, you guys, all of you." She waved the four of them down.

They all got to their knees, surrounding the headstone. Mary continued, "My two grandsons fought for this stone; they shed blood for it. These two women sacrificed their blood and family for this stone. Henry, we're sorry your blood and sacrifice went unrewarded. Please don't let our family suffer anymore."

Sydney felt the wind blow softly across her face.

Mary placed the ring in the hole, and with her hands, she pushed the dirt back in and placed her hand on top. "Come, everyone, place your hand on it."

One by one, they placed their hands, one on top of the other. They all closed their eyes.

Sydney felt a stronger breeze this time; it whipped her hair across her forehead. Then she saw it.

It was Mary standing in a church. A woman walking down the aisle, Mary's face covered in sheer happiness, tears streaming down her cheeks.

Then it was Roxy. Her hair was peppered with gray, and wrinkles lined her eyes. She handed a gray-haired Brady a mug of coffee as there were babies playing at their feet.

Then it was Asa. He was with a little girl with long black hair on a purple bike with training wheels. She was dressed in a pink dress, and he was showing her how to pedal the bike. Love sprung from her chest at the sight. The little girl looked back and said, "Look, Momma, Daddy's showing me."

It went dark, and there was a man and a woman, hand in hand. They were dressed in seventeenth century clothes. They were both smiling. The man whispered, "Thank you."

Her eyes sprung open, and she fell back on her bottom. The vision was so strong that her head was spinning. She looked around at the group. They all were looking around in amazement at each other.

"I think it worked," Roxy said. She wiped a tear from her eye.

"Me too," Mary said. She had tears racing down her cheeks, and she pulled a tissue from her pocket.

Asa stood and reached down to her. He pulled her up and in for a tight hug. "I love you," he said.

Now she was crying. "I love you, too."

"I guess I can do this now." Brady went down on one knee in front of Roxy. He pulled a ring from his pocket.

"Roxy Wright, you're the smartest and most beautiful woman I have ever met. Will you do me the honor of being my wife?"

Roxy's face turned bright red, but she smiled. "Yes." She nodded, her smile growing wider. Brady jumped up and spun her in a hug.

Mary clapped her hands together. "This is the best day of my life. Roxy, welcome to the family." Mary pulled Roxy from Brady's arms and hugged her; Sydney joined them.

"Really, brother, the cemetery? You couldn't wait to ask her somewhere a little classier?" Asa smacked Brady on the back and pulled him in for a hug. "Congrats, man."

Asa walked over to Sydney. He wrapped his arm around her shoulder and leaned in. "Don't worry; my proposal will be way more romantic."

She gave out a choked laugh, her heart full.

They made their way back to the car. "Hey, Roxy?" she shouted to her sister. "We have to invite Marcy to your Sinclair wedding." Roxy turned, a big grin on her face. "She's going to be so pissed."

The End